SCOOPED!

A sorrowful moan mingled in the night air with the tragic bouquet of the fragrance of roses. I tensed again, catching movement beyond the house, just outside the circle of bushes that surrounded the Holloway family cemetery. What the hell was that? I put a hand to my eyes to remove the glare from the porchlight and squinted into the darkness. I squinted harder when I saw a splash of white, stark and pallid against the dark backdrop.

"Scooby freakin' Doo!" I whispered. "Holy Halloween!" I watched, unbelieving, as a wispy sheet of almost transparent white appeared to float across the back yard, soft whimpers of heartache providing macabre accompaniment. "Loralie?" I whispered.

I was, like, totally on the verge of embarrassing myself at this point. Good thing I was alone. Well, sorta. Kinda.

A sudden movement from behind caught me off guard. Hot breath singed the back of my neck.

"Loralie?" I squeaked.

"No. But I'm by far your biggest nightmare," a deep voice declared.

GHOULS JUST WANT TO HAVE FUN

KATHLEEN BACUS

LOVE SPELL NEW YORK CITY

LOVE SPELL®

October 2006

Published by

Dorchester Publishing Co., Inc.
200 Madison Avenue
New York, NY 10016

ISBN 0-505-52694-8

The name "Love Spell" and its logo are trademarks of Dorchester Publishing Co., Inc.

Printed in the United States of America.

Visit us on the web at www.dorchesterpub.com.

ACKNOWLEDGMENTS

As a writer, it really goes against the grain to parrot what others have said before me, but in this case, I'll gladly make an exception. So, here goes:

"No one writes in a vacuum." Books don't appear simply by pulling one out of a hat or by virtue of crossed arms and an *I Dream of Jeannie* blink. There are so many wonderfully gifted and talented folks who work so diligently behind the scenes to put out the best books possible—often under impossibly tight deadlines and amid massive workloads, so a thank-you to those folks is long overdue.

My sincere appreciation goes out to Tricia, Daniel, and the entire Editorial, Art and Production departments for their commitment to excellence in all that they do—and for being so easy to work with. A big thanks to "go-to gal," Brianna, Manager of Public Relations, for always being so quick to respond to this newbie's SOSs (and for having all the right answers) and for being incredibly patient and so darned nice that she makes this ongoing learning process painless. And to Brooke and Tim, who get the books into the hands of our readers so efficiently—what would we do without you?

It goes without saying (but I'm saying it anyway) that I owe a huge debt of gratitude to my superb editor, Chris Keeslar, without whose total acceptance of a story and characters that refused to fit neatly in any one genre gave me permission to write outside the lines and introduce readers to a cast of characters I truly love to create stories for. Thank you so much for taking a gamble on two small-town, good ol' girls. Your vision provided the opportunity for a little filly called Tressa to kick up her heels— and a chance for a somewhat longer-in-the-tooth brood mare named Kathy to prove she isn't just a one-trick pony. Thanks for betting on us, Chris.

And to my all-knowing and all-seeing agent, Michelle, who never doubted for a minute that I could meet a deadline tighter than thigh-high hose, thank you so much for believing in me. We did it, kiddo!

And lastly, to my brother, Gary, a fellow monster movie aficionado, remember those monster stories we wrote as kids? Guess what? Your Tree Monster story beat my Wolfman story all to heck. Go figure.

GHOULS JUST WANT TO HAVE FUN

CHAPTER ONE

A blonde, a brunette, and a redhead went out for lunch. After a stimulating, healthful meal, all three decided to visit the ladies' room, and found a strange-looking woman sitting at the entrance, who said, "Welcome to the ladies' room. Be sure to check out our newest feature: a mirror that, if you look into it and say something truthful, will reward you with a wish. But be warned, if you say something false, you will be sucked into the mirror to live in a void of nothingness for all eternity!"

The three women quickly entered and, upon finding the mirror, the brunette said, "I think I'm the most beautiful of us three," and in an instant she was surrounded by a pile of money. The redhead stepped up and said, "I think I'm the most talented of us three," and she suddenly found the keys to a brand-new Lexus in her hands. Excited over the possibility of having a wish come true, the blonde looked into the mirror and said, "I think . . ." and was promptly sucked into the mirror.

1

* * *

Name a dumb blonde joke—any blonde joke—and chances are I can recite it backwards. I'm rather an authority on the genre, having been the inspiration for more than a few since I first made my appearance as a bouncing baby blonde on one snowy April-first morn twenty three and a half years ago. For those of you who subscribe to astrology, that of course makes me an Aries—and the target of year-in-year-out harassment for having been born on April Fools' Day. As if folks need a reason to harass me.

Those of us born under the sign of Aries are described with such alluring adjectives as "brash" and "bombastic"—the latter I had to look up just to make sure it wasn't some unpleasant gastrointestinal condition—not to mention quaint descriptive phrases like, "Aries strut their stuff with more moxie than most can abide." Ouch. Now that hurts.

I was born at the ungodly hour of 4:06 A.M., making my rising sign—whatever that is—Pisces. According to one Internet site, that means I'm supposed to be intuitive and possessed of psychic powers. Ha! That's a good one: "intuitive" in reference to a person who was generally the first one out at dodgeball in elementary school (this before they made us quit playing after the second-worst player, Chubby Chad Dinkins, suffered a mild concussion and his folks threatened to sue) and who had to watch *The Sixth Sense* six times before she figured out Bruce Willis was dead all along. Oops. Sorry I've spoiled the ending for those of you who populate caves and survivalist camps and have never seen the flick.

I'm one of those people who love to be scared to death in a movie theater with a hundred-plus other moviegoers, sucking down Coke and licking butter from their fingers. But when I'm home by myself watching a horror flick on one of Snoopy's infamous dark and stormy nights? Well, let's just say the sound of the furnace kicking on can get me running to the doors to check the locks, and to the kitchen to make sure all the sharp knives are present and accounted for.

Hey now. Come clean. You've done the old look-in-the-closet-or-under-the-bed move yourself a time or two, haven't you? It's okay. I won't tell a soul. Honest. We 'fraidy cats have to stick together, you know.

It's not that I've personally had any "close encounters of the paranormal kind" that would make me particularly susceptible to supernatural suggestion. But I did have a great aunt who loved to scare the pants off her "favorite" great nieces and nephews with spooky ghost stories and who swore up and down that she'd been visited regularly by the spirit of her dear, departed, dead sister, Misty Sue, who had tragically passed away at the age of five from a brain tumor. Aunt Eunice even showed us family photos taken years after little Misty Sue had passed, and would point to faint blurs in the photo and insist those blurs were Misty Sue. Aunt Eunice also had a rather disturbing practice of taking her camera to funeral home viewings of folks she knew and snapping pictures of them in their caskets "to remember them by." Bleah. Like, how creepy is that? She kept a photo album of her stiff snapshots that she'd bring out to show off like a new parents' brag book whenever we visited. So, while I'm not strictly a believer in every sense of the word, this youthful indoctrination in things-hereafter was compelling stuff for an impressionable young girl with a vivid imagination and a history of chronic mis-

3

adventure. So, while my mouth might say something is total hooey, the heart beating a mile a minute in my chest declares otherwise.

All things considered, I've elected to abstain from all forms of dark entertainment this Halloween season due to a series of, shall we say, unfortunate events that have seriously impacted my ability to watch slasher movies or to read any book that doesn't feature the words "cowboy," "bride," or "baby" in the title. I've sworn off anything remotely related to zombies, vampires, werewolves or clowns. Yeah. You heard right. Clowns. Hmm. I guess I should explain.

After playing a leading role in my own hometown murder mystery earlier this spring—a role that I assure you I did not audition for or aspire to—I headed off to enjoy two weeks of down-home good-time fun at Iowa's annual celebration of great food and simple pleasures, only to end up in my own nonmusical— and strictly PG-rated—cockeyed-cowgirl version of "Calamity Jayne Does the State Fair," complete with a supporting cast of characters only Mel Brooks could love. From my dweeby cousin Frankie, out to clear his name, to a pair of geriatric Joe Fridays, to an insult-spouting midway dunk-tank clown gone way off the deep end, the fair was one wild ride for which Dramamine was of zilch therapeutic use. The effects, I'm sorry to say, have been lasting. Even now I can't watch *Scooby-Doo* without someone else in the room. How sad is that?

After having my face plastered across multiple issues of Iowa's capital-city's daily newspaper during the summer season, I was ready to fade from the public eye, content to feature other folks' mugs—or mug shots, depending on the story—on the front of the

Grandville Gazette, the small daily newspaper where I sporadically found myself employed.

I'd been let go from the newspaper previously due to technical difficulties relating to the labeling of obituary photos. It's a long story, but let's just say that my publisher's wife took offense at having her favorite aunt identified as Stubby Burkholder, the strange little man who for years used to cut grass in area cemeteries while wearing what looked suspiciously like a ruffled frock. Personally, I always thought Aunt Deanie benefited by the photo mix-up. She'd never looked better.

Mowing graveyards must be a nice, quiet, relatively safe vocation. You sure wouldn't get any complaints from residents about your job performance. Still, how creepy would it be bouncing over the graves of hundreds of people for a living? And since, in my present frame of mind eating Count Chocula cereal gave me the willies, I was hardly signing up to take Stubby's place.

As a rookie cub reporter for the *Grandville Gazette*— the newspaper's founders garnering a D-minus for creativity but a B-plus for having the cojones to actually go with such a lame name—I had finally attained by-line status for a series of eyewitness articles relating to the bizarre crime spree I'd been embroiled in the previous summer. Now that autumn was in the air, I found myself surprisingly satisfied to cover school board meetings—okay, so this assignment was a total yawner—sports events, and the occasional human interest story. I shied away from the crime beat, though, and not just because I was still freaked out by my past brushes with danger. I was also trying to mend some fences with local law enforcement officials over what they lovingly referred to as "multiple counts of interference with official acts" during the course of my earlier mission to gain a little hometown R-E-S-P-E-C-T. Okay, so I may have undertaken what many considered Mission: Impossible with a little more, uh, enthusiasm than law enforcement authorities anticipated. Or could stomach. That's what happens when a slightly grumpy cowgirl-type fed up with being taken about as seriously as a rent-a-cop at a rock concert discovers a corpse in her car, loses the corpse and can't get anyone to believe it was there in the first place. Well, anyone except the killer, that is.

Anyway, at least for now, I was okay with writing short articles on the employee of the month at the local hospital, reporting the successes (and failures) of the high school cross-country teams, and doing a fluff piece on the candidates for homecoming queen. I'd inherited the assignment from a fellow *Gazette* contributor who, once he'd interviewed the king candidates, decided he wasn't up to doing the same with their frilly female counterparts.

It was this gem of a story that brought me to my former high school on a chilly late-October morning. I was finishing up my interview with queen candidate number four, Kylie Danae Radcliffe, a perky, over-the-top brunette (I *so* have a problem with perky brunettes, but that's another story) with teeth so bright I was tempted to stick my cheapo Bargain City sunglasses on my nose and pull my Dairee Freeze visor down low on my forehead to combat the glare.

In case you're wondering, my uncle Frank owns the Dairee Freeze, a local ice cream establishment where I currently put in at least twenty hours a week—more when I really need the moolah, which is, like, all the time. It was hawking Uncle Frank's dairy delights at the state fair in August that had reinforced my earlier aversion to clowns and to slithering serpents that invade the sanctity of private living quarters, and had heightened a sense of tension of both a sexual and a nonsexual nature between a certain gorgeous if exasperating ranger-type and me. Rick Townsend is an officer with the Iowa Department of Natural Resources. He's an avid sportsman, he loves to hunt and fish, and he loves to play games. With me. I've known Townsend— or Ranger Rick, as I like to call him—since before he grew hair in manly places, and when a six-pack meant a half-dozen cans of Coca-Cola.

I have issues with Rick Townsend. He's the jerk who stuck me with a nickname that's proven harder to lose than a bad credit rating—or weight from that stubborn thigh area. I was called Calamity Jayne so much in high school, at graduation Daniel Tremont had to give me a poke in the ribs when they called Tressa Jayne Turner up to receive her diploma.

I'll admit to having some pretty steamy daydreams— okay, and some pretty hot night ones, too—over the sexy ranger; however, I'm not ready to make any great leaps of faith—or into bed—with a man who has a soft spot for reptiles and who not so long ago had me convinced he was falling for my cover model, could-be-rocket-scientist little sister, Taylor.

I'm playing what used to be called "hard to get" with the good ranger. I figure if he's "the one," he'll hang in there long enough for me to figure it out. And if not, he never was. Does that make any sense?

Let's just say that for my own heart health I'm taking it slow and easy with Rick. And believe me, ladies, if you saw Ranger Rick, you'd agree that such über-amounts of self-restraint and sheer good-girliness ought to more than qualify me for sainthood—right along-side Mother Teresa and Pope John Paul II, God rest their souls.

"So, why would *you* make the best homecoming queen?" I asked the prep sitting across from me at a table in the commons area of Grandville High School. "What sets you apart from the other four candidates?"

With a toss of her head, Kylie shook a long, shiny length of dark hair over one shoulder, and I winced. Don't you just hate when girls do the hair-toss move? That annoying pivoting of the head like the girls in the shampoo commercials do, where their silky hair fans out in all its glory and makes all us frizzy-haired females jump into our cars and head for the nearest hair-care aisle in search of a miracle cure for split ends and flyaway hair? Okay, so I admit I'm totally jealous because I can't do the Pantene flip. My hair is a bit on the wild side. If I tossed it around like that, I'd hurt someone.

"I'm, like, a shoo-in for queen," Kylie said, clicking a set of perfect black-and-gold-decorated nails on the off-white tabletop. "Everybody likes me. I'm nice to just about everyone I meet. I'm in the top ten percent of my class. I'm a member of the GHS dance line—front row—and the National Honor Society. I'm also a football cheerleader. I'm in Chamber Choir and sing the national anthem at all the basketball games. I've had the lead in the school musical for the last two years. I play varsity basketball and volleyball, run track and play golf. I volunteer regularly at Grandville Nursing Home—the residents just love to hear me sing—and I work at Shady Pines Country Club. My father is a family practice physician at Grandville

Community Hospital and my mother is vice president of Central Iowa Savings and Loan."

Kylie Radcliffe rattled off her resume like I recite my to-go order at China Buffet on my way from one job to the next. *I'll have the pineapple chicken, fried rice, two egg rolls, half a dozen crab Rangoon and sweet-and-sour sauce on the side.*

Oh, buddy, I thought, suddenly making a connection between the candidate for queen and a certain banker I'd had occasion to deal with recently. Conflict-of-interest time. I knew Kylie's mother. She'd turned me down for a car loan six months back when I'd badly needed to distance myself from an '87 Plymouth that held some not-so-great memories for me.

I wrinkled my nose. I'd lay odds that little Ms. Shoo-in here wasn't driving around in a beat-up white Plymouth Reliant. But I put my car envy on hold and focused my attention on the matter at hand—retaining regular employment so that I could suck in that new used-car smell down the road.

"But what is it about Kylie Danae Radcliffe that makes her a better candidate for queen than, say"—I looked down at my notepad and searched for the name of the only candidate I hadn't yet interviewed— "Shelby Lynne Sawyer?" I asked.

Kylie gave me a "duh, are you for real?" look. Trust me. I've seen it before. I usually identify it by brows that suddenly meet above the nose, and by the repetitive rapid eye blinks.

"You're kidding, right?" Kylie asked. "Like, have you ever met Shelby Lynne Sawyer?"

I shook my head. "No. Not yet."

Kylie conducted a sensory sweep around the commons area, similar to the sweep my gramma performs when she's about to pass along a bit of idle gossip. Or invent it.

"Her queen candidacy is someone's sick idea of a joke," Kylie said. "A bunch of kids thought it would be a hoot to get Sasquatch on the ballot."

I blinked. "Sasquatch?"

"That's Shelby Lynne's nickname. She's over six feet tall and her feet are, like, bigger than Herman Munster's. And she had this real nasty overbite and has been in braces for, like, ever. Somebody got the idea that it would be funny to see Sasquatch and Tom Thumb on the royal court together. Frankly, I think it's insulting to the rest of us with bona fide royalty credentials."

My tongue slid over my own front teeth, and I winced. I myself was not all that many years away from a what's-up-Doc situation that had been corrected only by enduring four long years of painful orthodontic treatment and metal-mouth jokes from a adolescent horse's behind turned carp cop DNR employee.

I shook my head to clear it. "Uh, who's Tom Thumb?" I asked.

"Tom Murphy. He's the shortest kid in the school. He had some disease or something that stunted his growth when he was in elementary school. He was homeschooled until this year, but his folks thought he needed some socialization and decided to send him here for his senior year. He's barely five feet tall, but he's got a chip on his shoulder the size of a bowling ball. Some wise guys thought it would be fun to see Sasquatch and Tom Thumb paired up on homecoming night like something out of a Saturday afternoon horror movie. To tell you the truth, I really resent these people turning my senior homecoming into a freak show."

Queen-candidate Kylie's well-modulated my-wish-for-the-world-is-peace-on-earth beauty-contestant voice became fractured and shrill. It boomed off the walls of the large, open commons area even louder than the intercom days of *"Tressa Turner to the office"* I remembered so clearly. Ah, memories.

A shadow fell over the off-white table between us. Like, a really long shadow.

"Freak show, huh? I guess I'm in the right place, then."

I looked to my right and up. And up. And up. Right into the armpit of a girl who'd give any basketball coach who ever dreamed of a state championship a championship-sized woody. Not because she was gorgeous, you understand; carrot-colored hair and copper-colored freckles aren't exactly a sought-after look. But, man, she was gargantuan. All she had to do was stand in front of the basketball hoop with her arms up, and the opposing team didn't stand a chance. I knew my mouth was wide open, but honest, I couldn't stop myself. State tournament, I thought, here we come!

"Can't you see that we're busy?" Kylie greeted her competitor with one of those someone-didn't-use-their-roll-on looks.

"I think I've got enough material," I told Kylie, and stood to greet my final interview subject of the day. I was a bit taken aback when my head only reached Shelby Lynne's shoulder. And I'm no squatty body. "Thanks, Kylie. And good luck in the voting," I added, though I'd already decided Miss Radcliffe would not receive my vote—if I'd had one, that is. I'd really wanted that new used car.

Kylie shoved back her chair and got to her feet,

shooting a dark look at Shelby Lynne. "I can't imagine why you don't withdraw," she told Shelby. "You're only humiliating yourself, you know. And it's just going to get worse."

Shelby shrugged. "No pain. No gain," she remarked, and I raised an eyebrow. Maybe she wasn't homecoming queen material, but she could definitely be the queen of snark. Finally, someone I could relate to. I'd gone through the roster of king and queen candidates, reliving my own girlish angst at not being considered good enough or popular enough or pretty enough to serve as "Her Royal Highness," recalling instead how I'd assumed the role of homecoming court jester and feeling some slight embarrassment—okay, and some level of pride—at the jokes I'd played on the prepettes who were cut from the purple royalty swatch. Like my little sis, Taylor, the Turner version of a little princess.

"I'm Tressa Turner from the *Gazette*," I said to Shelby, sticking out my hand. "As you know, we're running a feature on the homecoming king and queen candidates, and I just have a few questions."

"Answer one: I'm six feet two. Answers two through three: No, I don't play basketball or volleyball or throw the shot-put, so you can put any state championship dreams away until the next Amazonian high schooler—hopefully one more athletically inclined than I am—enrolls. And answer four: There's absolutely no reason anyone would vote for me. Like Kylie said, my being nominated is a big joke." Shelby Lynne crossed her long arms. "So, get enough for your article? Did you bring your long-angle lens? You know—to snap a picture of me. Of course you might have to run it in sections one *and* two to get it all in."

I felt a smile lift the corners of my mouth. Sarcasm is something I understand. As a matter of fact, I earned As in Intro to Sarcasm through Advanced Sarcasm during high school. Not that I'm proud of this accomplishment, you understand. It was just the way it was. Just the way *I* was. And in lots of ways, probably still am.

Being back in my old high school, coming face-to-face—okay, face-to-upper torso—with someone who, rather than hide her flawed but human self behind a blond-bimbo mask, chose to hide in plain sight as the jolly mean giant sort of freaked me out. I was just starting to come to terms with certain things about myself. About why I'd played it safe—and dumb—for so many years. And how to give myself permission to risk letting folks see the "sensitive, feeling" Tressa once in a while. Okay, so I was basically a work-in-progress with the mushy stuff. God knew there was still enough Calamity Jayne in this country girl to wreak havoc with good ol' Grandville, USA. And I liked it that way.

"Not to worry," I replied. "With computer technology, we can resize you." I motioned to the chair Kylie had vacated. "You got a minute?"

Shelby shrugged and took a seat. I sat, too, happy that I was now able to maintain eye contact without getting a crick in the neck.

"If you think this is all a lame joke, why not withdraw as Kylie suggested?" I asked. "Why put yourself through it?"

Shelby rolled her broad shoulders again. "To mess with people's heads. Jerk them around." She paused and eyeballed me. "Or then again, maybe I really do want to be queen. Can't you just see me in heels and a tiara?"

I nodded. "Yeah. Like I can see me on the runway modeling the latest Versace fashions."

Shelby threw me a surprised glance. "Aren't you supposed to be kissing up to me for your article?" she asked, her eyes narrowing.

It was my turn to shrug. "Kylie gave me enough material for an entire series," I said. "Besides, a newspaper reporter lives for truth. It's the lifeblood of journalism."

Shelby had the uncouthness to snort. "You call writing about something as banal and prosaic as homecoming king and queen 'journalism'? I call it bourgeois and stereotypical tripe. But, hey, who am I? Just a representative of the reading public who doesn't get their news from MTV or *Saturday Night Live*."

I'd have to look up "bourgeois," "banal" and "prosaic" later just to make sure Sasquatch was really saying what I thought she was saying, but "stereotypical tripe"? Even I could interpret that message loud and clear.

I started to get that weird spastic sensation, characterized by twitching in my right eye and blood pooling in my cheeks (facial), that generally occurred just before I was about to do or say something that would require me to draft letters of apology—or recite huge mea culpas. Since neither of these came easily for me, I generally tried to avoid putting myself in situations where I might have to extend them.

I raised my eyebrows. "Oh? And this assessment from someone who—what? Worked on the high school yearbook committee, jotted soulful ditties in iambic pentameter for English class and scribbled little woe-is-me dear-diary entries in her journal about how much life bites? Thanks for the critical analysis, Miss

14

Sawyer. If there's extra space in the article, I'll be certain to add your insightful quote."

Shelby gave me another incredulous look and then started to laugh. "Geez. And I thought *I* had an attitude, Miz Calamity," she said. "Or do you prefer to be called Jayne?"

My eyes crossed. I'm fairly certain of this, as I suddenly saw two Shelbys, and neither was vastly appealing.

" 'Scuse me?"

"Calamity Jayne. That's your nickname, right? You're actually pretty famous around here. Or maybe I should say infamous. Not everybody discovers multiple murder victims in small-town Iowa, or is stalked by a felonious clown at the state's premier tourist attraction. With such impressive credentials, I guess I thought you'd be writing better material. You know. More hard-core stuff."

I looked at her through narrowed eyes. Hard-core? What kind of writer did she think I was, anyway?

I said, "What were you expecting? Something along the lines of 'Desperate Homecoming Queens'? 'Confessions of a Teenaged Homecoming Drag Queen'? Sorry. I'm a *serious* journalist." Or aspired to be one someday. When I grew up. And finally finished college. And could cover the cost of my shoe binges with something other than plastic with interest rates higher than my age.

Shelby Lynne leaned forward in her chair. It protested with a loud squeak. "Prove it," she said.

I threw her a "huh?" look. I should protect this particular facial expression with a trademark. It's been invented, improved upon and perfected by yours truly over a span of twenty-three years and counting.

"Prove it," Sasquatch—I mean, Shelby—repeated. "Prove you're a serious journalist."

I fought the urge to find out if the neck across from me was capable of being spanned with two hands. Purely for scientific purposes, you understand.

"How?" I heard myself saying.

"By nabbing the interview of a lifetime," Shelby Lynne replied, her remarkably pretty green eyes all of a sudden bright and alert.

"Interview? With who? One of the throng of presidential hopefuls who'll bring their dog-and-pony shows to Iowa to press voters' palms just in time for the Iowa caucuses? Sorry. Politics really isn't my specialty."

"What about famous authors?" Shelby Lynne asked. "What about *New York Times*–bestselling *reclusive* authors who haven't been seen in public for almost twenty years and haven't given an interview in well over a decade? Would that kind of story be your specialty?"

I could feel my spit dry up in my mouth and my ticker pick up the pace. Anyone who'd ever read a book was familiar with the unparalleled career and accompanying bizarre story of Elizabeth Courtney Howard, whose books flew to the top of the bestseller lists with the speed of my gramma to the potluck tables once the minister had blessed the food and said amen. A perennial favorite with critics and readers alike, Howard had suddenly disappeared from public view two decades ago, but had continued to pen her thrillers and chillers with clockwork regularity.

"You know E. C. Howard?" I asked.

Shelby shook her head. "Not exactly. But I know where she is. Or, I should say, where she is going to be in the not-too-distant future. Of course, information of this magnitude does not come without a price."

I gave her a you've-got-to-be-joking look and pointed to my white Plymouth beater parked illegally right outside the front doors. "That's my mode of transportation. You think I can afford your asking price?" I said.

Shelby Lynne shook her head. "I don't want cash. I want to meet Elizabeth Courtney Howard. Be there when you interview her. Talk to her. Pick her brain about writing. She's been my inspiration since I discovered her when I was a child. Nobody writes like E. C. Howard."

I nodded. Howard's earlier stuff could scare the Shinola out of me in broad daylight while I was sitting in a church pew in the sanctuary reciting the Lord's Prayer.

"She's awesome, all right. Or was when she was on her game. Her last several books got tanked by the critics. The reviews sucked."

"Doesn't matter. She's still the best writer ever. And I just have to meet her. But finding a way to do that? Well, that's the dilemma. I figure since you're a member of the local press and have a reputation for, uh, persistence, you might have a shot at getting an interview. And all you have to do is take me along. You won't even know I'm there."

I rolled my eyes. Like anyone could miss a six-foot-two redhead with freckles, Bugs Bunny chompers, and a 'tude that only Roseanne Barr could love.

"Okay," I said. "I'll bite. So where is E. C. Howard, reclusive mystery writer and all-around enigma, going to be in the very near future?" I was thinking that maybe I was being taken for a ride, but on the off chance this was legit, I was in for a penny, in for a pound.

"Oh no." Shelby got to her feet and stuck out a

17

freckled, long-fingered hand. I shook my head. With a paw like that, how could the girl *not* play basketball? Sacrilege! "Serious journalist type that you are, I must insist we shake on this deal before I divulge further information."

She looked so serious that I wanted to laugh. Who did she think she was, anyway? Deep Throat? And let's face it, I was not what you'd call Woodward/Bernstein material.

"I'm in," she said. "For any and all interviews or attempts at interviews with E. C. Howard. Do we have a deal?"

I hesitated briefly. "How old are you?" I asked.

"Eighteen and legally entitled to enter into binding contracts and legal agreements," she said. "Just in case you thought you could slip one over on me."

Rats. The girl was too darned shrewd for my own good.

"I'm hurt, Shelby," I said. "Really hurt."

"You'll live," she replied. "So do we have a deal?"

I wondered what I was letting myself in for, but decided that on a bad day I could handle a homecoming queen candidate—even a six-foot-two bogus one with a personality only a mother could love.

I put out my hand. "Deal," I said, slipping my hand into the much larger one. "So tell me, where do we find the elusive Elizabeth Courtney Howard?" I asked.

Shelby Lynne gripped my hand with such intensity that pain shot up my forearm to my elbow. "She's taking up residence at Holloway Hall on Dead End Lane," Shelby announced, her hand continuing to grasp mine with bone-breaking force.

"Haunted Holloway Hall?" I shouted, a noticeable quiver in my voice. "Holy shit!"

Principal Vernon, who'd been hovering in the corner keeping a watchful eye on yours truly, walked over to us and gave me a curt nod. "I believe this concludes your interview session, Tressa," he said. "I'm sure you know the way out."

I nodded, familiar with the drill—and the exit. The guy had personally shown me the door a time or two during our four years together.

Shelby Lynne tucked a crumpled-up piece of paper in my hand as I headed for the doors. "My cell phone number," she said. "Call me for more details." She gave my hand a final painful squeeze.

I waved at her and exited the high school under the watchful eye of Principal Vernon. I sat in my car and stared at the multicolored leaves still clinging to their last precious moments on the tree before a gusty north wind would catch them and rip them from the branches and they would become mulch, and I railed at the perverse injustices inflicted on those frustrated wannabes of the world who just want to get ahead.

Finally. Finally I got the chance at a serious journalistic coup that didn't involve guns, knives, dead bodies or clowns gone cuckoo, and what happened? My story was hiding behind the walls of a house only Norman Bates could love.

CHAPTER TWO

"Are you sure of your source?" Stan Rodgers, my sometime employer, and publisher and editor in chief of the *Grandville Gazette*, sucked on a star mint and peered at me across his cluttered desk, over the top of glasses that looked like someone had run out of materials before they finished making them. You know the ones—those half-glasses that have lenses the size of postage stamps.

I nibbled my lip. I really didn't want to admit to this seasoned professional that my source was a bushy, pushy queen candidate with goaltending capabilities.

"Sure I'm sure," I bluffed. "Who could make up a story like this?"

Stan bit down on the mint. "Those words have a familiar ring to them," he said. In fact, I'd recited those very words to Stan back in June when I'd been trying to barter a story about a stiff for a third chance at a reporting job. "On the off chance there is a story here, just make sure your source doesn't decide to share the wealth with our competitors. We don't want Van

Vleet over at *New Holland News* or his jackass son, Drew, getting a whiff of this. That guy is still chafing over our coup with the Palmer murder and your little state-fair exclusive. He's looking for something big to stick it to me with. And this story—if it's the real thing, that is—could be the ideal weapon. New Holland's version of the Louisville Slugger. I don't want them knockin' anything out of the park," Stan said.

Stan loves sports analogies. Stan and Paul Van Vleet, his counterpart at the *New Holland News*, are what you might call not-so-friendly competitors. Their one-upmanship is a natural extension of a long-time rivalry that has existed between the two cities since the Dutch first settled here and turned their heritage into a rather prosperous tourist attraction.

Dutch influence is everywhere in New Holland, from the yummy S-shaped almond pastries called Dutch Letters that keep you coming back for more to the yearly tulip festival to the Dutch architecture that is part of the New Holland landscape. You can't erect a building in New Holland without the town fathers rubber-stamping your blueprints. In Grandville, we go more for function over form. You know—if you build it, we can tax it.

I made a big production of putting my fingers to my lips and making like I was turning a key in a lock. "Mum's the word," I assured Stan.

He frowned. "Just make sure 'grand mum' isn't the word," he replied. It was my turn to frown.

"Huh?"

Stan leaned back in his chair and put his hands behind his head. "Your grandmother. Hellion Hannah. Better known as Ye Olde Town Crier," he stated.

I winced. I love my gramma, but the only secrets

she's been able to keep are her age—from everyone but the Social Security Administration and Medicare—and how many contraband gummy bears she consumes each week.

"Like I'm gonna tell my grandma about this," I told him.

"She'll wheedle it out of you. And let's face it, Turner, it don't take much. Shove a Krispy Kreme in front of you, and you'll sing like a bird."

I sniffed. "I'm a professional journalist," I reminded him, suddenly recalling how I'd uttered those very words only hours earlier—and how they'd been received, and ridiculed by my supersized source. "I know how to work a story." I hoped my nose wasn't growing as I said this.

"And you're sure there's a story?" Stan asked. "And if so, why haven't I heard anything about it? Hell, my wife is a real estate agent, and she hasn't mentioned anything about anyone occupying the Holloway house. As a matter of fact, there's been considerable speculation that Jerry Rivas over at J.R. Development is set to buy the place. Though why he'd want that old mausoleum, I'll never know." He laughed. "We used to call it Collinwood when we were kids. Different strokes for different folks, I guess."

"Collinwood?"

Stan threw his glasses on his desk. "*Dark Shadows*," he said. "Before your time. Soap opera from the late sixties and early seventies that ran at three o'clock each afternoon," he explained. "We used to race home from school so we could watch the last fifteen minutes of it."

I raised my eyebrows. "You ran home from school

22

to watch a soap opera? Stan Rodgers, the tough-as-nails news guy? The man who strikes fear into the hearts of reporters who can't spell and paperboys who deliver to the wrong addresses? *You* hoofed it home to watch a soap?" I grabbed a pencil out of a jar on his desk, and picked up a notepad. I licked the tip of the pencil. "Let me write that one down," I said. "Note to self. Give Stan a subscription to *Soap Opera Digest* for Christmas."

"Hell, this was no ordinary soap," Stan said. "This one had vampires and werewolves. And one very hot witch," he added with a wink.

I blinked. "Get real. They had *Buffy* soap operas back in, like, the Stone Age?" I asked. "How cool is that?"

"Barnabas," Stan said.

"Excuse me?"

"Barnabas, not Buffy. Well, Barnabus was the vampire. Angelique was the witch and, if I remember correctly, Quentin was the werewolf. No Buffys, but Angelique had a pretty good set on her." He sat back in his chair with a goofy faraway look and sighed.

I stared at Stan. I wasn't sure if he was on the level or not. With Stan, unless you see the veins bulging on a grossly enlarged neck or his ears turning red, it's kind of hard to be certain just what he's thinking. Besides, all this talk about how Holloway Hall reminded him of some dark shadowy place where ghostly inhabitants dwelled was making me just a wee bit uncomfortable. And since it appeared that I was going to have to visit Munster Hall in the very near future, I was trying my best to shrug off the house's rather colorful reputation. Stan's trip down memory lane with a buxom witch and a vampire who happened to have a

23

name more appropriate for a purple dinosaur than for a blood sucker wasn't helping.

I cleared my throat. "Does Mrs. Rodgers know about your, uh, history with this supernaturally endowed sorceress—Angela?" I said, snapping my boss back to the present and out of his prepubescent reminiscences by tossing my notepad on the desk in front of him. I'd drawn a set of collagen-enhanced lips with long fangs protruding, complete with little droplets of blood.

He sat up and glanced at my artwork, put his elbows on the desk and gave me a dark look. "Angelique," he corrected. "So, you think the story is legit?" he asked again.

"I'm fixin' to find out," I said, and stood.

"Just remember what I said," Stan reminded me, and he made a lip-locking motion of his own.

I nodded. "I know. Loose lips sink ships," I said.

"I prefer 'Flapping gums promote job loss,'" Stan replied, sticking his glasses back on his face and turning back to his computer monitor.

I rolled my eyes. Jeesh. Everyone was a comedian these days.

I tried the cell phone number Shelby Lynne had given me, but got her voice mail. I left a message for her to call me ASAP and left my cell phone number. I looked at my watch. Four fifteen. I hadn't eaten in—what—well past two hours. I was a growing girl. I needed sustenance. Something to tide me over 'til supper.

Okay, I should tell you here that I like my food—and most of the time it likes me. Likes me well enough to cling to my hips and thighs like a one-year-old clings to her mother when introduced to a stranger. Or at vaccination time.

I do exercise. Well, at least I think about exercise. And when I can no longer zip up my Levi's without cutting off circulation to everything south of my belly button, I'll actually do it.

I left the *Gazette* and strolled down the street to Hazel's Hometown Café, where you can get a warm slice of apple pie with a generous dip of cinnamon ice cream and a bottomless cup of coffee to wash it down, and all for three and a half bucks. If you aren't offended by the smell of manure, that is.

To be fair to Hazel, I suppose I should explain. You see, lots of farmers frequent Hazel's. Many of them have finished combining by now, and they generally get together this time of year to compare their respective yields. That's bushels per acre for you city folk. There's lots of talk about nitrogen fertilizer, soybean rust and corn rootworm. Yum, yum!

I headed straight for the circa-1950s counter and dropped onto a stool. I picked up a menu, even though I could tick off the breakfast and lunch items from memory, including daily specials and respective prices.

"Well—afternoon, Tressa." Donita Smith greeted me with a cup in one hand and the coffeepot in the other. She placed the cup on the counter and poured it full. I sniffed appreciatively. Nary a cup of stale coffee is poured at Hazel's. But don't look too closely at your cutlery.

Hazel of Hazel's Hometown Café has long since retired. She passes her time socializing at the senior citizen center during the week and pulling slots at the capital city's racetrack/casino on weekends. Her daughter, Donita, and her offspring run the family food business.

"How fares our local celebrity?" Donita asked, returning the pot to its place under the Bunn coffee-maker. "Any Calamity capers to share?"

I blew the steam from my coffee and took a careful sip. "Sorry, Donita. You're gonna have to wait and read all about it in the *Gazette*," I replied, thinking the chronic "Calamity" references were about as funny as *Full House* reruns. Talk about torture. You strap me in a chair and force me to watch hour after hour of Bob Saget being, well, Bob Saget, and I'll tell you everything you want to know. And some things you don't.

"So, you *are* working on something. Something big?"

I pondered the question. I supposed you could call a six-foot-two-inch queen candidate big news.

"I'm doing a feature on the homecoming queen and king candidates," I finally answered. "You know. Real in-depth stuff. Very cutting-edge."

Donita rolled her eyes. "Yeah, I can see it now. The odd couple crowned king and queen. May I present Paula Bunyan and Danny DeVito. Or should I say Sasquatch and Tom Thumb?" Donita shook her head and giggled.

I set down my coffee cup with a loud thump, spilling the contents onto the counter.

"Say what?"

"Oh, I've heard all about it. My niece, Tawny Sue, is up for queen. You know Tawny Sue. She helps out here sometimes. She's my sister Dora Lea's daughter."

I nodded. Tawny Sue was the superjock candidate who had offers on the table from three colleges, in three different sports. All she had to do was decide if she wanted to play volleyball, basketball or softball. Ah, if only all life choices were so clear-cut. "Sure, I know Tawny. Nice girl. Sounds like she's got a great future ahead of her."

"Can you imagine the school going along with such a mean trick?" Donita asked. "What on earth can they be thinking? To subject those poor things to public ridicule. They ought to be ashamed."

I was about to tell Donita that I didn't know about Tom Thumb, but the female half of the "poor things" was more than capable of kicking the competition's butt—literally—but I didn't want to take the chance that I'd say more than I should. I decided I needed something in my mouth to occupy my tongue and teeth. Something sweet. And fruity. And packing more calories than Victoria's Secret models consume in a week.

"Give me a slice of apple pie, warmed up and à la mode," I said.

"A scoop of cinnamon, right?"

I nodded. "A big scoop," I added as Donita went to irradiate the pie. I'd need some serious energy reserves if I planned to drop in for a visit at the creepiest house in the county. Plus, a necklace of garlic and a cross might not be amiss.

"And a Bible," I muttered.

"A Bible? I'd ask what you're planning, but I don't think I want to know."

The stool beside me swiveled, and I turned to see Ranger Rick Townsend settle his tattooed tush upon it. Tattoo? Well, you see, the good ranger and I made this over-the-top bet concerning the outcome of a certain double murder case. Townsend lost and, as a result, sports an adorable but classy raccoon tattoo on his cute bum. How do I know the raccoon tattoo is adorable? Well, I did have to verify that Townsend hadn't welshed on the bet, didn't I? The cute bum? Well, when you view a work of art, you do tend to notice a spectacular canvas. Everybody knows that.

Townsend was in uniform, his long legs cloaked in dark green fabric with black stripes down the sides. Now that fall was upon us, the hunky but vexing officer had switched to his winter uniform, including long sleeves and a tie.

"Why aren't you wearing my birthday present?" I asked, casting a pouting look at Townsend's totally lame tie tack with the DNR logo on it. "I put a lot of effort in locating that raccoon tie tack, you know. It was almost a perfect match for your tattoo. I'm hurt, Townsend. Really hurt."

Rick grinned. "Not state-issued, I'm afraid. But I was touched you remembered my birthday. As I recall, that's the first gift you've given me. If you don't count the horse shit you wrapped in a Godiva chocolates box and left on my doorstep several years ago."

"How do you know that was me?" I asked. "I'm certain there wasn't a card attached. 'To Rick. Enjoy this poop on your special day.' Besides, there must be tons of people out there who like you enough to give you crap on your birthday."

Townsend laughed. "But only one has given me enough crap to fertilize the high school football field until my twentieth-year reunion."

I shrugged. "I still say, prove it," I said.

"Well, afternoon there, Rick." Donita greeted Townsend with a grin and placed a large slice of pie with a generous scoop of ice cream on the top on the counter in front of me. The ice cream was beginning to melt and seep down the sides of the newly nuked pie. Just how I like it. I picked up my fork and shoved an unladylike amount into my mouth.

"What'll you have?" Donita asked Ranger Rick.

"Just give me a glass of milk and a fork," Townsend instructed. "I think Turner here has more than enough to share."

I gave the demented ranger a dark look. "You touch my pie, you die," I told him.

Rick raised an eyebrow. "On second thought, Donita, I guess you'd better bring me my own slice— about half the size of that one." He nodded at my plate. "I've learned not to get between Tressa here and her sweets—especially during certain times of the month. I still bear scars from the time we battled over the last chocolate cupcake at the Coffee Clatch opening."

I stopped shoveling pie long enough to defend my actions. "Hello, it was creme-filled," I said by way of explanation, and shoveled in another mouthful followed by a long swallow of coffee.

"So, Ranger Rick," I said, "what's up with you? Is the hunting community behaving itself? Is everyone wearing those lovely orange vests and hats so they don't get mistaken for some poor unsuspecting stag?"

Townsend took a drink from the tall glass of milk Donita had placed in front of him. I found myself staring at the taut line of his neck and the way his Adam's apple bobbed up and down. I shook my head. I was totally pathetic.

He set down the glass and wiped milk from his lips. "So far so good. A few near misses, but nothing out of the ordinary. How's the news business? And the retail sideline? Oh, and the ice cream hawking, too. I expect with the weather getting colder, most folks aren't eating much ice cream."

We both looked down at the remains of gooey cinnamon ice cream on my plate. I resisted the urge to lick the saucer. Hey, I'm not a totally uncouth hillbilly.

"Ice cream sales have tanked," I acknowledged, "but it's that way every year at this time. But we still sell a lot of ice cream cakes, and all year long the sales of dogs, burgers and tacos are steady. I just hope Uncle Frank doesn't decide to close down during the winter. He's talked about it for years, but he's never done it. Still, now that Frankie is busy with community college courses and courting Dixie the destructor, I'm wondering if Uncle Frank will decide this is the time. If that happens, I'm in deep financial doo-doo." I relied on the income from my job at the Dairee Freeze to take care of my tiny herd of horseflesh and two golden Labs with serious tartar buildup.

"You've heard the saying 'don't borrow trouble from tomorrow, 'cause it's got more than enough of its own'?"

I nodded. "Yeah. Sure."

"Well, that's my advice for you here. When it happens, if it happens, worry about it then."

I looked over at Townsend—just to make sure it was Townsend. These words of wisdom ran counter to everything Rick had drilled into my head for the past five years. *You gotta think down the road, Tressa. Look beyond today. Live with a care for all the tomorrows to come, Calamity.* Now, all of a sudden, Townsend was, what—telling me to stop and smell the freakin' roses?

I put down my cup and swiveled on the stool to face him. "Okay, Mr. Ranger, sir. What gives?"

Townsend drained the last of his milk and looked at me. He had a Groucho-sized milk mustache, but didn't bother to wipe it.

"I'm actually really glad we ran into each other, Tressa," he said, and I watched his tongue sweep over his lip to retrieve some of the milk.

Glad we ran into each other? I felt my cheeks grow warm—and not all because of the tongue thing. "Oh yeah?" I said. "Why is that?"

The ranger leaned in my direction and put a tanned, lean hand on the back of my stool. "There's something I've been wanting to talk to you about," he said.

The ranger wanted to talk? I felt my body move not-so-subtly in his direction. Hey, I warned you I was pathetic.

"Oh yeah?" I managed. "What is that?"

"It concerns both of us."

I moved closer, my nerve endings crackling. "Oh yeah? How so?"

"Because it also concerns our families—people we are very fond of."

Ranger Rick's milk breath fanned my face. I imagined my cinnamon-coffee breath was assaulting his olfactory orifices, too.

"Is this about Craig and Kimmie?" I asked. "Because if it is, I'm ready to accept your admission that you were totally out of line taking off with Craig for some dumb moose hunt in Canada when Kimmie was ovulating."

My brother and sister-in-law had been having some issues relating to parenthood. Craig wasn't sure if he was ready for a child, and Kimmie was tired of living only with one who got a five-o'clock shadow. And

Townsend hadn't helped matters by whisking Craig off to the wilds of Ontario with the issue still unresolved.

He shook his head. "I'm not getting in the middle of that mess, and I'd advise you to steer clear, too. No, this is about other beloved family members."

Holy-moley. Where was this leading? I pressed closer. I could see light flecks of amber dancing in irises of rich brown.

"Oh yeah?" I felt my breath catch in my throat. Was the announcement of a permanent truce about to pass Townsend's lips? Maybe, God help me, a real declaration of affection, even? "Like who?"

"Our grandparents, of course," Townsend said. "Who else? I think they may be moving too fast in the romance department."

"What!" I thought about Townsend's sermon on borrowing trouble for about as long as it took for my hands to reach out for his thick, clueless neck, but unfortunately my butt had run out of chair. I slid over the side and the stool tilted, dumping me to the floor. I heard a loud rip as I descended.

"Ye gods! I hope that was your pants and not a ligament," Townsend said, reaching down a hand to help me up.

I stood and put a hand to my backside, which was beginning to feel a bit drafty. "Shoot. I just got these pants," I said, pulling off my zippered hoodie and tying it around my waist. "They sure don't make clothes like they used to."

Or, sadly, men.

I grabbed my purse, threw money on the counter and headed for the door, but Townsend stopped me on the sidewalk outside.

"Were you aware that since the end of the state fair, my grandfather and your grandmother have become almost inseparable?"

I kept walking. "Yeah? So?"

Townsend ran a hand through his dark brown hair. It settled back into place as if by magic. If I did that, I'd never see my hand again. Unless someone shaved my head.

"Doesn't that concern you at all? Have you even noticed?"

I shrugged. "I've been busy, Townsend. Besides, they're both consenting adults. What they do together is none of our business." I pushed the pedestrian button on the traffic light pole and tapped my foot.

"Your grandmother stays over," Townsend said.

My toe-tapping faltered. "What are you talking about?" I asked.

"Your grandmother. She's been staying over at Granddad's. At night." He raised his eyebrows. "All night," he elaborated.

"Yeah, so? Maybe it got late and Gram didn't want Joe to drive. I didn't want to mention this to your granddaddy, Townsend, but I think I left some things behind in his vehicle on the few occasions I've ridden with him. Look for them the next time you're in his car, would you?" I asked.

He gave me an absentminded glance and ran his other hand through his hair. "Yeah, sure. What did you leave?" he asked.

"My fingernails," I told him.

We crossed over and headed down First Street.

"Very funny," Townsend said. "I think I laughed about as much as I did when I opened my grandfather's medicine cabinet and found that bottle of K-Y lubricating oil," he said. "Or, as you're fond of saying, hardy har har."

I winced. What were my gramma and Townsend's grandfather up to now? And did I want to know?

"That stuff has a variety of uses," I told Townsend. "It could be purely medicinal. Totally innocent."

Rick took hold of my elbow and stopped me. "Innocent? When Hellion Hannah, grandmother of Calamity Jayne, local celeb, finder of stiffs and the state fair queen of intrigue, is involved? Fat chance." He let go of my elbow and took my hand in his. I wished I'd taken the time to do my nails that morning. My peach frost nail color was chipped, and it really didn't go all that well with my tan hoodie and black pants with a butt-crack rip. "You've got to have a talk with your grandmother, Tressa. It's been less than a year and a half since my grandmother died, you know. I think Granddad needs to take things slow and easy. Keep things light and loose."

I shook my head. Slow and easy? Light and loose? Did Rick Townsend know Joltin' Joe Townsend at all?

I looked up at him. "You want me to have the sex talk with my seventy-five-year-old grandmother?"

Townsend suddenly grabbed me and gave me a quick bear hug. "I knew I could count on you, Tressa. Thanks!" he said, and he was off before I could tell him he still had a bit of a milk mustache. Served him right. Cheeky ranger.

"Uh, you rang?" a deep voice rumbled to my left. I turned to find a figure every bit as intimidating as Lurch from *The Addams Family*—and only slightly more animated—looming over me.

"Yeah," I said, looking up. "I rang. I need more information. About our special visitor. You know—the who, what, when, where, why and how of it all. We journalistic types live by those six little words."

"Or die," Shelby Lynne Sawyer replied.

I winced. The last thing I needed was to be reminded of just how close I'd come to buying the farm six months earlier.

I grabbed Shelby's arm and steered her to my car, the white Plymouth that is as conspicuous in my hometown as Hawkeye black-and-gold on the Cyclone side during the annual football showdown. I ran around to the driver's side of my car and opened my door. Shelby stood on the sidewalk near the front and stared for a moment before she shook her head and climbed in the passenger's side.

"You weren't kidding about the pay, were you?" she said, getting in and tossing aside a Sonic bag.

" 'Fraid not," I told her.

She sniffed. "This car smells like dog."

"Two dogs, actually," I agreed.

I put the Plymouth in reverse and backed out of the parking space. Shelby gave me a sidelong look.

"So, where are we going?" She asked.

I put the car in drive. It stubbornly hesitated a bit before the traditional backfire. I tossed Shelby a copy of Elizabeth Courtney Howard's last book, *Satan's Serenade*.

"You tell me, Deep Throat," I said. "You tell me."

CHAPTER THREE

My old jalopy *chug-chugg*ed along the rutted lane leading to the Holloway house. The once-stately home was on a hill on the outskirts of town, up a poorly maintained, dead-end gravel road.

"Are you sure this car will make it up the hill?" Shelby Lynne asked, pulling at her seat belt and trying in vain to get it to lock into place.

"Why? You volunteering to get out and push?" I asked.

Shelby shook her head and chuckled. "You are so weird," she said. She opened the hardback book I'd handed her, and looked at the back cover. "I wonder what she looks like now," she said.

I looked over at the black-and-white author photo. It showed a plain-looking middle-aged woman posing with her chin resting in one open palm— also known in some quarters as "writer's chin."

"What do you mean?" I asked. "There's her mug shot."

Shelby shook her head. "This picture practically

came over on the *Mayflower*," she said. "She's used it for over a decade now. I wonder if I'd even recognize her if I passed her on the street."

I made a *tsk-tsk* sound with my tongue. "Vanity, vanity," I said. "But it's probably not all that unusual for an author to keep the same publicity photo. Face recognition and all that. Personally, I figure if you luck out and get a picture that doesn't make you look like one eye is higher than the other or you have something disgusting caught between your teeth, you'd better stick with it. Besides," I continued, "who would want their wrinkled old puss on the cover of a gazillion books when they can simply halt the aging process and use an oldie but goodie from the past? Plus, Howard has that recluse thing going, so maybe she's camera-shy, too."

Shelby sighed. "I suppose you're right. But somehow it seems beneath the great Elizabeth Courtney Howard to pawn off an old picture on the reading public." She stared at the photo for a few seconds longer, sighed again, then reverently closed the book, resting a palm on the front cover. "So, what are we doing again, exactly? My source tells me that Howard and her entourage aren't due to arrive until tomorrow."

Shelby's "source" turned out to be her mother, Judy Sawyer, who operated a house-cleaning business and had been employed by the probate attorney handling the estate of Benjamin Holloway to clean the house and ready it for temporary occupancy. Judy had been told to keep the identity of the occupants secret; however, she obviously hadn't made allowances for a daughter with an eye at the keyhole or an ear to the heat vent. Or, considering Shelby's stature, both.

I reached into my pocket for a mint I'd pilfered

from Stan's candy bowl, unwrapped it and popped it in my mouth.

"We're conducting a preinterview reconnoiter," I stated, managing to get this out without choking on the hard candy. Shelby gave me a confused look. "It's a military term," I clarified. "Meaning to explore an area to gather information."

Shelby still looked confused. "What information do you plan to gather? No one is there yet."

I sucked on my mint. How did I explain to this high school girl, who was probably suckled on corn-fed beef broth and could toss me and break shot put records, that I wanted to make my initial visit to Haunted Holloway Hall in the light of day and with an able-bodied companion by my side to dispel the long-term aversion I had to the old house? To diminish the mystique of the place. Okay, okay. What can I say? The place creeped me out.

"I just want to get the lay of the land, so to speak. You know, get a feel for the setting. So I can include my impressions in my article, of course." I was proud I'd made my little preinterview visit sound so innocuous.

"*Our* article," Shelby reminded me.

I frowned. This girl listened to each word I said like she was a closed-captioner. "Whatever," I said.

My plucky Plymouth made it up the incline without external help, and I pulled into the circular driveway, which ran through the front yard and past the now-gray peeling columns of the dark stone structure. I put the car in park and stared at the rambling three-story facade, feeling a sudden thickening in my throat that had nothing to do with the mucus-producing dairy product I'd just consumed. The drapes on all of the house's windows were pulled shut, upstairs and down.

On the second floor, French doors led to a flat roof that was home to an outside terrace of sorts. It was surrounded by a black fence made of bent iron and twisted rails.

A dark cat passed lazily by my car door and stopped to bask in the warm afternoon sun, smack-dab in the middle of the rocky lane. I took a loud, shaky breath and saw Shelby glance over at me. I rolled down my window and sucked in another breath, then tapped my chest and burped at will—one of various little talents I happen to possess.

"Indigestion," I said. Shelby raised an eyebrow.

"So, how does this preinterview reconnoiter work again?" she asked. "I'm hoping there's more to it than staring down an old building. Did you even bring a camera?"

I'd left it at the newspaper office, but I wasn't about to admit that to my young apprentice.

"What do you suggest as being pictureworthy?" I asked. "The crow poop on the stoop? The yard that hasn't seen a good weeding since ol' Ben Holloway expired? The black cat licking its nether regions?" I watched as the cat in question slowly finished its ablutions, performed a slow I'm-all-that stretch and proceeded to cross the road in front of us. Damned cat. (Can you tell I'm a dog person?)

"No, but maybe that graveyard over there is worth a Kodak moment."

I'm sure both of us could hear my accompanying swallow. "Graveyard?" I followed the direction of her nod.

"Family cemetery. Lots of families had their own cemeteries back in the day," Shelby Lynne told me. "Especially the rich, snobby ones who didn't want their remains to decompose alongside the commoners. Care to check it out?"

I didn't even try to swallow past the wad in my throat. Instead I made a gaggy, coughing noise to clear it.

"Sure. Why not? No harm in taking a peek, right?" Yeah. That's what I'd told myself when, back in June, I'd opened a trunk looking for a jack and a tire iron and instead discovered one dead-as-a-doornail lawyer with a really awful toupee and a hole the size of Shelby Lynne's fist in his head.

Shelby opened her door and got out. She scooped up the cat and cuddled it while I surveyed the front of the house now shrouded in gloomy shadow. Shelby gave the cat a final squeeze, put it down and came to my window. "Is there a problem?" she asked.

Only with my fine motor skills. My hand did not want to grasp the door handle, and my feet wanted to stay right where they were—among discarded the gum wrappers, stale fries and pebbles that populated the floor of my front seat.

"No problemo," I said, pulling the handle, laying my left shoulder into the door and shoving. My door has a tendency to stick. I don't mind. Sometimes the nudge I give it is the only exercise I get.

I exited my vehicle, leaving the door slightly ajar. Getting the door open from the inside is easier than getting it open from the outside. One icy winter morning last winter I slid all the way under the car trying to get the driver's-side door open.

I pulled a notepad out of my pocket and followed Shelby around to the back of the Holloway house. Brown leaves crackled underfoot as we made our way to the tiny cleared area surrounded by a circle of the thick hedges where Holloway ancestors no longer living were laid to rest. The cemetery, like the sprawling yard, was unkempt and untidy. Tall unpulled weeds framed both weathered and polished marble headstones like fragile, brittle sentries.

I shivered and rubbed my arms. The only thing more depressing than a neglected cemetery is neglected pets and kids. Not necessarily in that order . . .

I wondered if Shelby Lynne experienced the same level of uneasiness I did staring down at the lonely headstones. That question was answered seconds later when she pulled weeds away from the front of an ancient headstone and whistled.

"Man, here's an oldie for you. Roswell Benjamin Holloway. Born 1797. Died 1853." She whistled again. "Oh my gawd! Here's Loralie's headstone! *The* Loralie Holloway! You know, the lady in white!"

I felt some more of my spit dry up. "Is that right?" I managed.

Shelby grabbed my hand and pulled me down beside the tiny flat stone that served as a grave marker.

"Surely you remember the story of Loralie Holloway: the spinster who is rumored to have been rejected by her lover at the altar—after dear old dad, Roswell here, paid him off, that is—and lived out her years a lonely, bitter old woman wandering about the family estate in her faded wedding gown clutching a wilted bouquet of forget-me-nots and bloodred roses to her chest. The virgin specter that, to this day, still walks the grounds of her ancestral home humming the wedding march and pining for her long-lost love."

"Oh. That lady in white," I said, a sudden shiver sending the willies down my body. I looked at the modest headstone. "Loralie Amelia Holloway," I read.

"Born April first, 1827." I blinked and slowly got to my feet, feeling a bit unsteady. "We have the same birthday," I said, totally weirded out by the coincidence.

"You were born on April Fools' Day, too?" Shelby brushed dirt from the lettering. "And look. She died on Halloween. Like, how freaky is that?"

I continued to look at the writing on the stone for a second longer.

"I think I've seen enough," I said, and made my way with long, hurried strides out of the shadows of the cemetery and into the light of the afternoon sun.

"They say Loralie walks the night in search of a lover," Shelby said, catching up to me with little difficulty. "Some people swear they've heard a woman weeping in despair and loneliness, and the next day lonely little red rose petals are blowing about the yard."

I shrugged. "We do grow roses here in Iowa," I pointed out.

"Ah, but this was in the dead of winter," Shelby clarified. "Can you imagine how those red rose petals looked on fresh, unsoiled snow? Like blood droplets falling on a blank canvas."

I stopped. "Do you have to be quite so graphic?"

"Graphic? That's a good thing for a writer to be, right? It lends authenticity to one's story. A sense of realism. Of being in the moment."

"Sure. Yeah. That sounds right," I said, hurrying to my car, pulling the door open and jumping in.

"What's your rush?" Shelby asked, folding her legs and arms into the Plymouth.

"I've got an appointment," I told her. "Family stuff."

She slid her seat belt across her middle and fought

with the fastener until she had it secured. "I guess I'd better get home and start my homework. So, what say you pick me up around six-thirty tomorrow and we come out and set up surveillance? There's a lane down the road a piece where we can stash the car, and we can come up on foot and watch the place from the grove of trees. That way we won't miss her arrival if she comes in early."

"Six-thirty?" I was still in full pillow-drool mode at that hour of the morning. I looked over at Shelby. "Don't you have school?" I asked.

"I'm a senior. My first class is at ten. Besides, if something comes up, you can pretend to be my mom and call in sick for me."

Yeah. Like that was gonna happen. No way was I gonna be called into the principal's office at my age.

I pulled around the circle driveway, past the dark front of Holloway Hall, and headed for the dirt road at the end of the lane. I gave the house one more look in the rearview mirror as I prepared to pull out, my eyes drawn to the French doors on the second floor of the old house. You know, the doors that led to the small terrace. The doors that had been shut, drapes closed, when we'd pulled in. The doors that were now ajar, the curtains swaying in the suddenly chilly afternoon breeze.

I quickly looked away, deciding that if a ghostly white apparition wearing a white gown and clutching red roses appeared, I didn't care to see it.

Let's see. Just what does an ace cub reporter with a nose for news do when confronted with a seemingly newsworthy phenomenon? I hit the accelerator like someone had waved a green flag in my face—or a dozen krispy kremes with chocolate frosting and a gooey white center. The Plymouth skidded sideways out of the driveway and onto the road, gravel spraying and striking the hubcaps I had left and the wheel wells on the tires that went without, and we narrowly missed crashing into the ditch on the other side of the road.

"What the—?" Shelby slid to the side, and her seat belt popped out of the catch and smacked the passenger window.

"Guess I need to fill up the power steering fluid," I said, giving her a wobbly smile.

"Power steering, like hell," Shelby Lynne said, righting herself. "Get rid of the lead foot, would you?"

I nodded. And I'd do it, too. Right after I shed the yellow streak a mile wide running down my back.

I don't believe in spooks. I don't believe in spooks. I don't. I don't. I don't. I don't believe in spooks.

"Are you sure you don't want something to eat, Tressa?" My mom was clearing the supper table when I popped my head into the kitchen over the bar that separated it from the dining room. "Meat loaf and cheesy potatoes," she added.

I rubbed my stomach. "Who made the meat loaf?" I asked.

My mom bit back a smile. "Your grandmother did the honors," she said.

"Maybe later," I said, knowing my grandmother's love for green peppers and onions. "Where is Gram, by the way?" I asked, picking up the pan of potatoes and snitching some with a finger. My mother picked up the meat loaf pan and carried it to the kitchen. I followed.

"She's getting ready to go out. Again," my mother said, setting the meat loaf pan on the stove with a loud thump. "Third night she's been out this week." My mother is a CPA and does bookkeeping and taxes in her basement office. She tends to lean toward economy in conversation.

"Bingo?" I asked.

My mother shook her head.

"Funeral home visitation?"

Another shake of the head.

"Church? Water aerobics? Senior night at the VFW?"

My mom grabbed the potatoes from me, stuck a plastic lid on them and shoved them in the fridge.

"Joe Townsend," she said, and slammed the refrigerator door shut. "Every night for the past two weeks. Except for the nights she doesn't come home at all. Frankly, I don't see where the woman gets the energy." She shook her head. "I told your father he needed to have a talk with her. Her behavior seems a bit . . . obsessive."

Obsessed was more like it. And with Ranger Rick's grandpappy, of all people.

"You know Gram and her phases," I said, trying to comfort my mother, who, with my father at work all day, inherited the dubious honor of being my grandmother's keeper much of the time. "Remember the time she was bent on joining that commune?"

"Nudist colony, you mean," my mother said.

"Or how she had her heart set on auditioning for *American Idol*?"

My mother shook her head. "How could I forget? It was just last season."

"And the time she swore she'd contacted Clark Gable on her Ouija board and sat for two days straight in a turban and beads, trying to reestablish the connection?"

"Lord help us," my mother said, and sat down at the kitchen table.

"So maybe her spending time with Joe Townsend isn't such a bad thing after all." I patted my mother on the shoulder, deciding I probably shouldn't mention the K-Y lubricating oil. "At least Joe is living and breathing—and wears clothes." If neon-colored sweat suits that could blind you in the sunlight counted positively, that is. "Besides, I think it's kind of cute—the two of them—in a blech sort of way."

"Who's cute? That Ranger Rick fella you wouldn't know what to do with even if he came with an instruction manual, step-by-step directions and a CD tutorial?"

My gramma tromped into the dining room, wearing short black boots with two-inch heels that would have crippled most women her age. You gotta hand it to her. Despite having fallen a half-dozen times in the past few years, Gram insists on wearing heels. She's hoping to hide the fact that she's lost several inches in height due to osteoporosis. My mom calls it foolhardy. I call it classic Hellion Hannah.

"We were talking about Joe," I said.

Gram pulled a chair out and sat down. "Joe? Joe Townsend?" She snorted. "He's not cute. He's macho."

I had to grin. The idea of calling bony Joe Townsend macho was akin to calling me Trump *Apprentice* material.

"Are we talking about the same Joe Townsend?" I asked. "Pale, skinny guy with Polident breath and superhero fantasies? A legend in his own mind?"

"A legend like John Wayne, you mean," Gram said, pulling out her compact and checking lips outlined with dark black lip color that brought Kelly Osbourne to mind. "You remember how he rode shotgun with you on that Palmer case? Tailing suspects and flushing out the bad guys? How he helped you discover that dead body? The second one, wasn't it? How he backed you up the night you about bought the farm? The first time, that is. Or was it the second?"

I could sense the escalating tension in my mother's shoulders. I gave them an awkward squeeze, wishing as always that I had inherited a natural ability to offer comfort.

I'm not the most affectionate person in the world. With people, that is. But my critters? I lavish attention on them like a twenty-year-old starlet does on a rich but ancient and ailing husband. I cringe to think what Dr. Phil would say about this behavior. Probably something along the lines of my overcompensating with my pets to make up for a lack of physical closeness with people. Like I need a TV shrink to tell me that.

"So how is Grandville's number-one nosy neighbor doing?" I asked. "Still packing unregistered heat?"

My mother jumped to her feet, mumbling something about husbands who were in serious denial, and left the room. I sat down in her chair and found myself staring at the collection of rings that adorned my gramma's arthritic fingers. Her faux nails were painted an ominous black, to match her lips. She opened her purse—which looked more like an overnight bag, I thought—and brought out a zippered mauve-colored cosmetic bag. She removed some makeup and refurbished herself in her compact mirror.

"Not bad for a woman of a certain age," she said, patting her blue hair. "I think it's that daily fiber therapy I'm on. Food moves through me quicker than beer through a pimply-faced teen boy taking his first drink.

47

Last time they shoved an endoscope up me, I was clean as a whistle. Said I had the colon of a fifty-year-old."

I wrinkled my nose. Way too much information.

"Mom says you're going out again tonight," I said.

Gram gave her reflection a sour look. "Tattletale," she hissed.

"Now, Gram, she's only concerned that you might be overdoing it a bit," I told her. "She's just looking out for you."

"More like looking to cramp my style," she snapped. "I can't help it if she prefers to spend her time in front of a big illuminated electronic square. Me? I prefer human contact."

I rolled my eyes. Gram's favorite chair had a permanent imprint of her butt cheeks from hours spent in front of the tube, watching her TV heartthrob, Bob Barker, plus a seemingly endless selection of daytime soaps and Court TV.

"Mom's computer is her workplace," I reminded my gramma. "Besides, it's getting darker earlier, and the folks just want to know you are in for the night, safe and sound."

"I don't need a warden," Gram said. "As a matter of fact, I've been getting along so well, I've been thinking about moving back into my place. You wouldn't mind a roommate, would you, Tressa? Two single gals sharing digs?"

I suddenly knew what it felt like to be thrown into the middle of one of your worst nightmares, lock, stock and serial killer. I'd taken up residence in my grandmother's double-wide mobile home after several tumbles there necessitated Gram's full-time supervision. My grandma's double-wide is not your typical extra-long trailer on wheels; it's more like two really big trailers stuck together. With two bedrooms, two baths, and the requisite eat-in kitchen, as well as a respectable sized living room, the domicile is large but homey. Like a ranch-style house. The switcharoo was a win-win situation for all of us. Well, except for my mother, Warden Jean Turner, her mother-in-law's keeper. I was out of my folks' house and on my own. (Okay, so I was just a short walk across the driveway from them.) And my grandmother had help available at all times. The idea of sharing even a hotel room with my gramma for one night—let alone a domicile, forever—left me reaching for a handful of Excedrin with a Pepto chaser.

"You want to move back into the double-wide?" I asked, hoping the somebody-kill-me-or-wake-me-up edge to my voice wasn't apparent. Gramma sat across from me, reapplying dark lavender lipstick to her upper lip with generous strokes.

"I'm thinking about it," she said. "It's certain I won't be cramping your style," she went on. "All you ever do is work, eat, sleep, feed critters and pick up their droppings."

I felt the noose tighten. *Kill me. Kill me now.*

"But what if you take another spill? The last time, you were on the floor so long that the linoleum pattern was imprinted on your face," I reminded her.

"Yes, but they have those gizmos you can wear to alert people when you take a tumble. Elvis shoulda had one of those. It mighta saved his life. He keeled over in the bathroom."

I raised an eyebrow. "You swore you'd never wear one of those. You said you'd feel like you were on electronic monitoring like some pervert or two-bit thug," I pointed out.

Gram shrugged and replaced her compact. "I may have been hasty. I've got me a full-time jailer now, so what's the difference? Besides, I was thinking maybe we could do some double-dating: the Townsend men and the Turner women out on the town."

Why did the sound of that bring to mind images of King Kong in New York City or Godzilla wreaking havoc on Tokyo?

"I just don't want to see you make a decision I— you—may live to regret," I said. "There are some perks to staying here, you know."

"Yeah, and Frau Kommandant doesn't let me forget it," Gram said, casting an eye at the door that led to my mother's basement office. "So, what are your plans for this evening, my dear? Work, as usual, I suppose. Cones to dip and sundaes to drizzle. Did you mention my offer of help to Frank? He's never contacted me."

Imagine that.

"It's our slow time at the Dairee Freeze, Gram," I said, sidetracking her. "Things won't pick up till spring. And I'm off tonight for a change. But I'm working on a story for the *Gazette*."

I had Gram's full attention now. Damn. Me and my big fat trap.

"What kind of story? Not more fluff and stuff on homecoming queens, I hope."

I rolled my eyes. Everyone was a critic.

"Actually, it is a seasonal piece," I said, suddenly realizing that I had one of the best sources in the tri-county area for information sitting right across the table from me. "Uh, I'm trying to put together something, uh, appropriate for the Halloween season that has some local flavor. Someone suggested doing a story on the history of the Holloway house." I was making it up as I went—in the best tradition of journalism, some might add.

"Haunted Holloway Hall!"

Oh, buddy. Another country heard from.

"I don't have fond memories of that place," Gram said. "Almost soiled my bloomers there once. Your grandpa Will, God rest his soul, didn't have as much control over his bodily functions, poor dear."

"Huh?" I said, beginning to think I should've kept the zipper shut on my mouth. Like they make a zipper strong enough for that job.

Gram took out a tissue and blotted her lipstick with a pronounced smack of the lips. "It was that damned lady in white, Loralie Holloway," she said. "Flitting about, pale as a ghost. That mournful cry. It really spoiled the mood."

"Huh?"

"The romantic mood, Tressa. You know. Lovers' Lane. Parking. Making out." Another wrinkle joined the legion on her forehead. "You are familiar with the concept, aren't you, girl? Or do I have to get out the Magna Doodle and draw a picture?"

Clearly one of those "I'll pass" moments.

"Romance. Parking. Making out. I gotcha," I said, wondering how the heck the talk I was supposed to be having with my grandma about sex and the single senior had turned into a lecture on sex and the sex-starved single girl. "Go on."

"Well, we were sitting in the car at the end of the Holloway lane and, at a rather inconvenient moment, we heard this sniffling sound."

I frowned. "Sniffling?"

"Like Frankie gets when he's around mold. Or

51

mildew. Or dog hair. Or cats. Or horses. Or soap. Or dust."

"I get the picture, Gram." My cousin, Frank Barlow, Jr.—or Frankfurter, as I like to call him—is basically allergic to life. "Go on," I said again.

"Well, naturally, we stopped to listen, and it was then we saw her."

"Her?"

"Loralie, dear. Try and follow along, Tressa. Well, your Paw-Paw Will and I raised right up and, once we wiped the steam from the car windows, we spotted Loralie garbed in a hideous wedding dress I wouldn't have been caught dead in, sobbing up a storm and dribbling red rose petals in her wake. Your grandfather was startled, and, well, the rest as they say is history. By the time we got ourselves righted, Loralie had am-scrayed, leaving behind a few rose petals and two lovers badly in need of new tighty whities."

I closed my eyes, trying to get a picture of a young Paw-Paw Will and his gal, Hellion Hannah, parked on a dark country road only to be interrupted by a dead wannabe-bride in search of a runaway groom. I did one of those fake laugh numbers that folks use to discount information that is presented to them. "Yeah. I can see it now. You and Paw-Paw Will out on a hot date in his souped-up hot rod. Parked on Lovers' Lane late at night in front of the most notorious house in the county. Whooooo! Spooky!" I said.

My gramma gave me a confused look. "Hot rod?" she said, with a lift of her eyebrows. "Hardly. It was Paw-Paw Will's Buick."

I stared at her. Paw-Paw Will had bought the Buick just three years before he died. At the ripe old age of sixty-eight. I put my head in my hands. Way, way too much information.

Gram stood. "You know, if you want to learn more about the old Holloway place, you should ask Joe. His family was pretty tight with the Holloways years ago. And the family ordered some roof repair materials from Joe's lumber company back in 'ninety-three when we had that doozy of a windstorm."

I resisted the temptation to pull out a hank of my hair or rip some clothing. The last time I'd partnered up with the self-styled Neon Green Hornet, I'd ended up a murder suspect and on a certain ranger's short list of people who should never be allowed within spitting distance of his granddad.

"Joe knew the Holloway family?" I asked.

Gram's brow crinkled. "I seem to remember he had a couple of dates one summer with someone connected to Haunted Holloway Hall. Some gal who went on to become famous or something. An actress. Or maybe a writer. Nothing came of it, of course. Joe is hardly the artsy-fartsy type."

I looked at Gram through my fingers. "Joe dated Elizabeth Courtney Howard?" I said.

"Who?" Gram asked.

I began to rub my temples. "So, where did you say you were meeting Joltin' Joe?" I asked.

Gram looked at me. "Oh, Tressa! How wonderful! You've decided to double-date!"

I looked down at my feet to make certain I wasn't bleeding all over my mother's dining room floor from shooting myself in the foot. "Double-date?"

"With Rick. Oh, Tressa, Joe will be tickled to death. I'll call him and tell him to pick up Rick on his way over!" Gram got up and clomped into the living room like she was leading the Charge of the Light Brigade.

"You do that, Gram," I yelled out to her. "You just do that."

I smiled. One of those naughty Natasha Fatale smiles. Rick had a Texas-sized soft spot for his grandpappy, which made it almost impossible for him to tell Joe no. Of course, it was difficult for anyone to tell Joe Townsend no. However, with the ranger's concern over the amount of time the two seniors were spending together, it was a safe bet he wouldn't turn down the opportunity to play chaperone.

I grinned again. I would have loved to be there to see the audacious ranger's face when Joe picked him up for our double date.

Oooh. I'm such a bad widdle girl.

CHAPTER FOUR

I could detect the I'd-like-to-strangle-you vibes wafting my way as soon as I entered the backseat of Joe's gold Buick. It emitted from the dark figure beside me and permeated the air like the delightful scent of Gay-Ben I mean Ben-Gay—that collected in the living room after my grandmother completed her morning exercise routine with the *Sunrise Stretches with Sally Show* on PBS.

"Isn't this nice?" my grandmother chirped as she settled into the front seat alongside her date. "The four of us out on the town together!"

Something that sounded an awful lot like the snarl my dogs make when Gram's cat, Hermione, strolls by, pierced the darkness to my left. I cast a quick look in that direction, but decided it was best not to further antagonize the shadowy silhouette I knew was already staring daggers at me. Besides, I never like to antagonize on an empty stomach. All right—so I don't like to do much of anything on an empty stomach, except maybe try on swimsuits. Or ride the bull at the Wild

Side, a favorite boot-stompin' country-western bar and grill in the capital city.

"What's on the agenda, Joe?" I asked the driver, scooting up on my seat to get a better look at his weird hat, which resembled a Dick Tracy castoff. "The all-you-can-eat buffet at Calhoun's Steakhouse? The China Buffet? Or do we feel like going a little south of the border this evening? Whatever you and Gram have in mind is fine by me," I assured him.

This was no put on. Frankly, there isn't a menu in print that doesn't include something that appeals to my rather culturally diverse palate. The snort from the silent yet seething man to my left was impossible to miss, but I decided to ignore it.

"I'm sure glad to hear that, girlie," Joe Townsend said, craning his neck around to get a look at me, " 'cause we've got a real special night planned. The senior center is having their annual joint Halloween get-together with the New Holland seniors, so we'll be dropping by there. We always hold it a couple weeks before Halloween. Weather, you know. As unpredictable as the length of the Sunday sermon."

If possible, the negative aura next to me intensified to a level where safety warnings probably ought to be issued for everyone in the immediate area.

"Halloween get-together?" I repeated.

"Of course, I don't plan to do any of that lame pumpkin-seed spitting or bobbing for apples they insist on peddling off on the older set. It's like they think that just because we're getting on in age, we've reverted back to our childhoods. But I sure as heck won't mind cutting the rug with a sexy vampire, I can tell you."

"Vampire?" For the first time, I noticed that my

grandmother appeared to have grown a significant amount of black hair in the past thirty minutes.

"Dat's right, dahlinga," my gramma responded in a way bad accent that had more Midwestern nasal twang than Transylvanian tongue. "I vant to drink your blud," she said, holding up one of her blue-black-nail-painted hands and stroking Joe's right shoulder.

"For the love of . . ." I heard muttered under someone's breath, but I wasn't sure if it was mine, Townsend Junior's, or, God forbid, Townsend Senior's.

"And let me guess. You're supposed to be Count Dracula, right, Joe?" I asked, thinking that getting the goods on Elizabeth Courtney Howard was not going to be as easy as I'd hoped.

Joe snorted. "You gotta be kiddin', girlie." He flipped on the interior light. "Do I look like Dracula?"

I gave the old guy a once-over. Pale skin. Sunken cheekbones. Red-rimmed eyes. Yeah. He could pass for an anemic bloodsucker. Or Skeletor.

"No? Yes?" I answered.

"Think, gal. Think. See the hat? See the long dark cloak?" He pulled out a silver cross. "This help at all?"

I made a face as if concentrating, but frankly I had no idea who the old guy was dressed up as. I made a note about the cross, though. It might come in handy down the road.

"I give," I finally said. "Who are you?"

"Van Helsing, of course!" he said. "Only the most bitchin' vampire hunter in history. And pretty darn sexy, too," he added with a look at my grandmother.

I silently apologized to Hugh Jackman. After this evening, I'd never look at him quite the same way.

"So you chase down vampires for a living and my

grandmother is a vampire," I said, getting a not-so-pretty preview of coming attractions. "You don't plan on, like, chasing my grandmother all night, do you, Joe?" I asked.

He chuckled. "That all depends," he said, casting another quick look back at me.

"On what?" I asked.

"On whether I run," my grandmother said and Joe growled.

I scooted back into my seat and silently cursed with powerful—but unprintable—words the price one had to pay for fame. I'd better get some useful info about Elizabeth Courtney Howard.

"At least you didn't ask if he'd brought along silver bullets," the other backseat occupant observed, a heaping dose of resignation in his voice.

I winced. Knowing Joe, he not only had the silver bullets but was also packin' the means to use 'em.

"You know, Tressa," Ranger Rick said, shifting his length perceptibly in my direction, "if you'd wanted a date with me so badly, you didn't need to use Van Helsing up there to fix us up. You could've just picked up the phone and called. I've never known you to be shy."

I felt Townsend's body heat reach out and wrap itself around me like a warmed towel after a shower. His arm found its way along the top of the backseat.

"What are you talking about, Mr. Moose? This isn't a real date," I hissed. "It's more like work!"

A tug on my hair told me Townsend was winding a strand around his finger. "Oh, so going out on a date with me is work, huh?" he said. "Nice."

"That's not what I meant," I said, thinking that this guy was the only person I knew who could get my juices going. And not just in a sexual way. "I meant that I'm, uh, mixing business with pleasure tonight."

I knew Townsend's eyebrow had done one of those skyward movements. I just knew it.

"What kind of pleasure did you expect?" he asked, moving a fraction closer.

"Why, the pleasure of giving you a hard time," I said, thinking that was a pretty nifty comeback.

Townsend gave another little tug on my hair. "I'm disappointed, T," he said. "I thought you were going to say the pleasure of my company."

"Isn't it the same thing?" I asked.

"When my pain gives you pleasure? I think there's a not-so-nice name for that," he said. "It involves black leather and some interesting little accessories, if I'm not mistaken," he added.

I looked over at him. "Trust you to know about such things," I said. "And keep your voice down, would you? We don't want the characters from *Creepshow* up there to get any ideas. But I'll admit there are times when you're cool to hang with."

"Let me write that one down," Townsend said. "We might have a story here. Let's see. 'Ranger Rick can be cool to hang with.' How about some supporting details for my article, Ms. Turner?" he asked. "Some examples that support the premise that there are actually times you enjoy the pleasure of my company. I want to record this moment for posterity."

The palms of my hands grew moist with dangerous-territory-ahead perspiration. Conversations about feelings and emotions always made me a little anxious. Maybe because I wasn't good at expressing them. Or maybe because I wasn't good at reading them accurately in other people.

You know, I've often wished people had tails. You can tell right away when a dog is happy or sad by his tail. Wag, wag, wag. Happy dog. No big mystery there. But people? People are much harder to figure out. Especially those of the male persuasion. And especially the male to my left breathing down the side of my neck like a blast furnace.

"What was the question again?" I asked with a slight breathlessness to my voice.

"I asked for some examples of how my company provides you pleasure—apart from being your dartboard, that is."

Dang. Apparently I didn't have the same effect on Townsend that he had on me: Sometimes when I'm around him, my brain turns to wet lo mein noodles.

"Oh, the usual ways," I said, hoping he didn't notice the sweat beads popping out above my upper lip.

"As in?"

"What do you want? A list of your esteemed attributes from A to Z?" I asked, suddenly so hot that I felt like I was standing over a grill at the Dairee Freeze, wearing a Gore-Tex winter parka.

"I doubt we have that much time," Townsend said, a grin evident in his voice. "But you could start with A, and we can see how far we get." His right hand came to rest on my right shoulder. "Or maybe we should skip right to F," he said.

I gave him a surprised look. "What the . . . ?"

"F, for fantastic kisser," he elaborated with a low laugh. "What did you think I was gonna say, T? You naughty, naughty girl," he added. "Disappointed?"

"Why, you . . . you A-is-for-asinine ass!" I responded by taking his hand off my shoulder and tossing it back at him.

"It's true, you know," he said. "Even if you won't admit it."

I looked at him. "That I'm disappointed? Not hardly, pilgrim."

"That I'm a fantastic kisser," he corrected with a shake of his head. "Surely you haven't forgotten those heated kisses we shared at the fair earlier this summer."

"Uh, like the place was on fire," I said. "Literally!"

He chuckled. "Keep telling yourself that, Cleo," he said, and I shrugged. Queen of Denial or not, I was gonna make darned sure that I knew right where the good ranger stood before we went and shared this bowl of alphabet soup—or anything else, for that matter.

"Hey, you two! Keep a lid on it back there, would you?" Joe Townsend called from the front seat. "You're steamin' up the windows so much my defroster can't keep up! I feel like I'm in that movie *The Fog*. Don't mind tellin' you I'm getting a bit claustrophobic!"

I shook my head. Townsend men would be the death of me yet.

Surreal seemed a pretty apt way to describe the transformed senior citizen center as we entered the facility, a bona fide collection of assorted freaks. Outside, once I got a look at my grandma's getup, I tried to do an abrupt about-face and skedaddle, but Townsend grabbed my elbow with an "Oh no you don't!" and kept me snared firmly by his side. When his grandfather came around the car in full vampire-hunter regalia—and carrying a nasty-looking hook in one hand and what looked like a dead bird in another—I was forced to return the favor, grabbing hold of Townsend's waistband to keep him from running off.

"What the hell are those?" Townsend asked, gesturing at the hook and bird in his grandfather's hands.

"It's a Halloween costume," Joe said.

Townsend raised an eyebrow and crossed his arms. "For who?"

"Well, for you, of course," Joe said, moving towards Townsend and clamping the bird down on one brawny shoulder. "You can't attend a costume party without a costume. "I wore this costume three years ago. 'Course, I went all out with the mascara and colorful clothes. Even wore a wig with two little braids and jewelry."

"You went as Pocahontas?" I asked, puzzled.

Joe gave me a dirty look. "I went as Captain Jack Sparrow! You know, from *Pirates of the Caribbean*. I even grew a little goatee to add to the effect. Hannah, grab that wig for me, would you?"

"Are you sure that wasn't *The Pirates of Penzance*?" I asked, starting to giggle when I saw the look of horror on Townsend's face.

"Wig? Wig? I am not going to wear a braided wig," he said, putting out a hand and backing up.

"We can take the braids out," Joe said. "Right, Hannah?"

My grandmother, the undead and undeterred, stepped forward. "Well, yes, but, you know, I rather like the braids," she said, putting the wig up to Townsend's face and dangling a braid alongside his ear. "They make a certain statement."

"Yeah, like, 'Can Rickie come out and play dress-up with us?'" I said, laughing so hard that tears came to my eyes.

"No way," Townsend said. "Nobody said anything

about a Halloween party or costumes when I agreed to this little date."

I looked up at him. "You agreed to a date?" I asked, suddenly feeling very not-amused—and slightly nauseated.

"I'm here, aren't I?" he said. "And someone had to keep an eye on Gomez and Morticia there. But no way in hell am I donning a braided wig and a molting bird and going out in a public place where I can be seen. I have a reputation to think about."

"So you'd do it in private?" I asked, trying to get my footing back after the ranger's rather surprising revelation.

Townsend looked over at me and grinned. "For the right price," he said with a wink.

"You're probably out of my range," I said with a sigh. Most delicious things, including studly rangers in rough pirate garb, generally were.

"You might be pleasantly surprised," Townsend said, and I broke eye contact first.

"We'll lose the wig," Joe told him, tying a bright red kerchief around Ranger Rick's forehead and plopping a dark gray tricorn hat on his head. "Here, pull up your sleeve and take this." He handed his grandson the plastic hook. "Grab hold of this and then lower your sleeve over it. Looks authentic, doesn't it? But I warn you. Be careful. You can almost forget you're wearing it. I had a near miss in the john last time I had it on."

I smiled at the sudden wince of pain on Rick's face.

"You'll need a bit of eyeliner," my grandmother said, stepping forward with her smoky gray makeup. "On the eye that doesn't have the patch, that is. Which eye are you planning to cover, dear?"

"Both," Townsend said.

"Let's put the patch on the left eye. The left eye is always weaker, you know. Now, just a touch—"

Townsend grabbed her hand in midair. "Uh, I think we'll let your granddaughter do the honors," he said, taking the pencil from my gramma's hand and holding it out to me. "T? If you would be so kind?"

I gave him an uncertain look. My feet felt heavy as I moved toward Townsend. The idea of doing something so . . . so intimate for the ranger made my spit disappear faster than my gramma when the minister made a surprise home visit. My hand shook as I took the eyeliner.

I stared into the ranger's gorgeous brown eyes, amazed at the trust he'd placed in me. Calamity Jayne. The girl most likely to create havoc out of serenity. Waves in a farm pond. Who struck terror into the hearts of car wash robots everywhere. I put the eyeliner up to his eye.

"Tressa?" Rick said with a soft, soothing voice.

"Yeah?"

"You put that ridiculous makeup on me and I'll leave all my reptiles to you in my will!" he said.

I thought about it for a moment. Seeing Townsend in smoky gray eye makeup was the stuff dreams were made of; however, there were other things to consider. Like the nature of this particular ranger and the creative nature of the pranks he'd pulled on me our whole lives. Ultimately I decided to heed the warning.

"There!" I said, stepping back and motioning at the petulant pirate. "All done!"

My gramma squinted at Townsend. "I normally use a heavier hand, dear," she said. "You can hardly tell he's wearing any."

I handed Gram her eyeliner back. "I'm going for that understated look, Gram," I said. "We don't want Townsend here looking like a crackhead, do we?"

Gram considered for a moment and then turned away with a grunt. "Guess not," she said. "But just so you know, Johnny Depp wasn't so full of himself that he was above wearing mascara," she pointed out.

"The millions of bucks he earned didn't have a thing to do with it, I suppose," Townsend said.

Oooh! The man had apparently been taking a few sarcasm lessons of his own on the side.

"You're next, Tressa."

I blinked. "What?"

"You're next, Tressa."

My throat felt like somebody had their hands on my neck and were squeezing. Three small, insignificant words. Just three little words. Yet when placed in this context and uttered by my rather unpredictable gramma, those teensy words struck fear into the heart and mind of this suddenly contrite cowgirl.

"Huh?"

"Your turn. And I have the perfect costume for you."

More words of doom and gloom.

"That really isn't necessary, Gram," I said, backing away.

"Oh, arrr—but it is, matey," the POed pirate piped up, grabbing my hand and pulling me away from the car I'd been hoping to take refuge in. "Time for yer makeover, darlin', or walk the plank, ye will."

I gave Rick a squint. "Like, who are you trying to be? You sound like a cross between that Aussie croc hunter and Austin Powers."

"Here, dear."

Gram approached, holding out a long black garment

65

and a tall witch's hat. I breathed a sigh of relief. Witches were cool. Tabitha was cool. Samantha Stephens was really cool. And odds were I'd be the sexiest witch at the senior center.

"Your Paw-Paw Will wore this the last Halloween he was on this earth," she said, handing me the costume. "I never could bring myself to wear it, but he'd want you to have it," she said with a sniffle.

I looked at the pointy witch's hat and back at my gramma. "Paw-Paw Will was a witch for Halloween?" I said.

"Well, he couldn't be Dorothy now, could he?" she replied.

I blinked. "Guess not," I said.

"Naturally, I went as Dorothy. Complete with ruby slippers and picnic basket. We caused quite a stir that year."

I nodded, wondering if there wasn't more to Paw-Paw Will than had met the eye.

I took the hat, stuck it on my head and wiggled into the black costume.

"No, no! You need your wig first!" Gram said, thrusting an long, gray, ungodly wig in my direction. "Glinda, the good witch, had the blond hair. Not you!"

"Yer the naughty witch, wench!" my annoying pirate friend ad-libbed. "So don yonder hairpiece, or I'll tickle ye with me one good hand!" He raised his hook and scratched his cheek, and I felt a smile tug at the corners of my mouth.

"You didn't have to wear a wig," I said. "Why should I?"

"Just do as yer told, witch, or yer fish food!"

I rolled my eyes. Rick was really getting into his pirate role.

"Hurry up, Tressa. We haven't got all night!" Gram said as I reluctantly took the wig and plopped it onto my head, trying to right it when long gray strands completely covered my face. I imagined I looked a whole lot like that movie character who crawled up out of the TV set and sucked people's faces off. A world away from Townsend's suave, sexy pirate—but I was thinking I'd still gotten off more easily than I expected.

"There. Happy?" I asked.

"Not yet. You need your nose."

"Come again?"

"Your nose, dear. You have to have a warty witch's nose. Have you ever seen a bad witch who didn't have a big pointed nose with an ugly wart on it?"

"And your point?"

"Not my point! The nose's point. The nose is the point. You can't be a decent witch without a pointy, warty nose."

"Is that, like, written down somewhere? Witch rules or something?" I asked. "'Cause I'm thinkin' I'm more of a *Bewitched*-type witch as opposed to a cackling, scare-your-pants-off, smoke-and-sulphur witch. Don't you agree?" I turned in Van Helsing's direction for some support. "Help me out here, Joe."

He hesitated. "I do have an extra costume I threw in, just in case Rick here balked at the pirate one. You're welcome to wear it."

"Thank you, Joe!" I gushed, thinking that it was a safe bet Joe's other costume embodied someone dashing and courageous. "So what is it?" I asked. "Superman? RoboCop? Spider-man? Or your personal favorite, The Green Hornet?

Joe held up what looked like a plaid skirt. "William

Wallace from *Brrravehearrrrt*," he said, sounding like a rrrreally rrrrotten Sean Connery.

I thought about the kilt and the no-underwear thing, then grabbed the warty green nose from my grandma and stuck it on, securing it in place with the elastic band.

"For the record, I coulda bade a bitchin' Sapantha," I said, the witch nose pinching off my nostrils and making me sound like I had a snot wad the size of a Ping-Pong ball plugging up my nostrils. I shoved the witch's pointy hat back on my head and tossed a long length of gray hair over one shoulder in one of those Cher moves. "Just bitchin'," I said.

"There's always William, lassie," Joe said, holding up the plaid.

I shook my head. Great choice. An old hag or a dude who lost his entrails, along with his head. Decisions, decisions.

"I'll stick with old witchie-poo here," I said. "I find I'm suddenly in the mood to cast a few spells. So, where's my magic wand anyway?" I asked. What self-respecting witch would be without her wand?

My grandma pulled out a hot-pink wand, complete with bright-colored sequins and shiny beads. I made a face.

"What is that? You mug Richard Simmons or something?"

Gram sniffed. "I misplaced the witch's wand. This was the only one I could find. It belonged to my tooth fairy costume. Damn. Why didn't I think to bring that? You'd have made a bitchin' tooth fairy, too, Tressa, but I was in a hurry and the Wicked Witch was the first costume I came to in the closet."

The warty green schnozz was looking better all the

time. And believe me, from where I stood, it was a wonder I could see anything else. The wart was the size of the gum balls we stock in the giant machine at the front of Bargain City. "I guess I'll pass on the wand," I said. "I need to keep my hands free."

"What for?" Townsend asked. "To strangle Morticia there?" He motioned at my gramma.

I sighed. "Not an option, Hook," I replied. "She's already dead. Remember?" I frowned. "Or is that undead?" I scratched my head beneath the wig, which was already beginning to make my scalp itch. "Uh, you wouldn't be interested in trading costumes, would you, Townsend?" I asked. "After all, my Paw-Paw Will didn't think it was beneath him to dress up as the Wicked Witch of the West. So, what do you say?"

Townsend gave me a decidedly roguish grin. "Arrrh, matey, but methinks me makes a bitchin' Jack Sparrow, so I'll be turnin' down your gen'rous offer."

Crap.

"Townsend," I said.

"Yeah?"

"Your parrot is molting," I said and stomped away, wishing for those damned ruby slippers so that I could click my heels together three times and wake up in a more amusing locale.

Like Sheboygan.

CHAPTER FIVE

I'd sashayed around the yellow brick dance floor of the senior citizens' center with the Tin Man, the Scarecrow, the Jolly Green Giant and two Elvises. One Elvis wannabe, obviously patterned after Elvis's beefier days, kept gasping and flinching when the collection of chains around his neck caught on the not-inconsiderable chest hair covering a torso that could have benefited greatly from a bottle of Nair. And a support bra.

Due to my exertions on the dance floor—plus the fact that the hairy Elvis had generally grossed me out—I hadn't had time to eat more than a handful of candy corn as I'd hoofed it by the refreshment table. I bid adieu to my latest dance partner, Michael Jackson, thinking he needed a few more lessons. "Michael" had spent the better part of the dance walking on my toes rather than on the moon.

I thanked him for the experience and hurried to the refreshment table. Nabbing a cold can of pop from the cooler, I placed it against my fevered forehead.

"Aaaah!" I was sweating worse than the guy wearing the furry-lined parka who'd come dressed as Nanook of the North. I eyeballed the goody table, trying to decide what I wanted first. I frowned as my gaze took in carrot sticks, broccoli, cauliflower and low-fat dip. Bran muffins and fake butter! Whole-wheat crackers with the butt-ugliest cheese ball I'd ever seen, and cookies made from what looked suspiciously like shredded wheat.

"Hello. What the heck kind of Halloween spread is this?" I asked to no one in particular.

"The kind meant for folks with hypertension, diabetes and congestive heart failure," Townsend said from behind me.

"I thought you were Sinbad the Sailor, not Dr. Jekyll," I said, yanking my witch nose down to hang like a freaky green necklace. I pulled the tab on my soda can and took a long swig. "Ugh!" I looked at the can. "Sugar- and caffeine-free! No wonder it tastes like cough medicine." I set the can down.

"Have you had an opportunity to speak with your grandmother, Tressa?" Rick asked, grabbing a carrot and dipping it in the low-cal ranch dressing. I gave him a look.

"What's the rush?" I asked. "It's not as if she can get pregnant." I chuckled.

Townsend didn't appear to see the humor in my jest.

"It's just that the longer we wait, the harder it will be for them both to take a step back. Slow things up a bit. Gain some perspective."

Townsend had been in his pirate garb too long. He was already going off the deep end. The last time my gramma had taken a step back was when she walked into an elephant's behind at the Shrine Circus.

"I think you're overreacting just a bit, Townsend. What harm can the two of them getting cozy really do?"

Townsend gave me an are-you-for-real look.

"Are you forgetting the Keystone Kop comedy of errors at the lake last June? Or the fair fiasco? Hell, just last week my granddad asked me if I knew of any divorce attorneys who needed investigators to get the goods on cheating spouses, and wanted to know if I knew where he could get hold of a stun gun real cheap."

I winced. This was probably not the time to tell Townsend I'd caught my gramma on www.security 4seniors.com. "At least they've ratcheted down the firepower from real guns to nonfatal electrical charges," I said. "That's a good sign, isn't it?" I asked.

"Talk to your grandmother, Tressa," Townsend warned. "Or I will."

I was hurt by Townsend's heated opposition to the idea that his granddad and my grandmother might actually hook up. And more than a little indignant. Where did he get off dictating who his grandfather spent his time with? Who was he, Match.com?

"Don't worry, Townsend," I said, spotting what looked like honest-to-goodness turkey sandwiches—albeit on whole grain bread—down at the other end of the table. "I'll do my best to keep my dangerous, designing woman of a grandmother away from your dear old grandpappy. And I'd appreciate it if you would return the favor. In case you hadn't noticed, the bulk of this romantic pursuit has come from a Townsend-powered vessel, el capitan. Permission to fill my face, sir?" I performed a cockeyed salute and made my way to the turkey sandwiches.

They weren't so bad. Not after I slathered them with one-third-less-fat cream cheese and dipped them in the lite ranch dressing three or four times. I was working on a triple-decker creation when I caught a whiff of the unmistakable scent of Polident. Not surprising. The room reeked of it. That and Absorbine Junior.

"Havin' a good time, girlie?" Joe asked.

I shrugged. "The food could be better. How do you stand it?" I asked.

"I usually sneak into the kitchen now and then and grab something from the bucket of chicken someone bought."

My eyes widened. "There's fried chicken in the kitchen? Here? Now?"

He nodded. "A variety bucket. Popcorn chicken. Chicken strips. Original. And some wings."

I felt saliva pool near the corners of my mouth and caught it before I embarrassed myself—or soaked the little man beside me. "You are the man, Joe!" I said, grabbing hold of the old fellow and dancing around him like he was a maypole. Which, come to think of it, he could almost pass for.

Forgetting my turkey concoction in favor of artery-clogging fried poultry, I suddenly realized that I finally had Joe to myself, and I could pump the ol' guy for information about the mysterious mystery writer and the subject of my Pulitzer Prize for Journalism winning feature. I debated my options. Fried chicken or career building? Honey-barbecue wings or network coverage? Face-feeding versus fact-finding. I considered it a moment more and finally decided on the only grown-up course of action: I'd see how much I could get out of Joe, but if I saw Elvis the enormo heading in the direction of the fried fowl, I was in that kitchen quicker than flies on fresh horse dung.

"Uh, Joe, I was talking to someone earlier today and this person told me something really interesting about you," I began, trying to figure out how to get the information I needed without giving any away.

"Oh, yeah? What was that?"

"Well, it was about a kind-of famous woman you mighta had a date with once," I said. I could tell from the sudden glitter in his eyes that I'd gotten his interest.

"Damned interloper," Joe snarled. "Brawny buttinsky."

"What?" I looked around expecting to see Ranger Rick. "Huh?"

"Romeo Rivas over there," he said, motioning at my grandma monster-mashing it up with a tall, silver-haired Zorro type. "He's movin' in on my territory."

"They're dancing, Joe."

"He's making the moves on Hannah."

I wanted to assure Joe that my gammy only had eyes for him—well, now that her cataracts had been dealt with—but remembered Townsend's edict regarding a cooling-off period between the two.

"If that's the case, Joe, she doesn't seem to be objecting," I said, feeling like pond scum when I saw uncertainty reflected in Joe's eyes.

"His wife only passed away six months ago. He didn't waste much time grieving. 'Course, he was hot to trot when she was alive, but no way was Jack gonna walk away from that marriage. She was the one that brought him the family business. Real estate agency and land developers. His son Jerry runs the show since he retired. Always thought ol' Casanova there was on the shady side. Now I can see I was right." Joe gave a disgusted grunt.

I wished I'd never opened my big mouth. I also wished I had a dime for every time I've thought that. If I did, I'd be soaking up warm rays on a white sand beach somewhere, waiting for Orlando Bloom to come apply a fresh coat of suntan oil and nibble an earlobe.

"It's just a dance, Joe," I reminded him.

"That it is, witchie-poo," he said, and pulled me out on the dance floor just as the last echoes of "he did the mash" evaporated. "That it is."

"Tough luck, Joe," I said, thankful to be spared the exertion of the lively dance. I'd just counted my lucky stars, but the music began again. "Is that a tango they're playing?" I asked with a bemused blink.

"That son of a bitch!" Joe said. "Hell yes, it's a tango. And Romeo Rivas over there requested it!"

Rrrawr! I thought. If Joe and ol' Romeo Jack were girls, we'd soon be chanting, *"Cat fight!"* My money, as always, was on the underdog.

"Come on, witch," he said. "Let's tango!"

Duh, duh, duh, duh, duh, duh.

The seductive chords of the tango, coupled with the outlandish costumes my dance partner and I had on, made me feel like I was in an episode of *Dancing with the Stars* meets *The Addams Family*.

"Walk with me, witch," Joe instructed, pulling me to him with a flourish and planting one Old Spice–soaked cheek to mine. "And step and step and step and plant."

"Uh, Joe, about that old girlfriend," I managed between the stepping, planting, sweating, huffing and puffing.

"What girlfriend? And one, two, three, slide, slide, step and plant."

"Elizabeth Courtney to you. Elizabeth Courtney Howard to like a gazillion and one faithful readers."

"And bend and bend and dip."

I heard a pop as Joe pushed me backwards, and I could only hope it came from one of my joints rather than from one of his bones. I wavered in midair, and I thought for a moment Joe would drop me on the hardwood floor.

"Elizabeth Courtney? I mighta had a date with her once," he said. "She went on to become a famous writer. And pivot and step and slide and plant and dip."

I was prepared this time and kept my footing.

"Did you keep in contact? Ever exchange Christmas cards? E-mail? Hemorrhoid remedies?"

Duh, duh, duh, duh, duh, duh.

"We used to get a Christmas card from her. Until about ten years ago, when they just stopped. Ruthie knew her better than I did. Like I said, we only had that one date. She was five years younger than we were. It was a pity date, really. She didn't have anyone to attend prom with, and Rick's grandmother asked me to take her. We had just started dating at the time. Ruthie felt sorry for her. Liz was an odd duckie, she was."

Duh, duh, duh, duh, duh, duh.

I don't know how it happened, but somehow I'd come to be leading Joe in the sultry dance. "And slide and step, and dip." I bent Joe over backwards in an elegant dip, if I do say so myself, and he gave me a surprised look.

"You're pretty strong," he observed.

"Hay-baling and manure pitching," I explained. I've got shoulders most men require steroids and a personal trainer to sculpt. I can't wear shoulder pads in anything. I look like I'm ready to suit up for the Minnesota Vikings' offensive line. Which, by the way, could probably use me, considering their recent season records. "Odd how?" I asked.

"What?"

"You said Elizabeth Courtney was odd. How so?"

I dipped Joe again and we smacked our faces together. I could feel the bristle of his cheek against mine.

"Why are you so interested in Elizabeth Courtney?" Joe asked. "She hasn't been back to these parts since high school graduation."

My slide faltered. "Uh, I'm just trying to get a handle on Howard," I said. "It's always intrigued me how such a famous best-selling author came from our little slice of hillbilly heaven."

"Don't try that hoodoo on me. There's more to it, witchy woman," Joe said, taking back the lead. "So what gives?"

I considered the pros and cons of taking Joe into my confidence. Lots of cons, obviously. After all, Joe was a major-league legend in his own mind. That delusion apparently ran in the Townsend family. But there was also one very compelling pro: He had known Elizabeth Courtney when she was a young girl. Had even taken pity on her and escorted her to the prom. She owed him. And that was one payback I wanted very badly to be part of. And to exploit, if possible. Of course, Joe didn't need to know that just yet.

"She's coming back to Grandville," I said, as Joe prepared to dip me. "There could be a story there," I went on, as if the idea of a gargantuan scoop was as commonplace as brushing and flossing. "And it might be a great opportunity to, uh, renew old acquaintances," I added, casting a telling look at my gramma, Vampyra, and Romeo Rivas, her masked Don Juan.

Joe's eyes followed the track of my gaze.

"Hmmm. Yes. I see what you mean," he said. "Couldn't hurt, could it? Renewing old acquaintances."

Duh, duh, duh, duh, duh, duh.

"You know, Joe, it's probably wise to keep this under your hat—until you find out if she's even willing to see you again, that is," I explained. "No point putting yourself up for public humiliation like that if Courtney Howard's gotten too high and mighty to remember old friends," I told him, feeling like something you scraped off your boots after mucking out the stalls. "And, remember, you did say she was odd even back then. No telling what time and celebrity has wrought." I was sooo bad.

Joe gave my grandma another intent look.

"And what do you get out of it, girlie?" he asked.

"Why, the pleasure of seeing you reunited with an old friend, of course," I told him, hoping I didn't end up a smoking pile of smelly, singed clothing like my Oz counterpart.

"Right. And a pretty juicy story, to boot," Joe said.

"Well, the moment does deserve to be recorded for posterity," I agreed, borrowing from Townsend's earlier quip.

"Posterity's posterior," Joe said. "Don't think I don't know what a journalistic coup it would be for you to get an interview with Elizabeth Courtney Howard and why you want this kept on the q.t.," he said. "Just don't forget who the founder of the feast is," Joe told me.

I gave him a narrow look.

"And don't you forget whose gramma you've got

the hots for, Van Helsing," I reminded the lovestruck senior.

Duh, duh, duh, duh, duh, duh.

One more dip by Geriatric Joe. I saw his intent a half second before my butt hit the hard floor.

"Guess your weight got too much for me," he said, looking down at me.

I stared up at him, not believing the guy who'd plied me with brownies, doughnuts, coffee cake and liquor now had the gall to call me fat.

"That's okay, Joe," I said. "Not everyone can be built like Romeo Rivas."

Joe stomped off. I rubbed my butt. Okay, so I was no Samantha Stephens. Get over it. I was about to get up on my own when a hand was extended to me.

"Well, look who we have here! If it isn't Calamity Jayne. What brings you to the senior center? Looking for a date? Gotta tell you, I don't think anyone's that desperate."

I wrinkled my nose as if I smelled something bad. Okay, so I did smell something bad—the competition.

I let Drew Van Vleet help me to my feet. I dusted off my black cloak, straightened my hat and pulled my nose out of my cleavage.

"Maybe I'm looking for a story," I told the blond-headed, fair-skinned, college graduate know-it-all who bore a strong resemblance to the youth who appeared on the Dutch Boy paint commercials and paint cans.

"Here?"

I shrugged. "A human interest piece, maybe."

Van Vleet gestured about the room. "I don't see many humans of interest here," he said, and for the first time I noticed what he held in one hand. A honey-barbecue chicken wing. *My* honey-barbecue wing.

My eyes on the wing, I asked, "So what are you doing here, then?" Besides pilfering from the Colonel's bounty, that is.

"I'm here to take a few pictures of the old folks recapturing their lost, lamented youth," Drew Van Vleet said. "It's good for business. Plaster pictures of the dinosaurs in the newspaper, and it increases the advertising stream from their doting families."

I frowned, wondering how a guy this young could become so cynical and jaded. So manipulative. Then I remembered how I'd just exploited Joe Townsend's affection for my gramma. I was worse than pond scum—I was Drew Van Vleet's evil twin.

"You give up on your fledgling journalistic career yet?" my unfriendly rival continued. "I can't believe Rodgers has kept a no-talent hack like you on." He brought the wing to his mouth, then paused. "You're not doing him, are you?"

I corrected my earlier assessment. Okay, so I was no Pollyanna, but compared to this guy I was a freakin' Snow White. With cooler clothes, though. And a huskier singing voice.

"Nice, Drew. Does your boss Daddy know you talk like that?" I asked.

He laughed. "Piece of advice here. Stick to cone dipping and burger flipping, blondie, and leave the reporting to the trained professionals," he said. "You know—someone with postsecondary education whose high school diploma doesn't come with the disclaimer, 'This graduate's performance does not necessarily represent an accurate assessment of GHS academic standards.'"

He brought the chicken wing to his lips and ripped into the meat much like I felt like doing to his pale white neck. I looked around, hoping my gramma was nearby. Her vampire teeth would come in handy right about now. Seeing that she was occupied with Romeo Rivas and the Tin Man, I decided to utilize the only other weapon I had available—and the only one I possessed that was never unloaded. Yep, you guessed it: my motormouth.

"Yeah, I can see how you'd need specialized training to cover the Rural Water Department's monthly meeting and the Quilting Circle's quiltathon to raise funds for the Butterfly Garden. Compelling stuff," I said. "Still, I imagine the heat is on over at *New Holland News*, seeing as how this past year the *Gazette* has broken the two biggest news stories that the county has seen since Tom Arnold and Roseanne Barr tried to open that loose meat sandwich joint," I said. "But, hey, look at the bright side. You've still got the Senior Citizen Monster Bash here to cover. And guess what? Elvis is alive and well and stuffing spoonfuls of lite sour cream dip in his face as we speak. So there's your big scoop! You're a professional—get on it, man! Nail that sucker! Make Edward R. Murrow proud."

Van Vleet tossed his mangled chicken wing on the table, his hand shaking from rage. Or laughter, maybe. Sometimes it's hard for me to tell one reaction from the other. I get both so frequently.

"Funny stuff," Drew Van Vleet said. "You might have a career in journalism, after all. Too bad *Mad* magazine is defunct. You could always try an Internet blog."

Danger. Danger. Sensors were picking up anger in the area.

"Maybe I will. It's bound to be more exciting than what folks read in the *New Holland News* as of late," I replied.

Drew picked up a soda from the table. I didn't bother to warn him it was diet. Let him find out the hard way like I had. He opened the can and took a long drink, then looked down at it in his hand. Ha.

"I feel I should warn you, the story I'm working on now will make your little fair feature and stiff story look like items from the Grandville High School rag. This story has major worldwide appeal," Drew promised, taking another swig of his pop and then making a face.

"What a coincidence," I said, unable to seal my lips before they got me in trouble. "I'm working up a pretty high-profile feature, too."

"Is that so?"

I nodded. "So I guess we see who puts their story to bed first," I told him.

"That's paper to bed, Einstein," Drew said, then walked off, shaking his head.

I remembered his gnarled chicken wing and hurried to the kitchen, only to discover the Colonel's bucket was bare and all that was left of the wings was some honey-barbecue sauce on the bottom of the box. I ran a finger through the sauce and stuck it in my mouth. It was soothing as a pacifier.

Drew Van Vleet thought he was so superior. Just because he had a college degree and his daddy owned the paper didn't give him the right to ridicule my credentials or my standing as a newspaperwoman. I had a pretty impressive portfolio going. Okay, so more of it than I'd have liked was due to dumb luck, but I'd thought I'd gotten past having to meet a burden of proof every time I stepped out as Tressa Turner, ace cub reporter. I thought of the slogan on the coffee mug my sister-in-law had given me for my birthday last year: *Whatever women do, they must do twice as well as a man to be thought half as good. Luckily, this is not difficult.*

I stared at the bottom of the chicken wing box as a call to arms gurgled up from my cavernous stomach. A cry for retribution. A challenge to accept.

I brought my hands together, wringing them in true Wicked Witch of the West form.

"I'll get you, my pretty," I cackled. "And your stupid newspaper, too! Aaaaahhaaaahhhaaa!"

CHAPTER SIX

Joe dropped Gram and me off before ten. The drive home was eerily quiet—especially given the fact that three-fourths of the car's occupants were usually vying for airtime. Joe was cranky and out of sorts. Gram was distracted—more so than usual. I was secretly plotting my revenge on a certain chicken-stealing cretin and trying to incorporate the flavor of the season in my payback. Smashed pumpkins on his driveway? Too traditional. A burning bag of poop on his front step? Done to death. An outhouse chained to his trailer hitch? Drew Van Vleet wasn't worth that much effort.

Townsend was in the best mood of us all, smiling and jovial. I wanted to slap him upside the head. No doubt he'd taken Romeo Rivas's dance with my gramma and the silence in the front seat as proof positive that I'd had "the talk" with Hellion Hannah and effectively applied the hand brake to the couple's runaway romance. Poor daft fellow. He needed a Dr. Phil reality check.

Inside, I sat at my tiny kitchen table and doodled drawings of scary, bare, leafless trees, with a huge moon in the background and pumpkins with various jack-o'-lantern faces. My golden Labs, Butch and Sundance, must have sensed my preoccupation, because they paced the kitchen floor like my mother's clients during tax season. Or me before I summon enough courage to open my credit card statements.

I thought again about Drew Van Vleet's insults. His put-downs. His superior attitude. The total dismissal of my accomplishments as if they were all results of happenstance or luck. Okay, so I'd already acknowledged that I hadn't actually gone looking for either of my big news stories, that they'd come looking for me, but still, what I made of those opportunities ought to count for something, right? Something more than "Calamity Jayne is at it again."

What would it take for me to live down twenty-two-years of *I Love Lucy* antics? I tapped my pencil on my pad.

I thought about that. In some ways, did I even want to? I had to ask myself. I loved Lucy. I got Lucy. She was an original. No one could duplicate her style. And look where it got her. A good living. A nice-looking Cuban crooner husband. A chance to meet my personal hero, John Wayne, and a plethora of other stars. Plus the opportunity to squish grapes with her bare feet and stuff her blouse with chocolate. Not many actresses can put that on a resume.

Okay, so maybe my methods were a bit unorthodox. Perhaps I didn't have the highest academic performance. Maybe I didn't graduate in the top fifty percent of my class. Maybe I wasn't the sharpest knife in the set, but I had something Drew Van Vleet didn't.

I had Lucy Ricardo. And that, my friend, was more than enough.

I grabbed my car keys, a flashlight and a black denim jacket from the coat tree. Oprah had done a show about phobias several weeks back and, by the time the show was over, a girl who was petrified of spiders was letting a tarantula crawl up her arm. The key, the phobia expert said, was to confront your fear head-on. Don't give it power over you, but take back your power over it. The man who was cured of his fear of public restrooms made a believer out of me.

I was going to take that lesson to heart. I was going to drive out to Haunted Holloway Hall that very minute. Drive right up that driveway, get out of the car and walk back to that creepy cemetery. I was going to face my fears and take back my power. And get on with life.

I shoved the dogs out the door with me and herded them into the backseat of the Plymouth. I jumped behind the wheel and twisted around to look at my pets.

"I'm going to confront my fear tonight, fellas," I told the two dogs, who listened obediently. "Look it straight in the eye and not flinch. There's only one thing I need from you two," I said. "Butch. Sundance. Please, one of you guys, bark me out of it!"

My pooches just looked at me.

"Oh, great," I said. "You two get the opportunity to raise a ruckus and what do you do? Become civilized."

I started the car, and it belched a couple times before firing. I really needed a new car.

"Woof! Woof!" came from the backseat.

"Oh, so now you two have something to say," I said. "Nice."

I threw the car into reverse and backed out. I wondered if the fellow on Oprah who was terrified of rest-rooms felt as nervous as I did now, when he walked through that restroom door at O'Hare airport. He was lucky, though. At least he had a convenient place to tinkle in case the jitters got too much for him. Me? I'd have to find a place to squat if I got the urge. My luck, I'd end up with poison oak on my butt.

I stepped on the brake and stopped the car, suddenly wondering if losing my 'fraidy cat status was worth all this.

"Woof! Woof!"

I rolled my eyes. Another country heard from. "I'm going. I'm going!" I said, and put my foot back on the accelerator. "Backseat drivers," I scolded.

My speed decreased significantly the closer I got to the house on the hill. I already had to pee, and the bossy mongrels in the backseat were getting restless, too.

"It's your fault, you know," I told them. "All you had to do was bark me out of it. But oh no. You two sat there like those pets whose owners have them stuffed, posed and preserved after they die. Like, totally silent. By the way, don't expect the taxidermy treatment. Much as I love you two, it's rather costly. Besides, it's really gross!"

I pulled alongside the road just down from Holloway Hall and killed my lights. I checked my watch. Eleven fifty-five. Five minutes before the witching hour. Perfect timing, Tressa. It had taken me longer to get to the other side of town than it did for me to drive to Des Moines. And back. I supposed confronting one's fear was not a matter to be rushed. It took time. Thought. Oh, and courage.

"Okay, so here's the plan, fellas," I addressed Butch and Sundance again. "We get out, stroll to yonder cemetery. We stand there for a minute to prove I'm not chicken—a minute ought to be sufficient time to prove I'm brave, right? Then we're back in the car and heading home and it's Miller time!"

Butch and Sundance barked their agreement. Or maybe their reluctance. Who can really know for sure except Dr. Dolittle?

"So what do you think, fellas? I'm excited about this plan. Are you excited? I'm excited." Uh, in case you hadn't noticed, I tend to babble when I get nervous.

I got out of the car and left my door ajar, and opened the back for the pooches to pile out. The beasties sat and looked at me.

"Come on, boys! Let's go, fellas!" I urged. Butch and Sundance began to whine in stereo. "What is it with you, two?" I asked. "Don'tcha wanna get out and run?"

More whining. I grabbed hold of Butch's collar, since he was closest to me. "Come on, Butch. Let's go!" I said, and tried to pull him toward me. He was having none of it. I finally gave up.

"What the heck is wrong with you two? We're a team here. Like the Vikings. Okay, bad example. How about the Three Musketeers? Do I hear Moe, Larry and Curly?"

The dynamic duo stuck to the backseat tighter than my uncle Frank sticks to his checkbook.

"Come on, guys. Help me out here." I was not above a little whining myself. Unfortunately, it fell on ears unable to appreciate the carefully placed inflections.

I tapped my nails on the car door. "Roy Rogers's wonder dog, Bullet, wouldn't cower in the car," I pointed out. "Rin Tin Tin would be out of there and ready to rock and roll in a heartbeat," I said. "Heck, I bet the Taco Bell Chihuahua would even be game." I waited. I couldn't even shame the suddenly timid two-some into action.

"I'll remember this the next time I fry up a pound of bacon," I told the craven canines. "And at your next bath time." I shut the door and grabbed my flashlight, trying to ignore the shaking of my hand.

This was nothing, I told myself as I concentrated on putting one foot in front of the other, moving at an old lady's pace up the driveway to the house. No big deal. Take a casual meander up the drive of a house reported to be haunted, meander back to the family graveyard, count to ten, then hightail it back to my car and drive home and pull the tab on a cold one to celebrate my triumph over trepidation. Don't you just love the thesaurus? Like, when will I ever have the opportunity to use the word "trepidation" again?

I crept— Wait, that sounds way too cowardly. Let's make that "moved stealthily." It's more heroic, don't you think? I moved stealthily up the driveway, dousing the light when I saw a dark cargo-type van backed up to the side of the house. Holy bat guano! Did my eyes deceive me, or was the author in residence?

I moved to the right of the driveway and hid—took cover—uh . . . secreted myself behind some thick lilac bushes now somewhat devoid of greenery, yet with branches still thick enough to hide . . . er, conceal me.

I could pick up the low, hushed tones people seem to use when it's dark out, no matter whether their nearest neighbor is next door or like twenty city blocks away. Like we were. With no one around to hear them for miles and miles. Like we were.

I was suddenly getting a not-good feeling about my little symbolic self-improvement campaign. Like, it would tank like Michael Dukakis's presidential campaign. (See? I do remember some stuff from school. Especially when public figures make asses out of themselves.)

I watched as two figures emerged from the front door of the house. Lights from the porch revealed a man and a woman. My eyes were immediately drawn to the woman. I couldn't help a nervous intake of breath. Could this be the famous but unsociable Elizabeth Courtney Howard? I took in the dark shoulder-length hair and approximate age of forty or thereabouts, and decided this could not be the world-renowned author. Too young. Too not-gray.

I checked out her companion. I'd never been good at judging age, but I guessed he was probably in his early to midthirties. Cropped dark hair. Muscular build.

The man walked around the side of the house, stopped at cellar doors that lay flat against the ground, and grabbed hold of a handle, lifting and opening first one door and then the other. He said something to the woman, but I was too far away to make it out.

He met her at the back of the van, and they opened its doors. More conversation. They appeared to be in the process of unloading something. The van bounced a bit as the two struggled with whatever it was they were trying to remove. A grunt followed by a colorful curse, both courtesy of the man, pierced the eerie silence of the night.

And the next thing I knew, the two were on the move and heading in the direction of the cellar doors, the man walking backward, the woman at the other end.

I finally thought to look and see what was so important that it had to be unloaded in the dead of night. I

stared at the long wooden box between the two figures, and felt the sudden urge to tinkle in my pants.

Uh-uh. No way. Couldn't be. That was *not* a coffin
being carried down the stairs and into the cellar.

It was a crate. A storage box. A trunk. Illegal drugs.
A box of automatic weapons. The missing weapons of
mass destruction. Anything. Anything but what it appeared to be.

A thick, heavy scent of roses reached my nostrils,
and I looked around. I stood there shivering, silent as
the grave—uh, silent as my uncle Frank at tithing
time. Or my dad most of the time. A sorrowful moan
mingled with the tragic bouquet of the floral fragrance
in the night air. I tensed again, catching movement beyond the house, just outside the circle of bushes that
surrounded the Holloway family cemetery. What the
hell was that? I put a hand to my eyes to remove the
glare from the porch light and squinted into the darkness. I squinted harder when I saw a splash of white,
stark and pallid against the dark backdrop.

"Scooby freakin' Doo!" I whispered. "Holy Halloween!" I watched, unbelieving, as a wispy sheet of
almost-transparent white appeared to float across the
backyard, soft whimpers of heartache providing
macabre accompaniment. "Loralie?" I whispered.

I was, like, totally on the verge of embarrassing myself at this point. Good thing I was alone. Well, sorta.
Kinda.

A sudden movement from behind caught me off
guard. Hot breath singed the back of my neck.

"Loralie?" I squeaked.

"No. But I'm by far your biggest nightmare," a
deep voice declared. "Partner."

I winced.

"I have a very good explanation for this," I said, keeping one eye on the lookout for the filmy white object I'd observed earlier—which now appeared to have vanished—and one on the hand that had a tight grip on my arm.

"I look forward to that," Shelby Lynne replied, and I could have sworn I heard the sound of cracking knuckles.

As I walked back to my car, stopping to look over my shoulder not more than—what? Ten or twelve times? I thought that getting Shelby to put the blame on Oprah was going to be much easier than convincing her there was a coffin in the cellar and a ghost in the graveyard.

Gee. Those sound like really rockin' book titles, don't they? Too bad I was too cowardly to write the books.

Thirty minutes later Shelby Lynne Sawyer looked no less menacing than before, arms crossed, one size-eleven foot tapping in a dum-dee-dum-dum rhythm that didn't bode well for the good ol' girl who'd done her wrong. In a nonsexual context, of course. Considering her extreme length, I should've known Shelby Lynne would go to extreme lengths to protect her interests in the story.

After she'd caught me in the act of cheating, so to speak, she'd followed me back to my humble abode, sticking to my bumper so close I could've seen the whites of her eyes in my rearview mirror—if I had a rearview mirror, that is. Mine fell off some time ago. I figure if I really need to see what's behind me, I can just stick my head out the driver's-side window and take a look-see.

Shelby stood at the sink in my cute but compact kitchen, taking up a considerable chunk of square footage. The expression on her face was not unlike the ones directed at me by various police personnel upon the recounting of my stiff-in-the-trunk story earlier that summer. It's a cross between the look Dick Cheney wears much of the time and the one John Kerry wears when Senate business forces him off the ski slopes.

"So you saw two people unload a coffin and carry it into the cellar at Haunted Holloway Hall. Was this before or after you saw the ghostly white apparition? And after you took your Xanax, I presume. Or maybe you saw what you saw because you're off your meds."

I gave her a rather weary version of my eat-dirt look. I usually reserve it for Rick Townsend, but I thought the occasion—and the recipient—called for it.

I drained the glass of water I'd poured and gave Shelby another disgruntled look—one that clearly showed my displeasure but wasn't so defiant as to get me bench-pressed. I'd really wanted the light beer I'd promised myself earlier, but figured with an under age person on the premises, I'd better pass on the alcohol. Still, with Shelby's size and weight, I had no doubt that she could probably drink me under the table with relatively little difficulty.

After careful consideration, I was ready to concede that perhaps I'd been wrong about the ghostly manifestation near the cemetery. For all I knew, I'd mistaken a clothesline sheet or a loose piece of plastic blowing in the wind for something supernatural. I do tend to have a rather healthy and active imagination. Especially when I happen to be on the grounds of a house that has had more spooky tales associated with it than the Tower of London does.

But the wooden box? Now that puppy was definitely not the product of an overly stimulated—albeit naturally squirrelly—imagination. Nor was it linked to drug use, legal or otherwise, or related to a history of mental illness. That's not to say my family tree doesn't include a few branches that are home to members who occasionally forget where they hide their nuts, and who, from time to time, like to indulge in a game of road tag on the state highway.

"The only meds I take go plop, plop, fizz, fizz when you drink 'em," I told Shelby. "And I didn't say it was a coffin, exactly. It just looked like one."

"And the ghost?"

I shrugged. "I suppose I might have been mistaken about that," I acknowledged. "I did have that hot dog with sauerkraut and a side of onion rings for lunch."

Shelby grunted.

"And you know, Shelby, it's not as if I went out there at that hour of the night with the intention of getting an interview or anything like that," I pointed out.

"Right. You were on your vision quest," she said with a giant-sized sneer.

"I went to face my fears," I explained again. "To vanquish my phobia. To take back the night."

Shelby sighed. "You pull another Lone Ranger act on me, Kemosabe, and I'll take this story back—all the way to your friend Drew Van Vleet in New Holland."

"Excuse me?" I said and got to my feet. This was one of those throwin'-down-the-gauntlet moments. Or, to go with the season, the equivalent of a mooning-your-athletic-opponents moment. "You'd conspire with the enemy?" I asked. "Join forces with Attila the Dutch? Betray your own heritage and hometown and throw your lot in with the wooden-shoe brigade? Have you no loyalty?"

"I'd tiptoe through the tulips with a whacked-out two-hundred-pound Tiny Tim to meet Elizabeth Courtney Howard. You think I won't enlist the aid of your competitor if you won't honor our agreement? I'll do it quicker than you can say Dutch Letter, girlfriend," she announced.

I winced. Hoisted on an almond pastry.

"I have every intention of keeping you in the loop, Shelby Lynne," I said, deciding a pinky-swear gesture at this point would probably only succeed in getting me a broken pinky. "Like I said, I had no idea anyone would be there at that time of the night. Who would? You'd already told me they wouldn't arrive until tomorrow. I just had an issue or two I felt I needed to resolve so I could give my best to our little joint endeavor."

Shelby shoved away from the sink, and I forced myself not to back up. We stood eye to unnaturally thick neck. A crick developed near my collarbone, but, warrior woman that I am, I ignored it and stood my ground.

"See that those little 'issues' don't interfere with our journalistic extravaganza, or you'll be reading all about it in the *New Holland News*," Shelby Lynne advised. "Understand, partner?"

I nodded. "Roger that," I said.

She backed off, seeming satisfied at my capitulation. "So, what time are you picking me up, again? For the return to Haunted Holloway Hall," she elaborated before I could ask, "Huh?"

I made a face. She made it sound like one of those

hokey horror-movie sequels. Uh, not exactly what I wanted to hear right about now. At least my next visit would be in broad daylight. Everything that went bump only bumped in the night, right?

"Pick me up at six-thirty sharp," Shelby instructed. "And be punctual. My naturally sunny personality turns cranky when I have to wait on people," she added.

I rolled my eyes. I must've blinked and missed her Mr. Rogers moment.

"Make it seven-thirty," I said, feeling the need to at least put on a show of being the grown-up here. "I'll need to make a coffee-and-doughnut stop. Stakeout essentials," I added for her edification. "We may need nourishment."

Shelby nodded, and I thought I sensed a fellow Krispy Kreme fan.

"I take my coffee black," she said. "And no jelly filling. I prefer pudding or creme."

I nodded my understanding, thankful that I'd discovered something else we had in common besides an affinity for sarcasm. And, curiously, I got the feeling that before our little odyssey was over, I might find that Shelby Lynne Sawyer and I were more alike than I ever expected.

And that was the scariest thought yet.

CHAPTER SEVEN

Orlando Bloom was whispering sweet nothings in my ear, his hot breath inflaming my cheek, a finger tickling the love handles I vowed to have liposuctioned away if the diet and exercise routine I planned as New Year's resolutions tanked. I giggled. "Stop that," I said, reaching out to slap his hand away in a mock show of resistance. The poking resumed. "Behave yourself, you naughty, naughty boy," I said and laughed, grabbing the persistent finger, preparing to bring it to my lips.

"You havin' one of them wet dreams?"

I blinked. Orlando had apparently relied for too long on writers to put words in his mouth. His extemporaneous romance dialogue sucked big-time.

"I've been up for hours, Tressa. Waiting for you."

"You have?" I came close to swallowing my tongue. There was hope for the guy yet, I decided, in a let's-get-naked-and-dirty sort of way.

"You're darn right. Now, if you're done slobbering on my hand, I need to tend to my ficus."

I tried every way I could to decipher the hidden—and erotic—meaning behind Orlando's latest remark, but the ficus reference totally threw me.

"Is there someone else?" I finally demanded, thinking his fiction about ficus-tending was about as lame as they came.

"Who else you expectin'? That ranger you'll probably let slip through your butterfingers?"

"Ranger Rick?" How had my little encounter with Orlando turned into a ménage à trois?

"So where do you suggest I stick it?"

Okay, that one did the trick. I went from drool-drying-at-the-corner-of-my-mouth slumber to near panic that the first sex I'd had in way too long was about to be with a partner who needed a diagram of human anatomy to figure it out.

"Uh, it's not a good time," I said. "And I, like, have the nubs."

"Is that like crabs?"

I opened my eyes to find my gramma bending over me.

"Don't you have to get to work somewhere? You know. Pick a job. Any job."

I blinked the remaining sleep out of my eyes and stuck my head beneath my pillow, moaning when I put the past few minutes of my life on rewind and then rolled the tape forward. I didn't think I could face my gramma ever again.

"Then you're off today? Good. You can help me bring over some of my other things. And we still need to decide about the ficus."

That brought me out of my blanket cave like my mother's chocolate-chip pancakes brought me to the breakfast table on Sunday mornings.

"What? What things? What ficus? What are you talking about, Gram?"

"Why, what we discussed earlier, of course. Me moving back in. No time like the present, they say."

"They? Who's 'they'?" Let me at 'em. I wanted to kick their butt but good.

I glanced at the window. It was just beginning to get light outside. I cast a hurried look at my clock radio. Six-thirty. I needed to shake a leg or, if I wasn't careful, Shelby Lynne would be gnawing on my other one.

I threw off my blankets and hopped out of bed. Butch and Sundance pranced underfoot, eager to answer their respective calls of nature.

"Those dogs will have to stay outdoors, you know," Gram told me. "They're always underfoot. I'll be flat on my back faster than that old slut Abigail Winegardner. Besides, Hermione can't abide your dogs."

Uh, the feeling was mutual.

"Gram, can we talk about this later? I have to shower and get to work. Plus, I need to make a stop on the way." No way was I going to tackle a tough story without my java and pastries.

"Which job are you going to? Frank's Freeze? Bargain City? *Gazette*?"

"The paper," I said, opening my underwear drawer and hoping I had clean undies and bra. Sometimes I get a little behind with my laundry. I snared my last pair of bikinis—black ones to match my mood—and a bright red sports bra. "And I'm running late."

"We still haven't decided about the ficus."

Hurrying to the front door to let Butch and Sundance out, I told her, "We'll figure it out tonight." Along with how I'd convince her that moving in with me was not the girls-go-wild good time she seemed to think it was.

"You'll need to be a bit tidier, you know," Gram said, hot on my heels. "And we'll have to come to an understanding about having male friends over. Devise some kind of sign or signal to alert each other when we're entertaining. You know. Maybe one of them DO NOT DISTURB signs on the door. Or a big red heart."

"How about one of those bare-butted Cupids?" I joked with a snort.

"Oh, I like that."

I rolled my eyes. This move couldn't happen.

I jumped in the shower and loofahed up, quickly lathering my hair and rinsing off. I did a quick towel dry, donned my mismatched undies and hurried out of the bathroom and into my bedroom.

"Uh, what are you doing, Gram?" My grandma had her head and half her torso stuck inside my closet.

"I'm checking out your closet. To see if you have any clothes I might want to borrow. Roomies do that, you know—swap clothes. But, to tell you the truth, Tressa, I can't see anything in here I'd be interested in wearing. Everything's too tame. Except maybe this little number."

Gram pulled out a deep red lacy Victoria's Secret teddy that had gotten my attention on a shopping trip to the Mall of America a year ago. It had been marked how-low-can-you-go low. Optimist that I am, I figured an opportunity to wear it would present itself sometime before I was too fat, too wrinkled or too old to have the guts to put it on. Of course, given the fact that my seventysomething grandmother had her eye on it, I guessed the age factor was pretty much moot.

I pulled on a pair of gray hip-hugger slacks, a white T-shirt and a black zippered hoodie with white stripes down the arms, and pulled on black socks and a pair of black harness boots. I applied my makeup with my usual flair and pulled my hair into a ponytail at the back of my head, then nabbed a black Hawkeyes hat, putting it on my head and pulling my ponytail through the opening at the back. I grabbed my book bag, which also did duty as purse and makeup bag, and headed for the front door.

"What time will you be home?" My grandma stuck her head out the front door. "I'll put on a chicken!" I found myself feeling like a husband going off to work, leaving the little woman home to cook and clean.

"Don't wait up," I heard myself say. Man, was I losing it or what?

"I still don't see why you get first dibs on the chocolate bismarck," my surly associate mumbled.

"Maybe because I bought it," I said.

"Yeah, and you got that coconut one for me on purpose, didn't you?" Shelby said. "No one likes coconut sprinkled on their doughnuts. Everyone just pulls it off. You did it to get back at me. Admit it."

I had, but no way was I gonna let her know that. It was my low-risk way of saying, "Bite me."

"Shelby, Shelby, Shelby, I was in a hurry," I explained. "I didn't want to keep you waiting. There was a long line at the doughnut dispenser, so I just reached in and grabbed the first doughnuts I could get a hold of. It wasn't planned or anything. And once I'd pulled out that coconut-covered one in front of God and everybody, it wasn't as if I could just stick it back in again. Come on. Who'd want to buy a doughnut someone else has rejected?"

"If it was coconut-covered? Nobody would be dense enough to pull it out in the first place."

We'd been sitting in my car on the lane adjacent to the driveway of Holloway all for just over an hour, and instead of planning our next move, we'd spent the time haranguing each other over sweets neither of us needed.

"The van is still there," Shelby said. "Shouldn't we just go up and knock?"

That was my usual MO. I'm a seat-of-the-pants-let's-see-how-this-works kind of reporter. However, for some reason in this case, my trial-and-error, try-everything-but-the-kitchen-sink method of journalism didn't appeal as much as it usually did. Maybe because I really, really cared about looking like I knew what I was doing in front of the venerable Elizabeth Courtney Howard.

"Okay. And say what? 'I'm here about the coffin in the cellar. Do you have a permit to store bodies on the premises'?"

"That we are from the local newspaper and we'd heard that E. C. Howard was currently residing here, and wondered, since she's a local girl who made it big, whether she might be willing to break her silence of the last eighteen years and give her old hometown newspaper the mother of all interviews."

I had to hand it to Shelby. It sounded like a pretty good intro for a novice.

I picked up the binoculars my grandma had left behind in the hall closet when she'd made the move to the big house. She'd insisted she'd used them for bird-watching, but frankly, my gramma couldn't tell the difference between an eastern goldfinch and a purple martin. Plus, she'd been known to use them to read people's lips across a filled auditorium or at a church picnic, and, on at least one occasion, was caught spying on Abigail Winegardner, her longtime enemy.

The drapes were closed, but I could detect light behind them. I took that as a green light.

"Let's do it," I said, grabbing my bag and checking to make sure I had my digital camera and notepad and a writing utensil. "And let me handle the conversation. You are here solely as an observer. Okay?"

Shelby rolled her eyes. "Just nail this story. Otherwise . . ."

"I know. I know," I said. "There's always the *New Holland News*."

Shelby nodded. "And I bet Drew Van Vleet doesn't stick his confidential informant with the coconut-covered doughnut," she groused.

"For the love of God, just let it go, Shelby," I said. "Just let it go."

"Fine for you to say. You've got a chocolate-covered, creme-filled pastry sitting in your stomach." She heaved a heavy-duty sigh. "Can we go now?" she asked.

At the prospect of lassoing this story, I felt a certain excitement similar to the sweaty palms and numb nose I always felt before I competed in barrel-racing events. The slightly upset stomach and gotta-go-right-now nervousness that accompanied my somewhat episodic risk-taking. I raised my Styrofoam coffee cup in a toast. "Let's go make history, Shelby Lynne," I said.

She tapped her cup to mine, raised it to her lips and took several long successive gulps, draining it. She crushed the cup in one king-sized hand and tossed it over her shoulder and onto the floor of my backseat. "Let's do it!" she said.

"Hey, that isn't a wastebasket," I pointed out.

Shelby looked in the backseat and then over at me. "Are you sure?" she asked.

A few minutes later we stood beneath the overhang of the second-floor terrace, and I looked over at my current business associate who towered over me, her red hair and freckles standing out against the pale backdrop of her complexion like paprika on a deviled egg. See how I'm always making connections to food? I can't seem to help myself.

"Aren't you going to knock?" Shelby asked.

Was I?

I looked around for a doorbell like the one at the Addam's Family abode that sounded like a sick foghorn. I didn't locate one, but I did spot the door knocker and was pleasantly surprised to find a somewhat tarnished silver horse's head knocker rather than Jacob Marley's face staring back at me. I lifted a shaky hand to raise the knocker assembly, which was the bit for said silver horse. I brought the knocker down several times.

"Nobody home, I guess," I said. "I'd better get you to school."

"Try putting some stank on it," Shelby Lynne said, and grabbed hold of the horse's bit and slammed it down hard half a dozen times.

I raised an eyebrow. "Thanks."

The curtains at the door moved, and through a slit in the opening I saw an eye peek out at me. I couldn't help but think of Cousin Itt.

A few seconds passed, and the door finally opened. I held my breath. I heard Shelby Lynne's own intake of air beside me. It seemed both of us were waiting to see if we were about to come face-to-face with a legendary literary giant. And both of us feeling the same level of tension at the thought.

"May I help you?" The door opened wider, and I recognized the crate-carrying woman with the page-boy from last night.

Disappointed, I fumbled around in my bag, trying to locate my ID card.

"Uh, hello there," I said, first whipping out a half-filled sticker card good for a free sub sandwich when filled, followed by a half-exposed pink plastic-wrapped minipad. I gave up. "Hello. My name is Tressa Turner, and I work for the *Grandville Gazette*. This is my, uh, associate, Shelby Lynne Sawyer. We received information that former Grandville resident turned best-selling author Elizabeth Courtney Howard has taken up residence here at Haunt—Holloway Hall to attend to some family estate business. Naturally, this is big news, and the *Gazette* would love to have an opportunity to visit with Ms. Courtney Howard and do a special feature on this small-town girl who made it big."

I thought I'd done a pretty professional job of presenting my bona fides, but had to wonder when the woman's eyes got big and she got a look on her face like I do when I walk into the house and discover that one of my pooches has gotten sick and hurled on the floor. Always on the carpet, never the tile.

"Where did you get this information?" she asked, giving away nothing.

"We're reporters. It's what we do," Shelby Lynne piped up and I noted with an understated eye roll her mercurial rise in status from associate to reporter.

The black-haired woman seemed to consider her options for a moment, then stepped out of the house and onto the front porch, shutting the door behind her. "Do you have some identification?" she asked, and I bit back a teensy curse and fumbled in my bag until I located my press credentials. Okay, that's a pretty fancy term for a laminated picture ID card that made my driver's license photo look like a Glamour Shot.

"And you?"

The brunette motioned to Shelby Lynne, who whipped out a nicely laminated card that looked more legit than mine. The things these youngsters can do with a computer and printer these days.

The brunette looked from Shelby Lynne to me, and I got the feeling she was still contemplating her next course of action. I really thought a phone call to the sheriff's department was near the top of her list of viable options. Ugh. I'd had enough dealings with Knox County's finest to last more than nine lifetimes.

"I'm Vanessa McCormick."

"Are you related to Ms. Courtney Howard?"

She didn't respond.

"Look," I said. "We have reliable, incontrovertible information that Elizabeth Courtney Howard is in town on a probate matter. It's big news. As you would expect, for obvious reasons, we'd like to keep this fact under wraps, as we're hoping to persuade Ms. Courtney Howard to favor our newspaper with an interview, but I'm sure you understand that if word got out, there'd be half a dozen satellite trucks parked out front by lunchtime. Think O.J. trial." Okay, so Shelby Lynne wasn't the only person capable of a little self-serving blackmail.

The dark-haired woman gave me one of those head-to-toe-and-back-again looks. The ones that make you feel as if you're standing there in holey skivvies. Or no skivvies at all. I could almost reach out and touch the fog of indecision that clouded the air between us. The woman threw an uncertain look over her shoulder at the house and then crossed her arms, rubbing her biceps with her fingertips to keep the chill off.

"I've been Ms. Courtney Howard's administrative assistant for over fifteen years," she finally said, holding out a hand to me. I took hers and pumped it. It was like grabbing hold of a cold crappie.

"Nice to meet you, Ms. McCormick," I said.

"Ms. Turner, was it?" she asked, then extended her hand to Shelby Lynne, who stared at it as if even the idea of shaking the hand of her idol's secretary was suddenly too much to grasp.

I nudged Shelby Lynne, and she covered Vanessa's hand with a large paw. "Hi," she managed.

"Ms. Sawyer," she greeted Shelby.

I held my breath, hoping she didn't recognize the name and make the connection to Shelby Lynne's mom—our unsuspecting source.

"So, is Ms. Courtney Howard available for a sit-down?" Shelby asked. "Or is it too early? We can come back. When's a good time?" Talk about your nervous chatter. Clearly I wasn't the only one with a motormouth run amok.

"I'm sorry. An interview is out of the question," the adamant administrative assistant declared. "If you know anything at all about Ms. Courtney Howard, you know she doesn't give interviews—hasn't given an interview in years. I don't anticipate that will change just because she happens to be back in her childhood hometown for a few days. I am sorry."

"But you won't know until you ask her. Isn't that

right?" I figured I'd better inject myself back into the conversation. After all, I was the real reporter here. And okay, you can quit laughing now.

"I've been with Ms. Courtney Howard a long time. I think I am well qualified to speak for her. In fact, she insists on it."

"But you will ask her? As a favor to us. We'll wait, of course."

Add Vanessa McCormick to the list of people who got that brow-wrinkling put-out look after limited exposure to me. Hey, you gotta admit I was polite to a fault. I did offer to wait for a response rather than doing an "Elizabeth, Elizabeth! Wherefore art thou Elizabeth?" from beneath her window à la *Romeo and Juliet*. I filed that away in my list of possible contingencies just in case.

Ms. McCormick looked from me to Shelby Lynne and back. She bit her lip.

"I suppose it wouldn't hurt to check if Ms. Courtney Howard is up and around," she said. "And, if so, I'll see if she is interested in talking to you. But I warn you not to get your hopes up. She hasn't been well this past year. She has a very tight deadline to meet, and when she's in the middle of a project, she likes to immerse herself in her story. She really can't abide distractions when she's writing and is a stickler for her writing rituals."

"But you'll check. Right?" I thought I'd better remind her of what we expected before she talked herself out of it. For the first time I wondered if Courtney Howard might be a bit of a tyrant to work for. A bit of a prima donna. Still, if that was the case, why would McCormick remain a faithful employee for so many years?

"Wait here." Vanessa spun on her heel and entered the house again.

"I take it that was one of the bearers of Count Dracula's remains," Shelby Lynne said. "Funny. She doesn't look much like a familiar."

"You didn't see her at the stroke of midnight after you'd spent the evening in the company of Van Helsing and Lily Munster," I told her, garnering a puzzled look.

"Just think. In a few minutes we could be sitting down to pick the brain of a world-renowned author." Shelby put a hand in front of my face. "See that? I'm shaking as if I'd just seen your lady in white," Shelby Lynne said. "This is not like me at all."

I smiled. It gave me a sort of sadistic satisfaction to see the unshakable Shelby Lynne quaking in her shoes. What can I say? I can be a tad bit petty at times.

"I suppose that smile means you're cool, calm and collected?" Shelby inquired with a look of skepticism.

My smile broadened, but truth be told, the armpits of my shirt were ready for the spin cycle.

"Naturally my experience has taught me to keep my composure in stressful situations," I lied.

Shelby nodded. "Ah. Was that the same composure that had you messing your panties last night?"

Oooh. Score one for Sasquatch.

"Hey, I don't need this abuse from you," I said. "I've got people taking numbers for a chance to take a cheap shot at me." Including one very experienced ranger.

Shelby chuckled. "You are so strange," she said.

We cooled our heels in the crisp morning air as the sun continued its slow ascent into a sky that promised a picture-perfect fall day. After about half an hour, I started to get antsy. I looked at my Bargain City bargain watch again.

"So what do you think? What are our chances?" Shelby asked.

I shrugged. "Maybe fifty-fifty," I said.

"Maybe it's a good sign that it's taking so long. It would take some time to get Elizabeth up and around if she's still in bed. And she would have to get dressed and spiffed up. So it's good that we're still waiting. Right?"

I found myself a wee bit touched at the wistfulness in Shelby's voice. This was really important to the young woman. And for some reason I couldn't put my finger on or comfortably define, I found myself really caring that Shelby Lynne might be disappointed. Almost as much as I cared that I might not nab this interview. See? I'm growing. Learning. Scary thought, huh?

I blew on my hands and shoved them into the pockets of my hoodie and stamped my feet. Patience is not high on the list of qualities I possess. Okay, so it doesn't make the list at all. It's one of those characteristics I hope to add as I mature. I figure by the time I reach retirement age, I'll have enough time on my hands that I can afford to be patient. Of course, that little theory didn't hold true for my gramma. Most days she can't even stand to wait for a three-minute egg.

The door rattled and got our attention right away. My hopes took a nosedive when Vanessa McCormick opened the door and stepped out, pulling the door closed before I could even peek around her.

"I'm so sorry," she said with a glance up at the terrace window on the second floor. "I tried. But Ms. Courtney Howard was adamant. She does not want to give an interview. Hometown correspondents or not." She shook her head, and I sensed her frustration. "I wish I had better news," she added. "But Ms. Courtney Howard was very clear on the matter. And, naturally, whether I agree or not, I must respect her wishes."

"Maybe today just isn't a good time," Shelby said. "We could come back anytime. Tomorrow. The next day."

I winced at the unveiled longing in Shelby's voice. Like I sound when I really, really want a pair of Doc Martens strap boots and I've cut up my last credit card and my funds are how-low-can-you-go low.

"I'm sorry," Vanessa responded, "but no day is good for an interview as far as Ms. Courtney Howard is concerned, I'm afraid. Not today, not tomorrow, not next week. I'm so sorry, but those are her wishes and I must abide by them."

One look at Shelby's face, and I was ready to storm the castle and confront the chatelaine of Haunted Holloway Hall. Who did Courtney Howard think she was, anyway? She slid her Levi's on one leg at a time like the rest of us, didn't she? She'd once been one of us. Just a small-town girl. The least she could do was come down and give us the bad news in person. Sign her book for Shelby Lynne and then send us packing. Ms. Courtney Howard had just dropped on my author rankings to behind Madonna and just ahead of James Frey.

"I'm sorry to hear that," I told Vanessa. "Sorry that your employer seems to have forgotten where she came from and who is responsible for putting her where she is: her readers."

Vanessa nodded. "I understand your frustration. I wish there was something I could do, but my hands are tied. You have to understand that Ms. Courtney Howard is under a lot of stress right now. This is Ms.

Courtney Howard's last and final book. She wants it to be perfect, but she hasn't been well. I'm sure you can understand that this is the worst possible time to ask her to change a long-standing practice of shunning the media and agree to sit down with you. It's just not going to happen. I'm sorry you got your hopes up only to have them dashed, but I did warn you. Now, if you'll excuse me." Vanessa held out a hand to Shelby and shook hers, and extended a hand to me. "It was nice meeting you both. Now I must get back to work."

McCormick turned on her heel and reentered the house. She met my gaze briefly as she shut the door.

"Well, I guess that's it, then," Shelby Lynne said. "Her final answer. A big fat zip. No meeting. No interview. No signed book. No brain picking. No prize-winning journalistic collaboration. Nothing."

I turned to Shelby Lynne. "You remember the saying that goes something like, 'We have not yet begun to fight'?" I asked.

She nodded. "Yeah. So?"

"So it's time to bring out our secret weapon," I told her.

"Secret weapon? We have a secret weapon? And what would that be?"

"Who, not what," I said with a tight smile. Or maybe I was gritting my teeth. Who's to know? "And you wouldn't believe me if I told you," I added, not quite believing it myself.

I took a long, shaky breath. Did I really want this story badly enough to involve a senior whose traditional Christmas programming included *Die Hard* and *Die Hard 2*, and who was currently researching what it took to obtain a PI's license? Who had hooked up with Hellion Hannah at the fair a month earlier and taken close-up photos of the testicles of the big boar?

I took a look at Shelby, who was busy kicking the tire of my Plymouth with one Sasquatch-sized foot and muttering to herself. I thought I picked up references to "Drew Van Vleet" and "friggin' coconut doughnuts" and "brain farts," but I can't be sure.

Okay. Let's see. How badly did I want this story?

Badly enough to bring the Green Hornet out of forced retirement, that's how bad. And something told me I was gonna live to regret it.

CHAPTER EIGHT

I dropped off a bummed-out Shelby at the high school, making sure I dropped her at the side door so as to avoid any potential unpleasantness with Principal Vernon. I'd almost had to perform one of those blood oaths swearing I wouldn't make a move on Courtney Howard without her.

I dropped by the *Gazette* to provide Stan with my lack-of-progress report. He didn't appear to be surprised by the fact that I hadn't come in all excited with armfuls of notes and photos and a cocky I-told-you-so attitude to go with it. Still, having confirmation from Howard's assistant that the author was, indeed, residing at Collinwood—er, Holloway Hall— however temporarily, put a gleam in Stan's eyes I hadn't seen since he was nominated for medium-sized-market publisher of the year by the Iowa Newspaper Association. You can bet that little news item got front-page coverage, with a courtesy copy sent to a certain competing newspaper who did not receive a nomination this time around.

"Stay with it," Stan told me. "Although I probably don't have to tell you that, considering the way you hounded me to give you back this job in the first place. In other words, be as much of a pain in the ass to Howard as you can be to me until she agrees to the sit-down just to get you off her back. You're good at grating on people. Better than fingernails on a blackboard."

I started to tell him thanks until I realized I'd been royally dissed.

"You know, you really ought to be nicer to me, considering I've brought you the two biggest stories of your career in less than six months. I'm, like, a regular news magnet," I told him. "In fact, I'm thinking it's time to renegotiate my contract."

"You don't have a contract," Stan said.

"I don't?"

Stan shook his head.

"Shouldn't I, like, have one? To spell things out?"

Stan leaned forward in his chair. He removed his glasses and gave me the benefit of his bushy-low-brow stare. "To spell out what, exactly?" he asked.

I swallowed. "Terms?" I suggested. "Compensation? Benefits?"

Stan got to his feet. "Compensation? Benefits? Who the hell have you been talking to? That schleet-meister over at *New Holland News?*"

I shook my head. "It's just that I've been here six months, and I feel a raise in pay—compensation—is in order."

Stan frowned at me. "Are you sure Van Vleet or that arrogant ass of a son of his haven't tried to backdoor me here? Lure you away with false promises of," he sputtered, "terms, higher compensation, benefits!"

I stood. "Don't blow a gasket, Stan," I said. "We can revisit these negotiations at a later date."

Stan raised an eyebrow.

"Once I deliver on the Howard story, you'll be wanting to make me a full-fledged partner."

Stan's other eyebrow went up. "Oh? So you have money to invest in the newspaper?" he asked.

Money? Oh. Money.

"Well, no. But I will once I win the Pulitzer Prize," I told him.

"We'll talk then," Stan said, and sat down and stuck his glasses back on his nose—his silent signal that I was dismissed. "By the way, Joan has a couple of events you'll need to drop in at, take a few notes, snap a couple photos and get 'em back to me. Nothing urgent, but they need to be covered."

"Did I catch the noon Kiwanis this time?" I asked. They always served quite a spread, including at least four different kinds of pie.

Stan shook his head. "Smitty drew that one."

"Lions Club?"

Stan shook his head again.

"Breakfast Kiwanis? Optimists? Lion's Club?"

More no's.

"You didn't put me on the county crime beat, did you, Stan?" I asked. "Because Deputy Doug and I don't actually click, if you know what I mean."

"All you have to do is pick up the printouts from the PD and the sheriff's office, Turner. In and out," Stan said. "And that's Sheriff Doug now," he added.

I nodded. "I keep forgetting."

My recent experiences associated with the courthouse were memorable ones, but not in one of those scrapbook-keepsake kind of ways. Not by a long shot.

"And the contract negotiations?" I asked, knowing Stan expected me to forget we'd touched on this issue. With me, diversion usually works.

"I said, we'll talk," Stan said.

"You bet we will, cheapskate," I mumbled—just as soon as I got out of earshot. "You bet we will."

I opted to stop by the local police department first and pick up their activity sheets. Although they weren't huge fans, there wasn't the history of back-and-forth sniping and cheap shots that the former deputy—now sheriff—and I shared.

Deciding that it was never good to do something unpleasant on an empty stomach, and seeing that the time was getting on towards noon, I decided to stop at the Dairee Freeze to check things out, including, but not limited to, the Taco Tuesday special that came with cheesy tots and a drink. Not that I really have to pay, of course, but sometimes I feel like a bit of a mooch if I eat on days I'm not scheduled to work. So I always order the special, whatever that is, when I'm going to pay. I guess that makes me a bit of a cheapskate, too, now that I think about it. Hmm.

I parked Whitey back by the storage shed so the oil leaks would be confined to one spot, and entered the Freeze. Uncle Frank and Aunt Reggie had left Sunday for some well-deserved rest and fun in the sun in Vegas. Frankie and his girlfriend, Dixie, half woman, half beast, were covering the business in their absence.

Frankie was currently taking classes in criminology at a nearby community college. He'd had an epiphany during the state fair, when he had a chance to go deep undercover while trying to expose the treachery of a soft-serve saboteur targeting Uncle Frank's fair businesses. Frankie is now convinced he has the right stuff for a career in law enforcement, and plans to apply to the state public-safety academy when they begin seeking qualified applicants next spring.

Hunky trooper P.D. Dawkins was "mentoring" Frankie in his possible pursuit of peace officer credentials. Patrick Dawkins and I had become acquainted in the aftermath of the fair hijinks. We were keeping things on a "strictly friends-only" basis. For the present, at least. The trooper has the extraordinary habit of accepting me for who I am that endears him to me in a big way. While Uncle Frank is secretly hoping Frankie changes his mind and decides to continue serving the public as a supplier of ice cream rather than as an arrester of bad guys, I've noticed a certain swelling of Uncle Frank's chest whenever someone mentions Frankie's lofty aspirations. Of course, that could also be heartburn from too many Taco Tuesdays. Or angina from thinking about what his grandkids might look like with Dixie Daggett providing half the genetic material.

I suppose you've gathered that Dixie and I aren't each other's favorite people. Dixie has a personality similar to Peppermint Patty from *Peanuts*. Physically, however, she more closely resembles Charlie Brown. Hey, I could've been meaner. I could have said Snoopy. Besides, Dixie has been the queen of nasty to me. As a matter of fact, a few months ago Dixie wanted to fight me. Of course, she was drunk at the time and only ended up ralphing. So, yeah, there's a history there, too.

I entered the restaurant, pleased to see that the place was doing a respectable lunch business. Ice cream cravings might be slacking off due to the nip in the air, but the Dairee Freeze serves the best chili in town.

Frankie was taking orders at the drive-up and his significant other was at the front counter. I was thinking it should be the other way around. That way Dixie couldn't scare off customers.

I started to go around behind the counter, but Quasimodo stopped me.

"You can't be back here," she said, standing in my way. She was shorter than me but stocky like a wrestler. Sumo variety.

I looked at her. "You've got to be joking. I've spent more time behind this counter than your fiancé over there, and he's the heir to the family jewels."

"Jewels or not, you can't just waltz in here and take over when you're not scheduled to work. Besides, your hands aren't clean. You can't come behind the counter with dirty hands. It's state law. You know. Public health code."

I wondered what the heck Dixie was talking about. I'd never heard of this law. How the heck did they enforce it? Go around sniffing people's hands? Swab palms with Q-tips?

"Okay," I said. "Then I'll have the Taco Tuesday special."

"I'm afraid you'll have to step to the back of the line and wait your turn, ma'am," Dixie said with an evil glint to her eye. That's right. Eye. As in the one right in the middle of her forehead.

"Excuse me?"

"Please, ma'am, there are people who have been waiting longer than you. Please step to the back of the line."

"Yeah, no cuts." A pudgy little grade-schooler gave me a dirty look.

I looked down at him. "Aren't you supposed to be in school?" I asked.

"I'm homeschooled," he said, and stuck his tongue out at me.

Nice.

"I see that's working out well for you," I said, and slunk to the bathroom and washed my hands until the skin was red and raw. As I walked past Dixie, the gatekeeper, I held them up like surgeon's hands waiting for the nurse to slap on latex gloves.

"Do these pass muster, Ms. Inspection and Appeals Person?" I asked, somewhat familiar with the folks who were responsible for the yearly restaurant inspections. "Or do you want to perform a scratch-and-sniff test?"

Dixie snarled but permitted me to pass.

"By the way, did you manage to scare up a date at the senior center last night?" she asked. "Geez, Turner, if you wanted a date that bad, you should've let me know. I'm sure I could have found someone who was born after D-day and still has his own teeth," she said.

"How'd you hear about that?" I asked.

Dixie shrugged. "Drew Van Vleet was in. Said for you to check out the next issue of the *New Holland News*, and you might find something that interests you."

I frowned. I could only imagine what that jerk could cook up to splash across the pages of the *New Holland News*. I mumbled something about paybacks and headed over to my cousin.

"Hey, Tressa," Frankie greeted me from the drive-up cubbyhole. I immediately noticed the difference. Normally, Frankie responded in a nasal, monosyllabic monotone that included a lot of heavy sighs and poignant pauses. But since Frankie had acquired direction for his life—and a potential life partner of some species or another—he'd lost that hangdog look and even made eye contact on a regular basis.

"Hey yourself, Frankfurter," I replied. "How goes the restaurant business?" I asked, still holding my hands out in front of me, ready to have the latex slapped on. "No grease fires or E. coli, I hope."

Frankie gave a look around the restaurant. "Do not even joke about that here!" he scolded. "It's like yelling 'bomb' on an airplane."

Wow, was he taking his responsibilities seriously. A year ago, Frankie would have been the one yelling, "Mad cow! Come and get your mad cow!"

"You seem like you actually like the Dairee Freeze, Frankie," I said.

Frankie shrugged. "What I like is not having Dad breathing down my neck and criticizing everything I do. This is the first time he's gone out of town and left me totally in charge." He paused. "It feels good. May I take your order, please?"

"I'll take the taco special," I said, and Frankie shook his head at me and pointed to the metal headset stuck on his noodle.

I nodded. "I'll just get that myself," I said. I fixed a taco basket, filled a large cup with ice and diet cola, sidled past the chubby kid who was still waiting for his grub, and stuck my nose over my food basket and sucked in the smell with gusto. "Ahhh!" I shot the homeschooler a smirk before I grabbed an empty booth in the corner.

I had just started my second hard-shell when my cell phone began to play "Roll Out the Barrel." I'd changed the ring tone on my cell phone several nights ago after I'd polished off a quart of Bunny Tracks ice cream, hoping each call I received would remind me of how I felt afterward. You know—one of those behavior modification tools. Like taping a "fat" picture of you on the fridge. Or buying a to-die-for pair of jeans two sizes too small and hanging them on the corner of your bedroom mirror. Or taping your head to Paris Hilton's body.

"Hello?"

"Is this the intrepid investigative reporter who believes in the boogeyman?"

"This is Tressa Turner? Who's this?"

"Your 'associate.'"

"Ah. Funny. What can I do for you?" I was fairly certain I knew.

"I'm just checking up on you. So, where are you?"

"I'm having a bite to eat," I said.

"Where at?"

I shook my head. Who did Shelby think she was? My mother?

"I'm at the Dairee Freeze. Sheesh. Am I not allowed a lunch break?"

"Are you alone?"

"Yeah. Why?"

There was static in the phone. "Hello? Hello?" I held the phone out and looked to see if I'd lost the signal.

"Hello!"

Shelby Lynne slid into the seat across from me.

"What are you doing here?"

"Checking to see if you were telling the truth. Congratulations. You passed the test, partner!"

I tossed my phone down. "You could've saved a trip if you'd been more trusting," I told her.

She reached out and selected a cheese-covered tot

122

and popped it into her mouth. "Ah, but then I wouldn't have the pleasure of sharing this meal with you. Where do we stand? Is that secret weapon of yours ready to be trotted out and put to use?"

Joe was born ready.

"I haven't made contact yet," I told her. "But that's coming up soon on my to-do list."

"We're going to take another whack at her, huh?"

I nodded. "Think battering ram," I said. "What say I pick you up around four? That should give me time to test our weaponry for preparedness."

Shelby thought for a moment. "How about I pick you up?" she said. "That car of yours scares me."

I shrugged. It worked for me. With gas at almost three bucks a gallon and with a car that sucked go-juice faster than I consumed milk with my Oreos— Double Stuf, of course—the savings were significant.

"That's cool," I said. "What do you drive, anyway?" With Shelby Lynne's height, it had to be roomy.

"A Jeep," she said. "Actually, my brother's Jeep. He's in the service and is trying to sell it. I take it to school hoping someone will see the FOR SALE sign and buy it."

"When you say Jeep . . . ?"

"Wrangler. It's kind of cool, but could use more legroom. Well, I'd better get back to school. If I'm late to American Government, Mr. Nielson will spend ten minutes lecturing the class on the importance of punctuality."

I popped a tot in my mouth. "Beats lecturing on American government, doesn't it?" I asked.

She shrugged. "I don't know. I think learning how our system of government was formed and how it has evolved over two hundred years, and recognizing just how each branch has overreached its constitutional authority like an out-of-control octopus is fascinating." She looked at me with a sheepish smile. "I guess it's no secret that I'm a strict constructionist," she said.

"Hey, how you raise your kids is your business," I said.

She looked at me to see if I was joking, and I smiled. Okay, so I slept through most of American Government. Understandable. I had it first period.

"See you at four," she said, getting to her feet.

"Don't be late," I told her. "I'm thinking our secret weapon might need to eat around five to take his meds."

She gave me another uncertain look. "O-kay. See you at four."

"Roger dodger," I said, thinking Shelby Lynne was right about one thing. I was a wee bit strange.

I finished eating and tossed my garbage into the nearby trash bin. I considered leaving it on the counter for Dixie to clean up, but I knew there'd be a payback, and right now I was too busy with my siege on Haunted Holloway Hall to wage a battle on another front.

I jumped in my car and headed for Joe's house, debating the most effective way to get him to agree to assist me that wouldn't automatically commit me to dragging the old guy around during this sensitive and high-stakes operation. I already had Shelby Lynne Sawyer to deal with; I wasn't sure I could handle a third person fussing over a creme pastry.

I was fairly confident that I could convince Joe to play along, though. He was always up for a little private eye role-playing. I also knew he was concerned about Romeo Rivas moving in on his territory, so playing up the let's-make-Hannah-jealous card would probably work. Two birds, one stone. Or, rather, one old boyfriend equaled one big story. I hoped.

I rang Joe's doorbell, wishing I'd had enough sense to bring food along. Joe is as obsessed with eating as I am. Fortunately for Joe, he has the physique of a clothesline pole. I'm not chubby yet, but the Levi's don't fit like they used to. Especially in the thigh area.

The door opened.

"Hey, Joe. What do you know?"

"What do you want?" he snapped.

I frowned, really kicking myself for showing up on Joe's doorstep empty-handed.

"Uh, I need a favor," I said. "Is it a bad time?"

"What kind of favor?"

This was so weird. Joe usually had to coax *me* into his house with goodies.

"What we talked about the other night. You know. That super-hush-hush visitor to town." I looked around. "Can we discuss this inside?" I asked.

"Is this about Elizabeth Courtney?"

I shoved the old man into the house and shut the door behind me.

"Keep it down, would you? You never know who's listening."

"Not to worry. Most of the people in this neighborhood are deaf as doornails," he said. "I do most of the neighborhood watching, if you recall."

I nodded. He had a point. He was the only guy I knew who kept track of license plate numbers on strange vehicles on the street around his home.

"You're in a grouchy mood," I told him. "What's the matter—Mrs. Winegardner find someone else to share her sticky buns with?"

Joe crossed the room and sat down on his sofa. He shook his head. "Naw. It's your grandma."

I tensed. "Has something happened to Gram?"

Joe shook his head. "It's nothing like that. She just can't go out this evening. We were planning to take in a flick at the theater—Harrison Ford's latest—but she up and cancelled on me. Something about packing to do. Is she taking a trip somewhere?"

I felt my south-of-the-border stomach contents churn. Yeah. A trip to Casa Tressa.

"You know Gram. She's probably packing up her romance novels for the library book sale," I said, trying to put the ol' guy's fears at bay. "Or going through her closet again and sorting clothes to give to Goodwill so she can buy new stuff. I wouldn't worry, Joe." I, on the other hand, was ready to unroll a new package of Rolaids and crunch away. "And as luck would have it, the timing is perfect, because I have a very special assignment for you. One that will make the residents of Grandville, including my gramma, sit up and take notice. And the only man for this job is you, Joe. Only you."

Joe perked up. "And you say your grandma will take notice?" he asked.

I nodded. "You'll get more attention from Gram than Lawrence Welk does on a Saturday night on PBS," I told him.

"Then I reckon I am the man for the job," Joe said. "So what's my assignment? Nighttime surveillance? Intelligence analysis? Covert operations?"

"Flower delivery," I said.

Joe stared at me. "You're nuts," he said.

"How about if I included a box of chocolates?" I added.

He considered a moment. "Gift Shoppe chocolates from on the square, not those cheapo Bargain City boxes," he said. "And I pick 'em out. I can't abide the fruity ones, and the caramels stick to my partial," he added. "I prefer the cremes."

"Fine. Whatever," I said. "These chocolates aren't for you, anyway. They're for a certain special someone who is going to help both of us get what we want most."

"And what's that?" Joe asked.

"Companionship for you and a bargaining chip for me," I told him.

His eyebrows went up one level. "You got a deal, girlie," Joe said. "But remember, if this plan goes south and Elizabeth Courtney gets too hot for my bod, I draw the line at having sex. I'm not that kind of undercover operator."

I laughed, figuring Joe was probably safe where his old prom date was concerned. Unless, of course, she was the one occupying the wooden crate I'd seen that night and had a hankerin' for iron-poor blood around sundown.

I thought for a second. Just to be safe, we'd go before sunset.

Joe and I had just finalized our plan of attack, with Joe taking copious notes, when I heard the back door open and shut.

"Who's that?" I whispered to Joe. "Are you expecting someone?"

"It's probably Rick," Joe said. "He was going to stop by this afternoon to return some fishing tackle he borrowed for his Canada trip."

I wrinkled my nose. Home-wrecking trip, he meant. Kimmie was still furious with Craig, and I was feeling none too charitable toward Craig's best friend and enabler. I'd really been getting into the idea of being Auntie Tressa or "Aunt T," which I thought was a cute play on words. Now, thanks to Townsend and his jughead cronies, Craig had missed Kimmie's ovulation cycle, and he was backpedaling about his readiness for fatherhood. And all to go murder poor Mr. Moose. And people thought my priorities were screwed up. Hello.

"Hide the plans!" Joe said, and I scrambled to conceal any trace of our little conspiracy. I tossed Joe's legal pad onto the floor and was scooting it under the couch with my heel when Townsend entered the living room.

"Knock, knock," Rick said, standing in the doorway between the living room and the kitchen, looking pretty handsome for a homewrecker.

"Isn't it a little late to knock," I asked, "considering you're already in the house?"

Townsend shrugged. "No telling what one could walk in on if they don't knock. Especially with Calamity Jayne on the premises," he said. "Hey, Pops," he greeted Joe.

"Well, hello there, Rick!" Joe jumped to his feet and joined his grandson. "I'd forgotten you were going to drop by. How is everything? How's the job? How's the folks? How's Hunter? How's that snake colony? Everything copacetic?"

I wanted to commit a little elder abuse. Joe had apparently been taking notes on the fine art of babbling when hiding something. From me. He was prattling so much I was surprised his dentures didn't pop out. And Townsend was no fool. He was certain to know something was up. Joe's superfluous chatter was a dead giveaway.

"Everyone's present and accounted for," Rick said. "What are you two up to?"

Damn.

"We were just chewing the fat, weren't we, girlie? Just visiting over a cup of . . . a cup of . . ." Joe finally realized we hadn't been eating or drinking. There was a first time for everything. "Just visiting," he finished with a help-me-out look.

"Actually, we were just working on a top-secret project," I said, getting to my feet. I saw Joe's head spin in my direction so fast, I thought we might have an *Exorcist* moment going. "Top-level security clearance only. Sorry, Townsend, but you don't have that clearance, I'm afraid. Security briefings and clearance authorization were scheduled the same week you were following moose droppings in the wilds of Canada. Tough break, Ranger."

Townsend nodded. "I'm sorry to miss out," he said. "I'd really like to be a part of the excitement when you two finally discover a snack food you both like that doesn't contain trans fat."

I sneered. "You will be sorry, Townsend," I said. "I swear."

Townsend shrugged. "Story of my life," he said.

I spent a moment trying to decipher his hidden meaning, but it hurt my brain too much. "Whatever," I said, my standard line when I didn't have a brilliant comeback. Or any comeback. "I'll just be taking off then, Joe."

I walked to the front door and Joe followed me. "Thanks for dropping by," he said in a loud voice, then bent close to my right ear. "Remember, buttercreams are my favorite," he whispered.

"I'll do my best," I told him. "You just get rid of your grandson there, Van Helsing." Rick was one distraction I didn't need. Especially when I was involving his granddad in yet another field operation.

But this was different, I told myself. This was perfectly safe. Totally no-risk. No bodies. No drug dealers. No handguns. No fleeing felons or crazy clowns. It was a friggin' feature article on a sixty-eight-year-old author, for heaven's sake. What could possibly go wrong besides the callous rejection by an ego-crazed author of a suitor bearing flowers and candy?

"Ten-four," Joe said with a wave. "I'll ten twenty five you at eighteen hundred."

"Oookay," I said, having no clue what had just been said.

Anyone know a good—and cheap—shrink? I probably ought to have my head examined.

CHAPTER NINE

I called Shelby and changed the pickup time to five-thirty. I needed to pick up the flowers and candy, feed my critters and spend a bit of happy time with my pooches. Joe would meet us at Holloway Hall around six. I figured that was late enough not to disrupt the author's supper hour—we eat early in the heartland—and early enough that she wouldn't be in her jammies nodding off yet. Yep. That ol' early-to-bed-early-to-rise credo.

I did my chores in a hurry, wishing I had time to go for a short horseback ride, and promised myself I'd do just that once the weekend rolled around.

I cleaned myself up, then made a turkey sandwich, washed it down with a glass of milk, and gathered my Operation: Pulitzer supplies. My digital camera. Flashlight. Notepad and pencil. Minirecorder. Cell phone. Breath mints—just in case Joe partook of onions or garlic at supper. I made my list and checked it twice, then turned on TBS to wait for Shelby.

When a movie called *A Howling in the Woods* came on, I flipped the channel to *The 700 Club*.

Shelby arrived right on time.

"You shouldn't have," she said when she spotted the flowers and candy on the table.

"I didn't," I told her. "At least not for you. They're our ammunition."

She cocked an eyebrow.

"Ammunition? What the devil kind of secret weapon are you planning to use?"

"Romance," I said.

"Oh, brother, this ought to be good," she said, sliding into a nearby chair. "So, are you ready?" she asked.

"I was born ready," I told her. Secretly, I'd just as soon jump into my jammies, pop some popcorn, put on *The Sound of Music* and sing along with Maria von Trapp and the von Trapp children.

"Where is the secret weapon?"

I got up and grabbed my supplies. "We'll meet him there," I said.

Shelby gave me a sideways look. "Him? Is this going to work?" she asked as we walked down the front steps.

"I'm almost positive it will," I said, hoping the weapon didn't backfire.

"If not, there's always Drew Van Vleet," she said.

I gave her a dirty look. Well, I gave her back a dirty look.

"You're starting to sound like one of those repeating parrot toys," I said. "Get some new material, would you?"

Shelby's shoulders shook. I couldn't tell if she was laughing or getting ready to turn and pop me one, so I gave her a wide berth. She walked around to the driver's side of a bright red Jeep Wrangler. It wasn't in mint condition, but the paint wasn't chipped or faded. And the tires weren't bald.

"Sweet ride," I said. "How much does your brother want for it?"

"Around twenty-five hundred dollars. It's a 'ninety-four. Why? You interested?"

"I might be," I said. Right. Twenty-five dollars was more than I could afford to pay right now. Still, the idea of tooling around in a red Wrangler was, like, the shizz.

Shelby turned onto the road to the Holloway house and flipped her high beans on, illuminating a dark-colored Buick and a skinny figure beside it.

"Who is that?" Shelby asked.

Joe directed his flashlight beam in our eyes.

"Don't tell me," Shelby said. "*That* is our secret weapon?"

I nodded. "And he looks like he's primed and ready," I said.

"Are you sure you don't mean loaded?" Shelby asked.

Shelby parked the Jeep behind the Buick, and I grabbed the flowers and candy and hurried up to Joe. He had on what looked like a brown tweed jacket, which smelled faintly of moth balls.

"Nice tweed," I said. "But the cologne leaves something to be desired. Did you lose your tail?" I asked, and Joe turned around to look at his rear end. "No! I meant your grandson. Did Townsend follow you?"

Joe's shoulders straightened. "Nobody follows me unless I want 'em to, girlie," he advised.

"All right, all right. Don't get your joints in a

knot," I said, thinking I was already too late on this count. "Here." I handed him the bouquet of yellow roses and the box of chocolates I'd spent way too much money I didn't have on. Especially considering I probably wouldn't get to enjoy any of the chocolates.

"Yellow roses! Why'd you pick yellow roses?" Joe asked. "They're not romantic at all."

"It's the traditional color for friendship," I told him. "Everyone knows that."

Actually, I'd had to ask, but Joe and Shelby Lynne didn't have to be privy to that information.

"I hate the color yellow. It makes my skin look sallow."

"You're not going to wear them," I pointed out.

"But I have to stand there holding them right next to my face. I'll look like a walking corpse. Like that look will get me in the door to see a lady friend," he said.

"I'm sure you'll get in by virtue of your charming, affable personality," I snapped. "You're so full of it!"

"Just a minute, vixen. You need my assistance with this little assignment more than I need you."

"And you need my help steering my grandma away from rich Romeo Rivas," I reminded him.

"Children, children, please. Let's not argue."

I finally remembered my new associate, Shelby Lynne.

"Who are you?" Joe asked. "Who's she?"

"You didn't tell your 'secret weapon' about me?" Shelby asked. "Why am I not surprised?"

"What secret weapon? What's she talking about?"

I shook my head. "Joe, Shelby Lynne Sawyer, homecoming queen candidate and die-hard Elizabeth Courtney Howard fan. Shelby Lynne, secret weapon and die-hard *Die Hard* fan Joe Townsend," I introduced the two.

They eyeballed each other.

"You related to Homer Sawyer?" Joe asked.

"He's my grandfather," Shelby said.

Joe nodded. "Good man. Good customer. Always paid his lumber bills on time. You look like him."

"Joe!" I said.

Shelby smiled. "That's all right. I do look like him," she said.

"Joe has, uh, assisted me in the past on certain undertakings," I told her.

Shelby nodded. "You forget, I read all about it in the papers."

Who hadn't?

"Okay, kids," I said. "Here's our plan. Shelby Lynne, you set up out of sight in those bushes along the driveway. I'll position myself up closer to the house and see if I can get some pictures. Joe, here's the recorder. You know how to use it, right? Turn it on before you knock on the door. Make sure you take any change out of your pocket, or all we'll pick up is the sound of coins dancing around. Now, we've gone over this before. You heard Elizabeth was back in town. You knew her way back when. You even took her to the prom. You want to welcome her back to Grandville. Blah, blah, blah."

"No problemo," Joe said. "I'll turn on the old Townsend charm, and she'll be like putty in my hands."

Townsend BS was more like it, but a rose by any other name.

"Once you're in and you've renewed old acquaintances, then you start talking about how great it would be for the community if Elizabeth would consider giving an interview. Stress those hometown ties that bind. The values of the heartland. Yadda, yadda, yadda. Then, if she appears to be relenting, only then do you mention me by name. Be complimentary. Talk me up, but don't go overboard. Tell her how nice I am, what a hard worker, briefly touch on the Palmer story and state fair action. Hit the small-town-girl-trying-to-achieve-success angle, but be low-key. Laid back, but frank. Don't beat her over the head with glowing praise for me and my journalistic credentials."

Joe gave me a look. "Don't worry," he said.

"If she still seems to be hesitant, then you pull out the 'do it for old time's sake' bit. You know, lay on some guilt. After all, you took her to the prom out of the kindness of your heart."

"And for fifty bucks," Joe said.

I frowned. "Huh?"

"Her dad paid me fifty bucks."

"What? You said Ruthie wanted you to take her."

"She did. And she wanted this high-priced engagement ring from Jacobsen Jewelry," he said. "So it was a win-win for everyone involved."

"Except Elizabeth, whose father had to bribe her date to take her to the prom," I said. "I think you'd better leave that little tidbit out when you ask for your favor."

"Like I'm about to tell her that," Joe said. "Give me credit for half a brain."

"You got it," I said. "Give that man credit for half a brain," I told Shelby Lynne.

Joe snatched the roses and candy from me. "You ought to be paying me for cinching this story for you," he said. "Instead all I get are insults. Insults and yellow roses that make me look like I have a case of jaundice. You better hope I don't find out these chocolates are knockoffs," he said. "Or there will be hell to pay."

"Just remember Romeo Rivas," I told him, "and his moves on and off the dance floor! Now hightail it up there and charm that old lady author's socks off. For God and Grandville!"

"It wouldn't hurt you, either," Joe mumbled, and got in his car and headed up the road toward the driveway.

Shelby and I followed our secret weapon at a safe distance, separating when we got to the end of the driveway. Shelby cut to the right, and I headed for a fat evergreen near the front of the house.

Joe stopped the car in the circular drive close to the front door, and I watched as he got out, grabbed the flowers and candy, muttered something about yellow roses belonging in Texas, straightened his clothes and walked to the front door. He lifted the knocker and brought it down hard.

I held my breath when the porch light came on and the door opened. I peeked through the evergreen branches and caught Vanessa McCormick's profile. I heard Joe jabbering and saw Vanessa nodding, but couldn't make out what they were saying. I hoped Joe had remembered to turn on the recorder.

A few more minutes of conversation followed and, to my shock and delight, Vanessa opened the door to let Joe enter. I caught Joe's backward glance in my direction just before he entered the house. Man, would he be the cock of the walk when this was over.

Fifteen minutes went by. Another ten. I was feeling pretty good about my chances of walking away with a to-die-for doozy of a story. I could feel my excitement build. This could make me a household name. Cinch my status as a serious journalistic type. Get me a huge raise!

Just when I was ready to break out the champagne—okay, beer—and celebrate, the front door opened and Joe exited empty-handed. From the way he moved to his Buick, his strides long but jerky, his arm swings pronounced, I could tell he was agitated. That, along with the not-quite-under-his-breath mumblings that accompanied his exit from the house. I looked on as he got in the car, slammed the door shut, put the Buick in drive and shot away. He stopped at the end of the driveway, and I jumped into the backseat.

"What happened?" I asked. "Did you see Elizabeth? Is she willing to meet? Does she really look like George Patton?"

Joe pulled onto Dead End Lane, alongside Shelby's Jeep. Shelby jogged up and slid into the backseat beside me.

"So, how did it go? Did she agree to an interview? Is she just about the coolest person ever? I bet she's the coolest person ever," Shelby Lynne rattled on. "Am I right?"

Joe just sat there. This worried me. Joe is rarely quiet, unless he's stuffing something into his mouth. Or adjusting his dentures.

"Joe? Is something wrong?" I asked. "Are we going to get our story?"

Joe turned around in his seat. "Only if you go with a headline like '*New York Times* Bestselling Author Denies Being Pity Date.' Or maybe, 'Courtney Howard: From Hometown Girl to Rich Bitch.' "

I gasped. "Joe! I've never heard you talk like that! What happened in there?"

"She snubbed me," he said. "Gave me the royal raspberry. The old heave-ho."

"What are you talking about?"

"She denied even knowing me. Said she never attended the prom. Implied I was a scheming, two-bit fortune hunter."

I shook my head. "I don't understand. She didn't remember you at all? Are you sure you took this Elizabeth Courtney to the prom, Joe? Maybe you were mistaken."

Even in the dark, I could sense Joe's displeasure at my words. The growl cinched it.

"I am not mistaken. I took that mad hatter to the prom. She just doesn't want to admit it for fear the truth about her daddy's payoff will get out. It wouldn't make her look too good, given her daddy had to hire someone to go to the prom with her."

I shook my head. "I don't know, Joe. It doesn't seem to me that would be such a big deal after all these years. Who'd care that much?"

"*Entertainment Tonight. Inside Edition.* The *National Enquirer.*"

"And she didn't recognize you at all?"

I saw him put a hand to his head to smooth his hair. "Well, she didn't actually see me," he said.

"What?"

"I told her assistant who I was, proceeded to make my way through that whole spiel you gave me, and her secretary went upstairs to tell Elizabeth. I could hear them talking. She came back down after about twenty minutes or so, and that was when she told me that Elizabeth didn't remember me and denied going to the prom at all. I suggested that if I could speak to Eliza beth myself, if she saw me, it might help her remember. Miss McCormick went back up to try and convince her to see me, even took the roses and the candy with her, but the old fork-tongued story weaver wouldn't have any of it. I even called up to her and she ignored me. Wouldn't take a friggin' step out of that room even for a second. Old horse-face."

"So you didn't even get to see Elizabeth?" I asked. "Speak to her?"

"If you don't count me yelling up the stairs at her, then the answer is no."

I thought for a moment. "Vanessa did say her boss hadn't been well. Do you suppose she might be seriously ill? Maybe having trouble with her memory? That would explain her not remembering you, Joe." In my book, it seemed unlikely that anyone having met Joe Townsend could forget him. Unless they were suffering from a medical or mental ailment.

"I suppose anything's possible," he acknowledged.

"Wait here," I told Shelby and Joe.

"Where are you going?" Shelby asked.

"I want to check something out," I said. "A photo op."

I opened the car door and jogged back toward the house. If nothing else, I wanted to try to get a picture of Howard to run in the paper. Maybe if I shot a really unflattering photo of her, I could use it as leverage to convince the author that it would be in her best interests, public-relations-wise, to let me have a whack at her. For Main Street, USA, apple pie and all that.

I crept back to the evergreen and noticed that the curtains at the terraced windows were open and a light was on. I looked around for something that

140

would get me to window level, saw a rather large, full, maple tree with low-lying branches off to my right and wondered what the odds of my being able to haul my carcass up and into the branches were. I was just about to grab a branch and make like a squirrel when someone grabbed my arm.

I whirled around.

"What are you doing here?" I asked, recognizing Shelby's unmistakable silhouette. "I told you to wait in the car."

"Your secret weapon left. He gave me the recorder and said something about finding his own photographic evidence so he could confront the old buzzard, and he took off," she explained. "So I came to find out what you were up to. Besides, I'm too old to be told to 'wait in the car' like a six-year-old."

I looked at Shelby and then at the tree, and decided that whoever said necessity was the mother of invention was brilliant.

"Okay, then make yourself useful and give me a lift," I said, raising my foot in front of Shelby Lynne.

"What?"

I put a hand on her shoulder and pressed down. "Come on. Give me a handhold," I said. "So I can reach the branch."

"Why do you want to reach the branch?" Shelby asked.

"Hello. So I can climb the tree," I told her.

"Okay. Why do you want to climb the tree?" Shelby asked.

"Because I want to look in the bedroom window," I said. "The second-floor bedroom window."

"You're planning to window-peek into Elizabeth

Courtney Howard's bedroom?" she asked. "Isn't that illegal?"

"Only if you get caught. Do you think you can give me a boost into that tree?" I asked.

"Why are you the one who gets to climb the tree and window-peek?" Shelby asked. "Why not me?"

"Uh, because I have about as much chance of boosting you up to that branch as I do getting into last year's exercise outfit," I told her. "And it's spandex."

Shelby grunted. "Being six feet tall ought to have some advantages," she said, bending over to cup her hands. "I suck at sports. I'll never be thin enough or pretty enough to be a model. I hate house painting. Now I'm a friggin' stepladder. It's not fair."

"Quit yer whining, Nancy," I said, gripped her lowered shoulder, stuck my foot in her cupped hands and jumped once, twice, three times, reaching and grabbing hold of the nearest branch on my fourth hop. Shelby Lynne wobbled beneath me, and I struggled to get enough of a grip that I didn't plummet downward. I wasn't exactly keen on the idea of impacting with either the ground or with the girl who served as my human stepladder.

"Ouch! Watch out! I like my nose right where it's at, thank you very much," Shelby Lynne said with a loud grunt.

"Sorry," I said, with some not-inconsequential grunting of my own. "But if you can manage just one more boost, I think that will do it. And put some stank on it," I added, remembering her earlier remark about my wussie door-knocking.

A second later I was propelled upward with a shove from below that had enough stank on it that, had I not known better, I'd have sworn there was a trampoline under me.

I reached for a nearby sturdy branch, pulled myself up onto it and waited to catch my breath before ascending several more layers of branches, situating myself so that I could get a bird's-eye view of the windows leading to the second-floor bedroom. I was just thankful this particular maple still retained many of its fall leaves. I spent spent some time rearranging them so that I would have an unrestricted line of vision into the author's boudoir.

For a brief moment I had second thoughts. How low had I sunk? I was no better than the hated paparazzi who chased poor Princess Di all over the globe. The newshounds who stalked Jen and Ben (and baby makes three), Angelina and Brad (and baby makes—oh, I can't remember), who terrorized veteran entertainers on their beach outings, trying to shoot photos of their flabby midsections and cellulitic thighs.

Then I had a stern talk with myself. Tressa, I said, you're really performing more of a public service here, I told myself. You're trying to promote your hometown. Put Grandville on the map again—this time without the need for body bags. If at the same time you happened to put yourself on the road to journalistic credibility and financial freedom, who could fault you for that?

Once I got through lecturing myself, I decided it was all very upstanding. Very commendable. Altruistic, really.

Okay, so what I was really doing was trying to talk myself out of feeling like a shameless Peeping Tressa. What can I tell you? It worked.

"What do you see?" Shelby Lynne whispered up to me.

"Leaves," I said, hoping I hadn't crawled up into the domain of some nocturnal creature who couldn't abide company that didn't call ahead.

"Can you see inside the bedroom?"

I altered my position on the uncomfortable branch and peered through the foliage. "Yes. I can see the room. No activity yet," I reported, wondering if this was going to turn out to be a waste of time, effort and a plethora of bruises in rather interesting places all for nothing.

"Do you want me to come up? I think I can manage it."

"No!" I hissed, thinking the poor tree needed more weight on its limbs like I needed more around my waist and hips. I was about ready to shush her when a light in the room went out, leaving behind only the soft glow of a lamp.

"We've got action!" I said, making sure my camera was set to record history at the touch of a finger.

I shifted slightly on the branch, my butt already becoming stiff and sore from the narrow perch. I watched closely as a figure walked into the room from the open door on the opposite side. It was the guy from the other night. The one who'd helped Vanessa unload the van. I looked on, my mouth dropping open when the man reached up and began to unbutton his shirt. Just my luck. I'd picked the wrong room to window-peek into. Or had I? I know—naughty me.

The guy finished unbuttoning his shirt.

Okay, what now? I thought about it for a while. Long enough to watch the guy slowly pull the shirt from his shoulders and toss it to the side in a blatantly steamy look-at-me kind of way. All right, all right. So I looked. Tell me you wouldn't do the same.

I'd just decided I'd do the noble thing, the decent thing, and climb down and leave the guy to his little striptease show when I saw the fellow crook a finger in one of those come-here-you motions. I paused, finally getting it for the first time that there was someone else in the room. I know. Duh. Blame it on the altitude.

The door to the terrace was slightly ajar, and I could pick up the muted hum of voices. I stuck my head through the opening in the branches, trying my best to make out what was being said and who was saying it.

"So, *Lizzie*, you sent the old beau away, huh? Didn't want to rekindle any old sparks for old time's sake? That's not very hospitable of you."

I almost fell out of the tree. Lizzie? Lizzie! I couldn't believe my luck. The man was talking to Elizabeth Courtney Howard.

The response to his remark was inaudible, and I frowned. Speak up, Lizzie, I urged. And put some stank on it!

"Ah, Lizzie, what am I going to do with you?" the well-built dude said, and I cocked my ear in the direction of the window to enhance the acoustics. "I think I know. Don't I always know what my Lizzie wants?" he added, and I almost fell out of the tree when the man reached down, popped open the fastener at the top of his pants and slid the zipper down with a slow hand.

"Come here and I'll provide some inspiration for your next lovemaking scene, Elizabeth," he said, moving slowly out of my line of sight. A second later I heard a soft moan, and the lamp went out.

I stared at the darkened window with equal parts shock, puzzlement and a feeling not unlike the one I get when I think about my parents having sex. No wonder Joltin' Joe couldn't reignite his old flame. She had one hot tamale on her payroll to stoke her furnace.

Eeewww!

CHAPTER TEN

"What did you see? What did you see?" I was treated to Shelby Lynne's version of "Are we there yet?" all the way back to my house. I still wasn't comfortable putting to words the tryst I'd witnessed through the bedroom windows. Ugh. People ought to keep their drapes closed, I thought—and then reminded myself that if they did, I wouldn't have a story. I frowned. What was I saying? I didn't have a story. I had no pictures. No proof. Besides, who would be interested in the fact that a sixty-eight-year-old world-famous author had a boy toy? I gave myself a pinch. Uh, like everyone.

"What did you see?" Shelby asked again. "Did you see Howard? What was she doing?"

"Having the time of her life, no doubt," I said, thinking there was something definitely screwy (no pun intended) when a woman old enough to be my gramma was getting more sex than I was. I stopped. Heck, my gramma was probably getting more sex than I was.

"What does that mean? Did you get a picture?"

I shook my head. "I got, uh, distracted," I said, thinking that a man's unexpected naked chest certainly qualified as a distraction. "Something came up," I added, and winced.

"Like what?"

"I couldn't get a clear shot," I explained. "Too much . . . interference."

"Great. Another dead end." Shelby slammed a hand on the steering wheel. She pulled into my driveway, and I stared. Every light in the trailer was on. "So what do we do now?"

"We investigate," I said.

"Huh?"

"We investigate why my place is lit up like the Vegas strip," I said, opening the door and exiting the Jeep. "Uh, you're coming, too, aren't you?" I asked, remembering the time I'd come home and my house had been broken into. Let's just say trailer trash took on a new meaning that night.

"Me? What do you need me for?"

"There might be a burglar in there," I said.

"A burglar who turns on every light in the house? You probably left them on without remembering," Shelby Lynne responded.

"You picked me up and left with me," I reminded her. "Were they on then?"

She thought about it. "Okay, I'll come," she said. "But then we need to talk about what we're going to do next to get this interview."

"First things first," I said. "First, we defend hearth and home."

We climbed up the porch steps, and I could hear dogs barking in the house. Now, my pooches are smart, but I didn't think they had the motor skills to turn on light switches, although Butch will sometimes jump up and turn off the microwave when I'm popping popcorn. He hates the sound.

I turned the doorknob. The door was unlocked. I gave Shelby Lynne a quick look. "Be ready for anything," I said.

"Uh, you want to be more specific?" she asked with, I thought, a touch of skittishness.

"Just make like a Boy Scout and be prepared," I told her. I opened the door a smidgen. Then a bit wider. The barking grew louder. I opened the door wide enough to step in—and Grandma's cat, Hermione, tore by me, a blur of dark fur, and out the door. Butch and Sundance weren't far behind. They whipped past my legs, almost knocking me sideways. I looked around to see whether Shelby Lynne was still standing. She was. It probably took a NFL linebacker to get her off her feet.

"Butch! Sundance!" I whistled through my fingers, but the beasties were in hot pursuit of cat flesh and ignored me completely.

"I didn't know you had a cat," Shelby Lynne said. "You don't strike me as a cat person."

"I don't and I'm not," I said, stepping farther into the house and motioning Shelby to follow, then closed the door behind me.

"Aren't you worried the dogs will catch the cat and do what dogs like to do to felines?"

I shook my head. I wasn't worried about Hermione. She'd taken the dogs on many a wild chase before and had always managed to best the dynamic duo. What did give me paws—I mean pause—however, was why Hermione was in the mobile home at all.

"Hello?" I called out, and began to make my way through the house. I hadn't gotten far when I tripped over a large box sitting in front of the couch. "What the heck?" I bent over and opened the lid. I got a sudden uncomfortable sensation in the pit of my stomach. A definite queasiness. One of those Maalox moments.

"Oh, this is not good," I said, looking at the contents of the box. "This is not good at all."

Shelby Lynne moved around the end of the sofa and looked over my shoulder. "What is it? What's not good?"

I pulled out a DVD of Lawrence Welk and His Champagne Music Makers.

Shelby looked at me. "So? What does that mean? Someone broke into your house and left Lawrence Welk DVDs? What?"

"Tressa! Tressa, is that you?"

I heard my grandma's voice from the back bedroom, and I wanted to run out the front door faster than the pets had exited.

"That," I told Shelby.

"Tressa?"

"It's me, Gram," I said with a long exhalation of breath.

"I'm so glad you're home! I've been waiting to surprise you."

I nodded. She'd certainly done that. "Uh, what are you doing back there?"

"Why, I'm just putting a few things in the closet," she said. "I hope you don't mind, but I dumped your winter coats and twenty pairs of cowgirl boots on your bed."

I shook my head. I'd be lucky if I uncovered my bed by spring.

"You have twenty pairs of boots?" Shelby asked.

I shook my head. "I'm almost certain I don't." My eyes widened when Gram wandered down the hall, clad in a maroon velour sweat suit with matching fuzzy slippers. I glanced down at her hands and saw that she carried a piece from her collection of fertility gods and goddesses: one that had the unmistakable shape of a phallic symbol. Heaven help me. She *was* moving in!

"Gram, I thought we were going to discuss this move of yours before you took the leap. You know, come to some arrangement." Seek an emergency commitment order.

"The timing seemed right," she said. "So I jumped."

I rolled my eyes. "You were lucky you didn't break a hip. And how the heck did you get all this stuff moved?" I asked. No way would she convince my folks to help her. Well, maybe with the exception of the administrator of the "penal institution" from which my gramma was trying to escape. There were many days, I was sure, when my mother would gratefully turn her back that particular resident's jail-break.

"Oh, Rick helped me."

I looked at her. "What did you say?"

"Rick helped me."

I'm fairly certain that at this point I started to make the transformation from Dr. Bruce Banner to Incredible Hulk. Dr. Jekyll to Mr. Hyde. Without facial and body hair growth, of course.

"Rick Townsend? Rick Townsend helped you move?"

Gram nodded. "Joe told him I was thinking of making the switch, so he came over and offered to help me move a few things. Very thoughtful of him, wasn't it?"

"Oh. Very thoughtful," I said. I was sure Ranger Rick had put considerable thought into this little homecoming treat for Tressa—the conniving, low-life, two-bit, backstabbing brigand. I had a sudden compulsion to rip off my clothes and howl at the moon. "You can't imagine how anxious I am to thank him in kind," I told Gram. "You just can't imagine."

"Holy-moley, who's that?" Gram looked beyond me to where Shelby Lynne stood. "Do I know her? Do I know you? The face looks familiar."

"You probably know her grandfather, Homer Sawyer," I said. "This is Shelby Lynne. Shelby, this is my grandmother, Hannah Turner."

Gram looked at Shelby Lynne a second longer. "You've got your grandfather's face," she said.

"I guess I'd better give it back then, huh?" Shelby replied with a smile. "Nice to meet you." She turned back to me. "Uh, do you think we can get down to business now? Or do you have more personal dramas to play out? Intrigues to attend to? I've got homework to do."

"Business? What kind of business? Investigative reporting? I'm pretty good at nosing around, aren't I, Tressa?" Gram looked at me. "Did you tell her about the fair? How Joe and I cracked that case wide open?"

I shook my head. "There really hasn't been time—"

"Is this the same Joe who just left Haunted Holloway Hall? The jilted suitor?"

I made a hacking motion at my throat, but apparently Shelby Lynne wasn't privy to directorial hand gestures like "cut"—and I wasn't sure how else to demonstrate "shut your piehole" with easy-to-follow hand maneuvers.

"The little guy was fit to be tied when he took off," Shelby continued.

"Joe? Joe Townsend? You've been with Joe this evening? And what's this about a jilted suitor?" Gram pounced on Shelby Lynne like I do on Great-aunt Eunice's homemade custard pie at family gatherings. "Why were you at Haunted Holloway Hall?"

I took the rather well-endowed statue from Gram and grimaced.

"I told you, we were trying to put a story together about the history of the Holloway house, Gram," I reminded her, setting the fertility figure on the bookcase in the corner and turning it to face the wall. "Given the long-standing tradition of spooky tales associated with the house, rumors that a real estate developer has his eyes on the place make it topical. And, remember, you told me that Joe knew the family through the lumber business, so I thought he might have more luck getting us into the house to have a look around and maybe snap a couple pictures." I felt proud of myself. The seat-of-my-pants explanation sounded reasonable even to me.

"So what's this about the jilted suitor, then?" Gram asked. Hello. What did I expect? Of course she'd pick up on the "jilted suitor" reference. Gram went to bed with *True Confessions* and woke with *Modern Romance*. Gram was in love with love.

"Well, it's not exactly like that," I told her, "but Joe was a tad disgruntled that you were busy with Rom — Mr. Rivas last evening, and I expect that's what got him out of sorts. Not so much jilted suitor as a frustrated friend. He thinks Rivas is a bit of a skirt chaser, you know."

"I don't wear skirts anymore," Gram said. "Not since that Fourth of July that was so windy my skirt was around my shoulders. Remember, Tressa? I was on a float in the parade at the time," she added.

I did. It was five years ago, and Gram had been wearing red-white-and-blue-striped underwear. Patriotic to the core.

"I just meant that Rivas has a love-'em-and-leave-'em reputation, Gram," I explained. "I expect Joe just doesn't want anyone to take advantage of you."

"Let 'em try," Gram said. "You remember the frozen turkey legs we used as weapons at the fair, don't you? If I'da beaned someone with one of those, it would have inflicted some serious damage, so I reckon I'm able to defend myself."

I nodded. Up until the time my gramma started taking spills, I never for one moment fretted about her being able to look out for herself. I figured, considering her granddaughter was a younger, hotter, blonde version of Xena, the Warrior Princess (Okay, folks, keep the guffaws to a minimum here. You're disturbing my concentration.) that maybe my grandma was the original warrior queen. The apples don't fall far from the tree and all that, you know.

"How could I forget?" I responded.

"Well, that's sweet of Joe to be looking out for me, but like I said, I can take care of myself in the male department." She winked at Shelby Lynne. "That's *m-a-l-e*, not *m-a-i-l*."

Shelby nodded. "Gotcha."

Gram gave Shelby a long, measuring glance. "You

look like you've moved a box or two, young lady," she said. "Come with me."

Shelby gave me a questioning look, and I put up my hands.

"I've just got a few more things I'd like to move over this evening. And Tressa is strong, but she's a complete butterfingers when it comes to my collection of fertility gods and goddesses. She knocked the winkie off one of them. Never would stand at attention once I had to superglue it."

I gave Shelby another what-can-I-tell-you look.

"Come along, dear." Gram reached out and took Shelby's hand. "This won't take long."

I waved good-bye to Shelby Lynne, who looked like she was being dragged off to Merle Norman for a makeover. If I'd been feeling compassionate and nice, I'd have volunteered to rescue Shelby Lynne. As it was, I was still fuming over two-faced Townsend's duplicitous, underhanded dirty trick that definitely wasn't a treat for Tressa. So the guy thought it was hilarious to be a willing—even eager—accomplice to my grandma taking up residence with me, did he?

I had to admit: His treachery was brilliant in its simplicity and effectiveness. And it deserved a response that was equally inspired.

I chewed my lip. I'd have to do some heavy-duty brainstorming. This was war.

I sat down, opened my bag and pulled out my binder. The material from the Grandville Police Department slipped out.

"Son of a Buick," I said. Sidetracked by flower-selecting and candy-choosing, I'd totally forgotten to stop at the sheriff's department to pick up their call summary sheets. I looked at my watch. Eight-thirty. Still early enough to drop by the courthouse and have them buzz me in so I could pick up the printed-off information—and avoid a butt-chewing by Stan the man.

I debated rescuing Shelby Lynne before I left, but I knew she'd want to hash out a plan of action for the Howard situation and, I gotta tell you, I was running on empty there. I really had no clue what approach to use next, short of taking up residence in the tree outside Howard's window and settling for some salacious exposé rather than an in-depth, well-researched literary piece. Either way, I wasn't ready to face Shelby Lynne Sawyer when she came back carrying a box full of trinkets representing exaggerated body parts and demanding action.

I grabbed my backpack and hightailed it out the front door, hoping I didn't leave too many chicken feathers in my wake. I hurriedly filled the dog bowls with chow and water, then jogged to the Plymouth, casting a look at the red Jeep in the driveway. I didn't suppose Shelby Lynne would buy the fact that I was taking the Jeep for a test spin.

I shook my head, remembering what had happened the last time I borrowed an automobile. I jumped into my Plymouth, repeated my traditional "please start" mantra, and turned the key. It took a couple of tries, but the Reliant sputtered to life. I pulled out, hit the gravel road that ran along our little slice of the good life and headed to town.

What was it with guys these days? First Drew Van Vleet with the insults and insinuations; now Townsend and his moronic move-Gram-in joke. Men.

I whipped into a parking place on the square and

turned off the car, pocketed my cell phone and key, and headed for the heavy glass doors on the south side of the courthouse. I pushed the intercom button to the right of the door.

"Sheriff's Department. May I help you?"

I sighed, appreciating the crystal-clear quality of this communication device. The drive-up at the Dairee Freeze sounded like Darth Vader on lead vocal, with Snap, Crackle and Pop providing backup. "Tressa Turner from the *Gazette*. I need to pick up the county trip information and nine-one-one calls," I told the metallic box.

I waited for a few seconds while they apparently decided if they really wanted to buzz me in. Understandable. For a while there my visits to the courthouse corresponded to a rising body count. I was finally buzzed in. I opened the door, walked up a short flight of steps and made a left down the hall to the communications center of the sheriff's office. The right-hand hallway led to the operations offices that housed the sheriff and his chief deputy. The jail was located in the basement of the ancient courthouse. It had always kind of creeped me out as a child to see those barred windows from the courthouse lawn—like some criminal could be standing there looking up my dress. Well, if I'd ever worn a dress, I might have thought that. Still, the idea that inmates could watch us without our being aware of it was disturbing.

There's currently a move on to build a new jail facility, but opponents are hesitant to support something for prisoners that is more modern than they themselves can afford to live in. I think they've heard too many stories about cable TV in jail cells. At least I hope they're stories. Heck, I can't even afford cable TV.

I walked down the hallway and was buzzed through a second door where dispatch was located.

"Hey, Toni," I greeted the three-to-eleven dispatcher, who also worked a second job at the deli of a local grocery store. I know most food outlet employees on a first-name basis. "How goes it?"

Toni looked up at me from her big comfy chair in front of a panel of knobs and buttons that looked like something out of *Star Trek*. Her short black hair curled down over the collar of her white top.

"Can't complain," she said. "No one would listen. And you?"

"Same ol', same ol'," I replied.

"That bad, huh?"

I shrugged. "Depends on when you ask me. You got the printouts for the *Gazette*?" I asked. "I meant to pick them up earlier, but something came up."

Toni got up, walked over to the counter and collected the paperwork from a wire basket.

"Here," she said.

"Thanks," I replied as the phone rang.

Toni hurried back to her seat and answered the call.

"Nine-one-one. Sheriff's Department. What is your emergency?"

I decided to stick around, mainly because I inherited the nosy gene from my grandma.

"And he's still there? Is he intoxicated? Are there any weapons?"

I listened, intrigued by this front-row seat for criminal activity unfolding around me.

"Yes, ma'am. I'll send a car out right away. Sixty-six-eight, County." Toni spoke into the headset microphone she had on.

"Sixty-six. Go ahead, County."

"Sixty-six, we have a report of a ten-fourteen, possible ten-sixteen, eight-oh-seven 115th Avenue. That's the old Holloway house on Dead End Lane, Sixty-six."

My radar went up quicker than the Grandville PD's handheld radar unit when the high school drivers left each day. A call from Haunted Holloway Hall? I racked my brain with no luck trying to remember ten-codes from TBS reruns.

"Ten-four, County. Ten-seventy-six."

"Ten-four, Sixty-six. Ten-seventeen is Vanessa Mc-Cormick."

Egads! Enough with the ten-this and ten-that.

"Ten-fourteen is described as an older gentleman, Sixty-six. Brown tweed jacket, blue jeans. Possible ten-ninety-six."

Brown tweed? I'd joked with Joe Townsend not more than three hours earlier about the mothball scent that clung to the jacket like stagnant cologne. What the heck was Joltin' Joe up to now?

"Ten-four, County. Ten-seventy-seven ten minutes."

It didn't take a genius to figure out that part. I had ten minutes. Ten minutes to get to Haunted Holloway Hall and get Joe Townsend the heck out of there before all hell broke loose.

I grabbed the printouts and headed for the door, hitting the sidewalk outside the courthouse at a dead run. I hoofed it to my Plymouth and jumped in and prayed Whitey wouldn't fail me now. Two small, inconsequential, almost not even bad swear words and three backfires later I was headed west out of town en route to Haunted Holloway Hall.

I floored the Plymouth's accelerator, figuring it was safe enough, as the closest county mountie was ten minutes away. I reran the county dispatch conversation back and forth in my head. Ten-fourteen. Ten-fifteen. Ten-forty-four. No, wait, that was a federal income tax form. I shook my head. I needed to print out the ten-codes one of these days. At least maybe I'd find out what a ten-ninety-six was.

It occurred to me that maybe I didn't want to know.

I pulled down Dead End Lane and into the circle driveway of the Holloway house, and my worst fears were confirmed when I spotted Joe's Buick. I threw the Plymouth into park, jumped out of my car and hurried up the driveway. I almost jumped out of my black panties when a figure came from around the side of the house.

"Who goes there?" rang out.

I shook my head. Theatrical to the end.

"Joe!" I whispered as loudly as I could. "What the hell are you doing? Get over here! The cops are only about five minutes out!"

"Let 'em come," Joe said, stomping up to me in all his outraged tweedish splendor. "I want that woman's perfidy exposed."

He wanted what exposed?

I took his arm and guided him toward our vehicles. "Listen, Joe, you may want to right a wrong here, but the way to do that is not via county lockup," I told him. "So get in your car and let's get out of here. Now!"

Joe shook his head. "Fine thing. The old bat wouldn't even admit to the prom date when her assistant showed her the photo," he said. "Warts and all."

I frowned. "She had warts?"

"Figure of speech, girlie," Joe said, shoving a photograph in my face. "Let's just say fifty years ago she could've been arrested for mooning when she looked out a window," he added.

I shook my head and waved the picture away. "Maybe there's a perfectly good reason for her not remembering," I told him. "One thing I do know: There is no good reason for us to hang around here. Now move it, Van Helsing, or your vampire-hunting days are over!"

I shoved him and his photograph into his car and hoofed it back to mine. I jumped in and turned the key in the car. The motor turned over, but wouldn't start. I tried again.

"Don't do this to me now, Whitey!" I wailed. "I'll donate you to the Society for the Preservation of the Barn Owl, and they'll auction your butt off," I warned.

Joe drove forward around the circular drive and out onto the dirt road. At least he wouldn't be caught, I thought with relief, until I saw the headlights in my outside mirror. I turned around to see Joe pull in behind me.

"You old fool!" I muttered. "What are you doing?"

About that moment I felt his bumper collide with mine—a jarring jolt that didn't quite send my head into the windshield. I couldn't believe it. The guy was pushing me!

I didn't know what to do. I couldn't get out of the car, because it was in motion, and the guy behind the wheel of the car behind my car had the night vision of a glaucoma patient wearing sunglasses, so I slammed the gearshift into neutral before the maniac behind me trashed my transmission. I steered as best I could, negotiating the curve in the driveway with a wing and a prayer, thankful I'd had experience behind the wheels of farm tractors and other implements of husbandry that weren't equipped with power steering.

I kept turning the key of the Plymouth, hoping it would fire and take off.

We had just made it through the circle driveway and out onto Dead End Lane when another twist of the key brought success. The engine started, and I honked the horn and stuck a hand out my window.

I was ready to spin my tires and get the heck out of the place when I saw the lights coming straight toward me. No sirens, but the top lights were fully engaged. I proceeded slowly in the direction of the approaching patrol car, feeling like I was a participant in a high-stakes game of chicken and, I must admit, getting a wee bit of a high out of it—until I saw the driver slam on his brakes and the patrol car slide sideways in the roadway, effectively blocking any avenue of escape, that is.

I watched those oh-so-familiar revolutions of the patrol car's light bar, and shook my head.

Caught on Dead End Lane in front of Haunted Holloway Hall in the dark of night with a county mountie between me and freedom, and an old-timer with a heavy-duty bumper and ego issues backing me up.

I shook my head. I was trapped in one doozy of a tale to tremble by. Classic. Just classic.

CHAPTER ELEVEN

I slowed my car to a stop and stayed put. I'd learned that much from prior experiences with law enforcement. I hoped Joe followed my example.

I watched the progress of the officer as he exited his car, flashlight in his left hand, the fingers of his right hand hovering over the holster that was fastened to the gun belt. The gun belt that belonged to the county mountie that was about to bust our sorry hides. Seems to me I remember a children's story about a house that Jack built that went something like that.

I sat still and waited for the officer to make his way back to me. He came up along the passenger's-side door and flashed his light inside the car. I waved, relieved that it wasn't Deputy Dong—or Deputy Dough-boy as I called him. One of the nicer things I called him. He flashed his light in the backseat, and then I heard him talking into the microphone clipped to his uniform shirt. He rapped on my passenger's-side door, shined the light again—right in the ol' peepers—and let out with a long sigh.

"You want to step out of the vehicle, ma'am?" he called out. "Please."

Did I?

I nodded and laid my shoulder into the door a couple times, and it popped open. "It sticks sometimes," I explained when I almost fell out of the vehicle.

The officer flashed his beam in the direction of Joe's car, and I noticed Joe had gotten out of his vehicle and was approaching the officer. "You two havin' some trouble?" the officer asked.

"Car trouble," I responded. "This gentleman here was just giving me a friendly push." Right into the path of the coppers.

"I see. Can I see some ID?"

We both complied.

"So, what brings you out in these parts?" the deputy asked.

Good question. What did bring us out at the end of a dead-end road at nine o'clock at night?

"Would you believe we're lost?" Joe asked. I winced.

"You're both lost?" the officer asked. "How does something like that happen?"

"It could happen," I told the cop. "You know how men will never stop and ask for directions. Well, I could've been following him and he got lost and we ended up on this road." I ignored the look of indignation Joe gave me.

"I thought you said you had car trouble and he was giving you a push," the officer said.

"That's absolutely right," I replied. "My engine wouldn't start so he was giving me a push." I thought our story, as stories go, wasn't too far outside the realm of possibility. And most of it was true. And what wasn't strictly so, was carefully worded so as to be supposition and not really a falsehood, strictly speaking. And face it, Joe hadn't given me much to work with given the lame "lost" story starter he'd supplied.

"I see," said the officer. "Explain this, then. How did a guy you were following end up behind you to give you a push?" he asked.

Just my luck. A cop who thinks on his shiny black patent leather feet.

"You wouldn't by any chance be the reason that the occupants of that house over there called to report a prowler, would you?"

I shook my head.

"No sir, Officer. Honest," I said. My prowling activities had all occurred earlier in the evening—and, thankfully, gone undetected.

"Uh-huh. And what about you?" he asked Joe. I hoped Joe had come up with a better excuse than his last one for being out here now.

"The truth, Officer?"

Oh, no. What was happening? This couldn't be good.

"Well, I was out here earlier to pay a call on an old friend, welcome her back to Grandville, offer to buy her a cup of coffee and take her around the old hometown, but she didn't remember me. Well, Officer, that disturbed me. Especially when we were close enough to attend her senior prom together. So I got to thinking about that and went home and scared up that old prom photo of the two of us. I thought maybe if she saw it, it would jog her memory." A hankie appeared in his hand as if by magic, and he dabbed at his eye. "It's a sad thing, getting old and forgetting special friends," he said with a sniff.

I wanted to both applaud loudly and, at the same time, hurl in the nearest ditch. I had to give the old guy credit: He was good. He hadn't deviated from the truth, but hadn't blabbed information I'd rather keep from the local authorities. And he'd played the weepy-ol'-man card perfectly.

The deputy nodded. "And you?" he asked me. "Care to change your story?"

I looked at Joe, who wore a smug "top that, girlie" smile.

"I happen to be a friend of Mr. Townsend here," I told the deputy.

"I'm familiar with the nature of the relationship," he said.

In Grandville, who wasn't?

"I work at the *Gazette* and, as fate would have it, I happened to be in county dispatch picking up information for the paper when the call came in. From the description of the uh, ten-ninety-six, I had a good idea it was my friend Joe here. I figured I owed it to the old guy to try and see if I could keep him from getting into any trouble." I felt the unmistakable shifting of Joe's weight beside me. "I'm sorry if my actions have caused more harm than good, Deputy." I only hoped my little performance trumped Joe's boo-hoo, Horatio Noseblower act. "And my car really did need a push," I said. "Sometimes it gets a little temperamental."

"I see," said the deputy.

I hoped not.

"What's this about a ten-ninety-six?" Joe asked. "That means mental subject. Did that senile old bat report *me* as mental? 'Cause if anyone is missing a bookend, it's her."

I gave him a shut-yer-trap look. I should have guessed Joe would know his police ten-codes.

"You two stay put," the deputy told us. "I'm just going to have a visit with the folks up at the house."

"Thank you, Deputy—"

"Cooper," he said.

"Have no fear, we'll stay put, Deputy Cooper," I assured him, reaching out and pumping his hand. "We'll just sit tight. Hang loose. Wait patiently." I get all jittery around coppers. Can you tell?

"You do that." The deputy gave me a long look before he walked back to his car, jumped in and pulled into the driveway.

"Have you written your acceptance speech yet?"

I looked at Joe. "What are you talking about?"

"That was some performance. 'I'm sorry if my actions caused more harm than good'? Since when do you talk like that?"

"Oh? And your little sniff-sniff-boo-hoo 'getting old is soooo sad' production? I couldn't tell if you were going for comedy or tragedy," I countered. "Like, where do you classify something that is so absurd it makes you want to cry?"

"That's what I get for sticking my neck out to help you get your story," Joe said.

"What do you mean?"

"Why do you think I came back here? To lose another box of buttercreams?"

"I think you came back to bludgeon that old lady over the head with that prom photo," I said. "To prove you were right and she was cuckoo."

"So what if I did? That would still get me in the door and you your scoop."

"How would it help me if I didn't even know you were coming back here?"

"I planned to tell you when I'd cinched the deal," Joe said.

"Right," I said. "Right. So what happened? Why'd she call the cops?"

"She? You mean Ms. Dementia? I told you. She told her assistant that wasn't her in the picture. Implied I was trying to run a con on her. Of course, if I'd looked like something from *Dawn of the Dead*, I'd have denied it was me, too."

I raised my eyebrows. "How bad could it be?" I asked.

"How bad? How bad? Let me show you. But I warn you, you'd better have safety goggles on if you want to protect your eyes from retinal damage."

Joe hurried over to his car, opened the door and flicked on the interior lights. "Here, take a gander," he said, handing me a five-by-seven black-and-white photo. He pointed at the female in the photo—at least, I thought it was female. "Take a look at that mug and tell me when she was born the doctor didn't smack her face rather than her tushie."

I studied the photo for a second before I responded, initially taking more time to check out Joe than to check out his pity date. I had to admit Joe cut a rather dashing figure—not exactly Johnny Depp. More like a young Johnny Carson.

I braved a look at Elizabeth Howard and made a face. Joe hadn't just been acting ornery when he'd implied Elizabeth Howard was on the homely side. How ugly was she? She was so ugly, her face was pushed into the dough mixture when making monster cookies.

Weird. I didn't recall her author photograph being

all that bone-chilling. I guess some things did improve with age.

"So she wasn't a beauty queen in her younger days," I said, recalling some school photos of mine that would have served nicely as rodent deterrents if posted around the barn and tack room. "Big deal. What does she look like now?" I asked.

"How the heck should I know?" Joe asked, and I gave him a funny look.

"What do you mean?"

"I didn't see her, remember? She wouldn't leave her cave. I expect she was too busy hanging upside down."

"You didn't talk to her this time either? Didn't see her at all?"

"Nope. She made that assistant of hers haul her cookies up and down those stairs half a dozen times, only to have her tell me, 'Joe Townsend, I never knew ye. Now bugger off,'" Joe said with a snap of his fingers.

I shook my head. "I don't know. Something doesn't add up," I said, although math was never one of my better subjects. "It seems to me there's more here than meets the eye. Something Ms. Courtney Howard does not want the world to find out."

"Apart from the fact that they filmed *Gorillas in the Mist* in her shower, you mean?" Joe asked.

I gave him an annoyed look. "Yeah. Apart from that."

"What are you thinking? Some big scandal?"

I thought about it. There was the boy toy factor, but that alone wouldn't keep Courtney Howard from seeing an old friend. I considered this for a moment. Unless she really didn't remember the man who'd saved her from ultimate prom humiliation.

I remembered what Vanessa had said about Court-ney Howard not being well and facing a tight dead-line. Plus there was a decadelong record of isolation, as well as a string of mediocre reviews to consider. What it all added up to, I wasn't quite sure, but I had to think it had less to do with an unflattering photo from the past and more to do with lower sales ranks, poor reviews and killer deadlines. And the underlying reasons for these difficulties? Well, now, maybe that was the real story here, pilgrim.

"I'm not sure what the heck is going on, Joe," I said, "but the clock's ticking, and now that Courtney Howard knows someone is aware she's in Grandville, no telling how long she'll stick around."

I was about to ask Joe if I could take the photo and scan a copy of it into the computer at work to run with an article, figuring that might be as much of a scoop as I got, when I heard a soft whimper like that of a sad child or lonely puppy.

"Did you hear that?" I asked Joe.

"Hear what?"

I put a hand on Joe's sleeve and listened. Distant yet unmistakable sounds of crying reached me. I saw Joe look up and around.

"That!" I said. "Do you hear that?"

"Who the devil is it?" Joe asked.

I took his arm in a death grip. "Loralie," I whis-pered. "It's Loralie!"

I felt Joe's arm tense under mine.

"Loralie Holloway?" Joe asked. "But she's dead."

I shivered and moved closer to the old fellow beside me. "I know," I said. "That's the problem."

"I thought all that talk was just that—talk," Joe said, and I felt him inch closer to me.

"Me, too," I said. "Until the other night."

Joe looked at me. "What do you mean, until the other night? What happened?"

I peered at the inky darkness around us. "I think I saw a ghost," I told him.

Joe moved closer. We were packed together tighter than Cracker Jacks in a box. "What do you mean, you *think* you saw a ghost? Either you saw one or you didn't."

I kept an eye on the trees that bordered the road's edge. "I definitely saw something," I said. "Last night when I was doing some preinterview snooping."

"What did you see?"

I tightened my hold on Joe's arm. "The lady in white," I told him. "And she was weeping."

Joe's own gaze moved across the grove of tall, spooky trees that surrounded us. I suddenly caught a whiff of something vaguely familiar. I sniffed hard.

"Do you smell that?" I asked Joe.

"What? Your rose perfume? Smells good."

I felt my legs begin to do a nervous jig. "I'm not wearing rose perfume," I said. "I'm wearing Bargain City Vibrant Vanilla body splash. Loralie was fond of roses."

Joe gave me a long look, probably to make sure I wasn't pulling his leg. When he noticed the absence of a smile, he sprang into action.

"I'm outta here!" he said, jumping through the open door of his car. I piled in after him.

We sat silent as the—well, you know—staring out the windshield at the cloak of black around us.

"A little prior information about your paranormal observations would have been nice," Joe said.

"It could've been a sheet," I told him.

"Remember how it turned out the last time you kept information from me?" he reminded me.

"What are the chances that something bizarre like that could happen again?" I asked.

A sudden gust of wind rocked the car gently, whipping up dust and dirt in winding threads along the country road. I looked out the front windshield and squinted when I realized that this particular wind carried something else as well. I could only stare openmouthed at the object that had fluttered to rest right before my startled eyes. There on Joe's windshield was a solitary dark red rose petal.

"Is that a rose petal?" Joe asked as I continued to gaze at the object stuck to the glass.

I could only nod in response.

"Didn't you buy yellow roses?"

I nodded again. "Loralie favored red roses," I whispered.

"Oh." Several loud swallows followed.

A sudden noise sounded on the window to my left, and Joe and I screamed louder than the hometown fans when the refs had blown a crucial call at the football game last Friday night.

Deputy Cooper pulled the door open.

"You all right in there?" he asked, directing his beam back and forth between Joe and me.

Personally, I'd have to conduct a panty check before I answered. As far as Joe was concerned, he was on his own.

I looked over at the uncharacteristically quiet senior, not sure whether we should tell the officer why we were cowering in the car making like two burned-out Ghostbusters.

172

"Are *you* all right?" I asked Joe.

Joe looked at me. "If you're all right, I'm all right," he maintained. Ah, the Townsend ego.

"Then we're okay," I told Joe. "We're okay," I repeated to the officer. "Just got a little chilly standing out there."

The deputy nodded. "You'll be happy to know, Mr. Townsend, that the occupants of this residence have declined to file charges," Deputy Cooper advised. "That is not to say that you are in the free and clear. These folks have an expectation of privacy, and you've got to respect that."

I wanted to advise the deputy that politicians and famous persons basically couldn't expect the same level of privacy as John Q. Public. Being famous came with certain costs, privacy being one of them. And while I felt that some media types went too far, it didn't seem excessively intrusive to ask an author who owed her celebrity to her readers to conduct a short interview with a very nice, very easy to talk to home town girl hoping-to-make-it-big reporter-type. Of course, I kept this opinion to myself. Now didn't seem the time to debate freedom of press issues.

"It wasn't as if I climbed a tree and was peeking in bedroom windows," Joe humpfed, and I hoped the deputy didn't see me twitch. "All I wanted to do was show her the picture. Help her remember. Surely there's no law against that."

The deputy sighed. "For reasons of her own, the individual you're talking about has chosen not to meet with you, Mr. Townsend. There's no law that compels her to do so. Maybe she'll change her mind. Maybe she won't. But she has asked that she be permitted to work undisturbed for the remainder of her stay here in Grandville, and I've promised her that will be the case. Are we clear on what is expected?"

Joe shrugged.

"Like I have a choice," he said. "I'll tell you one thing. No matter what her next book is like, I'm posting a scathing review on Amazon."

I bit back a smile. Looked like the Hornet's stinger was primed and ready, and pointed in Courtney Howard's direction.

Ouch!

CHAPTER TWELVE

I followed Joe home, making quite certain he was in for the night, and reluctantly agreed to share a late-night snack of cherry cheesecake that Joe's neighbor lady, Abigail Winegardner, had brought over the day before. Okay, so maybe he didn't have to twist my arm. It was cheesecake, after all.

Joe gave me the prom photo so I could use it in the newspaper article. If all else failed, I'd run the picture with a story about Joe and his attempt to hook up with his former prom date. I still wanted one more crack at Courtney Howard, but wasn't sure what to try next. Short of breaking and entering—and unlike some intrepid reporters, I wasn't ready to go to jail for the sake of the story—I had no clue how to breach the stone wall that surrounded the reclusive author.

I left Joe's around eleven, wondering what I would find when I got home. I'd turned my cell phone off. I knew Shelby would call with more threats to switch to the wooden-shoe tribe than Gram had butt-ugly fertility statuettes to decorate the double-wide.

I decided to drop the county and city law enforcement call sheets off at the *Gazette* before I went home. I could scan the infamous prom photo and make a copy, and maybe Google Elizabeth Courtney Howard to see if I could turn up anything new. I hoped that by the time I got home, Shelby would be gone and Gram would be in her bed. Which was now just down the hall from me. Mere steps away. I grimaced. I had to have a talk with my dad about his mother.

I unlocked the back door of the newspaper office and flicked on a light, they dropped the paperwork into the appropriate basket. I walked by Stan's darkened office and snared a mint from his candy dish, looking at the comfy padded office chair behind the great big desk. Me? All I rated was a folding chair and a scarred-up old table.

Stan always kept his computer turned on, so I decided, for efficiency's sake, that I'd just use his computer.

I inched into Stan's office, feeling a teensy bit ill at ease, and made my way behind his desk. I pulled the chair out and swiveled it around, the nicely padded seat open and inviting.

I eased down into the chair. Nice. Very nice. I swiveled it back around to face the computer, scanned Joe's photo and printed a copy off, then spent the next forty-five minutes researching the chills-and-thrills author who'd given the willies to generations.

I printed off bios and books, searching for a recent photograph of Howard—anything more recent than the antique photo that accompanied the author's bio on her hardbacks. I thought I'd hit pay dirt when I located a shot of the author taken three years earlier, on the streets of the Big Apple, as she was entering her hotel on the arm of a well-built fellow. Unfortunately, Howard was wearing a full-length black leather coat with a scarf draped around her head, and dark glasses like some old-time movie star, so there wasn't much to see.

I checked out the guy, and blinked. I couldn't be sure, but it looked like the stripteaser from Howard's bedroom the other night. I'd have to see his chest to know for sure.

I printed off the photo, along with all the information on Howard I felt might be useful.

Courtney had married Kevin Howard when she was twenty-two years old. She'd been married for only a year when her husband died in a noncombat military plane crash. Courtney Howard had never remarried. No wonder her stories always carried elements of true love that lasted forever. She'd lived her own love-for-a-lifetime story—one that had been cut tragically short.

Her first books, romance novels, were written under the pseudonym Beth Howard. The author made a genre jump to the horror/thriller chiller genre in her midforties, with unexpected success, each book garnering more fans and a higher position on the bestseller lists. Readers, it appeared, would pay good money to be scared out of their wits. Ten of her books had made it either to the big screen or to made-for-TV-movie billing. Megabooks Megabucks. The stuff that dreams were made of. Or, in Howard's case, nightmares—that paid off big. Courtney Howard made her home in rural Connecticut on a large estate outside Essex, where she penned her novels in seclusion.

I finished up, logged off the 'Net and turned in the

chair to face the wide expanse of desk in front of me. The desk had a larger area than my bed. I noticed Stan's goofy half-glasses on the desktop, and I reached out and stuck them on the end of my nose.

Okay, I admit, this was feeling a wee bit weird, but I went with it.

"Turner, get your ass in here! Turner, for gawd's sake use spell-check! Turner, keep that damned cell phone charged up!" What can I say? I get a little carried away sometimes.

I soon decided a little role reversal was in order.

"Rodgers, get that fat butt in here!" I barked. "Rodgers, for gawd's sake, edit your copy, man! Rodgers, move that lard ass next door and get me a cappuccino!" I was really into my little reversal-of-fortune fantasy when I happened to look up to find my brilliant, caring and very understanding boss standing in the doorway.

"What the hell are you doing, Turner?"

I popped out of Stan's chair like it had an electric charge hooked up to the seat.

"Nothing! Work! Research!" I said. "See?" I handed him the sheets I'd printed off. "Courtney Howard research. I was hoping to find something that could help me storm the castle walls they've erected around that woman."

"And did you?"

"Well, not yet, but we are making progress." I told him about the incident at the Holloway house earlier that evening. "So I'll have something for sure to run. Maybe not the in-depth interview with major AP appeal I'd hoped for, but the *Gazette* will definitely have something no other news outlet has."

I removed myself from behind Stan's desk and edged toward the door, thankful that he didn't appear to have heard my one-woman performance.

"It seems there may be something to that real estate angle on the Holloway house after all," Stan said. "The wife says Rivas is definitely interested in acquiring the house. She thinks they might be looking to expand into a B and B. With the history of the house and folks getting a thrill out of staying at a place that is supposedly haunted, they figure they could keep the place filled year-round."

"Really?" I couldn't imagine someone wanting to spend money for a night in a haunted house. In all the movies I ever watched, people were *paid* to stay in the creepy house . . . and usually never lived to collect their moolah. "So yet another story I can follow and pin down," I said.

"Good luck confirming it. The wife thinks Rivas will pretty much want to keep it out of the news until it's a done deal, or others will jump on the bandwagon and try to outbid them. Rivas is said just to be waiting for the heir to sign off on the paperwork."

"By heir, you mean Elizabeth Courtney Howard."

He nodded.

"Very interesting," I said, thinking it was more than fortuitous that my gramma had an in with a certain Romeo Rivas that her granddaughter might be able to use to her advantage. One might even say it was predestined. Preordained. Meant to be.

All I needed was access to the house so I that could have a chance to plead my case to Courtney Howard personally. I had to think a small-town success who had fought her way to the top of the literary world was bound to have some empathy for a young woman trying to do much the same. At least I hoped so.

"I guess I'd better call it a night," I said, picking up my stack of papers and heading for the door. " 'Night, Stan."

"Just a minute, Turner. Aren't you forgetting something?"

I stopped in the doorway. "Yes?"

"Could I have my glasses back now?" Stan asked.

I looked down my nose cross-eyed and realized I still had the glasses that weren't really glasses resting on the end of my nose. I handed them to Stan.

"So, goodnight, then, Boss," I said, relieved that he apparently hadn't heard the worst of my role-playing. I had just left Stan's office when he called after me.

"Don't you mean 'lard-ass'?" he asked.

I ran to my car, deciding that whatever awaited me at my domicile had to be more enjoyable than explaining myself to Stan. Besides, even I don't know sometimes why I do the things I do.

I motored home, grateful to see that Shelby's Jeep was gone, and tiptoed past the dogs. They raised weary heads in "hello, how are you, we're beat" acknowledgment of my return, then went back to their slumber. I opened the front door slowly, cursing the creak that accompanied the motion. I stepped in and caught a whiff of something unusual. I rolled my eyes. Incense. I hated the smell of incense.

I hung my jacket on the coat tree by the door and moved cautiously inside. If I could just make it to my bedroom . . .

"Tressa? Is that you?"

Crap.

Gram's call came from the back bedroom. Her bedroom now, apparently.

"Yes, Gram. It's me."

"You alone?"

"Yes."

"Dumb question. Come on back."

I walked down the hall, my footsteps uncertain. Wary. I stopped outside her closed door.

"Are you alone?" I thought to ask, not wanting to open the door to see Joltin' Joe Townsend in my gramma's bed.

"Unfortunately, yes."

I shook my head and opened the door. "Knock, knock," I said, and stuck my head in.

The spare bedroom had been transformed from a second room devoted to my western clothing and horse paraphernalia into something out of the *Arabian Nights*. Gauzy dusty rose–colored window treatments matched the full-sized bedspread. My horse-head lamp had been replaced with a dark maroon-colored lamp shaped somewhat like a feminine figure, with long, sleek curves and no head. The lampshade was covered with the same dusty rose color as the curtains. I was amazed at the transformation. My gramma could accomplish more in one day than I could in a week—and never raise a hand doing it. Other than to point out where she wanted things put, that is.

"Wow, you've been busy," I said—meaning "busy" as in putting other people to work, of course. Gram was in bed, her sheet and blankies pulled up to her chin. Remembering that Gram liked to sleep au naturel on occasion, I was glad to see her covered up to her golly-getter in bedding.

"You like it?" Gram asked. "It's called Romantic Rose. I'd like to paint the walls the same color. Maybe just a scoosh lighter."

I swallowed. Painting? That meant she was settling in for the long haul.

"It's nice," I said. "If a bit on the dark side."

"It sets a certain mood, don't you think?" she asked.

I nodded. It set a mood that promised this bedroom was going to see more action than mine. "It sure does that," I said. "So Shelby must have been a big help." "Help" being a relative term here.

Gram sat up. "She sure was. Why, that girl can reach that storage space above my closet without a stool. She's a worker, too, if a little excitable."

I frowned. "What do you mean?"

Gram patted her head, which was encased in one of those sleep bonnets that help your hairdo stay done while you're sleeping, so you can avoid having one side of your hair flatter than the other. No more bedhead!

"When we returned to the house with our first load and she found that you'd skedaddled, she put up a hue and cry that set the dogs to howling. I almost dropped my Kokopelli. You remember my Native American fertility god. The one we had to superglue? The poor fellow couldn't have survived a second emasculation," she said, and I winced.

"I had to run a couple errands," I explained. "And something came up."

"Too bad my Kokopelli will never be able to say that," Gram said with a sniff. "Did you have newspaper business? Shelby thought you were backdooring her again. Whatever that means. She said if she found out you were keeping her out of the loop, she'd take that loop and—"

"I don't think I need to hear more," I said, putting a hand to my throat. "I'll give her a call. It's cool."

"So were you working on the Holloway story?" she asked.

I nodded. "Online research, basically." I thought I'd better leave out Joe's visits to the house, and how the second one had turned out. Best to let Joe handle the heavy lifting here. "Howard has had some sad moments in her life, with her young husband dying so soon after they were married. She never married again. I wonder if that's because her first was The One, and she knew she could never feel for another man what she'd felt for him." I really wanted to ask Howard that question. To have her speak of things she'd never spoken of publicly before. And to pick me to tell those things to. Hey, if you're gonna dream, dream big.

"Maybe she was just too picky," Gram said. "There's lots of good men out there. Or maybe she was actually a closet lesbian. That happens, you know. On *Maury* the other day they had this fifty-five-year-old man who'd been married for thirty years, the father of five kids, and now all of a sudden he tells his family he's been gay all these years and introduces them to his secret lover, Sven. So who's to know?"

"Sven?" I shook my head to clear it, then remembered I needed her help. "So, what's this with you and Jack Rivas? Is he one of those 'good men' you were just talking about?" I asked, hoping to get a feel for whether my gramma would be in a position to pick up any information about the pending real estate deal between Howard and J&R Development.

"He's an incredible dancer," she said. "He's got more moves than HawkI Moving and Storage," she said. "But he also has an ego that could fill Wells Fargo Arena."

"But you enjoy spending time with him, right?"

Gram shrugged. "He's a big spender. He made big bucks off his wife's family business. And he's still got his finger in that business."

Now this was what I wanted to hear.

"Stan heard that Rivas Real Estate may be involved in the sale of the Holloway house," I said, not wanting to bring up the bed-and-breakfast angle just yet. I started to say something along the lines of, "What I wouldn't give to get in that house to snap a few pictures for my article," when I looked at my gramma lying there all cute and wrinkled, and guess what? I couldn't do it. I just couldn't do it. If she and Joe Townsend really were meant to be together in their golden years, I didn't want to place her in another man's path solely for personal gain. There had to be another way to get my story. "You'd better get some sleep, Gram," I told her, bending down to give her a kiss on her soft cheek. "You've had a busy day." I came away with Oil of Olay–soaked lips. "Call if you need anything," I added.

She nodded. "That won't be a problem. I picked this up in town earlier." She picked up an item from beside her bed, and a short burst like an abbreviated sonic boom resounded through the room.

It took a second for me to pull myself off the ceiling. I decided I also needed to start wearing those disposable undergarments made for bladder control problems, if I was going to spend much time around haunted houses—including ones haunted by blue-haired seventy-year-old women with too much time on their hands.

"It's an air horn," she said, as if I hadn't come to that conclusion already. "If I need you, I'll just give a short burst on this puppy. It's loud enough to wake the dead."

I stuck a finger in my ear to clear it. "Good night, Gram," I said.

" 'Night, Tressa Jayne."

"What's that?" I asked, clearing my other ear.

"Good night!"

Yeah. Good night and good luck.

CHAPTER THIRTEEN

When I finally crawled into bed, I was wide-awake, and my tossing and turning had less to do with my story dilemma than with the symphonic snoring marathon originating from the room down the hall. My gramma snored louder at night than she did during a extralong sermon.

I punched my pillow. Townsend had a lot to answer for—the least of which was one night's lost sleep. I'd still be tiptoeing around ancient artifact reproductions and Zulu death masks at Christmastime. I had to plan and execute a suitable retaliatory strike. But what?

I finally gave up, stumbled to my bathroom, grabbed some cotton balls, wadded them up and stuck them in my ears. Uh, if you're a minor, don't try this. I once ended up with a painful ear condition when I stuck a Q-tip too far back in my ear. Who knew you weren't supposed to use those to clean your ears? I thought that's what they were for. Live and learn.

After getting a drink of water, I stuck my tongue out at my reflection and headed back to bed.

"Ouch!" My bare toes collided with a book on the floor of my room beside my bed. I sat down and picked it up. It was the copy of *Satan's Serenade*, by Elizabeth Courtney Howard, which I'd finished last week.

I opened the book and started it again, finding my mind wandering as I read. I frowned. The early books by Courtney Howard had kept me riveted. I'd stay up late at night, flashlight beneath my bedsheets, reading till the wee hours. Or until I scared myself to the point that I had to turn on my bedroom light and read the Bible instead.

My all-time favorite Courtney Howard book, *Shadows of the Night*, had been written twelve years earlier. Along the lines of *Jane Eyre*-meets-*Dracula*, with the Dracula dude being one hot but tortured vampire, *Shadows* was one of those books you just couldn't put down till you'd finished. So much so that I'd hid it behind my math book and read it until Mrs. Jameson, my math teacher, discovered my little deception, took the book and proceeded to read a portion to the class. Unfortunately, she chose a pretty steamy section that gave folks the impression I was really a girlie-girl with a softer side after all. So naturally I devoted the rest of that school year to dispelling that notion. I spent so much time after school that I started making phone calls home to notify my folks when I *didn't* have a detention.

It was *Shadows of the Night* that convinced me that bloodsuckers with fangs could be as sexy as professional rodeo riders—or a certain ranger who was on my hit-back-hard list.

I padded over to my bookcase —yes, I do have such an item in my room—and pulled the hardback from its place on the shelf, then got back into bed. I opened the book and began to read.

187

During the daylight hours I counsel myself to put the past behind me. To lay aside the cloak of grief and despair I wrap tightly round me like a dark cocoon, and to cast that heavy shroud of loss from me. I challenge myself daily to live again. And perhaps dare to love again. It's moments like this, however—when the dark shadows of the night close in about me and conjure up pictures in my mind of mists and secrets, good and evil, hope and redemption—that I realize that I will never leave the past behind. For it is part of me, and I am part of it. But maybe with the telling I can finally find a measure of peace. Of understanding. And perhaps then the loss will be easier to bear, the grief not so paralyzing.

It all began with a child. . . .

I was lost. Lost in the magic of a storyteller's spell. Hopelessly snared by the evocative prose. Hey, what do you know? I do have a sentimental side. Uh, just don't let that get out, 'kay?

I awoke the next morning to the unfamiliar chorus of clanging pots and pans from the kitchen. I sniffed a couple times. Oh buddy, there's nothing better than the smell of freshly brewed coffee to wake up to in the morning.

I checked the time. Six o'clock. I swung my feet over the side of the bed. A thud got my attention, and I bent down to pick up *Shadows of the Night,* which had fallen to the floor. I'd read into the wee hours, falling asleep just as the heroine was about to offer up her long, pale neck and life's blood, and all for the sake of a man. Ah. Ain't love grand?

I got out of bed and stumbled past the piles of boots

I'd thrown on the floor last night so that I could actually go to bed, and made a beeline for the kitchen and a caffeine fix. My gramma's backside greeted me. Her upper torso halfway in the fridge, she was bent at the waist, her velour-clad bottom framed in the open interior of the refrigerator.

"Uh, what are you looking for, Gram?" I asked, grabbing a big blue cup from the mug tree and pouring a cup of coffee.

"What most people look for in a refrigerator," she said. "Food. But I'm coming up empty-handed. All I've found so far is a half-eaten package of pepperoni that expired two weeks ago, a package of bagels that are hard as hockey pucks, fuzzy cream cheese and a couple cans of lite beer. You need to go shopping, Tressa."

I shrugged. "I eat out most of the time," I told her. "Besides, you know what happens when I cook. We're talking major *Backdraft* here," I said. I inherited my lack of culinary prowess honestly. My gramma used to make Paw-Paw Will do most of the cooking. He never seemed to mind. Especially after she exploded that turkey in the oven early in their marriage. When my gammy cooks, we pray *after* the meal.

"Well, that will have to change," Gram said. "We can't entertain gentlemen callers without food in the house. It just ain't done."

"Gentlemen callers?" The last gentleman who called at my house had come to suck poop out of the septic tank with a four-inch-wide hose.

"Remember, the way to a man's heart is through his stomach," Gram reminded me.

For me, that would read more like, "The way to the nearest emergency room is via Tressa's cooking."

"I don't exactly entertain that much, Gram," I told her. "I work three jobs. I'm lucky I have time to eat, myself."

"I'll make a grocery list," she said, and closed the refrigerator door. "But that won't help us with breakfast."

"There are Dairee Freeze chocolate-peanut ice cream bars in the freezer," I informed her. "Uncle Frank had a bunch of them to get rid of. They taste real good with a cup of coffee."

"That's hardly breakfast food," she said, but I saw her eyes dart in the direction of the freezer. "I don't think that's a proper way to start the day."

I shrugged. "Suit yourself," I said, getting up and heading to the fridge. I opened the freezer door, grabbed an ice cream bar, unwrapped it, tossed the wrapper and returned to my seat.

"It does contain milk," Gram said, watching me nibble on the ice cream confection. "And milk has calcium, so in a way I'd be helping fight my osteoporosis by eating ice cream. So I reckon eating one of them Dairee Freeze ice cream bars is actually promoting good bone health."

I raised my brows. That was a stretch. But one I'd remember when I was in my seventies and really wanting a peanutty ice cream bar.

I finished up my breakfast, threw on a pair of blue jeans and my grungiest cowboy boots and an old gray hoodie, and hurried out to do chores. Butch and Sundance tailed me down to the barn, stopping to sniff the ground, then letting loose with barks and running to catch up with me like I'd pulled a fast one on them. The goofballs.

I presently care for three horses, but I'm always in

the market for more, even if my wallet isn't. Two of the horses are mine. One belongs to my mother. With the names we give our horses, you'd think we were a family of gamblers. My mother's horse is Queen of Hearts, or Queenie for short, a sorrel quarter horse with a nifty white blaze. Her first horse was Royal Flush. I am the proud owner of Black Jack, a black quarter-mix, and Joker, an Appaloosa quarter. Talk about goofballs. Joker is one of those horses more on the order of a great big dog. He can just wrap you around his hoof. I really learned to ride on Joker. He's a horse you can make those amateur mistakes with and actually live to regret it. Dopey but adorable.

I checked the tiny herd's water supply, scooping off the green gunk that collects on top of the water when horses drink after consuming hay or grass. I replenished the hay and tossed some grain into the feed boxes in their stalls. I didn't have to whistle for them this morning, as they were already up from the pasture and milling about the lot. I threw open the barn door and, in procession, they pranced into the barn and into their respective stalls. While they ate, I forked poop into the spreader and thought about my living arrangements.

Now, don't get the wrong idea here. I love my gammy, but a twenty-three-year-old just isn't supposed to be living with her grandmother. I think it's written down somewhere. Unfortunately, my options were pretty limited. Even if I found an apartment in town that I could afford, chances were they wouldn't allow two hairy ponies on the premises without a hefty deposit. More important, I just couldn't sentence my two dogs to a cracker box existence in a small apartment. They needed room to run and play.

And to dig in the dirt and make big messes. Like all children.

I finished up the chores, herded my four-legged critters out of the barn and headed back to the house. I filled the dogs' bowls and hit the shower, then dressed in low-slung brown slacks, a white turtleneck and a khaki-colored denim jacket. Gram was sitting on the living room couch, watching *Get Smart* reruns and writing her grocery list, when I emerged as put together as I get.

"How much milk do you think we need?" she asked. "How much do you drink?"

I thought about it. "That depends," I told her.

"On what?"

"On whether you buy Double Stuf Oreos and Soft N Chewy chocolate-chip cookies," I said.

"I'll get a gallon," she said. Bless her heart. You gotta love her.

I kissed her good-bye, warned her not to walk over to the house unless she called Mom first and told her she was on her way, and headed out the door.

I snitched some petrol from my dad's farm tank. We don't actually have a farm, but my dad likes the trappings. Plus, it's nice to have a gas tank on the premises—especially if one is running low on gas and cash. As is often my SOP.

I drove to town in a surprisingly good mood, considering I'd gotten little sleep due to my snoring roommate and my late-night date with a certain sexy vampire. As I drove into town and by the middle school, I noticed toilet paper decorating the trees on the south side of the building. Classroom windows were soaped. I marveled at how the students managed to spell all the bad words correctly. Public education must be in better shape than I'd heard.

So far I hadn't spotted any outhouses yet, but it was getting much more difficult to snatch one of these little beauties. Folks who owned these gems had gotten smart and usually protected them from becoming Porta Potties. The spoilsports.

I parked in a small lot behind the *Gazette* and entered through the back door. I got as far as the layout room when Smitty stopped me. "I'd turn around and go out the way I came in, if I were you," he told me.

"And why would you do that?" I asked. "If you were me."

Smitty put down the advertisements he'd been editing. "Because Stan's greeting this morning was something along the lines of, 'Calamity Jayne is on her last roundup'—or words to that effect."

I frowned. He couldn't still be sore over that "lardass" remark? Could he? I decided not to risk it when I caught sight of the fluorescent lights reflecting off his shiny balding head.

"Turner. My office. Now."

Smitty gave me a see-I-told-you look that also held a touch of pity. "Good luck, kid," he said.

I nodded. "Thanks, Smitty," I replied. "And thanks for the heads up. Maybe we should come up with a system like Homeland Security has for terror alerts. You could hold up a green flag if everything is cool, a yellow one if it's an 'enter at your own risk' environment and a red one if it's a danger zone."

Smitty nodded. "We'd only need the yellow and red flags," he said.

"Turner! I'm waiting!"

I sighed. I sure hoped I wasn't about to get a pink slip. I already had a collection so thick I could make a decent flip book out of them.

I hovered in the doorway of Stan's office.

"About last night," I began, and Stan waved me off.

"This isn't about your audition for *Saturday Night Live* last night, Turner," Stan said. "It's about this." He tossed a sheet of paper onto the corner of his desk. "Paul Van Vleet just sent me this little gem. It's appearing on the front page of the Thursday edition of the *New Holland News*. Take a look."

Recalling Dixie Daggett's mention of Drew Van Vleet and the Halloween party at the senior center, I was pretty sure I knew what was on the page. Or should I say "who"? What I didn't know was how bad the picture was. And what the fallout to me would be.

"Do I have to?" I asked.

"Turner."

"All right, all right. I'll look at it." I walked over to the desk and picked up the paper. There in living color—or almost-living color—in side-by-side photos was yours truly, being dipped and subsequently dropped by an ancient vampire slayer. My witch's nose had slipped to my chin in the first picture, and I was rubbing my ass in the second.

"Care to explain that?" Stan asked.

Explain what? The green nose protruding from my chin? My ass-rubbing? Or being dipped by a guy who could appear as a "Before Geritol" poster boy?

"Well, you see, there was this costume party—"

"Party? Tell me, Turner," Stan said, "tell me how I explain to my advertisers that one of my employees has her picture on the front of our competitor's newspaper doing the hustle with a guy old enough to be her grandpa. You're supposed to be selling our papers—not the other guy's, you know."

"Tango," I corrected.

"What?"

"Tango, not the hustle."

Stan shook his head. "What the hell were you doing, anyway? Besides a tango that apparently went very wrong," he added.

I took another look at the pictures. "How do you even know it's me? It could be anybody in that costume."

Stan sat back in his chair and looked at me.

"Okay, so it's me. And, yes, it looks like I was dancing," I said. "And I was. Sort of. Kind of. But what I was really doing at the senior center Halloween party was working on the Howard story. For you. For the *Gazette*. For God and Grandville!"

Stan rolled his eyes. "So now you're auditioning for a role on *Masterpiece Theatre?* What did you hope to accomplish at the senior center on the Howard story?"

I reminded him about Joe Townsend's connection to the author and how I'd planned to exploit—utilize—that connection to gain access to the author.

"So when you think about it, I was on the clock and so I really should be paid for my time that evening," I pointed out. "And probably I should file a workers'-compensation report regarding the little spill I took. I did pick up a beauty of a bruise."

Stan continued to stare at me.

"We can talk about this later," I said.

Stan nodded. "Speaking of work, there's a special county supervisor's hearing I'd like you to attend." He slid a piece of paper across the desk to me. "Apparently there's a major disagreement over whether access to one of the old boat ramp areas should be restricted. Residents say folks are using the area for drunken parties and smoking dope, and even allege they've discovered the beginnings of a portable meth lab. Fishermen and nature enthusiasts object to a gate being erected across the road and say the residents pushing the restriction—who just happen to own land adjacent to government land, by the way—are trying to pull a fast one. Should make for a good story."

I took the paper. "The clash of opposing interests," I said. "What time is the hearing?"

"Ten o'clock. Snap pictures, of the board and of a couple of the more articulate folks who address the board, and quote 'em in your piece. And nail down that other story. Pronto."

I nodded. "I'm working on it, Boss," I said. "I'm working on it." I turned to leave.

"By the way, Turner, you do know if you file a workers'-comp claim, your injuries have to be photographed, right?"

I stopped. "Photographed?"

Stan nodded. "As in, documented for viewing by folks with the workers'-compensation board, as well as the employees here who do the paperwork."

"Injury? What injury?" I said, and left before I caused another red-flag moment.

I spent some time writing up an article to go with Joe's prom picture, giving some background about the situation leading up to the prom date and about Joe's unsuccessful yet plucky attempt to reestablish contact with the famous author. I couldn't help but be disappointed. The article could have been so much meatier and more substantive. (Yes, thanks to online dictionaries and thesauruses—or is that "thesauri"?—I am expanding my vocabulary daily.)

I finished up, grabbed my backpack and camera, and headed for the courthouse. The county supervisors met on the third floor, which meant either a long climb on worn stairs or a long wait for the lone elevator. When I saw the gaggle of folks waiting for the elevator, I opted to take the stairs. Besides, I'm always kind of ashamed to use the elevator unless I'm going, like, a gazillion floors. Especially when I see folks a lot older than I am climbing the stairs without wheezing like asthmatics when they get to the top. I know what you're thinking: "Stop eating the chocolaty, peanutty ice cream bars for breakfast, you twit.' I get it. I get it.

I made it to the third floor, found the correct meeting room—not hard, considering there was only one— and checked my watch. I still had ten minutes to kill, so I zoned in on the M&M dispenser and put in fifty cents for a handful of the candy-coated chocolates. I munched away and searched my brain for a great no-fail way to approach Courtney Howard for the interview. One that was legal, that is. Well, mostly legal.

I finished my candy and was searching for another quarter to get some peanuts from the other dispenser when a hand appeared in front of me, holding out a coin. I looked up. Drew Van Vleet smiled down at me.

"Need a quarter?" he asked.

I shook my head. "Not from you," I replied.

"Oooh, where's the hostility coming from?" he said. "I'm just trying to help you out. Do a good turn."

I looked at him. "You want to do a good turn?" I asked. "Go over to that railing and take a sharp left."

Drew grinned. "You saw the senior center photos," he said. "They turned out better than I hoped. I couldn't have planned it better myself. To have the old guy drop you like that. I'm sure it will give our readers a good laugh over their coffee and doughnuts tomorrow morning," he said. He checked his watch. "Are you covering the supervisors' hearing?" he asked.

I nodded.

"Stan sent you instead of Smitty?"

I frowned. "Yeah. So?"

He shrugged. "This can't be the big story you said you were working on," he said. "How did you put it? 'High-profile'?"

I shrugged. "You never know where you'll find a compelling story," I told him.

"Come on, Turner. You know you've struck out with your scoop of the century. It's time to step aside and let the professionals have a crack at it."

I blinked. Van Vleet knew about Elizabeth Courtney Howard? "Over my dead body," I said, and almost immediately regretted those words. Given my recent history, it probably wasn't the smartest response.

Van Vleet's eyebrows lifted. "I see you're still suffering from the delusion that you really are a reporter," he said. "Might I suggest therapy?"

"Might I suggest you bugger off?" I told him, picking up on Joe's earlier phrase.

Van Vleet straightened his collar. "See you in the funny papers, witchie-poo," he said, and walked into the hearing room.

I sneered at his back. I'd show Drew Van Vleet just what this reporter was made of. There was more to Tressa Turner than ol' beater cars, ice cream confections and a string of bad luck long enough to fly a kite to Omaha. And Elizabeth Courtney Howard held the precious key to proving that.

Why did I get the feeling that securing the brass ring in this case was gonna make rescuing Dorothy, Toto and the ruby slippers from a witch's castle guarded by flying monkeys and armed soldiers seem like a day at the spa?

CHAPTER FOURTEEN

Contrary to what Drew Van Vleet had implied, I was fully capable of following the rather heated discussion in the county meeting room. Between my scribbled notes and my tape recorder, along with my photos, I felt I had a representative sampling of both sides of the gate versus no gate issue. I was surprised at the vehemence of the fishermen who'd voiced their objections. Many of them had been fishing at that particular area of Silver Stone Lake for longer than I'd been alive, and I sympathized with them over the possibility of losing access to something that had become a familiar—and obviously long-enjoyed—tradition.

The hearing broke up around noon, and I hightailed it down the stairs, trying to decide where to eat lunch. That's one of the things I look forward to each day: deciding where I'll eat and what I'll order when I get there. Simple pleasures and all that.

I finally decided on the Meat Market, a mom-and-pop place that sold meats, cheeses and deli items, and also served lunch daily. I hurried into the store, hop-

ing to beat the rush of high school kids who descended on the place over their lunch hour. It was
Wednesday, so that meant the specials were chef's
salad and taco salad. Since I partook of a good share
of food items with south-of-the-border ingredients, I
decided to go with the chef's salad. Besides, it would
be a healthy change from my usual fare.

Unfortunately the high-schooler in line in front of
me sabotaged my healthful selection by ordering a
tenderloin with the works. Once I got a whiff of that
baby, my previous intention to dine on rabbit food
was but a fleeting memory.

I was sitting at a back table in the tiny seating area
and ripping into my tenderloin like a *Survivor* contest-
ant tears into the food they win in a reward challenge,
when I heard the bell on the door. I looked up to see
my friend Kari Carter hurry in.

Kari is a language arts teacher at the middle school.
She's been my best bud since elementary school.
We've made our share of mischief together. Okay, so I
was the one who actually initiated the mischief and
then dragged my friend Kari into the fray, but she was
more than willing to participate. Kari is engaged to be
married to Brian Davenport, a physical education
teacher at one of our elementary schools. The wedding is set for spring break. Originally Kari was supposed to walk down the aisle in December, over
Christmas break, but I think she realized having an
anniversary so close to Christmas wasn't a smart
move, gift-wise. You know, there's just way too much
temptation for the man to simply combine two mega-
gift-giving occasions. And with men who are notorious for not being power shoppers anyway, it was just
tempting fate.

"Kari! Yoo-hoo!" I called out to my friend. "Kari!"

Kari saw me and rushed over. "Tressa, hi! I'm on my lunch half-hour. Let me place my order, and I'll visit with you on my way out."

I nodded, stuffing more tenderloin into my mouth and washing it down with a swig of Coke. Kari was back in no time, sliding into a chair across from me. She'd ordered the chef's salad, I noticed.

She has an expensive wedding dress to fit into, I told myself, and then remembered I had a bridesmaid's dress to fit into, too. My chewing slowed until I reminded myself that I had five months to lose enough weight to fit into my dress. I decided to ignore the fact that the holiday season—along with all the stuffed turkeys, pumpkin pies and homemade candies that went with it—was just over yon horizon.

"So how are things at the middle school?" I asked. "Are you ready yet to do something a little less stressful? Like locate land mines or track terrorists?" I remembered what I was like during those adolescent years, and could only admire those brave souls who ventured into a classroom one hundred eighty days a year without regular, intense therapy. No wonder my folks gave my teachers such nice gifts each year.

"It's a crazy week, with homecoming. The sixth-graders are hyper about the dress-up days. And there's the parade and game on Friday, of course."

I nodded, remembering those fun homecoming traditions and creative pranks with a fond smile.

"And there's the mixer tonight," Kari went on. "You did remember that you agreed to be a chaperone for the youth project mixer this evening. Right?"

I needed to get a Palm. Or a secretary.

"Uh, sure," I said, searching my mental inventory

of excuses for all occasions, which I referred to on a semiregular basis, most frequently so that I could skip church and sleep in on Sunday mornings. "What time was that again?"

"Six to nine at the community center. You're not thinking of backing out, are you?" she asked, giving me one of those scary teacher looks that communicate the sentiment "don't make me get ugly" without saying a word. Can you believe it? A teacher for less than two years, and already she had the look down pat.

"I'll be there," I said. "But no way am I dressing up." I'd had more than enough costume parties to last for some time. Plus, I didn't want to open up the *New Holland News* to find I'd made the front page again.

"No costume required," Kari said. "But you may want to bring along some ranger repellent," she added.

"Huh?"

"Brian asked Rick to chaperone as well. Will that be a problem?"

Only for Rat Fink Rick.

"Not at all," I assured Kari. "In fact, I'm looking forward to visiting with the ranger."

"There isn't going to be any, uh, drama, is there?"

I put down my tenderloin. "Drama?"

"Between you and Rick. Children will be present."

I shook my head. "Any drama-queen baggage will be left at the door," I told her.

"Great," she said, and looked at her watch. "Oh, look at the time. I've got to go. See you at the center tonight. Come around five-thirty if you can, to help get set up."

"You got it," I replied. "By the way, what's on the menu?"

"Sloppy joes, chips, cookies and caramel apples," she told me.

She'd had me at sloppy joes, but the caramel apples closed the deal.

"See you there!" I said.

I spent more than an hour writing up the county supervisor story and called my house to check on my grandma. When I couldn't get an answer, I called my folks, but the line was busy. I figured since I'd be tied up that night, I'd go ahead and stop by home and do the chores. Plus, that would give me a chance to check up on Hellion Hannah and get cleaned up before I went to the mixer. I decided I'd take my camera along and shoot some pictures to stick in the paper. Secretly I was hoping to get a really terrible picture of Ranger Rick to run in the paper, but I knew the odds were against me. The guy was just too hot to be nonphotogenic. So not fair.

My cell phone rang as I pulled out of the parking lot. I made the mistake of answering it.

"H'lo," I said.

"Where the heck have you been?" It was Shelby Lynne. Her bellow almost blew out my eardrum.

"Duh. Working," I replied.

"What happened to you last night? I called your cell for hours."

Sometimes I missed the good old days when folks couldn't reach out and touch me twenty-four-seven.

"Low battery," I said—my patented excuse when I either forgot the phone or didn't want to chitchat.

"I want to know what's going on," she told me. "Did you go back to the Holloway house again without me?"

I turned on my radio and tuned it to an out-of-range

station that only picked up static. I put the cell phone over the speaker and let the static take over for a few seconds, then turned the phone in my direction. "You're breaking up, Shelby. What was that?" I turned the phone back to the radio. "Can't hear you," I said. "I'll call you back when I change location."

I hit the "end" button.

Hey, don't judge me. Tell me you haven't pretended to be the babysitter, your sister or your mother when someone calls who can't pronounce your last name. Same diff.

I'd just passed the Coffee Clatch, a nifty little eatery that served five different kinds of cheesecake and beaucoup varieties of coffee, when I spotted my gramma coming out. I almost ran into the car in front of me when I saw Romeo Jack Rivas follow her out onto the sidewalk. I sighed. Apparently Gram had been serious about entertaining male friends. Funny me. At the time, I thought she'd meant Joe.

I drove home, changed into grubbies, fed the horses, loaded poop, romped with the dogs and decided to check in at the "main house" before I took a shower and dressed for the mixer.

My dad was at work. He's worked for the phone company forever. My dad likes solitary work, going off and doing his own thing. He loves to putter around acreage, working on his tractors, planting and tending his garden, and hunting with my brother, Craig. My dad is also keen on trapshooting. No, I don't mean running off at the mouth. I mean, as in blasting bright orange clay targets with a shotgun. He's pretty good, too. He's even won several trophies. I tried to shoot trap once, but only succeeded in hitting the top of the trap house. Good thing they're like bunkers and made of concrete.

"Howdy! Anybody home?" I walked through the sliding doors off the cement patio at the back of the house and into the dining room. "Mom! You here?" I crossed the dining room, moved through the kitchen and stopped short at the living room door. "Mom?"

If I hadn't seen it myself, I wouldn't have believed it. There on the couch, with a box of pink tissues in one hand and a bowl of M&Ms in the other, was my mother. Clad in a gray Hawkeyes sweatshirt and gray sweatpants, she sat cross-legged on the sofa in front of the TV, dabbing red-rimmed eyes and blowing her nose.

"Mom?"

"Tressa!" My mother jumped to her feet, oblivious to the bowl of fall-colored M&Ms that flew in every direction—a kaleidoscope of orange, brown and tan that pelted the TV and hit the carpeted floor. "What are you doing here?" she asked, grabbing the remote control and hitting the power button to shut the set off. But not before I caught a peek of Humphrey Bogart and Ingrid Bergman.

I moved to the center of the room to make sure I'd seen what I thought I'd seen. An M&M crunched under my foot. Proof, indeed.

"Are you all right, Mom?" I asked. My mother never wore sweats. Never munched on M&Ms. And never ever sat in front of the TV watching sad movies and bawling her eyes out in the middle of the day. "I came by to check in. I called earlier but didn't get an answer."

My mother blew her nose and started to pick up candy. I knelt down to help her.

"What's going on, Mom?" I asked. "Are you okay?"

206

She blew her nose again. "You're going to think I've lost my mind," she told me.

Like, how bad could it be?

"Try me," I said.

My mom stopped collecting M&Ms and sat down on the floor. "I can't think what came over me. I was downstairs, working as usual, and I came up to check on your grandmother—I'd completely forgotten she was over at your place."

"My" place? That remained to be seen.

"And?" I asked.

"And I walked into the living room and it was so quiet and so inviting and so . . . so unoccupied that I decided, what the heck, I was going to take the day off, get into some grubbies, as you call 'em, and veg out. I stuck in *Casablanca*, and the rest, as they say, is history." She started to tidy the floor again. "Don't tell your father," she said.

"Tell him what?" I said, totally understanding the compulsion that from time to time forced women to seek out large quantities of chocolate and sad, romantic movies, and sob their eyes out; yet I was somewhat thrown by the fact that my ultradisciplined mother played hooky from work to do just that. It was a side of her she rarely let even her family see—one, apparently, she preferred to let out only when no one else was around.

I helped her collect the remaining evidence of her afternoon's activities, blowing the fuzzies off a handful of the candy and popping it into my mouth. Hey, remember the ten-second rule?

We got to our feet.

"So, how is it working out with your grandmother?" my mom asked, taking the bowl of M&Ms from me. "Should I talk to your father?"

I thought about it, took one look at the fuzzy socks my mom had on and shook my head. She deserved a bit of a break from the care and feeding of one very high-maintenance senior.

"Naw, we're cool," I told her. "Besides, my guess is, come winter, Gram will have decided that fireplace looks pretty inviting and will have her stuff moved back in and her chair by the crackling fire before you can say Jack Frost."

My mother nodded. "Just keep an eye on her, Tressa. She's one wily woman."

"Tell me about it," I replied, wondering what Gram had cookin' with Romeo Rivas on the side.

I left Mom to her last few hours of "me time" with a final promise to keep the incident to myself, and headed next door to shower and change into jeans and a gray hooded Grandville sweatshirt before heading out the door to the youth center.

I arrived twenty minutes after the mixer started, and wouldn't have been surprised at all to see Kari whip out her hot pink detention pad and write me up for being tardy. Instead she settled for one of those teacher looks again, and I was off the hook.

The aroma of the center was out of this world—a combination of beef and yummy sauce—which made it completely understandable that I gravitated in the direction of the food table, similar to the way my horses converge on an open barn door after I've whistled them in from the pasture.

I picked up a festive if somewhat ghoulish plate decorated with a collection of fiendish characters on the front, and headed for the sloppy joe assembly line.

"You're late," Kari scolded as I held my plate out for a sandwich. She plopped an open bun down and dumped a spoonful of sloppy joe mixture on it.

"A double scoop, please," I told her. "That'll save me from coming back for seconds," I added when I saw her hesitate. "Who needs the extra bread, right?"

She dumped another helping on my bun.

"Thank you, Ms. Carter," I told her like a polite young lady. I moved along in line and grabbed a bag of chips, a couple of chocolate-chip cookies and a can of soda, and made my way to a table half-filled with chattering sixth-graders. I put my plate down at an empty space.

"May I join you?" I asked, thinking I was being a really good role model.

"No. I was saving that seat for my friend Douglas," I heard, and turned to find the same mouthy little kid who'd accused me of cutting in line at the Dairee Freeze in the seat across from me.

" 'Scuse me?"

"That seat's for my friend Doug," he repeated.

"Oh?" I checked out the food line and didn't see anybody who I thought would qualify as a Doug. "So where is he?"

The chubby child gave me a dirty look. "He's not here yet."

I nodded, wondering if Doug was real or fantasy. "How about I sit here and keep Doug's chair warm until he gets here?" I said. "Will that work?" I took a seat and held out a hand. "By the way, my name is Tressa."

The kid looked at my hand like I had held out a big hairy spider. Or a glass of vegetable juice.

He touched my fingertips briefly.

"Hi."

"He's Stewart," a blond girl two seats down from me said. "I'm Ginny." She motioned to a dark-haired girl beside her. "She's Sofia."

"Hey," I said.

"I saw you at the ice cream place the other day," Stewart said.

I nodded. "I work there sometimes," I admitted, hoping to head off an unpleasant confrontation regarding my cutting him in line.

"What kind of name is Tressa, anyway?" the blonde named Ginny asked.

I'd gone home from school and asked my mom the very same question myself the day Kelby Kennedy told me I didn't look like a Tressa. When I found out my mom had named me after a doll with a button on her tummy to grow hair and a keyhole in her back to wind it back up, I decided never to divulge the origin of my name to a soul. Now that my mom is a serious CPA type, I think she prefers we keep the subject of how she selected my name between the two of us as well. For some reason the idea of my mom playing beauty-shop Barbie embarrasses her, I guess for the same reason she doesn't want folks to know she vegges out in front of the tube with a two-pound bag of M&Ms and furry purple socks.

"It's a family name," I told the blonde.

"It's fun," she said, and I nodded.

"So are you all having fun during homecoming week?" I asked, trying to make conversation. "Excited about the game?"

"I hate football," Stewart said.

I looked back at the little butterball.

"Who hates football?" I said. Apart from Vikings

fans, of course. "Besides, homecoming is more than just football," I told Stewart.

"Like what?"

I took a big bite of my sandwich. A glob of meat filling plopped onto my plate. "There are cheerleaders, parades, pep rallies and dances."

Stewart didn't look impressed.

I shoveled a couple of Doritos sideways into my mouth. "You've got popcorn, candy apples, walking tacos, and hot dogs," I said. "And don't forget, they throw tons of candy at the parade," I added, my mind automatically going to the gastronomical perks of the event.

"Are you calling me fat?" Stewart asked, his voice slightly raised.

"Huh?"

"Did you hear her? She just called me fat!" Stewart wailed.

"I did not!" I turned to Ginny and Sofia. "Did I, Ginny? Sofia?"

"Oh, Stewart. Get a life!" Ginny told him.

I looked at Stewart. His face was downcast as he stared at his plate. "Uh, Stewart, one thing you need to know about me—I like my food," I told him. "I tend to obsess over it."

Stewart looked up at me.

"Confession?" I said. "I only agreed to chaperone this evening when I found out they were having sloppy joes," I told him. "Am I pathetic or what?"

I caught a smile at the corner of Stewart's mouth.

"So you're not here because you enjoy hanging out with middle school kids?" Stewart asked.

"Are you kidding?" I told him. "It's all about the food, man."

I picked my sloppy joe up and took a humongus bite. More innards dripped onto my plate. "Ugh, I should have picked up a spoon," I said, looking down at the nummy meat filling on my plate.

"I'll go grab you one, Tressa," Stewart said, and jumped to his feet.

"Why, thank you, Stewart," I said. "What a gentleman," I told Sofia and Ginny. "If I was fifteen years younger—," I said, and left it at that. The girls looked at each other.

"Well, hello there, young ladies. Is there room for one more?"

I bristled at the sudden suave—and intrusive—tones of a ranger who had a lot to answer for. I looked over and caught Ginny and Sofia staring up at Rick Townsend, their tongues collecting more airtime than my pooches' did after a cross-country romp.

"One chaperone per table, Ranger Rick," I said between mouthfuls.

"Is that right, ladies?" he addressed the girls around me.

"No! You can sit with us!" Ginny said. "Please!"

"Sit here!" Sofia popped to her feet more quickly than I did when the microwave dinged to tell me my pizza rolls were ready.

"Well, if you're sure I'm not breaking any rules," Townsend said, taking the now open seat between Ginny and Sofia. "Everyone having a good time?"

"We were," I told him.

"So what did you two girls do? Sneak in here when no one was looking? You've got to be eighth-graders, right?" Townsend said, pouring on the charm thicker than I did maple syrup on the short stack at IHOP.

Okay, so I don't normally get the short stack, but you get my point.

"We're sixth-graders," Sofia, the cute brunette, told him. "I'm Sofia. That's Ginny." She pointed to her friend. "And you're really good-looking."

I rolled my eyes. Trust the brunette to go from "hello" to "you're hot" more quickly than my car's temperature gauge hit the red in midsummer.

"No! You're kidding. I thought you both were much older."

I was, like, gonna be sick. And I still had my dessert to eat. Lousy ranger.

"Here's your spoon!" Stewart handed me a plastic utensil, took a look at what was sitting between Ginny and Sofia, and dropped into his seat, his full attention on his plate once again. Neither girl noticed he'd even returned.

"Thank you, Stewart," I said. "Ranger Townsend, this fine young man is Stewart." Stewart gave a nod in Townsend's direction.

"Hello, Stewart. Nice to meet you."

"Tell me, Stewart, what exactly do you do at mixers?" I asked. "Dance? Play games? Meet and mingle?"

He looked up at me. "Since this is a Halloween party, I think they have some games planned. And they usually give out prizes."

"Sounds like fun," I said. "I hope they let chaperones participate."

"They usually do. We sometimes compete against the chaperones."

"You mean I have to be on 'his' team?" I said, making an "uh, gross" face.

Stewart smiled.

"At least if we're on the same team, I won't beat you, Tressa," Townsend said. "I know you're a sore loser."

"Who says I'd lose?" I asked. "I seem to recall I won our last friendly little wager."

He grinned. "Ah, but this is a game. A sporting competition. Men are naturally better at athletic events."

I saw Sofia and Ginny look at each other, then send Townsend a dark look.

"Sofia won the free throw competition at the city rec center the last three years. She beat out a bunch of boys," Ginny said with a lift to her chin. "And I can run faster than all the boys in the sixth grade."

Rick held up his hands. "Hey, I was just giving Calamity a hard time over there. No offense intended, ladies," he said.

"Calamity?" For the first time, Stewart made eye contact with Townsend.

He nodded. "That's Tressa's nickname," he told the boy. "Calamity Jayne."

Stewart looked back at me. "You're Calamity Jayne? From the papers?"

I gave Townsend a withering look. "Uh, some rather unenlightened individuals have called me that on occasion," I admitted. "But I assure you that tales of my past exploits have been greatly exaggerated," I added.

"You're the one who found the body in the trunk?" Sofia's eyes were as big as the chocolate-chip cookie I hadn't had time to eat.

"You're forgetting the second body she found at the marina," Townsend supplied, and I was ready to dump my plate on his head, cookies and all.

"And there was all that excitement at the state fair," Ginny chimed in.

Stewart slowly got to his feet. "I'm homeschooled. My mom made me come tonight to improve my social skills," he said, picking up his plate. "I don't think this is what she had in mind," he added, and moved to a table so far away I needed binoculars to see him.

Townsend shook his head. "Scared another one off, huh?"

"I hope you're happy, Townsend," I said. "I was just getting Stewart there to open up. Now he's cowering in the corner like I'm a regular Lizzie Borden. Or a representative from that Biggest Loser weightloss show recruiting for a new kids' version." I grabbed a cookie from my plate and bit off a big chunk. "You've got a lot to answer for, Townsend," I said, spraying cookie crumbs across the black paper tablecloths. "A lot."

"What? That kid? What'd I do?"

"Not Stewart," I hissed. "Grandma!"

Townsend sat back in his chair and cocked an arrogant eyebrow at me.

"Ah. Do I sense some difficulties adjusting to your new living arrangements?" he asked.

Adjust? I'd have more success adjusting if I moved into the new orangutan research facility south of Des Moines with the orangutans and bonobos.

"And why blame me? All I did was to extend a helping hand to a feeble old woman." Townsend put his hands out, palms up, in an I'm-an-open-book gesture.

"Ha. Try aiding and abetting," I replied.

"Oh, so your grandma moving in with you is criminal, huh?"

"No," I replied. "Not literally. But there ought to

215

be a law. And you stepped over the line, bucko, when you helped her in the back door while I was going out the front," I told him. "I was scared to death when I came home and the house was lit up like center ring at the circus." Which, come to think of it, was a pretty accurate assessment as to what life would be like sharing digs with my grandma.

"Some of those fertility gods *were* pretty terrifying," Townsend acknowledged, and leaned across the table in my direction. "Not to mention some of them could cause inferiority issues in a man if he wasn't secure with himself," he added in a low tone.

I remembered the Homo erectus I'd performed a Lorena Bobbitt number on, and almost grinned. Until I remembered how many of those little treasures I'd be seeing daily in the weeks to come.

"Don't think this is over, Townsend," I told him. "As you so often feel the need to point out to me, actions have consequences. So I'd be keeping an eagle eye out for your consequences, Mr. Ranger, sir. Just think how you'd like it if your granddad moved in with you."

"I'd kill myself." Townsend sighed. "I see you're bent on taking your pound of flesh, T, so have at me," he said with a smile that had the preteen girls around him needing drool bibs. "Do your worst."

I stuffed the rest of my cookie into my mouth and stood.

"If you'll excuse me, I need to help with the cleanup." I picked my plate up and marched to the kitchen.

My worst? The fool ranger had no idea.

CHAPTER FIFTEEN

It was time for the last game of the night. We'd bobbed for apples. Having the biggest mouth, I naturally won, but was disappointed that the prize was a basket of—you guessed it—apples. The sponsors, it seemed, were trying to incorporate a healthy element to the annual Halloween fun. Apparently, here in the breadbasket of the country, many of us are carrying some pretty disturbing breadbaskets of our own around our midsections, so I suppose the nutritious alternatives were a good thing. And hey, apples can always be dipped in peanut butter or caramel, and there's this really tasty fruit dip you can get at the grocery store that is to die for.

We had run sack races, performed charades, played *Jeopardy* with questions from the sixth-grade science, social studies, math and language arts curricula. (Kari had the teaching bug bad.) Wouldn't you know the prizes for *Jeopardy* were king-sized candy bars, and I was disqualified for repeatedly jumping out of my seat before buzzing in. Townsend was the game show host, and was an even better Alex Trebek than Alex Trebek. Funny, great-looking, witty, great-looking, clever. Have I mentioned great-looking? He even got Stewart in on the act, drafting him as his assistant and scorekeeper.

The last event of the evening was the apple race. I'm sure you know the one: Two teams of equal number line up one member behind another. The object of the race is to successfully pass the apple from one team member to the next by means of the chin and neck only. The apple is transferred neck-to-neck down the line. If the apple falls or if someone uses a body part other than the chin and neck, that team has to start over. The last person to receive the apple has to race— apple beneath chin—to the front of the room and drop the apple (still by means of the chin/neck maneuver) and drop it in a basket to be declared the winner.

Frankly, I wanted to sit out, but I didn't want to be seen as a party pooper. Besides, I really wanted to whip Townsend's butt. Figuratively, ladies. Figuratively. It's a children's get-together, remember?

We'd chosen teams and already completed a best-out-of-three competition. Townsend's team had beaten mine all three times. I'm not saying they cheated, understand, but when you get stuck with a kid on your team who doesn't actually have a neck—no, I won't be naming names—you have a wee bit of a handicap.

It was getting close to nine and the party was almost over, when the youngsters decided they wanted to have one last race—chaperones versus children. For bragging rights.

We lined up and I stuck myself at the end of the chaperone line. I figured the kids would probably be done way before the apple got to me, and I wouldn't even have to participate. I frowned when I noticed Townsend positioning himself in front of me.

"What do you think you're doing?" I asked him.

He turned around and looked at me. "I'm getting ready for the race," he said. "Is there a problem?"

I looked at his long, tanned neck, attached to a great chin. I'd lay odds that same neck and chin smelled wonderful, too. No way was I going anywhere near that neck and chin in public with a bunch of kids looking on. Nope. Wasn't gonna happen.

"You're nuts," I told Townsend. "That's the problem."

Townsend shrugged. "What's the matter, Calamity? Afraid you can't resist my charms? I understand. I'll move so you won't have to be tempted."

Oh, buddy, was it time to pull on the ol' hip waders or what? For sure, it was suddenly gettin' purty deep.

"You just stay right where you are, Mr. Ranger, sir," I said, pulling on the collar of his sweatshirt. "I wouldn't want it said the chaperones were stacking our team to gain an advantage. I'm pretty sure I can control myself where you're concerned," I told him. "You'd better hope I can," I added. "You better hope I can."

The whistle sounded, and the race was on. The city youth director was the first one to hand off—I mean chin off—the apple, to his wife, a short but chin-competent team member. She accepted the apple from her husband with little difficulty and turned to relay the Red Delicious to Kari's fiancé, Brian. This exchange proved to be a little dicey due to the differences in height. At well over six feet, Brian had to bend almost double in order to snare the apple with his chin and secure it close to his neck.

219

I took a quick look at the kids' teams and saw that they were keeping pace with us.

"Come on, Brian! Move that apple!" I found myself cheering. "Move that apple!"

I saw Townsend shake his head, but ignored him. I sometimes get carried away in the heat of competition.

"Move that apple!" was now a loud war cry among the teams competing for first place.

Brian finally managed the transfer of the fruit from the diminutive team member and carefully turned to his fiancé to bestow said fruit on her.

I frowned when Kari got this really dopey lovesick look on her face. I hoped she wasn't going to get distracted by her fiancé's closeness and botch the subsequent transfer, so I yelled, "Move your apple, Kari!" so loudly that Townsend put a finger in his ear to clear his eardrum.

Short seconds later, it was obvious that Kari and Brian had a lot of experience neck nuzzling, as their handoff—uh, chinoff—was smooth, flawless and fast. Kari turned to deliver the goods to Townsend, and I checked out the other team's progress. Stewart's team was neck and neck—I've been waiting to use that phrase here!—with the chaperones'. Stewart would be the last to receive the apple for his team.

I looked at him. He stared back at me and to my surprise reached out and cracked his knuckles, then proceeded to rotate his head as if to pop any kinks out of his neck. Or out of where his neck should have been. Uh, oops. I wasn't going to name names, was I?

I looked back at Kari and Townsend struggling to perfect their technique to move the Red Delicious.

"Move that apple!" I chanted, my passion to win turning on me like a rabid squirrel. "Move that apple!"

Townsend finally turned to me, the red apple tucked between his chin and chest like a really enflamed goiter, and I hesitated. Could I really get that close to Townsend without one of us getting maimed? Or both of us going up in red-hot-definitely-not-for-younger-viewers ashes?

"Come on, Tressa!" Kari shouted. "Move that apple!"

I looked over and saw that Stewart had moved closer to Ginny and was in the process of wedging his chins into place to accept the fruit.

"Move that apple!"

"No fair!" I yelled. "Stewart's using chin flab. Is that allowed?"

"Move that apple!"

"What the heck," I said to Townsend, stepping into the circle of his long legs. "If Stewart can do it, so can I."

"Sweet talker," Townsend managed, and I shook my head.

"Don't you dare laugh and drop that apple," I told him, moving in to place the tip of my chin against the side of his neck. I sniffed. Dammit. He did smell good.

I shook the smell of good-looking guy, aftershave and sloppy joe out of my head and focused on the task at hand. I maneuvered my chin under Townsend's and latched on to the apple. Man, even Townsend's breath smelled good. He'd obviously thought to pop a Tic Tac. And he hadn't even eaten Doritos. I could only imagine what my breathed smelled like.

I felt Townsend's hands cup my waist, and I sucked my gut in to my sternum, hoping he wouldn't try the ol' pinch-an-inch trick on me when I couldn't defend myself. His fingers moved ever so seductively against my body, and I felt the heat of his thighs against mine like the electric blankey my gramma left plugged in on the sofa.

I figured I could probably remain in this position for, let's see, only about an hour or two longer. Townsend was one guy a girl didn't mind being this close to. And an apple beneath the chin was no real impediment to my enjoyment of the closeness. I sniffed his scent again.

"Do you have it?" Townsend managed to ask through clenched teeth.

"Have what? Oh, the apple," I mumbled, also afraid to move my jaw muscles for fear the fruit would fall. "Yes. I have it."

"Are you sure?" I could detect amusement in his voice.

"I think so," I said. "I'm almost positive I have it." I slid out just a hair from Townsend to test my hold on the apple. So far, so good.

"I think I've got it," I said carefully. "I think I've got it." I moved a step away from Townsend, and the apple remained in place. "I've got it!" I said, and turned to head for the basket and the winner's circle.

And bumped into a big, hard, black wall.

"Oooommphf!"

"Don't drop the apple!" I heard Kari call out.

I let my eyeballs slowly move up the expanse of black that filled my vision. Past a torso so broad a tailor would need two tape measures to measure the width. Up, up, up to a neck that I couldn't span with three hands.

"Hey! They got an extra team member!" some kid shouted.

"And he looks like The Rock!" another child added. A boy, I thought.

I finally made the trip up to the face of the surprise team member, and my startled gaze came to rest on dark eyes and a chiseled face.

"Hey, Barbie doll," my now-and-again acquaintance Manny Dishman—or is that Manny DeMarco—said. "Got fruit?"

The apple slipped from its place between my chin and breastbone and plummeted downward. I shut my eyes and waited for it to hit the floor.

Instead I heard a crunching sound. You know, kind of like you make when you bite into an apple. I opened my eyes. Just like you make when you bite into an apple.

Manny held the apple—minus one man-sized bite—in one extra large-sized hand. He looked down at me, chewing slowly.

"Barbie trying to tempt Manny with an apple?" he asked. " 'Cause Manny just bit."

"We win! We win!" yelled Stewart's team as he successfully released his apple into the basket with considerable fanfare.

I watched a tiny bit of apple juice spill out of the corner of Manny's nicely shaped mouth and felt this totally crazy desire to reach up and wipe it away.

Blame it on that old black magic.

The party was over. The kids had all gone home. Once Kari got a look at a certain tattoo on Manny's rather massive triceps muscle, she instructed me to "get him out of here before a parent sees him!"

Townsend was giving off unmistakable don't-do-it-Tressa vibes, characterized by the repetitive shake of his head, eyebrows that met in the middle of his face, and tightly crossed arms.

I performed a wide-eyed what-can-I-do? number, grabbed Manny's paw of a hand and dragged him out to the parking lot.

"What in the world are you doing here?" I asked, pulling him over by my car. "The last time I saw you, you were behind bars and giving false names to cops. I gotta tell ya, man, I hardly think a Halloween youth mixer is your scene."

"Manny came to find you."

I frowned. "How did you know where I was?"

"Hannah told me."

Damn. That was the last time I did the responsible thing and left my roomie a note telling her where I'd be.

"Manny needs a favor."

Have I mentioned that Manny is built like a pro wrestler, has skin so dark he makes me look anemic and travels in some, uh, pretty rough circles? He also likes to refer to himself in the third person. I know. At first it weirded me out, too, but now I'm pretty much used to it.

I frowned up at him with a narrow look. "What kind of favor?"

Back when I discovered that stiff in my trunk Manny had been of particular assistance to me—in exchange for bailing him out of the Knox County Jail, I should add. We'd kept in touch from time to time, the latest being at the Iowa State Fair. Manny was one of those fellows you have a hard time saying no to.

"Piece-of-cake favor, Barbie," Manny said. "Take about half an hour. In and out. No big deal."

Did I also mention that Manny is a man of few words?

"You don't want me to, like, rob a convenience store or be a lookout, or anything, do you?" I asked, adding a laugh just to make it seem like I was joking. And I was. Wasn't I?

Manny leaned on the hood of my car, and the car groaned and dropped down a good foot. I wouldn't have been surprised to hear the undercarriage scrape the concrete.

"Barbie. Always good for a laugh," he said, but I noticed he wasn't laughing.

"So what is this favor you need?" I asked. "And remember, I'm a good girl, I am," I added.

Manny smiled. His teeth were very white amid the tan of his face, and the darkness of the night that surrounded us.

"It's like this, Barbie. Manny's great-aunt Marguerite is dying."

My first reaction, naturally, was one of sympathy. After all, I am a very caring individual. Most of the time, anyway.

"Oh, I'm so sorry, Manny," I said. My next reaction was one of surprise at hearing Manny talk about his Great-*ahnt* Marguerite. He sounded like someone who belonged in the Hamptons, not in the heartland. "Are you close to your aaahhnt?" I asked.

Manny nodded. "Aunt Mo raised Manny. Gave Manny a home when his mom died. Manny owes her."

I nodded. "I can imagine. I'm sorry. I'm sure you have to be hurting. But what does this have to do with me and the favor you need?"

Manny moved off the hood of the car. Was it my imagination, or did the Plymouth not have the clearance it did before he'd sat down?

"Manny wants to make Aunt Mo's last days happy

ones," Manny said. "Give her something she's been wantin'."

I found myself really touched by the big man's obvious love and concern for his great-ahntie Mo. I put a hand on Manny's arm.

"That's sweet," I said, patting an arm as hard and solid as our farm pond during a long, cold winter. "What can I do to help?"

Manny gave me a long look. "Marry Manny," he said.

CHAPTER SIXTEEN

I found myself staring at Manny, thinking I'd somehow missed a huge chunk of pertinent material somewhere.

"Marry you?"

Manny nodded. "Aunt Mo wants more than anything for Manny to settle down with a good girl. You just said you were a good girl. You'll do."

As proposals went, "You'll do" left something to be desired.

"You can't be serious, Manny," I said. "I can't marry you. We hardly know each other."

"Doesn't matter," Manny said.

"How can you say it doesn't matter?" I asked. "You're talking about spending a lifetime together! Isn't it kind of useful to know the person who is going to be sharing your bathroom—and probably your toothbrush without you knowing it—for, like, ever?"

"What about an engagement, then? Be Manny's fiancée. Will that work?"

I shook my head. "What?"

"Aunt Mo is in the hospital. She may not have

much time. She wants to see Manny with a good girl. Manny wants to give her what she wants."

"Yeah. So?"

"So Manny needs you to pretend to be his girlfriend."

I put my ear near Manny's mouth. "What was that? I don't think I heard you quite right."

"Manny needs a girlfriend for a couple hours to visit Manny's great-aunt Mo. Barbie'll do. She'll do just fine."

For the first time in my life, I wished I was Ken.

"You want Barbie—uh, me—to pretend to be your girlfriend at your aunt's deathbed?" I asked Manny. "To stand there and lie to a dying woman? To perpetrate a fraud on an unsuspecting old lady?"

"Good. Barbie's a quick study," Manny said. "So, what time should Manny pick you up tomorrow?"

I looked at him. "Huh?"

"What say two o'clock?" Manny suggested. "Or would you rather meet Manny at the hospital?"

I'd rather be having a pelvic exam.

"I'm not sure—"

Manny began to ring, and he pulled out his cell phone. He put a finger out to me. "Yo, Manny here. Yeah. Yeah. Hell no. Yeah. Right. Okay. See ya."

I shook my head. Monosyllabic didn't begin to touch it. Manny put a huge paw on my head, mussing my hair.

"Manny's gotta split," he said. "Manny'll see Barbie at the hospital gift shop at two."

I blinked. "Gift shop? Why the gift shop?" I found myself saying, instead of something along the lines of, "Hell no, Tressa won't go!"

"Can't visit Aunt Mo without flowers and a gift," Manny explained.

I looked at him. "What would a dying woman want with flowers and gifts?" I thought to ask.

"Aunt Mo don't know how bad she is. Walk in there empty-handed, and she'll know she's a goner for sure," Manny said. I winced. Manny patted my head again. "I'm outta here, Barbie."

I watched Manny's long strides take him to his crotch-rocket. Uh, before those who aren't Harley-literate think I'm being perverted here, that's slang for "motorcycle."

From a stint as the Wicked Witch of the West to a newshound on the scent of a high-powered story to a hospital room performance as Manny's Dream-Date Barbie. I really had to wonder what was next. *Hollywood Squares*?

I heard voices near the front of the community center and recognized one of them as belonging to Rick Townsend, and I yanked open the passenger's side of my Plymouth and slid across the seat, diving behind the wheel. The last thing I needed after Manny dropped his little betrothal bombshell on me was to face Ranger Rick Townsend.

The Plymouth sputtered to life, and I planted a kiss on the steering wheel. I could only imagine Townsend's expression in my rearview mirror as I peeled out. Remember? My rearview mirror is among the collection of items that move about the floor of my car, so I really did have to imagine his expression.

I headed out of town, looking forward to crawling into bed with a cup of hot cocoa (with marshmallow cream) and spending the evening with Elizabeth Courtney Howard.

I'd finally decided on a plan of action, which felt an awful lot like inaction to me. I'd decided to take the semidirect approach, and place a call to Courtney Howard the next morning to see if I could persuade Vanessa McCormick to give me one last shot at convincing her boss to give me at least a short interview over the phone. It wasn't what I'd hoped for, but time was running out, and I couldn't think of a single new idea to pull out of Tressa's bag of tricks.

I pulled into my driveway, and an itty-bitty, insignificant, hardly-bad-at-all swear word escaped my lips when I spied Shelby Lynne's brother's Jeep in the driveway, accompanied by Joe Townsend's Buick. Oh, terrific. Just what I needed. Joltin' Joe Townsend and Hellion Hannah and a houseful of erotic artwork.

Banished temporarily to the out-of-doors, Butch and Sundance almost barreled me over welcoming me home. With the affection these guys showed me, who needed a boyfriend?

Which got me to thinking again about Manny and poor dying Aunt Mo. I sat on the porch for a few minutes, playing with the hounds and just enjoying the peace and quiet of the night, knowing that when I opened the door to my home, it would be like stepping into a scene from *One Flew Over the Cuckoo's Nest*.

I gave my critters a final hug and stood for a moment, collecting my courage, then finally decided maybe I'd left it out back, so I headed around to the back door. If luck was with me, I could sneak in and make my way to my room without anyone's being the wiser. It sounded like a plan to me.

I moved around to the back, pulled my key out from underneath the rock that isn't really a rock and everyone knows it, and unlocked the door as quietly as I could. I opened the door just wide enough for me to slip through, closed it quietly behind me and prepared to tiptoe down the hall to take blessed refuge in my room. I'd gone about three steps when I noticed that the lights were out. Strange, since Gram obviously had company. I took another step down the hall, picking up a weird scent—a combination of cloying incense and other, as yet unidentifiable fragrances. I was about to take another step when an unfamiliar voice stopped me in my tippy-toed tracks.

"We wish to make contact with the spirit of Loralie Holloway. Loralie, please make your presence known."

I stood there for a moment. What in the world?

"Loralie, we come to help you find rest."

I considered making a right turn into my bedroom and crawling under the bed, thinking that if I was in bed, I could discount everything around me as merely part of a bad dream. But Tressa, Warrior Princess, that I am, I ventured forth into fray.

I came to the end of the hallway and had to lean on the wall for support. My living room was lit by more candles than we could safely put on my gramma's birthday cake. A card table had been set up in the middle of my living room, and four people sat hunched over it. Somehow I didn't think there was a high-stakes poker game going on, or a jigsaw puzzle marathon. The now-familiar smell of incense, mingled with the combined perfumes of what had to be twenty-five candles of different scents, made me a wee bit high.

"We wish to make contact with the spirit of Loralie Holloway. Loralie, please make your presence known to us."

I could only stand and stare, feeling like I'd taken a wrong turn in the way-wrong wardrobe and ended up in a twilight-years *Twilight Zone*. I took a couple more steps—close enough to finally see the Ouija board in the middle of the table and sixteen fingertips on the plastic indicator dial that receives messages from the beyond. Eight fingertips were from two seniors with a penchant for trouble, four were from a homecoming queen candidate with all the charm of Frankenstein in taffeta, and the remaining four? I had no clue who those fingertips belonged to, but he appeared to be the one attempting to establish the long-distance contact with someone way out of my calling area. I cringed to think of the roaming charges.

"Loralie, we come to help you find rest."

I looked at the table occupant who was commanding the spirit of Loralie to come on down. I'd never seen this Kreskin before in my life.

I decided I'd better to put an end to the fun before something bad happened and the call for Loralie really did go through. I crept to Gram's room, grabbed her mini–air horn and moved back to the end of the hallway, then gave a short toot.

Screams erupted from around the table, and the guy who'd been calling for Loralie fell out of his chair and crumpled to the floor.

"Uh, excuse me, but, like, what's going on?" I asked the discombobulated group.

"Tressa Jayne! You scared the wits out of us," my grandma scolded. Like between the four of them they had any wits to begin with. "Don't ever sneak up on someone like that again! And the idea of using that horn! Why, you scared poor Tom out of his chair!"

I blinked. "Tom? Tom who?"

"Tom Murphy, dear. He's a friend of Shelby Lynne."

"Oh. Tom Thumb."

"Nice." Tom Murphy got to his feet. At least I think he was standing. It was kind of hard to tell.

I put out a hand and gestured at the table. "Would someone like to explain all this?" I asked.

"Not me," Joe said. "I'm a guest."

"Shelby Lynne?"

"I plead the Fifth."

I looked at my grandma. "Joe brought a chocolate cake," was all she offered.

"With chocolate frosting?" I said, then shook my head. Focus, Tressa, focus.

"What about you?" I spoke to the conjurer. "What were you trying to do?"

Tom Murphy stuck his hands in his pockets and weaved back and forth on his wee little feet.

"We were just having some harmless fun," he stammered. "Getting in the holiday mood. You know. Just joking around. Right, Shelby?"

Shelby Lynne was suddenly the poster child for See No Evil. First time for everything.

"Harmless? You've got enough candles lit here to turn the ceiling black, and you're trying to raise the dead. Have I missed anything else?" I asked.

"Besides the cat hurling on the carpet, I can't think of a thing," Joe said. "How about you, Hannah?"

Gram gave him a dark look. "You were the one who fed her the cheese puffs."

"What's the deal with you people? Why on earth are you trying to contact Loralie Holloway?" I asked the four paranormalists—or, probably, that should be abnormalists.

"Joe here told us about the crying and the rose petals at Holloway Hall the other night," Gram said.

"And I told you about the time your Paw-Paw Will and I—"

I put out a hand. I didn't think I needed to relive that little trek down memory lane.

"And so? You thought you'd set up a psychic hotline in the living room and reach out and touch some dead people?"

"Not people," Joe pointed out. "Just Loralie."

I looked at Joe and saw for the first time how he was dressed. No neon sweat suit this evening: Rick's grandpa had on a brown turtleneck, khaki pants and the same tweed jacket he'd worn the night he'd gone bearing gifts for Elizabeth Courtney Howard.

"What else did Joe tell you about that night?" I asked, wondering if he'd spilled the beans about our author-in-residence to my grandma.

"Said he was helping you on that story you told me about the other day," Gram said. "Sounds to me as if Loralie is still up to her old tricks," she added. "That's why we were trying to contact her."

I nodded. "I see. So, just for curiosity's sake, what were the four of you planning to do if you did make contact with Loralie—or with something else out there in the great beyond?" I asked. "For curiosity's sake."

All four of the séance participants looked at one another.

My grandma finally spoke up.

"As for me, I'd be having a Dr. Phil moment with Loralie, that's for sure," she said.

Gram and I are both devoted fans of Dr. Phil. I love the way he talks. Like, "That dog ain't gonna hunt no more." You know, he's a good ol' boy who shoots straight and deals from the top of the deck.

"I'd be telling her that she needed to get a life and stop with the boo-hooing and rose-petal-tossin' and move on down the road," Gram said. "That's what I'd tell her."

"Isn't that like telling a ghost to drop dead? And aren't they already dead?" Joe asked.

I rubbed my temple, thinking it was extremely fortunate for all concerned that no contact had been made that night, or I might have come home and found four cadavers sitting around the card table.

"Uh, I think I've heard enough," I said. "This first and only séance is now concluded."

I was going to switch on the lights and start blowing out candles when the doorbell rang. Everyone in the room froze, and we all looked at one another.

"Who could that be?" Tom Thumb—Murphy—asked, his eyes as big as Pringles potato chips.

"Loralie!" Gram said.

I have to admit to feeling a little apprehensive, until I remembered that ghosts generally didn't ring the front doorbell. They liked to walk through walls and float around the ceiling and leave behind snotty ectoplasm or wet footprints.

I hurried for the front door, hoping word hadn't gotten out that Hellion Hannah's Haven for Those Halted in the Hereafter was open for business. Instead I opened the door to find Ranger Rick standing on my front porch. This wasn't happening.

"Oh, uh, hello, Townsend. We meet again," I said, trying to close the door before he could look beyond me into the living room and see that it had been turned into something from *Fright Night*. Townsend's big, brown hand on the door prevented me from accomplishing that, so I tried to block his view with my body. (But, let's not get nasty here. I'm not *that* broad in the beam.)

"What can I do you for?" I asked, moving back and forth whenever Townsend made a move to look around me.

Townsend frowned. "Are you all right? You're dancing like you've got ants in your pants."

I shook my head. "I just need to use the restroom, that's all," I told him. "Was there something in particular you needed?"

Townsend nodded. "A couple of somethings," he said. "First, a word with my grandfather, who if I'm not mistaken is probably trying to sneak down your hallway and out the back door as we speak. And second, a word with you about your friend Manny."

I gave up and opened the door with a flourish. "Enter if you dare," I told him in a scary-movie voice, motioned him into the living room and closed the door behind him.

It was fortunate that I wasn't right behind Townsend; he stopped so suddenly, I'd have been crawling up his back. Not too awfully unpleasant an activity, you understand. For me, that is. For Townsend not to object, I'd probably have to drop about ten pounds.

He looked around the room at the candles, spotted the card table and séance accoutrements, took in the kooky collection of participants and stood there for a second. I sighed, completely simpatico. I knew just how he felt. Trying to process a scene like this was harder than *CSI* trying to process a crime scene in the desert after a sandstorm.

"What the hell is going on here?" Townsend finally said.

"A low-budget remake of *Rocky Horror Picture*

Show?" I suggested. Rick gave me a dark look and walked over to the card table. He touched the Ouija board with a finger.

"Pops? Don't tell me you've been participating in a séance," he said.

"Okay," Joe agreed.

"Okay, what?"

"Okay, I won't tell you I've been participating in a séance," Joe said.

I could imagine just how Rick was feeling right about now. I almost felt sorry for the guy. Until I remembered that he could drop his granddad off at home and drive away, and I was stuck with an in-house matriarch with an air horn and gross statues.

"I've already read them the riot act, Ranger Townsend," I said, "and we were just getting ready to close down the séance shop permanently. Right, folks?"

Mumbled agreement was forthcoming.

"Who are they?" Rick pointed to Shelby Lynne and Tom Murphy. Standing side by side, they looked like the odd couple they were.

I made hurried introductions. "Shelby Lynne and Tom are homecoming queen and king candidates," I told Townsend, who raised an eyebrow.

Shelby Lynne must have caught that gesture and— not knowing that it was a chronic repetitive motion on Townsend's part—she took it the wrong way.

"Is there something wrong?" she asked Rick. "What? You don't think we're cut out to be homecoming royalty? What?"

Townsend looked at me. I looked away. He was on his own.

"Uh, I've really got no opinion on the subject at

237

all," Townsend said. "I'm sure you'd both make great, uh, royalty."

Shelby Lynne sniffed. "Right. Right," she said.

"If you all wouldn't mind," I said, "I'd appreciate it if we could wrap things up here so that I can, like, forget tonight ever happened." I started blowing out candles, thinking that I'd run out of air before I finished.

Shelby Lynne and Tom moved to help me, leaving Gram and Joe to pick up the Ouija board and box it up. I figured they thought the older pair might not have the wind for candle duty. Ha. They didn't know Hannah and Joe like I knew Hannah and Joe.

In ten minutes' time, all evidence that a group of wannabe spiritualists had met there to commune with the dead had been removed, and I was herding all non-residents out the door and my dogs back in.

"Where do we stand on the interview?" Shelby Lynne asked as she was heading out with Tom.

I gave her a direct look. "I wish I knew, Shelby Lynne," I told her honestly. "I wish I knew. But I'm still working on it."

She nodded. "I'll call you tomorrow," she said.

"Do that," I found myself saying.

Gram and Joe said their good-byes, and I was just glad said farewells didn't include any overt displays of affection. I didn't think I could handle that this evening.

When Joe trotted by with a cake carrier, I stopped him.

"Just a minute. You're taking the chocolate cake?" I asked. "Isn't it, like, customary for one to leave the goodies they brought at the host's house?"

"Not when the host kicks everyone out," Joe said.

The only thing that had gotten me through the cleanup and Rick Townsend's sullenness throughout was the prospect of cutting a generous slice of chocolate cake and pouring a large glass of cold milk and heading off to my room. Now the cake was walking out the door with a grumpy old goat.

"I bet Abigail Winegardner baked that cake," I told Joe in a voice loud enough to be heard down by the barn.

Joe stopped and looked around to see if my gramma had picked up on the reference to the infamous Mrs. Winegardner.

"Keep it down, girlie!" Joe snapped. "And for your information, I bought this cake at Town Square Bakery," he told me.

"Oh yeah? Well, then why is it in a cake carrier rather than a cake box?" I asked.

Joe dumped the cake into my hands. "Okay, okay. Here's the cake. Just don't point out the box discrepancy to your grandma," he requested.

I clutched the cake container. "The next time you have your cholesterol checked, you'll thank me for this, Joe," I told him.

"Fat chance, girlie," he replied. "I've probably got better cholesterol than you!" He headed down the porch steps and hoofed it to his Buick before firing it up and driving away.

"Better get a move on," I told Rick when he appeared on the porch beside me. "Your granddad has a head start on you, and he looked like he was gonna put the pedal to the metal."

Townsend shrugged and, to my surprise, took a seat on the bench on my front porch, looking a lot like he planned to stay for a while.

"He can find his way home," he said.

I looked down at the cake I was hankerin' for. Plus, I wanted to get into the surreal subject of Manny and his "great-ahnt" Mo like I wanted to run for the school board.

"Are you sure?" I asked.

Townsend motioned to the empty space beside him on the bench. "Come sit for a minute, T," Rick said.

I looked at the cake again and then at Townsend looking totally hot now that he had a ten-o'clock-shadow whisker thing going. I wasn't sure which was more tempting at the moment, the chocolate cake or the gorgeous ranger-type relaxing on my front porch.

"It's pretty late," I said. "And I need to check on Gram."

"Please," Townsend said, patting the seat next to him. I couldn't remember Townsend ever using the word with me. Unless it was like, *Puh-leaze, Tressa!*

I moved to the bench and sat down, feeling really, really nervous. We sat silently for a few minutes.

"This is nice," I said, trying to figure out what the heck was going on.

I heard Townsend release a long gust of air, and he rotated in his seat and stuck a knee on the bench between us, putting his arm across the back of the bench. Oh, buddy, here it came.

"Manny has a personal problem. Well, not exactly a personal problem. More like a family problem. A family member who has a problem. And he needs a teensy favor. It'll take an hour, tops. I'll meet him there. In and out. No big deal. And no risk."

I rattled off the information before Townsend could even open his mouth. Thank goodness I wasn't entrusted with any national security secrets. Townsend looked at me like I did people who wear socks with sandals.

"Nothing is no-risk when it comes to Manny Dishman," Townsend said.

"Does that go for Manny DeMarco, too?" I asked.

"What?" Townsend said, and I shook my head.

"Never mind. Besides, Manny just wants me to visit a sick relative of his at the hospital, is all," I said, leaving out the fiancé role he wanted me to play.

"Why does he want you to go with him? Do you know this person?" Townsend asked.

"It's Manny's great-ahnt," I said, trying the pronunciation myself. From the look on Townsend's face, it didn't come across as being me. "She's very ill, and he needs someone to go with him when he visits her."

"And he doesn't have family to go with? How well do you know this guy, anyway?"

Well enough for him to ask me to marry him.

"I don't know him all that well," I admitted, "but he's been very helpful to me in the past. I'm not sure about his family situation."

"What do you know about him—other than the fact that you've bailed him out once and he was jailed at least one other time? Oh, and that he uses an alias." Gee, Townsend was good.

I searched for a plausible excuse for me to accompany Manny to the hospital the next day. One that didn't include any references to phony engagements, lying to dying old women and last wishes.

"Uh, Manny has a thing about hospitals," I said, hitting on the only reason I could come up with. "He's scared to death of them. Hasn't been in one since his mother died when he was ten. Since that day, he hasn't been able to set foot in a hospital."

241

Okay, so I bent the truth a bit. Tell me your weight on your driver's license is accurate. Or that's your natural hair color. We all lie. And this lie could be true as far as I knew, so maybe it wasn't a lie at all. See how I think?

"You're telling me a guy big enough to perform the job of a hydraulic jack with his back has to have you hold his hand and lead him into a hospital? You've got to be joking." Townsend reached out and opened the top of the cake carrier. He stuck a finger in, snared some frosting and slowly brought it to his mouth. He consumed the frosting as I watched. I felt my heart pick up the pace like it does when I spot a clearance sign at the Fashion Bug at the mall.

"Uh, looks can be deceiving. Manny actually is more sensitive than you'd think," I said, watching as Townsend's finger descended on the cake again.

"I wouldn't have pegged Manny the Mobster as being the 'sensitive' type," Rick responded. "Of course, maybe that has something to do with his calling me Rick the Dick whenever we happen to cross paths," he added.

Townsend brought out another scoop of frosting. His finger stopped in front of my face. I looked crosseyed down my nose at it.

"Be my guest," Townsend invited. "It's fingerlickin' good!"

The mother of all understatements.

"It'll melt in your mouth, T," Townsend promised. Despite the chill of the autumn night, I was beginning to think the cake I was holding on my lap was in danger of baking a second time.

"What are you up to, Ranger Rick?" I asked.

Considering Townsend's displeasure with me at the

end of the summer and my own disapproval with him over his little Canadian expedition that had caused big-time problems between my brother, Craig, and Craig's wife, Kimmie, we'd kept a safe distance. We'd shared kisses and some pretty intense clinches in the not-so-recent past, but Townsend and I were such polar opposites (except for the fact that we were both total hotties, of course—hee-hee) that I seriously questioned whether we could collaborate on anything without inflicting serious hurt on each other. I'm talking the emotional kind here, folks. Well, for the most part.

All I knew was that before I invited any buckaroos to put their boots under my bed, I was gonna make pretty darn sure they didn't use them to tromp all over my heart afterward. In other words, they had to have staying power. No. Not that kind! Staying as in over the long haul. From this day forward. "Till death parts us" and all that sappy sentiment that means so much to us ladies.

Townsend and I had locked horns for so many years that a shift to making nice was like switching from a western saddle to an English one. You know—a little awkward at first. A bit tricky. Maybe even risky.

"What are you up to?" I asked again.

"Would you believe a peace offering?" he asked.

I felt my eyebrows rise. "Peace offering? Are we at war?"

He smiled. "It does seem as if we're always at odds," he said. "Always have been. And that was understandable when you were a rotten little kid who'd kick me under your family's dinner table or steal my car keys when I visited. You were just plain ornery as hell."

I winced. I still kicked him under the table on occasion. So what did that make me now?

"What is confusing to me is that we make some progress—or at least I think we do—and then something happens and we end up back at square one. I don't want to be your enemy anymore, Tressa," he said with an intent look, and brought the chocolate-covered finger to his mouth. I found myself reaching out and stopping him.

"Even though it's no pic-a-nic basket, I accept your peace offering, Mr. Ranger, sir," I said. I took hold of his hand and pulled it over to my mouth, taking his finger and gently sticking it in my mouth and sucking off the frosting. I heard his intake of breath as I gave his finger a last lick and released his hand.

"And you were right, Townsend," I said. "That's finger-lickin' good!"

He stood and pulled me to my feet. I kept my hands around the cake between us.

"I guess I'd better get going," he said. "You're right. I'll have to drop by and do a bed check on Gramps."

I nodded. I'd be performing one on my gramma, too.

"I'm not sure exactly what went on here this evening," Rick said, "but—" He stopped himself. "Nope," he said, shaking his head. "I'm not going to do it. I'm not going to say it. Fact is, I don't want to know what happened here tonight. Just, please, Tressa, don't let it happen again."

"Like I want this place to be known as Spook Central," I said. " 'Night, Townsend."

"I thought we'd gotten beyond Townsend some time ago," he said.

"Old habits die hard," I told him, not meaning just my manner of address. "But I'm trying. I'm really trying. Rick."

He tilted my chin up with one hand, and I looked

into his eyes. Rick has the nicest eyes. Rich brown orbs with flecks of amber.

"Good night, Tressa." He bent toward me, and his lips touched mine briefly. Too briefly.

"Good night," I said again, and reached up to give him another short good-bye peck.

"Good night," he said, and he kissed me again, this time longer. And hotter.

"Ditto," I said and found my lips on his again. This kiss was hot enough to curl my toes.

"Ditto," Rick said against my mouth as we continued to kiss.

I finally broke off the kiss when I realized this was moving faster than I was prepared to deal with. And me an engaged woman and all.

Besides, there was the cake to consider. It was wedged between us like a cocoa-flavored chastity belt. There was also the matter of one very nosy roommate who no doubt had her ear to the door and her eye to the peephole at that very moment.

"I'd really like to invite you in, Townsend," I said with a long sigh, "but, well, I've got a roommate now, so no can do." I patted his cheek and gave him a saucy grin. "Toodles." I blew him a kiss as I entered the house. "Good night!" I giggled as I shut the door.

Woo-hoo. I was one witchy woman.

Ten minutes later, after making sure Gram was in for the night, I remembered I'd totally forgotten to fill the dogs' dishes. Rick Townsend could turn my brain soft as the tapioca pudding my gramma loves to eat. I was about to step outside, when the phone rang. I picked it up.

"Hello?"

I waited for Shelby Lynne to vent some more over

the lost interview, or for Joe to ask for my grandma, or for my mother to remind me that my sister, Taylor, was coming home from college this coming weekend. Instead I heard crying. Soft, whimpering moans of sorrow and loss. (Waxing poetic there, wasn't I?)

"Hello?" I said again. "Who is this? Can I help you? Are you hurt? Do you need assistance?"

The crying went on for a minute or so longer. Then I got a dial tone. I frowned at the phone, wishing I hadn't been too cheap to pay for caller ID. Someone might be hurt out there.

Unsettled by the call, I turned on the porch light and stepped out to finish taking care of the critters' needs. Butch and Sundance followed me out, jumping and barking at the air.

I smelled the roses before I saw the red petals littered in a careless array across the front porch. I looked around the front yard. A sudden breeze scattered the dark petals around my feet. The dogs continued to bark, and beyond the house, somewhere in the darkness, an owl picked that exact moment to let out a long, drawn-out hoot.

I whistled at the dogs, pushed them into the house, and shut and locked the door behind us. Tressa, Warrior Princess, was in full retreat.

I know what you're thinking: Like a locked door is gonna stop a spook, Blondie!

Thanks for sharing.

CHAPTER SEVENTEEN

The next morning found me sharing my bed with two hairy fellows and their slapping tails. I'd locked myself in my room for the remainder of the night, keeping my pooches with me, along with a baseball bat, the Bible and, of course, the chocolate cake. I'd spent much of the night trying to convince myself that I'd imagined it all, and the rest of the night trying to explain it all away. I also spent considerable time blaming the Bring 'Em Back bunch who'd passed the evening trying to bridge the great divide for screwing with the supernatural and sticking me with the tab.

I checked the clock, saw that it was past six and forced myself to get up. The dogs were still sleeping, so I left them where they were and hit the bathroom (mine is off my bedroom) and unlocked the door to my room. The aroma of fresh coffee didn't greet me this morning, so I figured my grandma's extracurricular activities of the night before had worn her out.

I headed for the kitchen, surprised to see Gram at the table, cup in hand.

"I don't smell coffee," I said, motioning at her cup.

"That's because this is tea," Gram replied. "French vanilla tea, to be exact. Want to try a cup? It's not bad."

"Does it have caffeine?" I asked.

"I'm sure it does," Gram said.

I grabbed the teakettle and a cup. "Then count me in," I said, filling the cup with hot water and joining her at the table. She handed me a tea bag.

"You still sore about last night?" Gram asked.

I looked up from dunking my bag. "You know I can never stay ticked with you, Gram," I said. "But don't ever do that again. You never know what could happen. Whose idea was it, anyway?" I asked, curious.

"It was one of them general consensuses," Gram said. "The youngsters wouldn't go for strip poker, so we improvised."

I looked at her. I hoped she was kidding.

"Well, just don't improvise like that again. You could have burned the house down with all those candles," I added. "It was glowing so much, I thought we had a radiation situation."

"So, what do you have planned for today?" Gram asked. "Still trying to beat that dog of a story to death?"

"If you mean the Holloway story, then yes," I said. "I plan to work on it this morning."

I dunked my tea bag a half dozen times and decided, like it or not, that there was only one thing left for me to do: grovel. It stuck in my craw like Gram's Thanksgiving turkey three years ago, but I'd do it.

"If you want to snap some pictures of the place, you should do it this morning," Gram said. "There'll be nobody around."

Gram had my attention.

"What do you mean?"

"Jack Rivas says they've struck a deal with the heir to the estate, and they sign the papers this morning. They've got a big meeting at the attorney's office at ten."

"They? Do you know who 'they' are exactly?" I was thinking I could sit down the road from the Holloway place and follow the Howard entourage right through the town square. When Howard got out of the vehicle, I'd hit my knees and beg for an interview. Okay, so I'd checked my pride at the door on this one; I wanted the story bad.

"Just a minute."

Gram got up and went into the other room. I sat there and continued to dunk my bag.

"Let's see. Jack said something about someone named Vanessa who has something called a 'power of attorney'—I think that's a legal term, dear—and this Vanessa would be 'negotiating the contract on behalf of the heir.' Does that make sense to you, Tressa?" Gram asked. "'Cause it's all Greek to me."

I dropped my tea bag in my cup. If Vanessa McCormick was signing legal documents on Elizabeth Courtney Howard's behalf that morning, then that meant Elizabeth Courtney Howard would be without her keeper during that time. Of course, there was still the boy toy to consider, but it was possible he might have more influence with Howard than her assistant had, and could persuade Howard to talk with me. It was worth a shot.

"Did you take notes, Gram?" I asked, noticing the slip of paper she held in her hand.

"I wanted to make sure I got everything right. I knew you were interested in the Holloway real estate deal Jack Rivas still has his nose in that business more than that ol' bitch Abigail Winegardner has in Joe's. I knew Joe was helping you out on the story, so I figger maybe Hannah can be of some help, too. Did I do good?" she asked. "Does the information help at all?"

The sting of tears crept up on me without warning. My teacup was suddenly blurry.

"You mean you went out with Romeo Rivas just to help me out with my story?" I asked, feeling all choked up at the thought. "Oh, Gram. That's so, so touching. So giving. So—not like you," I said.

"Hell no, I didn't go just because of your story," Gram said. "The man can dance like a dream, and he spends a fortune on his dates. But I tell myself, while I'm milking this, I might as well see what I can find out for Tressa and her story. And it doesn't hurt to keep Joe on his toes. Although, I have to say, Joe Townsend can't match Jack Rivas's fancy footwork," she said. "I saw how he dropped you on your hind end the other night. But don't tell Joe. We wouldn't want to hurt his feelings."

"It'll be our little secret," I told her, and smiled.

Good ol' Hellion Hannah. What a pistol.

I took a fast shower, pulled my mane into a tight ponytail and dressed quickly in brown trousers, a white open-collared shirt, and a short brown tailored jacket. I slipped into a pair of tan low-top Converse shoes—I felt like Ellen Degeneres, but I went for comfort over fashion—and grabbed my backpack and was out the door by seven.

My first call was to Shelby Lynne.

"What a coincidence. I was just about to call you," she said.

"Must be some of the psychic phenomena you summoned forth last night," I told her.

"You'll never let me live that down, will you?" Shelby Lynne asked. "I wouldn't be surprised if you did a story on it. Especially since you've choked on the Howard one."

Oooh. There was that 'tude again. I decided to let it go. I'd have Shelby Lynne eating crow before the day was out.

"I called to see if you'd like to accompany me to the Holloway house," I told her, and filled her in on Gram's snoop surprise of that morning. "But I don't suppose you can miss school, so I'll just let you know how it all turns out."

Shelby's voice boomed into my ear, and I held the phone a foot away to avoid hearing loss.

"Are you sure? Oh. You'll pretend to be sick? Do you have fake barf?" I asked when Shelby Lynne had calmed down and explained how she would get out of classes that day. "You'll need fake barf. Oatmeal works good. Mix a little with chicken broth, and it looks just like stomach juices." Okay, so I'd used the fake puke a time or two. This time it was for a noble cause.

Shelby Lynne told me to pick her down the street from her house at eight. When I rolled up to the corner to meet her, I felt like a doper making a buy.

I rolled my window down. "Hey, little girl, want some candy?" I teased.

Shelby Lynne shook her head and got in the car. "You are something else, do you know that?" she said.

"I know," I replied with a shrug. "You look quite chipper for being under the weather. Did you have to use the fake puke?"

Shelby Lynne shook her head. "I miss school so rarely that when I do say I'm too sick to go to school, my mom believes me."

Ah, for that kind of credibility. After my folks caught on to my homemade hurl recipe, they threatened me with a rectal temperature check if I faked being sick again. That sure cured me of hookyitis.

"So Elizabeth Courtney Howard will be all alone in the house?" Shelby Lynne asked.

I shrugged. "At least her keeper will be otherwise occupied, so we have another crack at getting in the front door," I said.

Actually, I wasn't all that gung ho about going back to Holloway Hall. Especially after my little visitor the night before had scattered rose petals on my porch like a frustrated flower girl. But the stubborn side of me—another legacy from my grandmother's side of the family—wouldn't let me give up without a fight. For Shelby Lynne's sake, as well as my own.

We set up shop in a rarely used country lane just down from the Holloway house. I backed the Plymouth as far into the foliage as I could, to avoid being detected. For once I was glad that my car was dirty, as it helped the white color blend in.

I settled back to wait for traffic to drive by from the Holloway house. For once, I'd forgotten to pack provisions. In lieu of food, I searched for an innocuous topic to occupy my mouth.

"So, Shelby Lynne, tomorrow's the big day. Do you have your fancy duds all ready to go?"

Shelby Lynne looked over at me—probably to see if I was serious or being jerky.

"I have a pantsuit to wear," she said, and I looked back at her.

"You're joking, right?" I said.

"Not at all," Shelby replied. "It's a very nice pantsuit. Very formal."

"You're not wearing a dress?"

Shelby raised her eyebrows. "Now you're joking, right? With legs shaped like Rolo rolls? Yeah, right."

I smiled. It seemed Shelby had picked up my habit of bringing food into the conversations.

"You could always wear a long dress," I told her, and she bestowed on me a "get real, girlfriend" look.

"Nobody wears long dresses anymore," she informed me. "They all wear those cute little black dresses with spaghetti straps, or even go stapless. Putting a dress like that on me would be like trying to stretch a too-small tarp over a wide load with not enough rubber tie-downs."

I grinned. Shelby Lynne might write a book, at that. She certainly had a way with words.

"What about your makeup? Who's doing your makeup?"

"Makeup? I never wear makeup," Shelby said. "I'll probably just slap on some of my mom's liquid makeup, brush on some blush and call it good."

I shook my head. "You poor thing. You poor, poor thing. You can't show up as a homecoming candidate looking like death warmed over. Even this close to Halloween. Good thing I have some expertise in this area," I said. "And my gramma sold cosmetics for that company with the pink cars years ago, so she's really in the know about what colors to use. Between the two of us, you'll look like you were airbrushed for the cover of *Vogue*."

Okay, so I exaggerated a bit. Still, Shelby Lynne had a flawless complexion, tiny orange freckles notwithstanding. I was sure Gram would have a ball with Shelby Lynne's makeover. And I always enjoy taking a crack at someone else's mug for a change.

"As soon as we're done here, I'll call Gram and tell her to get out her supplies, and we'll do a practice run later today," I told Shelby Lynne. "And just a reminder. Beauty is pain. So buck up."

Shelby Lynne's expression was reminiscent of mine the first time I let Gram have a go at my face. The power of that moment had corrupted her, and she'd used a heavy hand with her makeup supplies. I'd looked like I was ready for a stint on a dark street corner when she was done.

"So, that was Tom Murphy?" I said to get Shelby's mind off the makeover. "He seems . . . nice. Are you two an item?"

"An item? *Item?*" Shelby Lynne did an eye roll. She had been hanging with me too much. "What decade are you living in? And you saw us together. You think there's a future there? The guy barely reaches my boobs. But he's a real nice guy, and we are friends. Outcasts thrown together by circumstance, as it were."

"Sounds like the premise for a book or movie," I said.

"What about you?" Shelby asked. "What's the story with you and Rick Townsend? Did you know all the girls in high school have the hots for him?"

Girls in the middle school and women in the local nursing home had the hots for Rick Townsend. Maybe that's why I had such a difficult time believing his interest in me was something more than the irresistible lure of a seemingly impossible challenge. Was I crazy for wanting to be something more than a summit conquered? A hard-won notch on someone's bedpost?

"Officer Townsend and I have a complicated past," I told Shelby Lynne. "Our cat-and-dog fights make Punch and Judy fisticuffs look like *Sesame Street*.

Changing the patterns of a lifetime can be a little tricky."

"But he's so . . . so . . . so . . . yummalicious."

I looked at Shelby Lynne. "Yummalicious" was not a word I had ever expected to hear come out of her mouth. Unless she was talking food again.

"That's what makes it so scary. One bite of that prime choice hunk, and can you imagine how hard it would be to have to go back to beanie-weenies?" I asked her. "See my dilemma?"

Shelby Lynne sighed. "That sucks," she said.

I nodded.

We sat in companionable silence until we heard the sound of a car. We both sat up in our seats. I grabbed my binoculars—Gram's binoculars.

"Don't make any moves that might draw anyone's attention," I cautioned Shelby as we caught sight of the dark blue van that had been parked at the Holloway house since the occupants' arrival. I put the binoculars to my eyes to check out the vehicle.

"Oh my gosh! It's Vanessa! And the boy toy is driving! Do you know what that means?" I turned to Shelby Lynne.

"Boy toy?"

"Forget it. It means Elizabeth Courtney Howard is home alone!" I said. "Like, how lucky can we get!"

We waited for a few minutes to make sure the van didn't come back, and then I made a left onto Dead End Lane. I pulled into the driveway and drove right up to the house. No more slinking or skulking about for this ace cub reporter.

I grabbed my backpack, pulled out my camera and snapped several pictures before Shelby and I proceeded to the front door. I was just about ready to lift the knocker and bring it down when I heard the crunch of gravel beneath rubber. Shelby and I turned to see a maroon SUV pull into the driveway and park.

"What the hell is he doing here?" That came from Shelby Lynne.

"You didn't maybe invite him?" I asked her. "You know, hedging your bets. A win-win for Shelby Lynne?"

Shelby straightened her spine, lengthening her advantage over me by another inch. "Do you really believe I would stoop that low?" she asked. I looked up at her. She had a point.

"Well, what's he doing here, then?"

A second later Drew Van Vleet joined us on the front doorstep, and I had the opportunity to repeat my question. "What are you doing here?" I asked.

"Probably the same thing you've been fumbling around trying to do for the past couple days," he said. "Get an interview with Elizabeth Courtney Howard. The difference between us, however, is that I plan to snag said interview. No matter what it takes." He pulled a fancy camera, complete with a zoom lens out of his expensive shoulder bag.

"Is that right? So how did you find out about Howard?" I asked.

He smiled. "Grease enough palms, and you'd be surprised at what you can learn," he said. "Besides, I knew you were working something you thought was big, so I decided that it would be a good idea to keep an eye on you."

"You followed me? That's low," I said. "What's the matter? You can't scare up your own stories? What kind of newsman are you, anyway?"

Van Vleet took a shot of the house and looked at the

result before he saved it. "The kind who will win journalistic awards and kudos when you're not even a footnote in that rag you call a newspaper."

"Oooh. Who wrote that line for you? A spinmeister for one of the major political parties?"

Van Vleet ignored me, opened his bag and stuck his camera back inside. I was just getting ready to knock on the door when I picked up the sound of weeping.

"Is that crying?" Shelby Lynne asked.

I tensed. "Yes," I said. "It is."

"Is it coming from inside the house?"

It took a few seconds for Shelby and me to realize the crying came from none other than Drew Van Vleet's leather shoulder bag. We both stared at him. He fumbled about in his bag for a second, and the crying suddenly stopped.

"That was you?" I asked. Understanding, when it finally dawned, was followed a heartbeat later by anger. "You were the crier? The whole time?"

Van Vleet had the good sense to look slightly embarrassed—by being caught in the act, if not for the act itself. It didn't last long. He simply shrugged.

"Seemed the thing to do at the time," he said. "I wanted to scare you off the story. The legend of Loralie offered the perfect opportunity to do just that."

"There's only one problem with that reasoning," I told him. "It didn't work." Okay, so I admit it might have worked, had I not wanted this story so much— and had so many folks going out of their way to help me get it.

He shrugged again. "It was worth a shot," he said.

Beside me, Shelby Lynne was performing some serious knuckle-cracking.

"This guy set out to deliberately scare you off the

story? You want I should take care of him?" she asked, and I felt like a Mafia boss.

I shook my head. "Unfortunately, it's a free country," I told her, "and I doubt he broke any laws. At least any that I can prove."

"So what do we do?" she asked.

"Stick with the plan," I said, and reached up and slammed the knocker down. "We stick with the plan."

To my surprise, the door swung open. No one was there. I looked at Shelby Lynne. I stuck a hand on the doorjamb.

"Hello!" I called into the house. "Anyone home? Ms. Courtney Howard? Are you home?"

The only response was the echo of my own calls.

"Hello!" Shelby Lynne called out. "Yoo-hoo! Anyone home?"

"I'm going in," Van Vleet said, preparing to shove past me.

"Excuse me? You can't just barge into someone's home," I told him. "That's breaking and entering. Right, Shelby?" Shelby Lynne looked at me in surprise. I surprised myself. Here I was, facing an open door leading to the scoop of the century, and I was worried about protecting the object of that scoop's privacy? Irony. Oh, irony.

"The door is open. How is that breaking and entering?" Van Vleet asked.

"Uh, maybe because you weren't invited into the house," I replied.

"Criminal trespass at worst," he said, preparing to enter. I put a hand on his arm, suddenly feeling very protective of the woman who resided there.

"This isn't cool, Drew," I told him. "Let's give her a

call and see if she picks up, tell her we're down here and handle it that way."

"I've done the calling route. I didn't even get the courtesy of a response," Drew said. "I've played the good old newsboy angle and got doors shut in my face. I'm going in. So, take your hand off my arm." He yanked away from me and entered the house.

"What do we do now?" Shelby Lynne asked.

"We go in," I told her. "To make sure Van Vleet behaves."

She nodded. "You should have let me thump him," she told me, and it was my turn to nod.

"Hindsight is always twenty-twenty," I said. "And cheer up. You might get your chance yet," I added.

Shelby and I stepped into the house, and I called out once again to alert the resident author that she had visitors.

The house was lovely, in an old-fashioned kind of way. We stepped into a small foyer, which was home to an antique pedestal table my mom would give her DVD-R for.

We moved on into the living room on a well-worn hardwood floor that had recently been polished to a dark sheen. A large, rather stern-looking stone fireplace was on the opposite wall, with built-in bookcases and shelves on either side. Two high-backed sofas with carved wood on the backs and arms faced each other with a large cocktail table between them. A couple of Queen Anne chairs completed the arrangement. A worn but obviously costly rug was on the floor.

At the far edge of the living room was a long, impressive curving staircase that led to the second floor. I stopped at the bottom and called up.

"Elizabeth? Are you there? It's Tressa Turner from the *Gazette*." Okay, so I took the liberty of being on a first-name basis with the author. It was something I could look back on and remember with some level of fondness. "The door was open. Could you spare a moment of your time?"

I frowned and looked at Shelby, who had joined me in staring up the staircase. Nothing.

I looked around the uncluttered room with a wistful eye. My house was so messy, the dust bunnies had dust bunny babies.

I noticed a sheet of paper in a garbage can near the stairs and reached in and pulled it out. Before I could take a look at it—I can be a bit of a compulsive snoop, especially when given access to a famous person's "gar-*baj*"—Drew Van Vleet nudged past me at the bottom of the staircase.

"I'm going up," he said.

I shoved the paper in a side pocket of my backpack, put my arms out like a school crossing guard or traffic cop to stop him. Tressa, the human shield. "You can't go up there! If Elizabeth wanted to acknowledge our presence in her house, she'd be down here," I told him.

"Try stopping me," Van Vleet said, shoving me to the side, only to be deterred by a roadblock he had zero chance of dislodging. Shelby Lynne stood with arms crossed and an I-dare-you look about her.

Unfortunately, Van Vleet was more resourceful— and more foolish than I thought. He dove between Shelby Lynne's legs and climbed the stairs doggy-style. I ran up after him.

"Get back down there!" I told him in a hushed voice. "There's obviously no one here."

Drew Van Vleet stopped in front of the door that led to the room I'd, uh, surveilled that night from the tree. He put a hand on the doorknob.

"Don't do that!"

He turned the knob. The door was locked.

"Ms. Courtney Howard? Are you in there?" he said.

I looked at the locked door, wondering why this door was locked and the rest were standing open.

I tapped on the door. "Elizabeth?" I said.

"Back off! This is my story," Drew Van Vleet snapped, giving my shoulder a shove.

Our confrontation was brought to a rather anticlimactic end—and a fortuitous one for Drew Van Vleet, since I was about to clobber him—when we heard the sound of a car pulling up the driveway.

"Shit!" Van Vleet apparently wasn't as sure as he'd been a few minutes ago that he hadn't broken any laws. "They're back!"

I ran to a narrow window at the end of the hall and peeked out. Sure enough, the blue van was pulling into the drive behind Van Vleet's SUV.

"Run!" I warned, with no idea where to run to. I just knew I didn't want to be caught inside the house with no way to explain being there that didn't end with an incarceration.

"Down here!" Shelby hissed from the bottom of the stairs. I ran down, Van Vleet on my tail. Shelby motioned to a door leading to the basement. "We can get to the basement back here, then crawl out the cellar door and hightail it to the cemetery once they've entered the house. We can pretend we've been there all along," she said.

As a plan, it had merit. Except for the fact that

Shelby Lynne wanted us to make our escape through the very same cellar I'd seen the oblong box carried into that very first night.

Still, knowing that Drew Van Vleet was responsible for the Loralie hauntings helped me haul this reporter's rear down the narrow, steep stairs to the basement with barely a flinch. I kept my eyes glued to Shelby Lynne's back, not taking a chance on seeing something I didn't want to see.

We made our way over to the stairs that led out through the cellar door on the side of the house, and sat breathless, waiting for the occupants to enter the house before we made our way outside into the sunlight again.

I shivered in the cold gloom of the basement. The door upstairs squeaked and then shut, and we heard someone call out. That was our cue. We climbed up the stairs one right after the other, opened the door and climbed out, shutting it behind us and running for the shelter of the cemetery.

I carried one thought with me as I sprinted for cover: Thank goodness I'd worn my Converse.

CHAPTER EIGHTEEN

While we caught our breath in the cemetery, I took the lead and outlined our strategy. I know. Boo! Scary!

"Okay," I said between wheezing breaths. "Here's what we do. Once they don't find us inside"—breath—"they'll come out into the yard to look for us." Breath. "We let 'em find us." Two breaths. "Act all surprised."

"Brilliant, Einstein," Van Vleet said. "How do we explain being back here?"

"You just have your camera out and pretend to be a reporter, and I'll take care of the rest," I told him.

Shelby Lynne gave me a this-better-be-good-or-I'll-squash-you look.

"This is insane," Drew Van Vleet said after a minute or two. "I'm not gonna cower in this grave-yard. I've done nothing wrong. I'm going to march up there and demand to speak with Elizabeth Courtney Howard."

"Is that right?" Shelby Lynne caught him by the collar. "You're the one who got us into this mess in the first place by going into that house when you shouldn't have. If you think I'm gonna let you put my future at risk, you're nuts. You're gonna do just what Tressa tells you," she advised Drew.

"Oh, yeah?" He looked at me. "And what if I don't?"

"Then Shelby Lynne and I both tell the cops how we warned you not to go into that house and how you ignored us. It may be simple trespass, but it'll still make an interesting headline in the *Gazette*," I told him.

Shelby Lynne reached into his bag and pulled out his recorder. "Besides, calling a person and playing sick jokes like this could be considered harassment," she pointed out.

Drew's Adam's apple made a couple quick trips up and down. "You win," he said. "For now."

"And I doubt very much if Publisher Van Vleet would be amused," I added.

I got out my camera and shot pictures of the house and of Loralie's headstone. Several minutes later we heard voices. Showtime.

"What are you doing there?"

I gave a little start—you know, as if taken by surprise—and turned to find Vanessa McCormick and Lizzie's boy toy standing watching us. Drew Van Vleet continued to shoot pictures. Shelby simply stood there, a rather large mime.

Come on, guys. Work with me. Work with me.

"Oh, hello again, Vanessa," I said, putting my camera into my bag. "How are you this dreary morning?"

"What are you three doing back?" the boy toy asked. He was shorter than I'd thought. Under six feet tall. Shorter than Shelby Lynne, for sure. And he wasn't pleased to find us here.

"Oh, good question," I said. "Good question." I walked over to the couple and leaned toward Vanessa. "We're actually working on a story," I said, a conspiratorial tone in my voice. I took her arm and led her toward the house. "You see, Vanessa, we know about the B-and-B."

She gave me a questioning look.

"Bed-and-breakfast," I whispered. "The real estate deal with J&R Development."

She looked surprised.

"We also know the sale was finalized today," I said. "Even though it's not the caliber of story that, say, an interview with your employer is, it's still big news for the county. By the way, Ms. Courtney Howard hasn't changed her mind about that interview, by any chance, has she?"

Vanessa shook her head.

"That's too bad," I said.

"Do we have enough shots, Drew?" I asked.

He shrugged. "Guess so," he grumbled.

"Excellent," I said. "Well, we'll just be on our way, Vanessa. And if Elizabeth changes her mind about the interview, be a dear and give me a call, won't you?" I wrote my cell phone number on a *Gazette* business card. "She can call me after she finishes her final book, if she prefers. Anytime. Day or night," I added.

Vanessa took the card and stared at it. I put out a hand to the boy toy. "And you are?"

"Leaving. As I'd advise you to," he said, and turned on his heel with a really nasty observation about reporters.

"I'm sorry if I've upset your friend," I told Vanessa. "We're leaving."

"That's Ms. Courtney Howard's driver," Vanessa

explained. "Tony. He's a bit protective of Elizabeth," she said.

I nodded. Tony the boy toy was protective of his employer, huh? So protective, he left her locked in her bedroom?

"We'll be leaving, too," Vanessa McCormick added. "We're heading back to Connecticut early tomorrow morning. Elizabeth's last book is a wrap."

"So, I guess that's that," I said. "Well, it was nice meeting you at least."

She nodded. "It was good to meet you, too," she said and walked back to the house. We all walked to our respective vehicles and got in.

I couldn't help but glance at Elizabeth's window as we drove away. This time, the curtains were closed.

It was getting close to the time when I was supposed to meet Manny at the hospital, so I offered to drive Shelby Lynne home first.

"I can ride along with you," Shelby said. "No biggie. I'm supposed to be sick, anyway, so it's not as if anyone would be surprised to see me at the hospital."

I could tell she was disappointed that the Courtney Howard story wasn't going to happen. I was bummed, too, but at the same time I was relieved that we'd avoided an ugly confrontation that could have landed us all in hot water.

I couldn't shake my unease over the locked bedroom door. Was it possible that Courtney Howard was being confined against her own will? Victimized by trusted employees who stood to benefit from controlling the older woman's finances and access to the outside world? I knew it sounded far-fetched. Vanessa McCormick didn't seem the type to take advantage of an old woman. But I'd learned fairly recently that you couldn't depend on anyone being what or who they claimed.

And what about Driver Tony? He seemed a little rough around the edges. Still, I supposed that bad boy image had a certain appeal. Which brought me around to Manny and my debut as his significant other.

I pulled into the hospital parking lot and turned off the Plymouth.

"You have a sick friend here, huh?" Shelby Lynne said.

"Never met her before in my life," I told her.

"You're visiting someone you've never met before?"

I nodded, grabbing my rearview mirror off the floor and holding it out like a compact so that I could reapply lip gloss. I never went anywhere without a heavy-duty coat of lip gloss.

"I'm doing a favor for a friend. It's his ahnt."

"Huh?"

"His aunt."

"And he needs you to go with him because . . . ?"

It was Rick Townsend's third degree all over again.

I turned to Shelby Lynne to explain, and noticed that her eyes were huge.

"Shelby?" I asked. "Is something wrong?"

She pointed past me. I started to turn, when the driver's-side door fell away and I tumbled out. I expected to hit the concrete, but strong arms lifted me before I struck the ground.

"Hey, Barbie Doll," Manny said, settling me on my feet. I straightened my clothing.

Shelby Lynne scooted toward the driver's side and leaned out. "This is your friend?" she asked, getting an eyeful. "Introductions, please."

"Shelby Lynne, Manny. Manny, Shelby Lynne."

Shelby held out one large hand. Manny seemed to stare at it for a second before he shook it.

"Good to meet you, Manny," Shelby Lynne said.

"Hey," Manny replied.

"I won't be long," I told Shelby Lynne.

"Take your time," she said with a wink. "Take your time."

Manny and I headed for the hospital entrance.

"Friend of yours?" he asked, obviously referring to Shelby.

I thought about it for a second.

"Yeah," I said. "Yeah, we're friends." Like, how did that happen? I gave Manny the short version of how Shelby Lynne and I had hooked up, and explained the homecoming controversy. "I'd give anything to see those preps lose big, and Shelby Lynne and Tom win," I told him. "So, how's your aunt Mo?" I asked as we approached the main entrance. "Is she improving?"

Manny shook his head.

"What's wrong with her?" I asked.

"Congestive heart failure," he replied.

"Sorry, Manny," I said. "That's tough."

He opened the hospital door for me, and we entered. We made a short stop at the gift shop, and Manny asked me to pick out a flower arrangement for his aunt while he picked up a box of chocolates. I couldn't resist selecting an ice cream cone vase with an assortment of white and pink carnations as faux ice cream. Trust me. It was adorable.

We made our way down the hallway to his great-aunt's room. Just outside the door, I grabbed Manny's arm.

"What am I supposed to say again?" I asked. "How

long have we supposedly been dating? Isn't she going to wonder why she hasn't met me before now?"

Manny shrugged. "Manny's a private person."

"And it's just going to be your great-aunt Mo we're telling, right?" I asked. "Not Great-uncle So-and-So, First-cousin What's-Her-Name and Second-cousin-Twice- Removed Whatever. Right?"

"Just Ahnt Mo," Manny said. "No sweat. Manny'll do most of the talkin'. All Barbie has to do is take my lead and play along."

I'm usually in for it when someone tells me what I have to do, and it starts with the word "all."

Manny suddenly grabbed my left hand and slipped a ring on my finger. Without warning he opened the hospital room door.

"Yo. Ahnt Mo."

Sounded like the beginning of a rap.

I tagged in on Manny's heels, sticking close behind him and staring at the rock on my third finger that had to be fake. It had to be. It was as big as a Skittle.

"Ahnt Mo's been wondering where her Manny's been keepin' himself," came from the bed. "Come give Ahntie Mo a big hug.

I saw now where Manny got his third-person-speak. I peeked around him at the figure reclining on the hospital bed. I also saw where Manny got his bulk.

Aunt Mo was heavyset but by no means fat. Dark hair that had probably once been jet-black but was now salt-and-pepper was pulled back in a tight ponytail. Aunt Mo had cast off her hospital bedsheet, but was wearing the traditional ugly light blue print hospital gown.

Manny released my hand and went up to hug his aunt.

"How you feelin'?" he asked, giving her a quick kiss on the cheek.

"Don't help to complain, so Ahnt Mo will just say never been better and leave it at that."

" 's good," Manny said.

Aunt Mo leaned to one side. "Who's that hiding behind Manny? I know Manny's shadow is bigger than that."

I was about to take a step to the side when Manny grabbed my hand and yanked me forward.

"This here's Tressa, Ahnt Mo," he said.

Aunt Mo looked at me for a long moment, one of those top-of-the-head-tip-of-the-tootsies numbers that make you feel really uncomfortable and wonder if your zipper is down or if you've walked out of the house without a brassiere. She finally looked at Manny.

"Tressa? Did you say Tressa? What kind of name is that, anyway? Tressa. Ahntie Mo never heard of no one called Tressa," she said, once again giving me the benefit of her appraisal. "Unless she worked in a beauty parlor." She leaned up in her bed. "You work in a beauty parlor?"

I shook my head. "I work at a newspaper. And at an ice cream shop. And every other weekend at Bargain City," I told her.

"Hmm. With a name like Tressa, you should open a beauty parlor. Tressa's House of Tresses. Don't that sound fine?"

"Very nice," I replied.

Her eyes narrowed and centered on my face.

"Manny never brung a girl home before," she said, and I couldn't tell if she was talking about Manny or

270

to him, so I just stood there. "What makes you so special?"

I looked up at Manny, completely blanking on how to respond to this inquiry.

"You know how you always tell Manny to find a good girl?" he said. "Well, here she is. Manny's good girl." Manny grabbed my left hand and held it up in front of Aunt Mo's nose.

"Oh my god! Is that an engagement ring? Oh my lordy! Are you two engaged? Oh my god! Oh my god. Oh my god! My Manny's found himself a nice girl! And a hardworkin' one! Oh my god, oh my god, oh my god!" The old woman's hands suddenly moved to her chest. Not in an oh-my-god-I'm-just-so-happy kind of move, but more along the lines of an oh-my-god-I'm-having-the-big-one number.

"Are you all right?" I asked her. "Is she all right?" I asked Manny.

He moved to his aunt's side. "Ahnt Mo, are you okay?"

She nodded, but she didn't look okay. And apparently the heart monitor thingy she was hooked up to agreed, because all of a sudden alarms started going off and people started running in and yelling something about someone coding. And they put the head of the bed down and shoved Manny and me out of the room.

"I've killed Ahnt Mo," Manny said as we waited for news of his aunt's cardiac episode. He must've been upset. He'd used first person.

I rubbed his broad back. "Look on the bright side, Manny," I told him. "You made her last moments on this earth extremely happy ones. In fact, I don't recall ever seeing anyone quite that happy," I added. "Ever."

The doctors came out about half an hour later, and I could tell Manny was poised for the worst.

"Are you Mrs. DeMarco's nephew?" a hospital-green-clad doctor-type asked, and Manny nodded.

"Ahnt Mo's gone, isn't she, Doc?" Manny said and I reached out and took his hand and squeezed it, and felt him squeeze back.

The doctor smiled. "No. As a matter of fact, your aunt is resting comfortably," he told Manny.

"Say what?"

"She had an episode with her heart there, called an atrial tachycardia. Fortunately for her, with her history of structural heart problems, the episode actually helped jump-start her heart out of the sluggish rhythm it had fallen into. As you know, with the medication not working, we were hesitant to use the paddles on her, fearing that might kill her outright, so believe it or not, this little episode was actually the perfect medicine at the perfect time."

I looked at the doctor. "You mean she's going to live?" I asked.

He nodded. "Not forever, but for now," he said.

I looked at Manny. He looked at me. We both stared at the ring on my left hand, fourth finger.

Manny and Tressa were screwed.

I dropped Shelby Lynne off at home before three-thirty, reminding her of her makeover appointment, and called Gram to make sure she was armed and ready. If Shelby noticed my preoccupation and the gem the size of a pea on my hand, she didn't mention it.

I stopped by the *Gazette* and threw together a piece on the acquisition and upcoming renovation of Haunted Holloway Hall into a bed-and-breakfast, and called it good. I decided to wait until the next day to do the article on Joe and his old acquaintance Elizabeth Courtney. It wouldn't run till next week, anyway. By that time, the reclusive author would be back home in rural Connecticut, and life in Grandville would return to normal—whatever normal in Grandville is.

I stared at the ring on my hand the entire trip home, wondering what it would be like to really be engaged to be married. I pulled into the driveway around five. On the way, I'd picked up a pizza from the Thunder Rolls Lanes, our local bowling alley. They have some of the best pizza in the county.

The pups picked up the scent of the supreme ingredients and frolicked hopefully about my heels all the way from the car to the house. I opened the pizza box, pulled off several cheese-covered sausage balls and tossed those over, promising the dogs any leftovers.

Yes, I occasionally have leftovers. Okay, so maybe not pizza leftovers. Anyway, all that bread isn't good for a dog.

I opened the door and called out to Gram that I was home and that I'd come bearing pizza. She was in the living room, watching the local news, cotton balls between the toes of one foot.

"You don't have cable," Gram said. "Why didn't I know you don't have cable?"

"I can't afford cable," I told her. "Besides, we live in the boonies. We can't get cable out here. Only satellite or DirecTV."

"You need one of those, then. All you get are the network channels."

"It's all I can afford, Gram," I said. "Besides, I'm not home all that much, and I don't have time to watch TV."

"I'll pay to have one of them big dishes stuck in the backyard," Gram said. "We'll beam in channels from Greenland."

"You do that, Gram," I said, carrying the pizza into the kitchen. "You do that."

"What time is Shelby Lynne coming over?" Gram asked, hobbling into the kitchen behind me, one foot still decorated with cotton.

"Any time," I said. "You all set to work your magic?".

"Hannah's House of Beauty is now open for business," she said.

I snared a can of light beer from the now fully stocked fridge, fetched a paper plate from the cupboard, sat down at the kitchen table and helped myself to a slice of pizza.

"Shelby Lynne won't know what hit her," I told Gram with a wink. "Will she?"

Gram also took a large slice of pizza, opting for a can of cream soda to wash it down with. She opened it and raised her can. "To makeover magic," she said.

I raised my can high. "That kind of magic I can live with," I said. "To Shelby Lynne!"

Poor, poor Shelby Lynne. She didn't know what hit her. The independent-minded young lady had already rejected two faces Gram had made up. The first one, she said, made her look like Howdy Doody. The second one? Howdy Doody's grandmother.

I sat in the living room, dressed in gray sweats, my feet up on the coffee table, finishing the last chapter of *Shadows of the Night* for only, like, the eleventh time in my life. I still couldn't get over the way I could so easily lose myself in the world Elizabeth had created.

She reached out and grabbed a reader from the get-go and didn't let loose until that very last word—leaving you content yet strangely melancholy that you'd finished her story.

"Now this this is a masterpiece," Gram said. "You'll have no cause to complain about this face. You look like you're ready for the red carpet like one of them Hollywood starlets."

I grinned, wondering when Shelby Lynne had last heard the term "starlet."

"Come take a look, Tressa. Did we do good?"

I got up and went over to the kitchen. I stopped in the doorway and almost tripped over my lower lip. Shelby Lynne looked . . . not bad. Gram had played up her peaches-and-cream complexion, and she had a soft, radiant glow about her.

"You look terrific, Shelby Lynne," I told her honestly. "You've got to let Gram make you up tomorrow night. You'll be a knockout."

Shelby Lynne gave an uncertain smile. "Are you sure? I wouldn't want people to make fun of me."

"Not to worry," I said. "Now, what about the hair, Gram? Up or down?"

"Up," Gram said.

"Down," Shelby said.

Circle the wagons. Here we go again.

I sat on the couch long after Shelby Lynne left Hannah's House of Beauty, having compromised on the great hair debate by going with a half-up-half-down do. Worked for me.

I'd picked up my copy of *Satan's Serenade* and found myself reading it again, seeing for the first time in black and white the subtle differences in Howard's earlier writing as opposed to her last several books. In her earlier work, Elizabeth Courtney Howard had a way of seducing her readers, reaching out and grabbing us by the throat with ribbons of sensuality and mystery rather with than violent imagery or shock talk. That quality was lacking in her later books, which, while okay reads, were hardly the compelling page-turners her earlier works had been. Her last books didn't have the depth of character her earlier ones had. Or maybe it was her characters who didn't have the depth of character. Which led this nosy Nellie to wonder if the changes in her writing could possibly be linked to a serious illness, which in turn could also provide a reason for her inability to remember her own high school prom and, I might add, her rather dapper prom date.

I continued to read her latest book, and shook my head. Used to be you could tell by the time you got to the bottom of page one that the book was an Elizabeth Courtney Howard book. There was just something unique about her writing. And while her later works held glimpses of that certain something, they fell just short of the certain something that earmarked her early books as one-of-a-kind Courtney Howard classics. It was almost as if they'd been written by someone else "in the tradition of" Elizabeth Courtney Howard.

I shook my head. Maybe she was just burned out. After all, the woman had written überbooks. Maybe the well had run dry.

I picked up my backpack and decided to call it a night. Tomorrow was homecoming, with all the associated pageantry. The parade, the pork-fry, the game, the popcorn, the crowning of homecoming king and queen, the caramel apples. And there was also the little matter of a pretend engagement to take care of.

I gathered up my paraphernalia and was ready to stuff it in my bag, when I noticed the folded sheet of paper I'd pilfered from the round file at Haunted Holloway Hall that morning.

I unfolded it.

"'*Ghostwriter*,'" I read. I scanned the one-page document and couldn't believe what I was reading. In my grubby little purloining hands I held what appeared to be the back-cover blurb for the absolute final Elizabeth Courtney Howard book. My palms grew sweaty as I read the short blurb.

What would you do when loyalty and passion war—
and you alone must keep a devastating secret that can shatter a multimillion-dollar house of cards?

Out of work freelance writer Tina Clarke can't believe her good fortune. She's just nabbed a job as live-in administrative assistant to Cydney Scott, beloved storyteller and record-setting author. Cydney Scott has sat atop all the literary lists that count. But far away from the publishing mecca of New York City, behind the closed doors of a mansion far off the beaten path hides a secret that, if revealed, will end the author's career. Tina's employer has a terminal case of writer's block—and a megabuck book deal pending—and she's just offered Tina Clarke the chance to ghostwrite her book.

Tina is thrilled to accept this once-in-a-lifetime

opportunity. But when one book turns into five and Tina's secret life threatens her real life—and sanity—it's time to stop the madness. Unfortunately for Tina, Scott's ghostwriter has taken on a life of her own.

Can you keep a secret?

I must have read the half page of material ten times before it hit me like a two-by-four between the eyes. All right, so sometimes it takes a mighty powerful force to make an impact on my skull. I couldn't believe what I was thinking, but deep down I knew I was on to something. Like maybe the truth?

And with it, the mother of all stories.

CHAPTER NINETEEN

I jumped up from the sofa and tossed my copies of *Satan's Serenade* and *Shadows of the Night*, along with the page with the cover blurb for *Ghostwriter*, into my backpack. I grabbed my cell phone, car keys and camera, and then remembered I was wearing my gray grungies. I tore down the hall and into my room, grabbed a pair of jeans, replaced the gray sweats with the jeans, washed my face, smeared on some shiny lip gloss and called it good. I stuck a black ball cap onto my head and checked the time. Ten thirty. Miss Manners would frown on the lateness of the hour, but breaking news, I reminded myself, had no timetable.

I remembered that I should probably leave a note for Gram in case she got up and wondered where I was, so I left her a short note saying that I'd gone out to work on my story and would be back for breakfast. It's hard to have someone keeping track of your comings and goings all of a sudden. I hadn't decided yet whether I liked it or not.

I raced out to the Plymouth, also picking up some

flack from my dynamic duo of dogs, who were grumpy at having their sleep interrupted. The wind was howling and a cold drizzle began to fall, so I took pity on them and let them into the house. Gram would rip me a new one the next day, but I figured it beat them howling outside her window all night.

I crossed my fingers, performed my little please-start ritual and started the car. I backed up and turned around in the drive and headed for town.

I called Shelby Lynne's cell and left a message for her to meet me at Holloway Hall if she wanted to get the real scoop on her idol, and drove like a bat out of you-know-where through Grandville and out the west side of town.

I drove up the driveway to the Holloway house, not bothering to kill the lights to hide my approach. The worn-out windshield wipers squeaked back and forth, leaving behind a fogged-up windshield. Through the raindrops on the windshield, I watched Haunted Holloway Hall come closer and closer, the dreariness of the night making the house appear even more ghostly.

The house was lit up both upstairs and down, and the blue van was pulled up close. I imagined they were packing up for the return home the next day.

I stopped my Plymouth, shut it off and opened the door. I grabbed my backpack and got out, leaving the stubborn driver's door open a hair so that I wouldn't have to walk around to the other side if the fool thing stuck again.

I turned toward the house. No more hiding in trees or skulking around bushes. No more creeping about in cemeteries or running scared through cellars. This was a main-door, no-subterfuge frontal assault.

I walked to the front door, raised the horse-head

knocker and brought it down on the door half a dozen times.

The porch light came on. Curtains to the side of the door moved. The door opened. Vanessa McCormick stood there, looking surprised to see me.

"Trick or treat," I said.

She stared at me.

"Ms. Turner! What are you doing out here at this time of night?" she asked.

"My job," I said. "We need to talk."

She shook her head. "It's not a good time. We're in the middle of packing. We leave in the morning, if you recall."

"All the more reason for concluding our business this evening, Ms. McCormick," I said. "Or should I say, 'Ghostwriter'?"

Vanessa McCormick's face grew sickly pale, like mine gets when I open my bank statement every month. Or when Gram asks me to take her around to all the cemeteries around the tricounty area for Memorial Day.

"What did you say?" Vanessa asked.

"I think you heard me."

She hesitated for a second, looking to her left and right, before she opened the door. "You'd better come in," she said.

I walked in, and she shut the door behind me.

"How did you find out?" she asked, moving into the room and motioning for me to have a seat on the couch. Instead, I chose the turquoise Queen Anne walnut wing chair. (My mum likes to go antiquing.) Vanessa sat on the edge of the sofa.

I shrugged. "I'm a reporter, remember?"

She didn't seem as impressed as I'd anticipated.

"The publisher has been hounding us for the premise of Elizabeth's last book. I knew it was just a matter of time before something leaked out."

"So what happened? Why does the incomparable Elizabeth Courtney Howard require a ghostwriter?" I asked. "Is it writer's block? Health? Dementia?"

Vanessa got up and moved to stand by the fireplace. "I'd been with Ms. Courtney Howard for more than seven years when it started. It was subtle at first. Fatigue. Memory lapses. Difficulty with her motor skills. Irritability."

"Did she consult a doctor?" I asked.

Vanessa shook her head. "Elizabeth refused to see a doctor. I begged her to go, but she said there was nothing wrong with her that exercise, a proper diet and writing wouldn't cure. But I think she just didn't want to face the truth. About six years ago, it got really bad. She was under contract for a book and still hadn't settled down with one story. Elizabeth has always kept files and files of story ideas, but this time she'd start one, write maybe a chapter of it and then abandon it. This went on for months. She was frustrated. I was worried. She was adamant that it was just a fluke, and that once she found the right story it would take off. And that's the way it usually happened. She'd try several stories until the one she was meant to write appeared."

"But it didn't happen this time."

Vanessa shook her head. "Her block only got worse, until she was really frantic and I was extremely concerned for her health. That was when she approached me about collaborating on the book with her. I'd helped with editing and polishing on her earlier books, and had even rewritten scenes that her editor requested without anyone being the wiser, so it really didn't seem like that big of a deal."

"So you wrote the books together?"

Vanessa looked up at me in the mirror above the fireplace. "She tried, she really did, but she just couldn't concentrate. Couldn't focus. And I had to take over. I'd grown up on Elizabeth's work, adored her way of telling a story, of connecting with the reader's deepest, strongest emotions. I was a student of her literature. I lived with it day and night. In early days sometimes she would dictate it to me and I'd read it back to her, and we'd laugh at the parts that weren't so good and cry together over the ones that were just right. It broke my heart to see her slip away into a lonely shell more and more each day."

I felt tears sting my eyes. Hardly the jaded reporter type, huh? The truth is, Elizabeth's story got me to thinking of my gramma retreating into a world I couldn't see or reach, and it messed me up. More than I'd expected.

I snitted and nodded. "That's tough," I said.

Vanessa smiled, but the smile didn't reach her eyes. "Elizabeth was like a mother to me. Before. And then all of a sudden . . ."

"You had to become a mother to her," I finished.

She turned away from the mirror and nodded. "*Ghostwriter* seemed a fitting way to end it all. To explain. To come to terms. To get closure. A catharsis."

Thanks to Dr. Phil, I knew what "catharsis" meant.

"I have to ask. Didn't her publisher or editor notice the difference in her writing?" I asked Vanessa. I had, and I didn't know a scene from a sequel.

Vanessa shook her head. "You have to understand—in the publishing business, name recognition counts for a lot. And Elizabeth's publisher knew anything with her name on the spine was guaranteed to be a moneymaker. And if the book wasn't quite what she usually dished up, well, she was getting up in years."

I supposed I could see Vanessa's point. And publishers couldn't catch everything. Look at the hoopla around that bestselling memoir that wasn't a memoir at all.

"So, just what do you plan to do with this information, Ms. Turner?" Vanessa asked, crossing her arms in front of her, ever the protective surrogate daughter.

I joined Vanessa at the fireplace. "It's a story with national interest, as you are well aware, Ms. McCormick." I also went with a formal, professional tone. Of course, when I caught a look at my reflection in the mirror and saw my sweatshirt hood jammed inside my back collar and my hair sticking out at weird angles, I had to concede that I hardly looked like a professional anything. Except maybe a plumber. Or handyman.

I'm going to ask you one favor," Vanessa said. "For Elizabeth's sake. Could you please wait to run the story until we're back home? I don't want the media to turn Elizabeth's story into a sideshow. And a day or two's delay on your part in releasing the story won't hurt you at all."

I thought about it. She was probably right. I'd still have my scoop. And I really didn't want Elizabeth to suffer any more than she already had.

"Okay," I said. "I reckon that'll work."

Vanessa gave me a broad smile. "Thank you so much," she said.

I picked up my backpack and remembered the books I'd brought along.

"I do ask one favor in exchange for holding off on the story," I told Vanessa, pulling out the hardbacks. "You remember Shelby Lynne Sawyer." I put my hand out about a foot above my head. "Tall, redheaded— Howdy Doody's daughter."

Vanessa nodded.

"She is just about the biggest fan of Elizabeth Courtney Howard as you could find. Would it be possible, do you think, for you to have Elizabeth sign these books for Shelby Lynne? It would mean so much to her. Really."

Vanessa stared at the books.

"I'm afraid that's impossible," she said. "Elizabeth is basically bedridden. I doubt very much if she could even sign her name. That's why I take care of all that for her."

I frowned. Bedridden? "Lizzie" had been ambulatory enough for boy toy Tony to suggest a little riding in bed several nights before. Then I remembered that Vanessa here had been doing some role-playing herself, and felt like giving myself a good-ol'-girls' slap upside the head.

"Lizzie" was standing right in front of me. Vanessa was Lizzie. By her own admission, Vanessa had become Elizabeth II when she started ghostwriting Courtney Howard's books. And Tony, the boy toy? He was Vanessa's plaything. On the night I'd climbed the tree, he'd been about to give Vanessa some technical assistance on her love scenes. Vanessa. Not Elizabeth.

So if Vanessa and Tony were the ones frolicking in the locked bedroom, where had the bedridden Elizabeth I been? And where was she now?

I watched Vanessa play nervously with her sweater, and it occurred to me that I only had Vanessa's word that Elizabeth Courtney Howard was ill.

But what if she wasn't? What if Vanessa was lying about the illness? What if she'd actually been controlling the old woman—and her fortune—for years? What if she'd kept Elizabeth isolated from everyone around her, forcing her to sign over her power of attorney to Vanessa? What if all the while Vanessa and her boy toy were living the high life, compliments of a victimized old woman, and I was the only one around to prove it?

I thought about my own gramma back home in the double-wide, leaving blue hair in the bathroom sink and snoring up a storm down the hall, and knew beyond a shadow of a doubt that I could not leave Haunted Holloway Hall until I knew for sure, with my own two big blue peepers, that Elizabeth Courtney Howard was okay.

"In that case, I'll be content with just taking a quick peek at the legendary author," I told Vanessa. "She won't even know I'm there. Really. I'll be quiet as my dad at family reunions," I assured her.

"That's not a good idea," Vanessa said. "She's down for the night—"

"I'm used to old folks," I went on. "As a matter of fact, my grandma is living with me right now, and she has her friends in and out all the time. So, believe me, I know how to get along with the older generation."

"But she needs to be rested for our trip back east tomorrow—"

"I'll just pop in and out. If she's sleeping, I won't wake her up. Girl Scout's promise." No snide comments here, please.

"I just don't think that's a good idea."

Vanessa McCormick was getting more and more

agitated the more and more I insisted on seeing her employer.

"You'd better go," she said. "Now."

"Or what?" I finally asked. "You'll call the police? Go ahead," I told her. "And when I tell them what's going on, we'll see whether they think it's in Ms. Courtney Howard's best interest to conduct a welfare check. I'm bettin' they will."

Vanessa walked over, picked up a cell phone off the coffee table and walked back to the middle of the living room. She flipped the phone open. I didn't budge.

She looked at me for a full minute, and then slowly shut the flip cover and put the phone down. She sat down in the Queen Anne chair. "You won't understand," she said.

I walked to the bottom of the staircase and looked up the dark and winding banister. I put my hand on the cherry wood and my foot on the first step. My heart pounded in my chest like the big bass drum that accompanied the football players out on the field. *Boom. Boom. Boom.*

I climbed the steps to the landing, then turned to continue my ascent. One. Two. Three. Four steps. I put my foot on the fifth and was suddenly grabbed from behind. I lost my balance and tumbled down the stairs.

I lay there for a few seconds, a forlorn fact finder, and adjusted the ball cap that had fallen forward over my eyes. When I could see clearly again, it was to discover boy toy Tony looking down at me. And from the look on his face—jaw muscle ticking like a time bomb and a dark scowl that said he wasn't a fan of the press—I knew I was about to become part of my story. Again.

"So, you want to see Elizabeth Courtney Howard?" Tony asked, and I decided it didn't have the urgency now that it had earlier.

"Uh, on second thought, Vanessa over there is probably right," I said, sliding to a sitting position. "It's pretty late, and old people do need their sleep."

Tony smiled down at me, but for some reason I wasn't put at ease. Or charmed by his dark good looks. Maybe that was because the smile showed too many teeth that were clenched. And it didn't reach his dark eyes.

"Oh, but a few seconds ago you were so concerned about Elizabeth that you were threatening to call the police yourself to check on the old lady. What changed your mind?"

I got to my feet. "You know how women like to change their minds," I said.

He looked at me. "Yeah. But sometimes that can be a fatal flaw." Yikes. This guy should be the one writing books.

I shrugged. "Whatever." I bent over to pick up my backpack, which had tumbled down the stairs with me. "I guess I'll say good night." I attempted to move around the blockade that boy toy Tony made, one hand on the banister and the other on the wall. "If you'll excuse me," I said.

Tony didn't budge. I was hesitant about getting in a shoving match with him. Without Shelby Lynne, I didn't stand a chance.

"Please," I said.

Tony shook his head.

"You want to see Elizabeth?" he said. "You really want to see her?"

288

Okay, so the guy was creeping me out. I stood there scared shitless—I mean, witless.

"No, Tony." Vanessa moved to put a hand up. "Let her go," she said. "Just let her go."

Tony's eyes didn't leave my face. "You want to see Elizabeth, you'll see Elizabeth," he said. "Who am I to deny access to the press? Am I right?"

He reached out, grabbed my arm and dragged me off the landing and down the remaining stairs.

I looked back toward the second floor. "Isn't . . . she . . . up there?" I asked with a pathetic phlegmy quaver in my throat.

Tony just shook his head and sneered. I'm hoping, with practice, I'll learn to sneer that well. He opened the door to the basement.

"No! Tony! Don't!" Vanessa ran to the basement door. "You can't do this," she said. "You're only going to make matters worse."

But apparently Tony was done taking orders. He pulled me down the stairs behind him, and I resisted. I felt like I was our closest neighbor, Verlin Little's, stubborn mule, Corky.

"Stop! Tony! Please!" Vanessa followed us down the narrow steps. Tony's fingers bit into my arms, and I yelped. That was gonna leave a mark.

He yanked me along like a rag doll and headed for a room at the northwest corner of the basement. He took out a key, unlocked the room and opened the door.

"You want to see the world-famous Elizabeth Courtney Howard?" he asked. "There she is."

He gave me a powerful push and I fell into the room face-first, my backpack the only thing that saved me from reconstructive dental surgery. That lasted only a second, as Tony reached out, grabbed the bag and ripped it out from under me. He slammed the door shut, and I heard the lock turn.

I was still for a moment and listened to Vanessa continuing to plead with Tony to think about what he was doing, and to Tony telling Vanessa to shut up and let him handle things for a change, as she'd gummed everything up.

Their voices grew faint as they apparently climbed the stairs and shut the basement door behind them. I heard another key turn and knew I'd been doubly locked in. But probably not for safekeeping.

For the second time in ten minutes, I picked myself up and dusted myself off. It was so dark that I couldn't make out my hand in front of my face. The room was as cold as a refrigerated meat locker. Or a walk-in freezer. (Trust me. I've had some firsthand knowledge of this.)

"Elizabeth?" I whispered, not really believing that they'd kept the old woman locked up in a room in the cellar, but I figured it gave me something to do instead of screaming in abject terror. "Elizabeth?"

Although I hadn't really expected Elizabeth to pipe up and say, "Who's there?" and would have wet my pants if she had, the idea that Tony expected me to find Elizabeth in the cold, dark cellar really twisted my innards.

I felt along the sides of the door for a light switch. The house was old, but I figured there had to be a light down here somewhere. I suddenly remembered that lots of old houses had old-fashioned lights on the ceilings, with long pull chains. Judging from the first time I'd been in the basement, I thought this house might be sufficiently ancient to qualify.

I got to my feet and felt around some more. I suddenly remembered my Bargain City indigo watch, and pulled up my sleeve and hit the button to turn on the light. I held it up.

"Let there be light!" I said, and began to move cautiously about the room. It's amazing how much light one of those cheapo watches will give off.

I played blind man's bluff for a couple of minutes before I found the light chain. I tugged on it, and the room lit up like Gram and I did at Bonanza Buffet with an all-you-can-eat five-dollar coupon in hand.

I took a look around the room—and for a considerable period of time thought I was going to do an Aunt Mo and have my own myocardial infarction. (Yeah, I Googled this.) There, positioned on two wooden sawhorses, was the wooden crate I'd seen Tony and Vanessa unload the night they'd arrived.

I moved to stand beside the box and looked down at it, debating on whether I should open it. The wussy part of me wanted to leave well enough alone. You know, what you don't know won't hurt you. Ignorance is bliss. My wussier self, however, didn't want to just sit there like a sap and have that crate cover slowly open up, and see an old, decrepit, rotting hand with black fingernails reach out and grip the wood. And Tressa, Warrior Princess? Well, she'd given up her throne and set up housekeeping with the warrior queen.

I took a deep breath, reached out and lifted the lid on the crate. A long, white linen cloth, a milky white shroud, covered the contents. I pulled the sheet away. Underneath, wrapped in what looked like a giant Ziploc bag, was a body. I nervously poked the plastic with a finger. It was cold to the touch. I winced as I moved to look down at the face beneath the plastic.

I shook my head.

"Ah, Elizabeth," I said, the prom photo coming to mind. "You haven't changed a bit."

CHAPTER TWENTY

I replaced the lid on the crate and, locating a jumbo roll of duct tape, proceeded to tape down the cover on the crate just in case. (Further proof that duct tape has innumerable uses.)

I looked around for any possible avenue of escape. For a second or two, I considered the tiny basement window. I could maybe get my head and shoulders wedged through, but my butt and thighs? No way were they sliding through, even if I stripped down to my skivvies, had waxed last night, and was greased down with Vaseline petroleum jelly.

I tried to pin my hopes on Shelby Lynne coming to my rescue. She knew I was here. Heck, my car was parked out front. And I was betting the minute she got my message, she'd hightail it out to Holloway Hall in righteous indignation that I hadn't waited for her.

I groaned. My car was parked out front with the door open and the key in the ignition. All Tony had to do was hop in and drive away, and all evidence of my ever being at Haunted Holloway Hall was erased.

I shook my head. Stupid, stupid, stupid. There was the note I'd left for my gramma, but after her late nights this week, no telling what time she'd be up and around to see it.

Upstairs the arguing continued. From what I could tell, Tony was winning. Suddenly the arguing stopped. Then, silence. I did what any ex-warrior princess would do under the same circumstances: I jumped up and started screaming at the top of my lungs and throwing paint cans, paint brushes and anything else I could get my hands on across the room.

"Help!" I yelled. "I'm in the basement! There's a body down here with me! Help!"

I screamed until I heard the door open at the top of the stairs. Holy shit. What had I done? If I wasn't mistaken, I was about to become bunkmates with Elizabeth. Roll over, Elizabeth; I always take the left side.

Okay, so I was getting a tad bit hysterical. I searched for a weapon, realized that the paint can was as good as it got and moved hurriedly to extinguish the light.

I positioned myself behind the door. My plan was simple. Step one: Reach out and bash Tony in the head. Step Two: Run like hell. Step Three: Okay, so I hadn't gotten to step three yet. I'd consider my options while I was hauling ass.

The lock clicked and I heard the doorknob turn.

"Some investigative reporter," I heard Tony say. "She couldn't even find the light. Blondes."

I raised the paint can above my head, thinking I'd just been handed more than what they call "adequate provocation" on the court shows. Whatever damage I inflicted was justifiable—as long as I had a jury of blondes, that is.

The door swung open. The light came on. I was momentarily blinded—long enough for me to discover there was a light switch by the door, after all; and for Tony to discover me, separate me from my paint can weapon and shove in a confused Shelby Lynne to join the little party.

"I believe this is a friend of yours," Tony said. He looked beyond me to the wooden crate, saw the duct tape wrapped around it and shook his head.

Ten minutes later, Shelby Lynne and I sat in the dark on the cold, dirty floor, duct-taped together like a pair of really grotesque-looking Siamese twins. Apparently Tony was taking no chances. He'd also duct-taped our mouths.

I worked my lips back and forth. Fool man. He must not have realized, Tressa Jayne Turner never ventured out without applying enough heavy-duty lip gloss to withstand a Hefty Gulp from the Git 'n Go, a French vanilla cappuccino from the Coffee Clatch, and a large fries from any number of places. I had enough gloss on my lips to wax a floor. In less time than it takes Gram to fall asleep when the news comes on, I had my mouth free.

Unfortunately, Shelby Lynne, who'd worn lip gloss for the first time the other night at Hannah's House of Beauty, was in danger of losing her lips altogether. Trussed together back-to-back as we were, it was almost impossible to move. Shelby Lynne hit her head against the back of mine.

"Ouch!" I said. "Watch it!"

She nudged me again.

"What? What do you want?"

She knocked her head against mine and mumbled something that sounded like "teeth, tape."

"What? I can't understand you."

She head-butted me again.

"Uh, news flash. That's starting to piss me off," I told her. I turned my head toward hers and our noses collided. Sharp pain. Instant headache.

"Are you happy? I think you broke my nose!" I said to the side of her face, feeling the duct tape that sealed her mouth next to my cheek. "Wait a minute," I said. "Turn your head this way as far as you can. More. A little bit more. I might be able to lift a corner of that tape with my tongue and then rip the rest off with my teeth," I told her.

I stuck out my tongue and started to work at the tape around her mouth, then stopped.

"Uh, we speak of this to no one, understand?" I told her. "And no *Brokeback Mountain* jokes or references. Agreed?"

I could feel her nod vigorously, and I set to work on the tape. Twenty minutes later I wished I'd left the tape in place.

"I can't believe she's dead! I can't believe Elizabeth Courtney Howard, my idol, the person I aspired to emulate, is lying over there in a pine box, wrapped in a Ziploc bag, stone-cold dead. I can't believe it!" Shelby railed. "It's just not right."

"I told you I saw a coffin," I said. "I told you, but oh no, you wouldn't believe me. You thought I had bats in my belfry. Well, I guess next time I tell you I saw someone unload a coffin, you'll believe me."

"Like that will ever happen again," she said.

I'd filled her in on what had led to my *Ghostwriter* discovery, as well as on Vanessa's explanation as to how it had all come about. There was still a rather big gap in the story. Like, how and when had Courtney

Howard died, and what was she doing in the cellar of Haunted Holloway Hall?

"How did you know I was still here?" I asked Shelby Lynne.

"Duh," she said. "White beater car."

I frowned. "Tony didn't move my car?" What kind of criminal mastermind was he, anyway?

"Oh, he was in the process of moving it when I drove in. Man, was he ever cursing. Vanessa was behind the wheel, and he was in the van pushing like crazy to get that car out of the driveway."

"Pushing it?"

"I guess it wouldn't start. You know, if I hadn't seen your car, I might have just thought I'd missed you, and left."

I suddenly fell in love with the ugly white Plymouth Reliant. If I made it out of this mess, we were going to celebrate with a case of Valvoline 10W30 motor oil.

The arguing upstairs intensified. Doors were slamming. Footsteps landed hard against the wood floor.

"Hurry! Get up! We need to break that lightbulb out," I told Shelby.

"Why?" she said, but as a unit we made it to our feet.

"The element of surprise," I said. "Tony can't see in the dark any better than we can. He won't expect to be blindsided. But we have to hurry! I think they may be coming!"

"How are we gonna break the bulb?" Shelby asked.

"We'll have to get on that pine box over there," I told her.

"Elizabeth's casket?"

"It's the only way we can reach the light."

"It'll break with our weight," she said.

"It's not as if she'll complain," I replied.

"What'll we use to break the bulb?"

I searched around and discovered an old plastic bucket on a shelf. "We'll use the bucket. One of us will have to put it on our head. We climb up on the pine box, smash the lightbulb with the top of the bucket, and it's lights-out time," I told her.

"I see. And who's going to wear the bucket and smash the bulb?" she asked. "As if I didn't already know."

"It has to be you. You're taller. Me? I'd have to jump up to hit the bulb."

"But tomorrow's homecoming!" she said.

I maneuvered her over to the shelf with the bucket. "If we don't break that lightbulb, maybe there won't be a homecoming—for either one of us!" I told her. "Now bend over and stick your head in that bucket!"

It wasn't pretty. In fact, I imagine we were a pretty gruesome twosome, but Shelby managed to get the bucket on her head. It was a tight fit, yet somehow, back-to-back, hands bound, we managed to climb the pine box summit.

"Okay, Shelby Lynne, on the count of three, you hit that bulb! And don't forget to close your eyes! One, two—"

Crash! Where were you when the lights went out?

Shelby Lynne and I stood huddled together in the cold. The temperature in the room grew colder. I could feel a body-length shiver along my back. I peered around at the inky blackness that surrounded us. A faint yet unmistakable scent of roses replaced the dank, musty, decaying smell of the room.

"Do you smell that?" Shelby Lynne asked. "It smells like roses."

298

It *was* roses. And I was fairly certain Drew Van Vleet was not responsible this time.

Shelby Lynne and I listened as the door at the top of the stairs was unlocked and opened. Someone was coming down. I held my breath. I felt Shelby Lynne's spine straighten next to mine.

"Now remember, Shelby Lynne," I said. "When that door opens, we rush the door and knock down whoever is in our way."

The room door opened again, and Shelby Lynne took off toward it. I tried to run backwards as fast as I could to keep pace with her, but I couldn't match her Bigfoot strides. I felt my feet go out from under me, and I found myself being carried like a human backpack.

Unfortunately, Shelby Lynne stumbled under my weight (don't even think about saying it), and that's all it took for us to go down, and go down hard.

"I'm sorry it has to be this way," Tony said from above our tangled, bruised bodies.

Me, too. I tried not to whimper. *Me, too.*

Tony shoved a bound and crying Vanessa into the room with us. "But five million dollars can ease a lot of sorrow." He sniffed. "What's that smell? Smells like roses," he said, and looked around suspiciously for a moment. Then he shut the door and locked it.

The front door slammed one final time, and everything was quiet.

Great. Now who we gonna call?

The female ability to bond under difficult, even bizarre circumstances never ceases to amaze me.

Once we were certain Tony had left for good—or,

in this case, bad—we set about freeing Vanessa's duct-taped mouth, utilizing the same technique I used on Shelby earlier, and only after securing the same understanding that what happened between us girls in the cellar of Holloway Hall, stayed at Holloway Hall.

Three women, sitting bound and helpless in a cold, dark cellar of a house purported to be haunted, with the dead body of a famous person three feet away, waiting for daylight—or help whichever came first, to show up—and you guessed it. The subject eventually had to get around to men.

"Tony was my guilty pleasure," Vanessa told us in the eerie quiet of the basement, while rain pattered against the brick exterior and wind whistled outside through the trees. "He was young, almost ten years younger than I am. And so full of testosterone—I couldn't help myself. I'd been with Elizabeth for two years when Tony came along. We fell in love. And it was magic. For a while it was magic."

It was probably good it was dark. I hate to see people cry. And I hate it more when they see me.

"Tell us about Elizabeth," Shelby Lynne said. "Tell us all about her."

Vanessa let out a long breath. "Where do I start? All I told you about Elizabeth before was true, Tressa," Vanessa said, her voice soft and hushed. "All of it. Elizabeth was wonderful. I remember the first time I met her. She smelled of lavender and coffee. She was gracious and kind, understanding and giving. I wasn't lying when I told you she was like a mother to me. She really was. But she was also my mentor. My teacher."

Vanessa's words were almost like a tribute, as if she was speaking at a memorial service. And maybe she was, I thought. Maybe she was.

"Why did she never go out in public for all those years?" I asked. "Why shun the spotlight and public acclaim she'd worked so hard to achieve?"

"Elizabeth never got over the death of her husband, Kevin Howard. She loved him deeply and took his death extremely hard. She said she'd never wear any scent but lavender, because that's what Kevin liked. Elizabeth told me all she needed were her books and her memories of her beloved husband. And it's true. She was content to the end."

"How did she die?" Shelby Lynne asked.

"And when did she die?" I added.

"Elizabeth had Alzheimer's," Vanessa said.

"How can you know for sure? You said she wouldn't go to a doctor," I said.

"There was a history in her family. Her father. Even before that, I think. She didn't want anyone to know, and she knew that Tony and I could care for her as well as any nursing home. She didn't want to be in an institution. She wanted to be in her home. Several years ago her condition deteriorated, but before that she often spoke about this house, about how she visited as a child. She'd tell me about the legend of Loralie, as she called it. She'd tell me about how Loralie had lost her love, too, and how when she died, she wanted to be buried not next to her husband but here with Loralie. Tony and I used Loralie's legend to try and scare you off," Vanessa said, and I frowned. Drew Van Vleet had tried the same dirty trick. No wonder I had self-esteem issues.

"Go on," Shelby Lynne urged.

"I had been planning for some time to make this book the last book. It's not the usual Courtney Howard fare. It's our story, you know. Elizabeth's and mine. Our memoir, really." Vanessa's voice trailed off into a poignant silence.

"And?" I prodded.

Vanessa stirred herself. "Tony and I put away our earnings as well as the royalties and earnings from the sales of the books I wrote—only the books I wrote—I would never, ever steal from Elizabeth," she said. "And we opened accounts in various parts of the world. Grand Cayman. Switzerland. We always kept our passports up to date. One morning last week, I went in to wake Elizabeth and discovered she was dead. She'd died peacefully in her sleep.

"We'd been putting off this trip to settle up the estate issues, and we decided this was perfect time to bring Elizabeth back to Holloway Hall for the last time. We'd planned to bury her near Loralie tonight—we'd already dug the hole—and we were going to take off for Omaha as soon as we were through. We already had tickets out of Omaha for the Cayman Islands," she said.

"But what about Elizabeth?" I asked. "Wouldn't people wonder where she'd gone to? Her publisher? Someone?"

Vanessa shook her head. "It was easier than you'd think. We'd finished the final book. All proceeds were electronically transferred to a bank account. Tony and I oversaw her finances very carefully."

"What does a limo driver know about finances?" I asked.

"Tony earned a degree in business and accounting," she said. "He's a man of many talents."

Yeah. I'd seen some of that talent on display from my little perch outside her bedroom window.

"What about back home? Weren't people back in

Connecticut bound to wonder about her? And what about her large estate?" I asked.

"Elizabeth had already said she wanted her home to be used as a writers' retreat when she was gone. A foundation has already been set up to manage the house and grounds."

"And so the eccentric, reclusive spinner of chillers and thrillers and supernatural stories just—what—disappears into thin air?" I asked.

"Elizabeth would rather have liked that ending, I think," was all Vanessa said.

We sat quietly for some time, but you all know I'm not a big one for prolonged silent contemplation.

"Why didn't you go with Tony?" I asked Vanessa. "Omaha's, like, only three hours away. You could have been in that big white bird out over the Pacific before anyone was the wiser."

"That's Atlantic, Finstein," Shelby Lynne said.

Since it was dark, I saved the dirty look for later.

"Why did you stay, Vanessa?" I asked.

More silence followed.

"Because people were getting hurt," Vanessa finally responded. "And I guess because I was Elizabeth's assistant and I hadn't finished the job. I hadn't put Elizabeth's gentle soul to rest."

Okay, first off, it's not cool not to be able to blow your nose when you're bawling. And it's really not cool when you have three women in the same predicament. There was so much sniffing and snorting and snot-sucking going on in that small room, the place sounded like an allergist's waiting room.

"Do you think you'll ever see Tony again?" I finally asked.

"Only in my dreams," Vanessa said. "Only in my dreams."

Sunlight crept through the tiny cracks in the door, and I roused. Every muscle in my body felt tight and achy, every joint in need of lubrication. I felt like Dorothy's Tin Man. I'd never known my bed to be this uncomfortable, even with two bed buddies with sharp noses. I opened my eyes and realized that my bed was Shelby Lynne, and we'd fallen asleep propped up in the corner.

Vanessa was asleep at the foot of the pine box. Not unlike a familiar from one of Elizabeth Courtney Howard's books, I decided.

"Good morning, sunshine." I nudged Shelby Lynne. "Rise and shine. This is your big day!"

"Buzz off, Blondie!"

Jeesch. And I thought I was crabby in the mornings.

"We've got to get moving. Get loose. Get help," I said. "And get you to school before they disqualify you from the voting!"

That helped.

"You can't think I'm going to make it to school after the night I've had! Besides, no amount of wonder cream from your grandma's bag of tricks is going to mask circles so dark they'll think I'm in costume as the Lone Ranger. And I'm not sure even ten showers will rid me of the perfume Eau de Death and Decay," she said.

I nodded. Elizabeth was beginning to get a little ripe.

"Don't be such a gloomy gus," I told her. "Think positive. Be upbeat! Get excited about your future!"

"Stuff a sock in it, Dr. Phil," Shelby Lynne said, and we struggled to stand.

"As I see it, we'll need to free Vanessa's hands first," I said. "Then, when her hands are free, she can untape us."

"Sounds reasonable," Shelby said. "So how do we unfasten the tape on her wrists when we're still bound?"

I thought about it.

"There's only one technique that might work," I told her.

"What's that?"

"Brokeback Mountain: The Story Continues," I said.

By this time Vanessa had awoken, and I explained our plan to free her.

"It'll work best if we all lie on the floor," I said. "Vanessa, you first. Hold your hands out behind you as far as you can. Okay, now Shelby and I'll just ma neuver ourselves so our mouths are even with your hands, and we'll take turns ripping at the tape with our teeth."

"What do you think we are? Vampires?" Shelby Lynne asked. "That's duct tape. People repair radiator hoses with that stuff."

I blinked. "They do? Okay, then, what's your alternative?"

"We could break the door down," Shelby suggested.

"With what?"

"Our bodies. We run at that door and bust it down."

"Yeah, I remember how successful we were at running together last night," I told her. "I say we try the teeth method."

"Whatever," Shelby Lynne said. "But you go first."

We got into position, and I began to tear away at the tape with my teeth. Good thing I drank a lot of milk when I was a little nipper. I had strong teeth. I also decided my four-year-long torture at the hands of Dr. Lecter, my orthodontist, had been beneficial, after all.

I made decent progress before I pooped out, and Shelby Lynne and I switched places. When she'd had enough, it was my turn again. We scooted and rolled, and I hunkered down to grab the length of loosened duct tape we'd managed to unroll, when I heard a squeaky noise. Like a tiny mouse.

"Oh my god! Would you look at that?"

Three gasps erupted from three prone women like the precursor to a violent volcanic episode.

We all wiggled around on the ground trying to get a look at the basement window. With the way we were hog-tied, it was physically impossible for both Shelby Lynne and me to get a view of the window. But in our wrestling match to gain advantage, I saw Sheriff Doug Samuels wiping dirt from the window and peering in at us.

"Would you take a look at that?" I heard him say.

Shelby Lynne rolled me over so she that could take a look.

"Is that who I think it is?" Shelby asked.

"Yep. That's our esteemed county sheriff, formerly known as Deputy Doug," I said.

"I don't think so," Shelby replied.

"Huh?" I did a flip move, putting my butt and thighs into it, and ended up facing the window.

There, framed in the tiny, dirty window, was Ranger Rick looking down at me.

"Uh, remember, ladies. What happens in Haunted Holloway Hall, stays in Haunted Holloway Hall," I said.

CHAPTER TWENTY-ONE

By the time Shelby Lynne, Vanessa and I were free and circulation had returned to various parts of our anatomy, quite a collection of county officials had gathered. From the county coroner to the county attorney, to my boss Stan, to Joe Townsend and Romeo Rivas (uh, not a comfy combo), the dead-end lane leading to Haunted Holloway Hall looked like a parking lot.

Once Deputy Doug—dang, I keep doing that— Sheriff Samuels and Ranger Rick Townsend entered the basement through the exterior cellar door and managed to gain access to our tiny prison and Elizabeth's makeshift crypt, we were more than ready to be rescued. The good sheriff, I noted, snapped photos of us before he assisted in our extrication. I had a sinking feeling those pictures would come back to haunt me down the road. Big-time.

We were ushered up to the living room of the house and, in turn, each of us explained our involvement in the Agatha Christie drama that had unfolded behind the brick walls of Haunted Holloway Hall.

I opted to go last. I figured that way there would be less for me to explain. Boy, was I wrong.

"So, this was the story you roped my granddad into assisting with?" Townsend asked, coming to loom over me as I sat beside Shelby Lynne on the antique sofa, waiting for my inquisition.

I raised an eyebrow. "Roped? Are you kidding? He came with his own lead rope and halter," I said.

Townsend shook his head. "I guess I can only be thankful I didn't find him duct-taped in the cellar like a Christmas package wrapped by a redneck," he said.

I nodded. "You gotta love those hidden blessings, Townsend," I said.

"I still can't believe I didn't pick up on the differences in the books," Shelby Lynne said, not for the first time. Next to me, Shelby Lynne was plainly having difficulty understanding how she could have overlooked what was now obvious to her. "I've read every Elizabeth Courtney Howard book at least five times, and until it was pointed out to me, I didn't suspect a thing." She looked over at Vanessa. "You're good."

"Ah, but remember, Shelby, I had the missing link, the final chapter, as it were."

She gave me a confused look.

"The back blurb to *Ghostwriter*, Elizabeth Courtney Howard's final book," I clarified. "Or rather Vanessa's book. That was really when I figured out what was what." Now *that* was clear as mud.

"How did you get that cover copy, again?" Vanessa asked.

I felt Shelby Lynne tense beside me. She must've had

a thought similar to the one that went through my head. Something along the lines of jailhouse orange not being a cool look. Especially for homecoming queen candidates—or their fashion and makeup advisors.

I did a hear-no-evil number and turned instead to the sheriff. I had a few questions of my own.

"How did you happen to be at Holloway Hall, of all places, this morning?" I asked the sheriff and his buddy Townsend.

"We were having breakfast," Sheriff Dougie said, and I wished he hadn't mentioned food. The last time I'd gone this long without eating was when I'd had my tonsils yanked. My belly growls had turned into full-fledged feeding-time-at-the-zoo roars. "I got a call about a ten-fifty. Possible PI."

Oh, great. More ten-code confusion.

"Translation, if you will?" I asked.

Samuels shook his head. "A report of a vehicle accident. With personal injuries possible."

I nodded. "Ten-four," I said, and Townsend rubbed his eyes.

"The report stated that a car was down the embankment off of the state highway just about a mile or so from here. So I rolled, and Townsend followed."

"How does a car in the ditch miles away bring you to the Holloway house?" I asked.

"It was a blue van," he said, and my eyes got big.

"Tony!" Vanessa jumped up from a Queen Anne chair. "My god! How is he? Is he hurt?"

"He got boogered up, but he'll live," Samuels said. "We got to looking in the vehicle and found the rental receipt for the van and other documentation that led us back up here. On the way, we spotted a very familiar white Plymouth Reliant in the ditch at the bottom of the lane."

"Ditch? My car is in a ditch?"

Samuels nodded. " 'Fraid so," he said.

"Is it damaged? Totaled, even?"

"With that car it's kind of hard to tell, but it didn't appear to be," he answered. "Put a hook on it and pull it out, and it ought to be drivable."

"That's good," I said. "Because it wasn't before."

Townsend shook his head.

"What made the van and Tony run off the road?" I asked. "Was it on account of the rain?"

Samuels looked at Townsend and then back at me. I hadn't missed the exchange.

"A deer probably ran out in front of him," Samuels said.

I frowned.

"Probably? Is that what he said?" I asked.

Samuels shook his head. "He was confused. He was injured. No telling how long he'd been trapped in that vehicle. It was cold. He was probably shocky. Out of his head when he spoke to us."

"Why?" I asked. "What did he say?"

"Tressa," Townsend said. "Let it go."

The two men had me curious now. And yes, I know what curiosity did to the cat, thank you very much.

"Come on. What did Tony say?" I asked. "Why'd he run off the road?"

"Yes. Please tell us," Vanessa added.

Sheriff Samuels sighed. "Mr. Camarillo stated he had just turned onto the highway and had only gone a mile or so, when he looked up and saw a figure in white right in front of him. He said he swerved to avoid hitting her, and the vehicle got hung up on the shoulder, flipped over and rolled down the hill. He was lucky he was wearing his belt, or there's a good chance he wouldn't be alive to tell the tale."

"Hold it a minute. You said he swerved to avoid hitting 'her'?" I pointed out, feeling a sudden case of the gooseflesh coming on. "What do you mean, 'her'?"

Samuels shrugged. "Camarillo said it was a woman. A woman in white."

"Are you joking?" Shelby Lynne's hot breath hit my cheek. "A woman in white?"

Sheriff Doug shook his head. "That's his story," Samuels said, "and he's stickin' to it."

Color me creeped out.

It was past noon when we were free to go—with admonitions from the authorities to make ourselves available for interviews the following day "as events warranted." I love the way cops talk, don't you?

Shelby Lynne's brother's Jeep had been driven around to the back of the house so that it would be out of sight, and she volunteered to drive me down the lane to the Plymouth. We walked around back and for some reason found ourselves making our way to the Holloway family cemetery one last time. We stood looking at the freshly dug hole meant to be the modest final resting place for the incomparable and never-to-be duplicated Elizabeth Courtney Howard.

"I believe Vanessa," Shelby Lynne said. "Don't you?"

I thought about it. I wasn't the greatest bullshit detector in the world, but it was hard to argue with actions. Vanessa had remained behind when she could have fled with Tony.

"Yeah. I believe her, too," I finally said.

"Do you think they'll bury Elizabeth here, after all?"

I shrugged. "Who knows? I suppose if Elizabeth wrote it down somewhere, they could. Sure as heck would give the B and B a huge tourist boom. And the events of this past week have given Haunted Holloway Hall even more notoriety." And me, too, I realized—as if good ol' Calamity Jayne needed more notoriety.

As we stood there, clouds rolled across the sun, blocking out the light, turning the cemetery dark and chilly.

"Do you smell that?" Shelby Lynne asked.

I nodded and looked around.

"Roses," I said, feeling my throat close up a bit.

Shelby shook her head.

"No. Not roses. Lavender," she said.

I found myself bracing for the sound of soft, sad weeping, but picked up something radically different. It sounded like . . . laughter. Girlish laughter. I looked at Shelby Lynne to see if she was picking up the same frequency. From the size of her eyes, my money was on the affirmative.

A breeze whipped up around us as we stood in the gloom of the cemetery, but this breeze was unexpectedly warm. Earthy and moist. It picked up fall leaves—oranges, browns and yellows—in a tiny cyclone of color and whipped across the open grave.

Shelby and I took a step and peered down into the new grave, the grave meant for Elizabeth. There, standing out starkly against the rich, black Iowa soil, were rose petals.

But these petals were yellow. For friendship.

It was the night of the big game—halftime and the presentation of the homecoming king and queen and their court were only a quarter away. So far the football game had been ho-hum, with Grandville down by seven. But I suppose anything that came after an overnighter with a corpse was somewhat anticlimactic.

The investigation into Elizabeth's death continued, and an autopsy would be performed the next day to determine the actual cause of death. I was certain the results would indicate that Elizabeth had died from from natural causes. Tony Camarillo was recuperating in the local hospital, and local authorities were in touch with law enforcement back East regarding possible charges of interstate transportation of a deceased person as well as fraud.

I wasn't too concerned about Vanessa. I figured she'd hook up with some slick celebrity attorney, plead out and do her time, then sell her story to the big screen for big bucks. I did wonder about one thing, though. Who would they get to play me?

With my inside scoop and Vanessa's promise not to talk to any other media types, I had a story that would hit the news services like gangbusters. Stan and I had finally agreed to talk about an adequate compensation package—contingent, Stan insisted, on my pursuing postsecondary credits in journalism. Conditions. Conditions. Always conditions.

I stood in line patiently waiting my turn to order at the busy concession stand, when the person behind me stepped on my heel. I turned around to give them a nasty look and discovered Drew Van Vleet, his camera bag slung over his shoulder.

"Looks like the home team has some ground to cover to bring off a win," he said. "Frankly, I don't think they can do it. Our boys have your boys outweighed in every position. Not enough meat on the lines."

I shrugged. "Our boys tend to be faster than the New Holland tackles, many of whom have had way too many Dutch pastries and spent too many hours clogging in wooden shoes," I said. "Talk about your bunions."

"I guess now's as good a time as any to warn you that my story about Holloway Hall will be in Tuesday's edition," Van Vleet said, and I turned around to look at him.

"Your story? And what story would that be? How you eluded arrest on breaking and entering charges?" I asked him.

He smiled and shook his head. "The B and B story. The Rivas real estate deal. And, of course, the story that will get me noticed: Elizabeth Courtney Howard coming back to her hometown to complete her final book."

I stared at him. The authorities really did have a lid on this story. Drew Van Vleet was, like, totally clueless. And me? I was totally lovin' it.

"Are you sure that's the story you want to run with?" I asked, feeling a tiny pinprick of conscience when I realized just how much notice Van Vleet and his newspaper would get if he went ahead and published a story he'd only have to publicly retract at a later date—and with considerable embarrassment, at that.

"Give it a rest, Turner. You've lost this round. And I've done the newspaper-reading public a favor and dealt you a knockout punch," Van Vleet said.

Over the public address system, spectators were reminded that results for homecoming king and queen voting were to be announced at the half, and the candidates were named one last time.

Van Vleet chuckled. "Not only did you lose the big

story, but your football team is going to lose the big game," Van Vleet said, "and your big friend with feet the size of snowshoes is about to lose the homecoming queen contest. Instead of Grandville, this town ought to be known as Loserville," he added, putting the final nail in his journalistic coffin.

"You know what, Van Vleet?" I said. "I was going to try to persuade you not to run that article, but guess what? I'm not going to do it. I reckon you've earned the right to print that story, bud, so you run with it. To the victor goes the spoils!"

I imagined Stan's reaction when he saw the *New Holland* story. I'd make a note to hit him up for a real desk and chair the day that little scoop hit newsstands, I decided with a grin. Trick or treat, Mr. Rodgers!

I made my way to Gram and Joe. We had reserved prime seats right smack-dab in the middle of the hometown section, and right in front of the place where the king and queen would be crowned. Actually, to reserve seats at our stadium, you go out early on game days and put your blankets down where you plan to sit.

"Shelby Lynne really looks nice," I told Gram, looking over at Shelby standing with Tom Murphy, who also looked rather sharp in his tiny tuxedo. "How did you manage to convince her to wear her hair up?"

"She said it still reeked of the stench of rotting flesh and mildewy basements, and the farther away from her nose, the better," Gram said. I nodded. I had my hair pulled back into a ponytail so tight I looked like I'd had an extreme face-lift gone way bad.

"It looks good," I told her.

"Hey, Joe." I leaned over and greeted Gram's escort for the evening. "You're awful quiet. That's not like you."

"He's dealin' with some guilt issues," Gram said, and I looked at Joe.

"Guilt? Why is Joe feeling guilty?" I asked.

" 'Cause he said all those awful things about Elizabeth Courtney Howard snubbing him, and all the time she was dead as a doornail," Gram said. I winced.

"Well, he didn't know that at the time," I pointed out. "And I thought some not-so-nice things about her, as well. As a matter of fact, I even crawled up a tree to peek into her bedroom," I told them. Realizing suddenly what I'd just said, I cupped a hand over my too-big trap. "Forget I ever said that. Wipe it from your memories like dry-erase markers from Mom's message board," I instructed.

"I guess I'm not as bad as I thought," Joe said. "All I ever did was talk. You climbed a tree and became a Peeping Tom. A voyeur. I'm not anywhere near that far gone."

I gave a fake smile. "I'm so glad I could make you feel better," I told the old character.

"Shush! Shush! They're getting ready to announce the winners!" Gram said, and we all got to our feet.

"And this year's homecoming king and queen are: Shelby Lynne Sawyer and Tom Murphy!"

Gram and I looked at each other, totally stunned by the loudspeaker's proclamation, and put up a whoop and a holler and hugged each other, dancing a little celebratory jig.

"I can't believe they won!" I clapped, looking through blurred eyes as Shelby Lynne went forward to accept her crown and bouquet of roses. "I can't believe it! I'm so happy for them both!"

I looked over at Joe and caught him wiping his eyes. I smiled. Sentimental old sap.

After the formalities were over and things had settled down a bit, Gram grabbed her purse. "I'm going down to congratulate her!" she said. "You comin', Tressa?"

I shook my head. "You go on," I said. "And give her this." I handed Gram a single yellow rose. "She'll know who it's from," I added.

"Oh, if you would, dear, visit the concession stand and bring me back one of them walkin' tacos and a pop," Gram said. "I'm feeling like I need some fornication."

I looked at her. "I think you mean fortification, Gram," I said.

She took Joe's arm and gave me a wink. "That's what you think, sister," she said. "That's what you think."

I blinked. Oh, buddy, things were heatin' up in Gramville.

"Talk about underdogs making a comeback. This is one for the record books." Rick Townsend slid in beside me. "Hope that holds true for the second half," he said. "It'd be nice to have a win," he added.

I smiled. "We already won," I said.

Townsend nodded. "I see that. Pretty amazing. Maybe looks and popularity don't count for as much as everyone thinks. We could be looking at a new trend. And that's a good thing, I'm thinking."

I looked over at the guy who'd been crowned homecoming king the year he'd graduated.

"You really think things are changing?" I asked. "Less focus on the outer person and more on the inner?" I wasn't sure whether I should be pleased or petrified.

"By the victory we've just witnessed, it appears likely. Nice to see folks having such a good time," he said and I followed the path of his gaze. He was watching his granddad get his picture taken with Shelby Lynne, Tom and my grandma. A smiling group, they locked arms and hammed it up for the camera.

"Uh, you know that little talk I was supposed to have with my gramma, Townsend?" I asked. "Well, you see—"

Townsend put out a hand and covered my mouth with his fingers.

"Forget it, Turner," he said. "I get the distinct impression that even the legendary Calamity Jayne, equipped with a magic lasso and mounted on the grand champion cattle-roping horse five years running, couldn't separate those two." He removed his hand and motioned at my gramma and his pops.

"I'm sorry, Townsend," I said. "But the way I look at it, they've earned the right to live their lives the way they choose. With adult supervision, of course," I added.

"Are you volunteering for duty?" Townsend asked. "It could be a full-time job keeping those two out of trouble, you know," he pointed out.

I looked over to see Shelby Lynne pick up Tom Murphy and hold him in her arms as Smitty, who was covering the event for the *Gazette*, took snapshots of the reigning king and queen. Gram and Joe were nearby snapping off shots, pointing and laughing.

I shrugged. "What's one more job when you have three?" I asked. "And never let it be said that Tressa Turner ever got in the way of true love," I added. Seeing Townsend's sudden, intense look settle on my face, I wished those words back in a heartbeat. He reached out and touched my cheek.

"So, Cupid, do you have any plans for after the game?" Townsend asked.

"Why? Did you have something special in mind?" I asked, trying to keep my tone light and casual when in reality my innards were dancing around like the Grandville fight song was being performed in my gut.

He raised his eyebrows. "A bunch of us are driving to Des Moines to take in a couple of Halloween haunted houses for kicks, and then we'll probably grab some breakfast. You game?"

"That depends," I said.

"On what?"

"Is there a full moon tonight?" I asked, dead serious.

Townsend smiled. "I sure hope so. It'll give me an excuse to bite that neck of yours," he said. "Like I wanted to during the apple race," he added.

I felt my cheeks grow warm. Yeah. I still blush.

"You in?"

I thought about it. I'd survived the night in an honest-to-ghoul haunted house with a real corpse laid out. I figured I could handle one where I knew the poltergeists were paid and the bodies were props.

"Sounds fun," I said. "Can Shelby Lynne and Tom tag along?" I asked, thinking it was better to be safe than sorry, just in case Townsend was serious about the neck-biting. Or, maybe, in case he wasn't.

Townsend grinned. "The more the scarier," he said.

"Great!" I excused myself to get Gram's goodies and left Townsend to save our seats.

I was ten-seventy-six (ten code for "en route") to fetch the food when the catty tones of a certain "shoo-in" queen candidate-type reached me, echoing my earlier sentiments on the voting results but with an altogether different—and disparaging—take.

"I cannot *believe* Sasquatch and that pipsqueak won!" Kylie Danae Radcliffe (aka, the loser) squawked. "I'm sure there has to be some mistake. That's the only way that Amazonian ape and measly midget could have beat me."

Ouch! Make that *sore* loser!

"I'm going to force a recount. For sure, my mother will demand one," Little Miss Perfect snarled. "And now that that knuckle-dragging nerd teamed up with that train wreck of a reporter from the *Gazette* and got lucky, she'll be the talk of the town for the rest of the year."

Train wreck? This was getting personal.

I followed Kylie and her companion for a few steps before I accidentally trod on the back of her stiletto-clad heel. Kylie whipped around, a scowl on her face that only partially faded when she recognized me.

"Uh, sorry, Kylie," I said. "About the heel and the queen thing. But I'm really glad I ran into you, because I have a question that I think many Grandville High School students and our local residents would be interested in having you answer."

She hesitated, a spark of interest—perhaps at receiving additional local PR—apparent in the sudden glint of her eye. "Yes? What question would that be?"

"Whether being such a rude, nasty, insulting loser comes naturally, or do you, like, have to practice?" Kylie Danae's mouth fell open. "On second thought," I said, stepping past her, "forget it. You're old news."

I was in line at the concession stand once again,

waiting my turn, when someone reached out and took my left hand.

"Barbie ain't wearin' her ring." I turned, and Manny was standing there looking down at my finger.

"It's at home. In a safe place," I replied. "By the way, that's not a real diamond, is it?"

"Could be," he said.

"How's your aunt?" I asked. "Is she feeling better?"

Manny nodded. "She's around. They released her this morning. Ahnt Mo never misses a homecoming game."

"She's here?"

He nodded again.

"Barbie sees Ahnt Mo, Barbie keeps her left hand in her pocket," he instructed.

"About that . . . ," I started. "Now that she's better, don't you think you'd better tell her the truth? About us, I mean? After all, she still thinks we're engaged. That could get a tad . . . awkward, in a small town like this."

Manny shook his head. "Too soon. Shock could kill her," he said. "Give her some time to get her strength back, and we'll see then. Oh, hey, Mick."

A young man appeared next to Manny. I blinked, thinking I was seeing double. No more than seventeen, the kid was nearly as tall as Manny, although he still had to go some before he had Manny's muscle mass.

"This is Manny's cousin Mick," Manny said, and Mick nodded.

"Yo," Mick said.

"This is Tressa," Manny said, and all of a sudden I saw a lot more of the whites of Mick's eyes.

"This is Tressa?" Before I knew it, Mick had picked me up and whirled me around three times. I was thinkin' he'd better stop, or I'd embarrass myself all over him with those two walking tacos I'd consumed.

"Wow. Cool meetin' you, Tressa!" Mick said.

"Mick here did a little bit of campaigning for your underdogs today," Manny said.

"Huh?"

"It wasn't nothin', coz," Mick said. "I just did a little pressin' flesh, if you know what I mean, asking people to vote for Murph and Sawyer. No big deal, homey."

I looked at Manny. "You asked Mick here to, uh, campaign for Shelby Lynne and Tom?" I asked. "I'm touched, Manny. Really touched."

Manny smiled briefly, and I was again struck by the whiteness of his teeth and the curve of his lips.

"Consider it an engagement gift," he said.

"There they are! There they are! Manny! Mick! Auntie Mo's been lookin' all over for you. Aunt Mo's seen royalty crowned, and she's ready to go home to her warm bed."

I looked up and saw Manny's great-aunt Mo, looking pretty darned spry for someone who had been knock, knock, knockin' on heaven's door the day before, making her way in our direction. I found myself slipping my left hand in my hoodie pocket.

"Tressa? Is that you? Is that Tressa, Manny? Oh my goodness. It is. Hello again, Tressa." She stopped and looked at me. "Did you do something with your face?" she asked. "You didn't have Botox, did you?"

I shook my head.

"Never mind that. You two give each other a big kiss for Auntie Mo. Come on now."

I swear to God, I was going to tell Auntie Mo the truth, the whole truth and nothing but the truth right then and there, really I was, but then I thought about Shelby Lynne's happy face and Tom Thumb's broad smile, and somehow my eyes were looking at Manny's mouth again, and before I knew it, I'd reached up on my tippy, tippy, tippy toes and planted a kiss on one very surprised homey.

What can I say, guys?

The devil made me do it.

KATHLEEN BACUS

CALAMITY JAYNE

Tressa Jayne Turner has had it up to *here* with the never-ending string of dumb-blonde jokes and her long-time nickname. Crowned "Calamity Jayne" by Iowa Department of Natural Resources officer Rick Townsend, Tressa's out to gain a little hometown respect—or die trying. She's just been handed the perfect opportunity to get "Ranger Rick" to finally take her seriously. How? By solving a murder no one else believes happened.... No one, that is, except the killer.

Yup, Calamity Jayne is in it up to her hot pink snakeskin cowgirl boots. Tressa would tell you her momma never raised no dummies, but the jury's still out on that one.